# VALKYRIES

BOOK ONE

## some through
### the fire

# VALKYRIES
BOOK ONE

# some through
# the fire

*a novel*

# JERI MASSI

MOODY PUBLISHERS
CHICAGO

Permission to reprint lyrics  on page 390 granted by K&R Music
Publishing, Ferrisburgh, VT

Library of Congress Cataloging-in-Publication Data

Massi, Jeri.
  Valkyries / Jeri Massi.
       p. cm.
    Summary: In the 1970s, behavior and family problems send
Tracey to a Catholic boarding school, where she struggles to
explore and practice her new-found belief in the Bible and
Protestantism.
    ISBN 0-8024-1513-X (bk. 1)
    [1. Christian life--Fiction.  2. Catholic schools--Fiction.
3. Conversion--Fiction.  4. Family problems--Fiction.
5. Schools--Fiction.  6. Protestantism--History--Fiction.
7. Catholic Church--Fiction.] I. Massi, Jeri. Some through
the fire. II. Title.

PZ7.M423855 Val 2003
[Fic]--dc21

                                                  2002010667


                   1 3 5 7 9 10 8 6 4 2

           Printed in the United States of America

*To All Good Valkyries and True*

# PART ONE
## JUNE 1973

# O N E

"Those girls are going to fight us," Jody said coolly, pointing to a small knot of girls leaning against the walls of the school building.

Alice, trying to sit comfortably on the teeter-totter fulcrum bar, looked at Tracey to gauge her reaction.

Tracey Jacamuzzi looked across the playground. She was new to all this, new to the lounging in the evenings at the public school yard, new to the casual way her companions bummed cigarettes from boys who came by, new to the jean jacket she wore and to the language she now used.

To hide her concern at the prospect of a fight, she fished a cigarette out of her pocket, lit it, and took a drag. "Three of them and three of us," she said quietly. She stood taller than either of her two companions, and she always made her best impression on them when she spoke calmly and carelessly. But inside she hoped there would be no fight.

In the pocket of her jeans she carried the latest letter from her eighth-grade teacher, Sister Edward Elaine.

She had been tempted to show it to Jody and Alice, but she had decided not to. There was always the chance they would despise her attachment to her former teacher, or that they would give vent to their disdain for the kids who had gone to school at St. Anne's. Jody and Alice had gone to the public school, Ezra Pound. They knew how to wear jeans and jean jackets. They drank beer whenever they could get away with it. And they didn't seem to care about anything. Nothing bothered them. Tracey desperately wanted to be beyond caring.

Two letters had come from Sister Ed that summer, but Tracey had not written back after the second one. She knew she never would, but she was not sure why. Maybe it was the new look she sported, which she knew Sister Ed would disapprove of. And see right through. She had let her short brown hair grow long and straight. She and Jody and Alice hung around the playground of Ezra Pound every night, bumming ciga- rettes and every now and then wrangling invitations to parties. Sister Ed would have seen more—the scratch marks on her neck that she hid with her hair or with turtleneck shirts, the bruising on her left shoulder where her father had hammered her with his fist at the supper table. Somehow, Sister Ed would have known the marks were there. One look at Tracey, and she would have known. Tracey was sure of it. Some deep instinct, deeper than any instinct she had ever felt, was operating to protect her from being seen and known that way. Better that nobody know, and better that she make herself into a person who could take it, a person who just didn't care.

Tracey and her friends had stationed themselves at the teeter-totters so they could talk to some of the players when the baseball game was over. When the game ended, the girls across the playground continued to eye Tracey and her friends. But a couple of the boys stopped at the teeter-totters and talked to them, accepted cigarettes, mentioned the game coming up the next day, and walked away.

Jody had her hopes set on one of them, a boy named Kelly who played first base and sometimes pitched. She and Alice and Tracey sat on the teeter-totters and talked about him.

Jody gave a confident flip of her dark hair. "Kelly said he might go to the St. Anne's dance next week." She was the acknowledged pretty one of their threesome, and her efforts to get Kelly's attention seemed skillful to Tracey. Jody knew how to dress. She wore earrings, and she wore makeup, and her jeans and sweaters were always short and tight. Even her jean jacket seemed tight. She wore it halfway buttoned up, and it was short enough to let her midriff show when she moved. With her dark eyes always partially obscured by her bangs, she had a pert, pretty, rather bold look.

"So maybe he'll ask you out," Alice said. Helpful Alice, with her enormous nose and straightened teeth, usually got along with Jody by flattery and encouragement. Occasionally, she resorted to whining, but Tracey was the only one who ever gave her any pity. Alice was skinny and short, and she still looked and dressed like a little girl.

Tracey wondered if she would ever be as pretty as Jody. She caught a glimpse of herself in the glass doors of the school, tall and thin, brown hair—but whatever she thought was interrupted.

11

The other girls sauntered toward them. There were three of them too. Tracey saw the bulge of the cigarette packs in their jean jackets. They stopped a few feet away and stared.

Jody stared back. "Yeah?"

"You guys are on private property," said a girl almost as tall as Tracey. She had bleached blonde hair and brilliant red lipstick.

Tracey felt a stab of both fear and excitement and quickly suppressed both. She assumed a careless attitude, forcing her body to relax. "I don't see any signs," she said, eyeing the girl from the ground up.

"Sign's on my hand," the blonde said. "Take a look."

That was an old trick. If you looked at the hand, you got walloped with it.

"That just means *you're* private property," Tracey said without looking.

"I doubt that," Jody said with a laugh.

The tall blonde knocked Jody off the teeter-totter bar. One of the shorter girls grabbed Tracey.

A coil inside Tracey exploded. She never knew how she did it, except maybe she owed something to her uncle Joe, who had once taught her to box and had even made her go a few light rounds with him when she was twelve. She did not pull hair. She punched: left, right, left, jackhammering her arms out as fast as she could at the other girl's face. Suddenly the other girl reeled away from her, stunned not only by the hard blows on and around her nose, but by Tracey's promptness with them, as though Tracey had been fighting all her life.

Alice and one of the other girls rolled around on the ground, pulling hair and screaming. But Jody had been knocked right off the bar. The blonde girl was getting astride her, with a fistful of Jody's hair held tightly. Tracey ran to help. She clouted Jody's attacker on the ear. When she looked up in pain and surprise, Tracey hit her dead center on the face. She screamed and cursed. She jumped to her feet and tried to grab Tracey's hair, but Jody pushed Tracey right into her. Tracey hit the tall girl with her shoulder and chin and knocked her away. Tracey punched the girl two or three times. Then she put her head down and hammered punches into the girl's body as hard as she could: lefts and rights. Then all of a sudden there was nothing in front of her, and she found herself hitting air.

Tracey straightened and looked around. The three girls were gone. She glanced at Alice, who sat on the ground with her face in her hands, crying.

Jody looked up at Tracey. For a moment none of them said anything. Then Jody smiled. "You never said you could fight."

Tracey felt a strong urge to cry, and another urge to throw up, but she mastered both and spoke evenly. "My uncle Joe taught me how to fight a long time ago. But I never—" She didn't know how to complete the sentence. She'd never fought; she'd never wanted to fight; she'd never known she could fight. It was horrible. But it was fun too. It made the pain of her father's blows seem a little further away. For a few minutes, she had stopped caring, had stopped thinking about the scratches and bruises he'd given her. She had passed them on to somebody else. So that's what she said. "I never knew fighting could be so much fun." It had been like a release.

"Only when you win," Jody said. "For crying out loud, Alice. Get up and quit crying. We beat them!"

"I never fought either." Alice sobbed as she stood. "And I didn't think it was fun."

"That's because anybody could beat you up," Jody told her.

"Jody!" Tracey exclaimed.

"Well, it's true," Jody said.

"You weren't doing much better," Tracey said.

"That girl was a foot taller than me," Jody complained. "I couldn't even reach her with her grabbing my hair." She ran her hand tenderly over her head. "It still hurts."

"What are my folks going to say?" Tracey wondered.

Jody stared at her. "Don't tell them, and they won't have anything to say."

"Parents always know when you've been fighting."

"No, they don't," Jody said. "Yours won't. You're not too messed up. Besides, they probably aren't home tonight, right?"

"I guess not. Come on, let's go tell my little sister Jean and get some ice cream out of our freezer."

From that day Tracey became a fighter.

There weren't many girls around the neighborhood who liked fights. But the tall blonde girl, whose name was Barbara, often started them, usually with Tracey. And she had friends who backed her up.

On some nights, keeping a station at the teeter-totters involved some heavy suspense, if not actual action. On other nights, the suspense ignited into a brawl.

Things got more complicated when some of the

boys on the baseball team took sides. The Ezra Pound playground was safe during the games, but afterward it became a battleground. That was fine with Tracey. Usually she could avoid getting beat up by a girl. She was tall, strong, and kept getting better at fighting. A few times some boys on the other side tried to fight with her, but she either managed to get the best of them or one of the boys on her side came to help her.

One night in early July, when both groups stood at opposite ends of the playground, eyeing each other and making plans, Jody spotted a police car that circled Ezra Pound. It slowed as it drove by them. She passed the word to Tracey. "Don't tell Alice," she added.

Tracey told Alice anyway, even though Jody shook her head at her. The three of them melted away into the woods on the far side of the school. They ducked down and scurried away, then took the long way back to Tracey's house in the growing dusk.

"That was close," Jody said once they were well away from the school.

"That cop wouldn't have done anything but yell at us," Tracey said. "They don't bust girls like us for fighting. You need knives and chains for that."

"You want to go back and get yelled at?" Jody asked.

"No, thank you." Tracey gave Jody a second glance. Jody had been willing to leave Alice behind—dumber, slower, weaker Alice, who stuck with them even though she cried every time there was a fight. She wondered why Jody would leave her best friend to take the rap for something they had all gotten into.

"It's still early," Jody said. "What do we do now?"

"I gotta go," Tracey said.

"Where?" Jody asked.

"Home. Jean is baby-sitting alone, and it's my turn," she lied. "I'll call you guys tomorrow."

Tracey hurried away from them.

Darkness was falling by the time Tracey started walking up the driveway. Her younger sister Jean sat out front on a lawn chair by the front screen door of the house. Jean, as short as Tracey was tall, was huddled on the flimsy chair, feet drawn up. Jean had hair so curly it was almost kinky. At the moment she looked like a defensive and nervous poodle, her large, dark eyes fixed on her older sister.

"Hi," Tracey said.

"Hello to you."

"What's wrong?" Tracey flopped down on the ground by Jean.

"You lied to me, that's what's wrong. I heard you've been fighting. Not just once, but all the time."

"I never lied about that," Tracey said. "Why do you care? Do you want to fight too?"

"No. I want you to stop," Jean exclaimed.

"Can't stop. I don't start the fights. They do," Tracey said.

"You're so dumb sometimes. What would old Mister

Ed say?" Jean demanded. Mister Ed was everybody's nickname for Sister Edward.

"I don't know," she said honestly.

"You two are writing to each other, aren't you?" Jean asked.

"Yeah, sure. I owe her a letter right now. I miss her a lot."

"She'll be back at the end of August."

Tracey looked up at her younger sister. "No, Jean, she's not coming back."

Jean's eyes showed surprise. "Has she been transferred?"

Tracey shrugged and looked out across the street. "She'll be at a school in Boston." The truth was, Sister Edward Elaine had left the convent. Tracey didn't understand why, but she knew that if she mentioned it, everybody would say Sister Ed was pregnant or had fallen in love with somebody. Neither was true. But for some reason she had quit. Stopped being a nun. Ended the vow.

"Why didn't you tell me?" Jean asked. "You never tell me anything!"

"I just did tell you," Tracey said. "I didn't say anything earlier because I didn't know until I graduated eighth grade. Sister Ed didn't want a big deal made of it."

"Man, you never tell me anything. I do everything for you," Jean said.

Tracey looked up at her again in the growing dimness. Jean was the pretty one of the two of them, and in a lot of ways she was more vulnerable. Anyway, right then she seemed more vulnerable.

"Where are your friends?" Jean asked sulkily.

Tracey laughed. "What friends?"

"Jody and Alice."

"Oh, Jean, they're not my friends. I don't know what they are."

"You don't have anybody else," Jean told her.

"I wonder what a friend really is," Tracey said.

"You guys have an argument?"

She shook her head. "No. But all of a sudden I didn't like them. I don't know." She looked up at Jean. "What is a friend, Jean? What would you say? You have lots of friends."

"Friends are friends," Jean said. She seemed flattered by the question. "A friend loves you. Tries to protect you."

Tracey nodded. "That sounds right." All of a sudden, without looking at her younger sister, she said, "What are we going to do about Mom and Dad?"

"I don't know. At least they aren't fighting anymore. It's just quiet."

"That's because they're never here."

"Mom says if Dad's at the office all the time, she shouldn't have to stay home alone, so she goes out to play bingo."

Tracey darted a look at her sister. Jean's serenity was a little strained, but it was obvious that she believed their mother was at bingo games all those nights.

"What about us?" Tracey asked. "What about you?"

"I don't mind if she goes out at night."

She was lying. But all of a sudden Tracey saw through the front on Jean's life. The whole front. Jean always took care of things. She would take care of the three little ones, just like she took care to get good grades and fit in well and cover for Tracey's misdemeanors. Jean would always provide what was missing. She was holding her whole world together, and she was doing it alone.

Tracey swore to herself, at herself, and pulled out a cigarette. She made her voice inviting. "You smoke, Jean?"

"Of course not! It's disgusting!"

"Well, you can if you want. I think you're old enough."

"Well, no thanks."

"Hey, you know what I do sometimes at night?" Tracey asked.

Jean couldn't help but show some interest. There was a normal kid under all that goody-goodness. "No, what?"

"I climb out on the roof over the garage where it's flat, and I lie on my back and look up at the stars. You ought to see them from the roof."

Jean seemed impressed in spite of herself. She never thought to do things like that. But she could enjoy them when Tracey suggested them.

"Can I do that sometime?" she asked. "I'll make you a deal."

"You don't have to make a deal for it. Come anytime you want," Tracey told her. "We'll do it tonight after Mom and Dad are in bed if you like. It's great out there. Some nights I lie out there all night. I just lie out there and smoke."

"Ugh. I don't want to do that."

"You don't have to then. But it's a great place to go, and nobody knows you're there."

"I ought to bring something to eat," Jean said. She

frowned in thought. Both of them were fond of keeping stashes of candy and cupcakes in their rooms.

"I got some candy bars," Tracey told her. "You can have them."

Jean looked at her and smiled. "Thanks, Tracey."

She shrugged and then smiled. "You're welcome. You've covered a lot for me this summer. Are the kids in bed?"

Jean nodded.

"I guess I'll go get a shower." Tracey stood and dropped her hand on Jean's shoulder, and Jean let her. "You're a good kid sister, Jean."

Tracey went inside. She decided not to tell Jean what she suspected. For one thing, she didn't know; and for another, it was better not to say it; better to bury it. She turned on the shower, fast and hot and hard, and stood in it for a long time. She knew that her mother was not attending the bingo games, even though she said she was. Tracey had ridden her bicycle up there one night at ten o'clock, all the way up there in the dark, and had checked for herself. The women who normally joined her mother for bingo were there, but her mother had not been there.

With the water flowing over her, she could cry and not sob, just sort of blend her tears in with the crashing water. Tears flowed down her cheeks, but she only had one question on her mind. *Do they really love us?* There was no answer to it. She didn't really believe a yes, and the no was too terrible to consider.

Tracey knew she didn't have the strength or ability to hold the family together without her parents. Unlike Jean, she didn't even want to try.

Jean was much closer to their father: a daddy's girl.

Tracey knew he would never hit Jean the way he hit her. For he had hit Tracey—really hit her, not just a spanking, and scratched her as she had run away from him. She did not understand why.

By the time Jean came into Tracey's room that night, Tracey had pulled herself together again. They climbed out onto the roof in the cool darkness.

"It is pretty," Jean said softly. They sat with their backs against the gable. Jean unwrapped a candy bar while Tracey lit a cigarette.

"It's like the whole world is all mine," Tracey told her. "Sometimes I even pray up here."

"I pray sometimes," Jean admitted.

"I think everybody does."

They sat quietly for a time, then Jean asked, "Did Dad ever really hit you, Trace? Hard?"

Tracey glanced at her. "Who told you that?"

"Mom did. She said he knocked you into the dish cabinet. She said it was child abuse. She said she thought you'd told me."

For a long moment, Tracey stared at her sister. In the faint glimmer from the stars, Jean's face showed all the fear of a small child. Tracey sat back against the wall. "Yes," she said. "It happened on graduation night."

"Why didn't you ever tell me?"

"Because maybe it won't matter," she said. "Mom had no right to tell you. Dad was sorry. And don't worry —he'll never do it to you."

"No, I wasn't thinking that," Jean said quietly.

"Why did Mom tell you that?" Tracey demanded. But the question wasn't to Jean.

"She came to my room one night after Dad took

me to a movie. You were gone, and Dad said I'd been watching all the kids every night, so he was taking me to a movie. Mom didn't seem to mind, but after I got home and went to bed, she told me about . . ." Jean began to cry the sputtering, quiet sobs of someone who doesn't want to cry.

Tracey leaned close and pulled a lock of Jean's curly hair gently toward herself so that Jean put her head on Tracey's shoulder. "I don't know why she told you, kid," she said. "But I'm all right. It wasn't that bad. Don't hate Dad."

"Do you hate Dad?" Jean asked in a muffled, weepy voice.

"Yeah, I do. And he knows it," Tracey said. "I started hating him that night, and it hasn't stopped. But I don't want you to hate him, and I don't want Mom to hate him."

Jean cried for a long time, long after Tracey had finished the cigarette. But at last she stopped, and then Tracey told her all about the many fights at the playground, about drinking beer and throwing up; and she got Jean to laugh at her.

"You guys always get into such trouble," Jean exclaimed.

"Not as bad as some kids I graduated with," Tracey told her. "Some of them smoke pot! Did you know that?"

"No! Not in eighth grade!" Jean exclaimed.

"Yeah, a couple of the boys did it this year. It's the seventies, Jean; things aren't like they were when Mom and Dad were kids. A lot of high school kids do pot and other stuff. But don't worry. I won't." She lit a fresh cigarette and threw her other arm around Jean.

"Some people have bad times in their marriages, I guess. We have to give them some slack. Things will get better." She hesitated and then said, "I'm not hanging around with Jody and Alice anymore."

Jean was astonished. "Why not?"

"Because they live for trouble, and I got tired of it. I like you better than I like them. A whole lot better."

Jean yawned and started on her second candy bar.

"Isn't this nice?" Tracey asked. "You come out here anytime you want."

"OK." With the confidence that came from having been comforted by her older sister, Jean leaned her head against Tracey again and took a big bite of chocolate. "Who will you hang around with?"

"I don't know. Someone new or you or nobody. I don't much care. High school starts soon, and I'll make friends there."

"Hmm."

They sat quietly together until Jean fell asleep. Using only her far hand, Tracey got a third cigarette out and lit it. It figured Jean wouldn't last until the sun came up, but that was OK. Jean was there, anyway. Asleep, but there.

# T H R E E

Tracey slept till noon the next day, then decided to go out. But she planned to avoid Jody and Alice. She took a shortcut through several yards and then walked up to the shopping center. She hung around there to see who she might meet from her eighth-grade class. Nothing much was happening. She walked around from place to place, finally ending up several neighborhoods away from her own. She circled around the long way to take a look at Ezra Pound from the vantage point of the woods.

She had a good idea where she was in relation to the patch of woods, and she started off confidently. But as she neared the school grounds, an uneasiness crept over her. To go back there might mean another fight, and suddenly she was sick of fighting. She resumed walking, now traveling unfamiliar neighborhood streets.

She noticed that a small group of people was congregating in a parking lot ahead. It was a church parking lot. A wooden sign out front advertised a tent meeting. She went around to the back of the building and saw that a brightly striped circus tent, its side panels rolled up and tied back, had been set up.

It was a Baptist church. She wasn't sure about Protestants and what they did, but her own church had plenty of bingo games, carnivals, and other activities. She decided it might be worth a visit. At least it would spare her from going back home or from running into people she'd rather not see.

Tracey sauntered back to the parking lot. Everybody in the knot of people turned around to look at her, and they smiled. Almost as if they'd been waiting for her.

One plump, gray-haired woman walked right up to Tracey. "Hello, dear. Can I help you?"

"Do you guys let Catholics into your tent meetings?" Tracey asked.

"Of course we do. Come along. You can sit with us. I'm Mrs. Murphy."

"How do you do? I'm Tracey Jacamuzzi."

Mrs. Murphy introduced Tracey to her husband, then led her to the tent. Inside, it looked a lot more like a church than a carnival. But she resolved to see what was going on. Sister Ed had left the convent for religious reasons, and Tracey had felt more misgivings about the church and God in the last few weeks than ever before. Maybe it was time to listen to somebody new. These seemed like kind, gentle people, the way she believed people were supposed to be.

Most of the women wore dresses and carried Bibles. She had neither. Mrs. Murphy shared her Bible with Tracey.

The hymns were another problem. Tracey flipped

26

through the hymnbook but only found three songs she knew: "Holy, Holy, Holy," "Praise Ye the Lord, the Almighty," and "Faith of Our Fathers." While the people sang unfamiliar hymns, Tracey stood silent, feeling like a dope. Finally, they sang "Holy, Holy, Holy," and she was glad to sing along.

One nice thing about tent meetings was that after the hymns were over, all you did was sit there. Nobody kneeled. Tracey didn't listen much as the minister preached to them. Certain words and phrases caught her ear, but she was too absorbed in looking the place over.

Everybody seemed so nice and so kind, and the women had children with them. The men looked sober and dignified in their white shirts, ties, and jackets. Somehow she knew these people didn't go to bingo games.

"Don't wonder if God can help you, brother, sister, or poor lost sinner," the preacher said. Tracey fixed her eyes on him. "Of course He can. He said so in this Book. In *the* Book." He had her attention then, and the odd thing was, he seemed to know it. He caught her eye as she looked at him.

"Yes indeed," he exclaimed. "Read this Book. Read the Bible for yourself, and you'll see the love of God."

*I wonder,* she thought, *if God really does stop the waves for some people. If He pulls them out. If He can reach them.*

Just then the preacher pounded his wooden pulpit, and she started in surprise. She'd never seen a priest get mad or excited when he gave a homily.

"The God who parted the Red Sea and the river Jordan for His people is the same God who rules today."

"Amen!" several people exclaimed.

*Maybe I should read the Bible*, she thought. She knew the Bible wasn't given for any private interpretation, but maybe it would be OK just to see it and think about it. She'd read some Bible verses in school, and they had seemed pretty straightforward. Even though a lot of people said that nobody could really understand the Bible, all of these people apparently read it. She thought there was a Bible or two somewhere on the bookshelves at home.

But the night was not yet over. After the sermon ended, three men came up to the pulpit. They didn't wear their suits and ties with the assurance of the preacher or the ushers. And they stumbled over their words.

One man said he'd been a heavy drinker for five years after his wife left him, and then he'd gotten saved just two years ago, and he hadn't had a drink since. He pointed out his two adult sons in the audience and said that God had saved them too, and now they were a happy family again.

The next man said that he'd served the Lord for thirteen years on the mission field and that God had provided for his every need. He quoted a Bible verse about the Lord being a refuge and then sat down. Tracey liked him best because he was briefest.

The third man talked about getting saved as a young boy, and then leaving the fold for many years. At last he'd been brought back by God's loving hand. He pointed to his wife in the audience and said that he thanked God for such a faithful and kind spouse. "Every man who has such a wife should thank God for such a blessing," he said.

Many other men called out, "Amen!"

Tracey jumped again and looked at Mrs. Murphy. She smiled and patted Tracey's hand. Mr. Murphy, who'd been one of the men who said "Amen," took his wife's hand and gave her a proud smile.

Tracey wondered how you joined this church. She already liked it a lot more than the Catholic church. Her mind reached back to the memory of Sister Edward. Was this the thing that Sister Ed had wanted and missed in becoming a nun?

*If God really is able to do all these things,* Tracey thought, *I wonder how you get Him to help you.* It seemed obvious that what you first needed to do was to join this religion. But she didn't know what that involved, aside from reading the Bible.

It was dark when the service finally ended. There had been a long plea from the minister for people to come forward and get saved, and Tracey's interest piqued. But she had no idea what that meant, so she decided to wait.

"Dear," Mrs. Murphy said as they walked down the aisle between the folding chairs, "can we give you a ride home?"

"Well, I'm not supposed to ride with people I don't know," Tracey began. "But I don't want to walk home in the dark, either. The service lasted a lot longer than I thought it would."

"You could call your parents from the church, and we'll ask them," she suggested.

Tracey shook her head. "My parents aren't home. It's OK. I'll ride with you."

Once in the car with the Murphys, Tracey asked, "Will any Bible do? Can I read the one I have at home?"

"It will do for a start," Mrs. Murphy said. "We'll find you a Bible of your own if you like."

"What's that *getting saved* mean?" she asked. "Saved from what?"

"From sin," Mr. Murphy told her. "And from hell."

"You guys don't believe in purgatory, do you?" she asked.

"It's not mentioned in the Bible," Mr. Murphy told her.

"It isn't? How come?"

"We think it's because there is no purgatory," he replied. "In fact, we're sure of it. The Bible gives no grounds for it."

"Look," she said, "can God really help people? Can He stop bad things from happening to them?"

"Yes," Mrs. Murphy told her. "But sometimes He chooses the bad things to happen to people. He uses hard times to try people, to purify them."

"But what about things that would really destroy someone? Can He stop it?"

"God can keep you in the fire and through the fire," Mr. Murphy said. "He may make you walk through it, Tracey, but He preserves you as you go through it. It just depends on what His will is."

When the Murphys dropped her off at her house, no other cars were in the driveway, but she knew she was just a jump ahead of her father. She thanked the Murphys and then hurried up to the house, to Jean, and to the sanctuary of the roof.

# F O U R

She really was just a jump ahead of her father. There was only time to tell Jean not to say anything and to promise to tell her on the roof about everything that had happened. Then she went upstairs to find a Bible if she could. She pulled open the resisting storage room door, groped in the darkness until she found the flimsy chain to the light bulb, and turned on the light. The storage room ceiling was low, and she had to keep her head down. She rummaged among the dusty cartons of discarded clothing, tablecloths, and Christmas decorations until she found the boxes of books.

Her father came home about five minutes later and came upstairs to see what she was doing.

Don Jacamuzzi was short and very broad. He was a clean-shaven man with thick black hair. Many people thought him distinguished-looking. At least, he was when he dressed up, but most of the time he was simply gruff, busy Don Jacamuzzi, whose thriving business had made it because of shrewd planning and not because the owner was a master handler of people or diplomacy.

"What are you doing up here?" he asked as he appeared at the storage closet door.

"Looking for a book," she told him. Books, as a rule, were things he approved of for the children.

"What's it called?" he asked.

"The Bible. Ever hear of it?" she countered.

He ignored the sarcasm. "A Bible? What for?"

"I want to read it." She stopped her search through the cartons of old books and looked up at him. "Isn't that OK?"

"Sure, read the Bible if you want. Maybe it will do you some good." He shrugged and trudged back downstairs.

He had long since stopped showing any embarrassment in front of her, but she avoided him as much as possible. He didn't seem to object to that. Maybe it was better for both of them if she stayed out of his way.

At last she found what she wanted, an old white Bible of the sort given to kids when they got confirmed. It was never really intended to be read, but it had a lovely white cover with HOLY BIBLE engraved in gold lettering across the front cover. She switched off the storage room light and walked back to her own room to read her new book.

For the first time she felt as though things might be working out for her. Maybe going to the tent meeting hadn't been just an accident. She remembered the prayer she had prayed on the roof so long ago, asking God for help. Maybe at last He was helping her.

Late that night, when Jean came to her door, Tracey brought the Bible out to the roof along with the cigarettes and candy bars. In the quiet darkness she told her younger sister all about the tent meeting, the Murphys, the men who had talked about God, and the Bible.

32

Jean took the Bible from her and looked it over. She looked at its cover anyway. "Always been there," she said at last. She handed it back to Tracey. "You think it works like they say? They sound like holy rollers."

Tracey handed Jean the candy bars and leaned back to light a cigarette. "Is there really such a thing as holy rollers?"

"Sure. That's how black people and poor white people do it—worship, I mean. They jump up and yell 'Hallelujah,' and then run around and drop on the floor and roll around. Some of them handle snakes."

"I've heard about that," Tracey said. "I wonder what for."

"I think Jesus told His apostles He'd give them power to tread on snakes."

"You know a lot about this."

Jean shrugged. "Only what I've seen on TV."

Tracey thought it over as she smoked. At last she said, "I don't think the Murphys are holy rollers. Nobody was yelling or rolling around. No snakes, either. They did all say 'Amen,' though."

"We do that," Jean said.

"Not like they do it. They just say it out on their own." Tracey looked at the Bible in her lap. "I can't picture the Murphys or those other guys rolling around. That'd be silly, and they weren't silly." *Corny, maybe*, she added to herself, *but not silly*. She could forgive the corniness or pretend it wasn't there. Because something else had been there. Like they understood some facts she'd never heard of. Facts about God and about life.

"They'll want you to quit smoking," Jean said.

Tracey looked at the cigarette in her hand and glanced back at Jean. "Drinking too?"

Jean nodded solemnly. "And fighting."

"I already quit fighting. See, I'm getting better and it's only been one night."

"What are Mom and Dad going to say if they find out you want to switch religions?"

"Oh, who cares?" Tracey put out the cigarette and took a candy bar. "You and me are the only ones who go to Mass, and that's just to take the little ones."

"Yeah, and it's usually me who ends up going," Jean mumbled.

"Protestants have church nurseries." Tracey shot a look at Jean. "Want to give it a try?"

"Don't try to get me into this," Jean told her. "I like being Catholic. It's beautiful."

Her stern reply startled Tracey. "You do?" she asked.

"Yes. I like Mary and St. Joseph and all the rest. They're good, and they're . . . I don't know. Beautiful."

"You really mean that, don't you?" Tracey asked.

"Sure. You gotta work at it. I did stations of the cross every day before school last Lent. But it did get to mean something."

Tracey thought about stations of the cross—that long, tedious walk through Jesus' path of shame from being condemned to being laid in the tomb. People slowly progressed up one aisle of the church and then down the other, stopping before each wooden plaque that commemorated another episode of His journey to Calvary. At each station they said a couple of prayers and read a little devotional.

Every Lent the whole school did stations on Wednesdays. At the service, only Father Theodore

34

moved from station to station while everybody else read the prayers. The boredom was relieved every now and then by one-stanza songs of four dolorous lines, sung quietly and slowly. The service wasn't too bad until he got out the incense. Lent was about the only time incense was used, and the parish's choice of scents was anything but heavenly. In late Lent, when the weather was hot and the sanctuary all shut up, some of the students passed out. Tracey could remember one time when Jean had been helped out.

"And you believe all that about the saints?" Tracey asked. "About St. Patrick and the snakes and all that? And the dogwood tree?"

Jean shrugged and said nothing, a sign that she didn't know and didn't want to admit it.

Tracey was silent for a moment too. She realized that her younger sister had tensed up. She dug a new cigarette out of her jacket pocket. "Don't worry," she said. "I'm not leaving the Holy Roman Catholic Church, with the priests and the nuns and the little bambinos. And of course old Top Wop All Up Top."

Jean glanced at her, unsure whether to laugh or get mad. Tracey imitated the pope as she always did when she told the TWA joke. "Hey, I'm-a the pope o' the whole-a Catholic-a Church, Mr. Newsman. I'm-a got all them *pisanos* under me—alla the priests and the nuns and the little bambinos." Jean smiled as Tracey added the punch line. "'At's-a why I ride-a TWA: Toppa Wop Aboard!"

They burst out laughing, and Tracey lit her cigarette. "I ain't joinin' no church that says I can't smoke," she told Jean. "Took me a year to get hooked, and I'm not breaking the habit now."

# F I V E

No man can come to me, except the Father which hath sent me draw him: and I will raise him up at the last day. It is written in the prophets, And they shall be all taught of God. Every man therefore that hath heard, and hath learned of the Father, cometh unto me. Not that any man hath seen the Father, save he which is of God, he hath seen the Father. Verily, verily, I say unto you, He that believeth on me hath everlasting life. I am that bread of life.

One thing was for sure, Tracey thought as she fumbled her hand along the rooftop in search of her glass of cola. Once you started reading the Bible, all the stuff about Mary and the saints went right out the window.

She had always suspected that. Anyway, it seemed like always. Unlike Jean, she had seldom felt the attraction to Mary or to a particular patron saint that so many of the nuns had evidenced. Elaborate stories of the sufferings of the saints and of Mary's purity and compassion sounded like tall tales. Mary, void of the passions of a woman, void of all sin from birth, void even of a sense of humor, had at times annoyed Tracey. She wasn't a real person. Even the one story that hinted that Mary was a typical mother, when Jesus stayed at the temple for three days and Mary rebuked Him, had been dampened when Sister Rose Marie had told them in second grade that Mary's rebukes to Jesus were justified. Sister Rose had explained that it was still too early for Jesus to be made a public figure because John had not yet come preaching.

As Tracey read the story herself, she realized that Jesus was well in control of Himself and the situation. If anything, the Bible made it sound like He was being patient with Mary and Joseph, not they with Him. She was glad. She was even glad for Mary. It was much nicer to be a real person than to be the waxwork doll Mary had become.

Tracey walked up to the Baptist church again on Monday night. Nobody was around; the tent meetings were over. When the pastor came out to lock up and go home, she talked with him. He gave her a book called *False Doctrines Answered*. Tracey hurried home and rushed up to the roof to check it out. Its first section contained nine chapters on the "Errors of Romanism."

Much of what she'd guessed was verified. Other more complicated things were spelled out, but it was missing a few things she thought were important. The thing that griped her most about the church was that the pope was so rich. It was a subject she had brought up to Father Theodore in the eighth-grade class discussions. He had thanked her for her participation and had said the pope didn't want that wealth; it was given in honor of the position of Holy Father. Tracey found that a little hard to swallow. After all, Jesus was God, and He hadn't demanded wealth in honor of His position. Hadn't He commanded that the first would be last and the last first?

There were a lot of things about the pope that bothered her. He was never in contact with real people. And popes—supposedly infallible—had contradicted each other. She remembered, when she was in second grade, Pope Paul had declared that St. Nicholas and St. Christopher weren't saints. Well, what about the popes who had made them saints? Somebody had to be wrong. She'd heard some eighth graders talking about it and had become convinced the pope was not perfect. So why did he still claim to be?

It was not a question she had put to Father Theodore. She already could have guessed his answer: The pope did not claim to be perfect. Only his position was perfect. His statements as pope were infallible, but his statements as a mere man were not infallible. Nobody had ever claimed that they were.

For crying out loud, all you had to do was watch a few episodes of *Star Trek* or *Mission Impossible* to know when people were using propaganda. It had bothered her more in sixth grade, when she'd learned that the high priests of the Aztecs and Incas had also claimed to be infallible in their proclamations of the gods. It all sounded like the same thing.

Her thoughts were interrupted by Jean's voice from down below. "No, Tracey's not in the house," she was saying.

Tracey rolled onto her stomach and lay flat. She heard Jody's voice but couldn't make out the words.

"You'll have to ask Tracey," Jean said defensively. After a pause, she said more loudly, "I'm telling you, she's not in the house."

Another pause, then Jean said, "I'll tell her you were looking for her."

Good old Jean, holding things together. After a few moments, Tracey sat up and returned to her Bible.

It seemed like, in the Bible, people who wanted to be Christians just came up to Jesus and asked Him. But it was different from confirmation or Acts of Contrition. For one thing, He always said yes, whereas with an Act of Contrition, you never knew if you'd been good enough or sincere enough for it to count for anything.

*If Jesus were really here,* she thought, *I could just go and ask Him.* But she dismissed the thought. She didn't think she would. What about the rich young ruler? What if the Son of God should look at her like He'd looked at that guy, and say, "Give up your cigarettes, your friends, your jean jacket, and come follow Me"? Or, "Give up your grudge against your father, stop running from your old friends, and help your younger sister." He could ask any one of a hundred things that she didn't want to do.

And yet she couldn't stop reading, couldn't quite dismiss it all from her mind. Maybe it was just that the people at that church were so nice, that the Murphys were so much what she wished her own parents were, that when they talked about God and holiness it wasn't like tall tales of fake saints and waxwork Marys.

She closed the Bible softly, stretched out on her back, and lit a cigarette. For a long time she watched the sunset sky. The sun hung as though pasted there, stark red against the cloudless, opaque blue, dipping toward gentle, misty ribbons above the horizon. It would soon fall below the horizon, harmonizing with the colors, the glow becoming gentler.

A clap of noise startled her as something struck the ground behind the garage. She tried to sit up but found she couldn't move. She listened. Someone was stepping up the woodpile, just as she had done several times, climbing up the sturdy chunks of tree trunk, then higher onto the less stable logs on top without hesitation. Whoever it was sounded very surefooted.

Had Jody determined to find her at last, to force her to a confrontation about why she had dropped her and Alice so quickly? She tensed at the thought but for some reason could not even lift her arm to defend herself.

She did not see the head of the person come up over the edge of the roof. Suddenly, there it was—or he was, or she was—standing upright on the very edge of the roof. A tall, straight figure, who seemed to be all face. There was a body, of course—arms, legs, hands, and feet—but the only thing Tracey saw clearly was the face. Even then, she never did remember the color of the eyes, or the type of hair, or even whether the person had eyebrows. She felt an urge to scurry for the bedroom window and get away from this stranger, but her body lay limp and paralyzed.

For its part, the newcomer recognized her and quickly crossed the roof to her side. Without asking permission or speaking a word of greeting, the creature either leaned over her or dropped to its knees alongside her, took the jean jacket by the lapels, and opened it as wide as it would go. The sides of the jacket fell on either side of her body like wings, draped over her useless arms. She felt a fear that this thing could take her by the throat, then a sharper fear that it would turn down her collar and look right at the scratch marks that were still just faintly visible on her neck.

But the newcomer did something that Tracey could not see, a gesture as though flipping a switch under her throat. She felt no pain, but she realized that somehow this creature was looking inside her, unhampered by the covering of clothes or skin or flesh. The creature looked for a long time. Its intentions did not seem unkind, but from the way its eyes flicked back and forth, it seemed to be reading something deep inside her, and she thought this reading might give her a reason to be afraid. And it did. As though following some map inside her, the newcomer reached for the collar of her blouse, gently pulled it aside from her neck, and checked the faint scars. Then it touched her shoulder and traced the exact pattern of the bruises—no longer visible to human eyes—that her father had given her weeks ago. The old injuries seemed to add to its information bank about her. The creature searched down her arms until it found her hands, then held them up to inspect. Her knuckles were bruised and bloody from all the girls she'd punched.

She suddenly realized that, though the passing of days had hidden the bruises and the blood from the outside world, the marks of her fights would always be there for any creature like this to see. It simply had to know where to look. She had been ashamed to have the creature so quickly identify where she had been hit. But now, when it looked at her hands, she felt a horror deep inside—a horror that this thing, who seemed intent and yet dispassionate, should see the blood of another person on her hands. It gingerly set the hands down, and it did seem daunted by them, subdued for the first time.

For a moment, the face of this intruder looked like Sister Ed, the expression indicating puzzlement over why Tracey had never written back. But the likeness faded. It leaned over her, studying her face. She closed her eyes and desperately wished it really were Sister Ed. She felt the scrutiny through her closed eyes, panicked, then suddenly found that she could move.

"Stop!" she yelled. She bolted up to a sitting position. She opened her eyes and found herself alone on the roof, the first shades of dusk stealing over her, her jacket safely buttoned over her as it had been. Her hands were supple and unmarked. The cigarette had burned out alongside her. Shaking, she dug another one out and lit it, waiting for the courage to move again, to resume her evening routine as though it had all been a dream.

On Sunday morning, Tracey passed her father as she hurried through the kitchen to grab a doughnut.

"What are you so dressed up for?" he asked.

"Goin' to church," she said as she crammed half of the doughnut into her mouth.

"Would you please eat like a young lady," he demanded.

"I'm in a hurry, Dad."

"What for? You can go to the next Mass and have time to eat nicely."

She finished the doughnut and wiped her mouth with a napkin. "I'm not going to Mass. The Murphys are picking me up to go to their church."

"What church?"

"The Baptist church on the other side of Ezra Pound," she said, grabbing her Bible.

"Who said you could go to another church?" he demanded.

She looked back at him. "Am I supposed to ask to go to church?"

"And who are those people?" he asked.

"Dad, I met them over a week ago at an outside thing their church was having," she told him. "I've mentioned them in front of you before, but you never asked. They told me they'd be glad to drive me over to their church, so I said sure. I like them, and I like their church—I think. Today's the first time."

"You listen to me, young lady," he exclaimed, pointing his index finger at her face. "If you have time to go to some other church, then you'd better make time to get to your own as well." She could see that he was annoyed, annoyed even to the point of anger. "Where's your mother?" he demanded. "Does she know about this?"

"You'll have to ask her," Tracey said evenly.

"What's that supposed to mean?"

"Just what I said. You'll have to ask her. I don't know if she knows or not. I told her, if that's what you want to know."

He looked at her with a long, calculating stare. This was not his look of senseless anger. She'd hit a button on him that had switched off the question of church for a moment. The silent stare between them was broken as a car horn beeped outside. Don Jacamuzzi snapped back to the present. "You heard me. You be in Mass today."

"All right, all right!" she exclaimed as she hurried out. "Anything to get out of here," she mumbled as she went out the door.

By the time Tracey got back from church, there were no more Masses to attend that day. She stayed quiet around her father and said little about church services or the Bible or the Murphys. But she couldn't wait to get Jean out on the roof and tell her about everything that had happened.

Every Sunday evening, her mom went to her bingo game, or claimed to, anyway. Her father stayed home and watched *The Wonderful World of Disney* with the three little ones. Tracey usually stayed holed up in her room, listening to records and thinking about eighth grade and Sister Edward.

But that night, her parents surprised her by going out to dinner together. They took the three little ones with them and wanted to take Jean and Tracey too, but the girls said no. They said it so adamantly that both parents gave up rather than argue, and left.

"How do you like that?" Tracey said as soon as the door closed.

Jean shrugged. "I told you it would be OK."

"Sure."

Tracey turned toward the living room and—feeling the liberty of having no parents or little kids at home—automatically reached for a cigarette. Then she pulled her hand out of her pocket.

"You gonna smoke?" Jean asked.

"No," she said.

"No?"

Tracey threw herself onto the couch. "I got saved today."

Jean rolled her eyes. "Oh, come on. Tracey, they did it to you!"

She nodded. "I know. But cheer up. We didn't roll around."

"What did you do?" Jean asked.

"It's not what you think," Tracey told her. "It's not anything like Catholic church. And what the preacher said made sense."

"So what happened? Did you see God?"

"Come on, cut it out!" she yelled. She stood up. "You're so out of touch, Jean. You're so hooked on the way you want things to be. Well, it doesn't work that way. I can't be Catholic now. And that stuff you like so much is stupid! I quit believing all that way before I started reading the Bible."

"So what happened when you got saved?" Jean demanded, challenging her. "Now that you've got the real thing instead of the made-up stuff? Come on, did you see God?"

"Just forget it," she said and went into the kitchen to make something to eat.

After a minute or two, Jean came in after her. "What did happen?" Jean asked.

"Nothing. Just forget it. I'm sorry I told you."

Jean sat down at the kitchen table and waited while Tracey put on a pot of Cream of Wheat.

At last Tracey said, "All the guys in the Bible just came up to Jesus and asked Him to help them. That's all they did, Jean. No priests, no sacraments, nothing. But they meant it. And suddenly, today, I meant it."

"And that's getting saved?" Jean asked.

"It's not like you're asking for a favor," Tracey told her. "It's a big change. It's asking Him to make you His, asking Him to make you good. Don't you see that nobody's good? Nobody. So what are Catholic people trying for? That's what makes the saints so fake. We all know that nobody could be that good in real life."

"Jesus was that good, and He's not fake."

"He's God," Tracey said. "And the Lord cried, and sometimes He got mad. Well, angry, anyway. He didn't act like those saints we read about. Even though He didn't sin, He was real. You know, even Mary called God her Savior in the Magnificat. Remember? 'I will rejoice in God my Savior.' So she needed to be saved from her sins, too. Just like me. And just like you."

"So now you're not Catholic anymore?" Jean asked.

Tracey hesitated, then said, "No, I'm not. It's all wrong. And . . . and it's bad too. It's corrupt."

Jean stood. "Dad is going to kill you if you tell him that."

"Well, I'll say it nice." Tracey poured the cereal into a bowl. "But it's true," she said softly. She knew it would be pointless to even try to tell Jean about everything that had happened that morning. One minute she'd been normal Tracey Jacamuzzi, and the next she'd seen it all for what it was worth. Her dad didn't like her anymore, and her mother was doing something worse than hitting her kids—far worse. Tracey's friends were gone, and she had plenty of enemies. Sister Edward was not only gone, she was gone forever. Just writing to her once had been an act of reopening that pain, and Tracey had realized that all summer she'd been trying to somehow forget that Sister Edward had left as a failure.

Suddenly, Tracey had been able to see that she was boxed in and helpless. Then she'd understood the conditions of the people who had come to the Lord on their knees. It was the same with all of them. That was why they could come on their knees and not care what people said. That was why they could do it and not seem like fakes. Because when you were desperate, that was when the Lord suddenly came through your town or walked up your road or rode by under your tree.

Without understanding how, she'd realized to a deeper level just how desperate she was. She'd understood that the Lord was not a stranger to her by coincidence or because she was so young. She suddenly could understand that she was a stranger to Him and had never cared all that much about Him before. But here was the door opening: She understood, she wanted, she believed, and she prayed. Then she knew what prayer was—not the empty words said on her knees at the rail, but real words that meant something.

She wondered what she would tell her father. Maybe she could keep it quiet for a while. Keep it quiet until she had read the Bible more and had covered more in the other books the Murphys and the pastor had loaned her.

Jean kept her distance for the rest of the evening. Tracey retired to her room and stayed there even when she heard the rest of her family get back. She took out the Bible and her *False Doctrines* book and sat and studied while the night outside lengthened.

At last she heard everybody going to bed. She waited another thirty minutes, grabbed her bag of miniature candy bars, and went out on the roof. Life without cigarettes was going to take some getting used to, but the roof was still her private domain, even if she no longer used it to catch a smoke.

The first week after Tracey had gone down the aisle was busy. She sent off a letter to Sister Edward and then immersed herself in reading and studying.

On Tuesday morning, her mother came up the stairs and found her up and in her robe, seated at the old, battered desk in the room. Her Bible and the textbook lay before her. "Studying?" her mom asked. "Do you feel all right?"

"Yeah, I feel OK."

Her mother bent over to pick up the small piles of dirty clothes that lay strewn around the room.

"You know I've been reading the Bible," Tracey began.

"Yes."

Her mom seemed in a pretty good mood this morning. Tracey ventured a question. "What do you think about a person's religion, Mom? Is it most important to be in a certain church, or to live what you really believe?"

"It's most important to live what you really believe, of course," her mother told her.

"What if . . . what if you believe something that's against your religion?"

Her mother straightened up. "Tracey, I don't have time for religious discussions. I have work to do."

"I'll help you with the laundry," Tracey said. She stood. Suddenly it was urgent that she get her mother's attention. Her mother stopped and turned around.

"I don't want help with the laundry. I like to do it my way and get it done right. If you want to help, make your bed and clean up your room."

"But what about religion?" Tracey asked.

"Tracey, be any religion you want." She turned around and walked out. Tracey sat back down again. The first hurdle was cleared, but it left a disappointment in her.

In spite of her mother's seeming carelessness, Tracey gradually realized over the next few days that her father was aware of a change in her beliefs.

"Hey," he said to her one night as she cleared the dinner dishes from the table. It was another one of those mysterious nights when neither parent was going out. And it was only a Wednesday.

"What, Dad?" she asked.

"What's this about you and that Baptist church?"

Even then, she didn't say the words "I'm saved," and certainly not "I'm not a Catholic."

The evangelical fire that had burned so brightly in front of Jean flickered a little. "I believe what they say," she told him. "And I respect them a lot. They believe the Bible, and so do I."

"I believe the Bible," he countered.

She stopped stacking the dirty plates long enough to shoot him a second glance, her eyes faintly defiant. "Have you ever read it?"

His eyes were suddenly cool and calm. "In college," he told her. He sounded self-satisfied. Then he added, "A lot of people misinterpret it in a lot of ways."

She was sure that he had never read the whole Bible, but she didn't say that. "Can I keep going?" she asked him.

He pushed his plate toward her. "It's like I said. You go to Mass, then you can go to their church. But every time you're in their church, you be in your own church too."

She nodded. "OK."

It took a week to get up the nerve to ask him to let her go to public school. "It's only July 23, Dad," she told him. "There's plenty of time for me to transfer."

"Are you out of your mind?" he demanded. "Do you know what goes on in public school? Those kids drink. I've heard that at least a third of the kids in our public school have tried smoking marijuana!"

"Dad," she exclaimed, "this is the seventies. Kids at St. Anne's tried pot!"

His face betrayed a look of astonishment that was almost comical. "Did you?" he yelled.

"Of course not!" she replied truthfully. She wondered what she would do if he asked about the smoking, the drinking, and the fighting. "Look, all that pot smoking and stuff goes around at Bishop Wood, just the same as in public school."

"Listen to me, young lady, those nuns at Bishop Wood take care of their students and watch over them like mothers. Yes, like mothers!"

"Oh, come on, Dad! Like Sister Rose Marie did? And Dominicus?"

"Hey, you! They're strict. That's all. That's good for you."

"I don't need a nun to keep me off pot," she told him. "The Lord can take care of me."

"The Lord can take care of you in a decent school then."

She gave up before she got him too mad. But she knew there would be trouble. After ten days of being a Christian convert, she already believed that kneeling in front of a statue and offering prayers to it or to any of the saints or to Mary was idolatry. What would she do when school started? They had first-Friday Mass every month; and the mornings, even in high school, began with an Our Father and three Hail Marys. On certain days, the Magnificat would be thrown in, the Apostles' Creed, the Act of Contrition, any of the rest of them. And then there were the May processions and the hymns to Mary that she now rejected.

When she went to Mass at St. Anne's before going to church, she simply sat in the last pew in the back and read her Bible. Her Protestant pastor had been quick to point out the idolatry of kneeling to the Eucharist or to any of the statues, and so she stayed seated through the whole Catholic service.

It was one thing to do that as a free layperson who had come in off the street. It would be something else again to do it in the Bishop Wood sanctuary, wearing the Bishop Wood uniform, surrounded by her classmates and teachers.

# E I G H T

Dear Tracey,

I was surprised and pleased to get your last letter. I was beginning to be afraid that you had dropped off the face of the earth! I'm very pleased that you've had a great summer.

I wasn't sure from all that you said in your letter exactly how your beliefs have changed, or where you differ with the church so much that you feel you can no longer be a Catholic. I have considered the Bible several times in recent months, and I own one, but I'm afraid that my progress through it has been slow. As I told you in June, I feel comfortable with being a Catholic for right now, and leaving the mission has given me great freedom to ask questions and to seek answers.

But I'm happy for you if this is what you think you should do. I don't feel any loyalty to any church simply because it is a church. Sincere religion is the best religion, and if your choice was between sincere religion and no religion, then I'm glad that you chose sincere religion.

I am happy with teaching summer school this year, and I am getting along well with my students. I have six gifted students in an accelerated science class in the late afternoons, and I enjoy them so much. We sometimes stay late if there is a project due, and I am glad to be able to afford treats like hamburgers or ice cream for them. Next month I will move out of my family's house into my own apartment, and I plan to get a cat. Can you think of any good names for her?

I miss you very much and hope that you will get a chance to come up and visit me. Please write soon.

Love,<br>Mary (Sister Ed)

One problem with letters was that sometimes they seemed impersonal. Or if not impersonal, at least not real. Tracey put the letter down with a sinking feeling. It felt as though Sister Edward was still thinking of her as a little girl.

Then Tracey gave herself a mental shake. She felt like she had grown up years since graduation day, but how would Sister Ed know that? Tracey had sent her only one letter before the last one. That first letter had been so emotional and gushy that Tracey blushed at the memory of it.

There was no way for Sister Ed to know how serious this was. Nor could she know how real.

August had come. She finished the *False Doctrines* book. In her Bible, she had read John, Luke, Acts of the Apostles, Romans, and First Corinthians. The only thing to do all day was either read or watch television, and though she might leave her reading for a while when it became dull to her, it always seemed to bring her back. The slow but steady unraveling of all the things she had once believed drew her like a magnet.

She was learning hymns at church and could get through two stanzas of "Just as I Am" and all the stanzas of "At Calvary." Other tunes and snatches of words came back to her all the time, but it was hard to learn so many new songs very quickly. She hated to look like a dope when everybody else was singing, so she took the few minutes before the service and a few minutes after to pick out hymns in the hymnbook and memorize the words.

She noticed, as August lengthened, that her mom and dad were now usually home on the weekends. They didn't really talk to each other all that much. They were nothing like the Murphys, who sometimes held hands in church and always treated each other like company. When Mom was home she was usually ironing or cleaning house with that strict, harsh method of hers that usually meant nobody could help her. When she was *really* cleaning and wanted you to help her, that was worse. Without fail, you made a mistake somewhere or spilled something or didn't do it to suit her, and then she got mad and yelled, and you felt stupid. Tracey had learned long ago to vanish when her mother was recruiting for big cleaning projects.

Her father usually spent the morning loafing around the yard, maybe working in his garden. By eleven o'clock or noon, he would take James, Gina, and John out somewhere—Grandmom's, maybe, or the park, or out for a special treat for lunch.

Tracey knew her dad was much better with little

kids than with bigger ones. He'd always been nice to her when she was small. Not like now, when they just about ignored each other. On Saturdays Jean either disappeared with her friends or went with the three little ones when their dad took them out.

Sunday was Tracey's day to disappear. After early Mass, she had the rest of the morning with the Murphys at church and, if there was time, a quick look through the church's small library.

"All I hear about is church, church, church," her father complained one Sunday afternoon when she came inside the house, her dress on and her Bible in her hand.

"Dad, they have three services there a week," she told him. "I only go to one. Is that too much?"

"Listen to me, young lady. Are you really going to Mass like I told you?" he demanded.

"Yes, I went to eight o'clock Mass," she told him. "Father Drew said it, and Stephen Magee and his little brother Joe were the altar boys. There was only one nun who showed up. I guess the others are all on vacation."

Eight o'clock Mass was when all of the nuns came in. It was the best Mass to go to, because you got to sit safe and sound and out of school with your family, where the nuns couldn't get you. You could watch them for once. That was how she had felt about it when she was a kid, and even now she felt the same.

It was also good to go to eight o'clock Mass because when the Murphys picked her up at St. Anne's, there was still time for her to go to Sunday School. She preferred Sunday School to church. There wasn't as much singing, but the class she was in answered her questions pretty thoroughly. The lessons were much more systematic than the sermons. Straightforward information was what she wanted. But though church bored her sometimes, she liked to sit by the Murphys. It was nice to have friends.

"Well, I think I'll just ask Father Drew to keep his eye on you," her father said.

"Fine," she told him. "He'll tell you that I'm always there." She went upstairs to get to the privacy of her room. Her mom was up in the storage closet in the hall. Tracey stuck her head in the door. "What's up, Mom?"

"Oh, I'm just getting a few things," her mother told her. She seemed cheerful. She was tugging at a stack of purses and hatboxes. "I thought I'd put away some of my spring clothes and try to dig out some things for fall." The prospect of new clothes and trying things on always put her mom in a good mood.

Tracey relaxed. "Need help?"

"Not yet. I might call you. I just need to look around and find things first."

"OK." Tracey bent her head to duck out the low door, and as she did, her eyes fell on a strip of paper lying on the floor. "I'll throw this out," she said, half to her mom and half to nobody. She went up the hall and absentmindedly put the rectangle of yellow paper into her Bible.

She wanted lunch, but most of all, she wanted to change. It took only a moment to throw off the dress and find her jeans and a T-shirt. After that, she went downstairs and made herself some turkey sandwiches on rye bread. She carried these on a plate up to her room and sat down with them at her desk. She opened up her Bible, right to the strip of paper she'd found.

She glanced at it as she reached down to find the trash can.

> ROOM SERVICE, dial "0"
> Sandwiches Fresh from Our Deli
>     Turkey Club
>     Reuben
>     BLT
>     Grilled Cheese
> Entrees Served with Salad and Roll
>     Sirloin Strip
>     Baked Chicken
>     Catch of the Day
>     Sorrento's Special Pasta Plate
> Sorrento's thanks you for your patronage.

It was new, unwrinkled, and unworn by any time spent in her mother's purse. Tracey turned it over and saw, in someone's handwriting, *Mary Anne, ran down to the desk to get towels, will get spare key from clerk. Jim.*

Her heart almost stopped. Mary Anne was her mother's first name. Her mind flicked over the town: the streets, the highway, the place where the turnpike entrance was. The Sorrento Motel was a nice, though dark and sheltered, place near the turnpike. Next thing she knew, Tracey was on her feet, the paper in her hand. In two strides she was at the door, and the cry to her father was almost in her throat when she stopped.

Just as quickly, she closed the door and locked it. She put her back against it and slowly slid down to the floor until she was sitting as a barricade against the door. It would never do to tell him. They would divorce. Where would that leave her, and Jean, and the three little ones?

But what if they did divorce? What if she left him for . . . for Jim, whoever he was? Or what if her father found out? He had to know. He had to at least suspect something. Even she, Tracey, dumb as she was, all caught up in church and the Bible and religion, had suspected something. Maybe he couldn't face it. Maybe Don Jacamuzzi, tough, cold, and hard, couldn't face that.

The idea that her parents were genuinely in love—in love like you saw it on the soap operas or in the movies—had always made her laugh. But for the first time she caught a glimpse of the awfulness of it: of sharing everything with a person and having kids and thinking they belonged only to you. And then suspecting. If the house, which had not been cleaned until recently, and the laundry not done, and her mom's preoccupation had worried her, what must they have done to him?

How could he face it? It really would mean a divorce, and it would mean putting all of them through a divorce. Not just her and Jean, but James and Gina and John too. And he would have to walk through his neighborhood—rich Don Jacamuzzi, the shrewd businessman—knowing that everybody knew his wife had dumped him for someone else. Everyone he had ever beat out in real estate would be there to laugh at him, and everybody he'd ever helped out would be there to pity him. She knew her father. Both would be awful for him.

She was even more afraid to confront her mother. Afraid to hear the lies she knew would come. It was like a cold dash of water in her face when the truth hit her that her mother had been lying to her and to all of them for nearly a year now. And furthermore, that she was really good at lying. She might have been lying to all of them for who knows how long. How could you know?

And she would lie, too, if Tracey confronted her. She might, if pushed to the wall, really hurt Tracey. Right now it seemed that all of their lives hung on her mother's decision whether to stay married to her husband. Tracey didn't want to push her.

"Oh, God, help me," she whispered. She clamped her lips together and shut her eyes and prayed the rest in her head. *Help me, help me. Don't let it happen. Why did You let me see this? I didn't want to know. I didn't want to know about this.*

# NINE

The only thing to do was walk and walk. Walk, and walk, and walk some more. If she stayed around Jean, she would tell her. Or Jean might see it written all over her face.

This was Thursday, the fourteenth of August. She had known for four days. All she could do was walk and think, and maybe pray, but keep walking. It was a cool evening, and her heart turned longingly to Sister Edward and to better days. Then she made her mind let those thoughts go. She had been a Catholic then, with no answers.

But she didn't know enough about Christianity to find the answers to this. Already in the rack of leaflets at the back of her new church, she had seen and taken several papers meant for "young people," as the teens were called in Baptist churches. In these papers, the teenagers always faced terrible, almost insurmountable, problems. They found a verse in the Bible that fit their lives exactly, and somehow they got the faith right away to make it through their troubles. That was what she was waiting for: the verse, the doctrine, the knowledge that would make her a good Christian who could deal with this. It was in there somewhere.

She had also taken a step backward. That morning she'd found an old pack of cigarettes in her other jeans. She was now smoking one, enjoying it while asking God to forgive her and explaining to Him that this was her last pack for life.

She was way past Ezra Pound by now. In fact, she was getting close to her church, and she realized that walking around with a cigarette in her mouth might not be a good idea.

She glanced around for a sight of anybody from church, and she saw two girls up ahead of her. She recognized one of them. It was Barbara.

The tall blonde girl saw her almost at the same time and nudged her friend. Tracey threw the cigarette to the ground. It crossed her mind to run for it, but she dismissed that thought. She didn't intend to fight, but she wasn't about to run, either. The part of her that felt the old thrill of excitement at the idea of a fight was a part she didn't acknowledge. It was impossible to believe she wanted to fight. She'd given that up even before she'd gotten saved.

"Well, look who it is," Barbara said.

"I almost said the same thing," Tracey told her. "Spotted you a block away by your lipstick."

The girls stopped a good ten feet away, and she stopped too.

"Seems like your friends aren't around tonight," Barbara said.

Tracey shook her head. "No, they aren't. That's OK."

"You think so?"

Tracey put her fists on her hips and stood with her feet spread. "Yeah, I think so."

"Don't you look tough."

"Barbara . . . and Barbara-ette." Tracey nodded to the shorter, younger girl. "You don't want to do this. Not tonight."

"I thought you might say that." Emboldened, Barbara walked slowly and deliberately toward Tracey. Her friend tailed along.

"I think you mistook me," Tracey said. Before Barbara was close enough to do anything, Tracey sprang at her. Waiting for the other person to hit first sounded nice in books, but Tracey knew that if you let two people against one start a fight, it was a sure thing they would finish it too. Their intent was clear, and she wasted no time.

Her sudden attack caught the other girls by surprise. Such wild, careless bravery was unusual. Even Tracey didn't possess it in normal circumstances. But she had it now, fueled by the despair and grief she'd been fighting all day.

Her jump forward brought her a little to the side of Barbara and out of range of the other girl. Before Barbara could grab her, Tracey punched hard with her right hand and followed it with her left. She danced back around the blonde girl, again out of range of the smaller girl.

It was like being wired to a power line. Suddenly she couldn't stop. They both rushed Tracey, and she darted to the side, staying closer to Barbara and away from the other one. Tracey kicked and felt Barbara's fingernails rake her ear and claw her hair, but then

Tracey punched again and felt the shock run from her fist to her shoulder as she connected solidly with the other girl's lips. She jumped away, and at last had a moment to clout the younger girl with her right forearm. Then she simply grabbed her by her jacket collar and spun, throwing her into Barbara.

They both turned and started to run away, but Barbara couldn't resist turning back to yell something at Tracey. It slowed her down enough so that Tracey tackled her and brought her to the hard asphalt.

"Let me go," Barbara screamed.

Tracey got astride her and hit her.

"Get off me!" She cursed at Tracey.

Tracey hit her again and then again. "Come on," she said to the girl beneath her. "You're the one who's not afraid to fight two on one. So fight, big mouth." She hit her again and then grabbed her by the collar front and shook her, back and forth, while her own eyes blurred and her mind went numb.

It was the sound of Barbara's gasping and sobbing that brought her back to what she was doing. Almost in a somersault, she leaped away from her.

"Somebody help me," Barbara sobbed. Her voice sounded weak and choked, but she got up on her elbows and rolled partway over. Tracey's heart felt a stab of thankfulness. There was blood on the other girl's face where her nose was bleeding and her lip was cut, but she was all right.

*I might have killed her,* Tracey thought. *I might have.* She fell down to a sitting position, struck weak with the thought of what she might have done, with the sudden glimpse of the beasts of rage that still lived inside her.

Barbara at last sat up, and she cried, "Look at me. Just look at me! I hate you!"

She pulled her knees up to her chin, hid her face in her hands, and rocked back and forth, crying. Blood dropped onto her jeans.

"You started it," Tracey said at last.

"I wouldn't have hit you this bad."

"I'm sorry," Tracey said. She didn't think she would have the strength to get up. Her legs felt like rubber. But she made it to her feet. "I am sorry," she told Barbara again. "But I warned you not to do this tonight."

"Get out of here! Get away from me!"

Tracey had half a mind to ask if she could help her home, even if it meant facing her mother. But when she took a weak step toward Barbara to offer help, the other girl screamed and cried harder. "Leave me alone! Leave me alone!"

"All right," Tracey said. "But I am sorry." She turned and made for home, limping—not from pain, but from the unsteady feeling in her legs.

When she got home, she was surprised to see that her mother had not gone out that night, and that her father's car was also in the driveway. Tracey checked her face in the car's outside mirror. She didn't look too bad for having been in a fight. She straightened her hair and went inside. Nobody was downstairs, but she heard voices upstairs. Her father's voice sounded angry.

*He found the paper,* Tracey thought. With an explosion of fear, she raced up the stairs. "Dad!" she heard herself call out. "Dad!"

At the sound of her voice, Don Jacamuzzi appeared at the top of the stops, his wife behind him. "There she is," he exclaimed. "What do you say now? What? Where have you been?" he demanded.

If Tracey's mind had been clearer, she would have kept her distance from him. But she was fixed only on that paper, on stopping them, if possible, from getting a divorce. She never saw his fist. She never—before the first blow—realized that this had nothing to do with the paper tucked safely away under her clothes in the bottom drawer.

She had nothing to fall back on, and her last feeling was one of horror, of falling down the stairs. But she couldn't even see the stairs, or the roof, or the crazily swinging banister. She only heard the crashing from far away as her feet knocked her mother's vases off the shelves that ran along one side of the steps.

The first thing she really felt was a sensation in her sinuses of having come up from underwater. Then her eyes cleared. She was lying on the bottom steps. Everything was deathly still. No, there was a sound from a tunnel far away. Garbled voices, faster and faster, that at last exploded into sensible words.

She flung up one hand and caught the banister and got up on her knees. The room and stairs swung. Another blow caught the side of her face and knocked her into the banister.

*This is how Barbara felt*, she told herself. She heard her head hit the rail. The yelling from her father was meaningless in her ears, but what she heard her mother say made perfect sense.

"I'll leave you."

With an effort, Tracey opened her eyes and saw them, her father foremost, her mother just behind him on the stairs, bent on stopping him from hitting her again.

"Tonight!" she shouted.

They stared at each other, but even Tracey could see her mother meant it. Some part of her didn't dread it so much now. Because he might kill her. Only her mother could save her, and that threat was the only one that would work.

"Get her out of my sight," he yelled. "Get her out of my sight! Take her upstairs. Take her to bed." He slammed past Tracey down the rest of the steps and stormed through the kitchen.

"Tracey," her mother said as she got under Tracey's arm. She was crying.

"Mom, what happened?" Tracey asked. She still couldn't see straight, and she let her mother half lead and half carry her up the steps.

"Father Drew called. He was very annoyed with you. He told your father that you just sit in church and read all the time."

"I do," Tracey whispered.

"Why are you doing this to us?" her mother moaned. "Why, Tracey? Why? Just tell me that. Why are you tormenting your father?"

"Doing this to you?" Tracey asked. The shock wore off and she began to cry. "Doing this to you?" she asked again. She cried harder. Suddenly her crying was as out of control as her fighting had been. "To you?" she asked. "Doing this to you? To you?" Until it was a scream. She couldn't stop.

"Stop, Tracey, stop. Stop. It's all right. I'm sorry. He's sorry."

Jean's face crossed her line of vision, white and terrified but determined to help.

"To you?" Tracey yelled. "Doing this to you?"

"I'm calling the doctor," she heard her mother say. Then there were footsteps as her mother hurried away. Tracey dimly realized that she was on her bed.

"Mom, don't!" Jean exclaimed.

"Your father left. It's all right."

"What am I doing to you?" Tracey screamed. "What am I doing to you?"

"Doing what to you?" Tracey yelled. "What? What?"

# PART TWO

FRESHMAN YEAR

# T E N

The bus station seemed almost empty. There were only three or four people left on the bus, and she was the only one to get off at the remote station out in the country. It had been a long seven-hour ride, and she had come alone.

A silent week had passed in that awful, silent house, and then her mother had given her all the instructions on what she must do once she arrived at the station. One of the sisters would meet her at the station. She would be taken to the school, which had already been in session for two weeks, and she must meet the acting principal, Sister Mary Mercy, as soon as she arrived.

For the first time since early morning, when she'd kissed her mother and Jean good-bye, Tracey felt tears sting her eyes. Her father and the three little ones had been absent. He had taken them out to breakfast, Tracey supposed, to avoid a scene. Maybe there had been some danger that he would have changed his mind. She might just have embarrassed him enough to make him relent.

Her mother's last act of comfort had been to spread expensive foundation makeup over her face, hiding what was left of the bruise around her left eye. It had faded considerably in seven days, and the makeup gave it an almost perfect cover. But if she cried, it would wash off. She did not want anyone to see what had happened, especially here, at this place of such reputation.

The Sanctuary of Mary and Joseph had once been a fine school for promising young girls, but now it was known as the place to send girls who "needed firm guidance and attention." Not quite reform school, but the next thing to it. The students would be tough, and the teachers would be tough, and Tracey would need all the toughness she could muster to hold her own.

There were a few people wandering around the postage-stamp–sized bus terminal. Most of them paced slowly up and down the wraparound wooden porch or sat on the faded, splintery benches. Nobody said anything to her, and there didn't seem to be any sisters among them. The driver expertly and quickly hefted her two suitcases out of the luggage compartment in the side of the bus, nodded to her, and climbed back on. In another moment the bus rolled away again. Tracey looked after it, wishing she had just stayed on and ridden with it all the way to the end, to wherever buses went.

A hand touched her shoulder.

"Pardon me, miss, are you Tracey Jacamuzzi?" a kind voice with an accent asked her.

Tracey turned and looked up into the face of a woman—a laywoman, to judge from her tailored trousers and summer sweater. Then Tracey remem-

72

bered that some orders permitted the sisters to wear street clothes when they went out in public.

"Yes, Sister, I am," Tracey said.

Something in Tracey's face must have arrested the woman's attention, for she seemed not to hear Tracey for a moment. Then she caught herself and said, "I've come to take you to the campus, dear. Are those your things?"

"Yes, that's all of them," Tracey told her.

The woman called over a porter and asked him to take the suitcases to her car. She handed him the keys and turned to Tracey. "I suppose that you must be hungry," she said. "You've come all the way up from the Philadelphia station, haven't you? That's a long trip for a girl all alone."

The bus had stopped twice for food, and Tracey had eaten both times, but a sudden, different kind of hunger gripped her, a hunger for kindness from somebody, and she said, "I am hungry, Sister." She wanted to see if this woman would give her something to eat, if there were a kindness and generosity in her that could be measured out and relied on during the stretch of days and weeks to come.

The woman smiled suddenly. "Dear, I'm not one of the sisters," she said. "My name is Maddie Murdoch. Father Williams asked me to come and get you. School is in session today, and none of the faculty could be spared."

Only then did Tracey identify the woman's lilting Irish accent. It was pretty. She was surprised and a little disappointed to realize that the woman was not a sister. "Do you work at the school?" she asked.

"Only as a volunteer. It's my ministry, I suppose you

could say. It's very nice to meet you." She offered her hand and clasped Tracey's for a moment. "Come on, then," she said with a smile. "We'll stop by McDonald's on our way to the school." Her eyes looked troubled for a moment. Nonetheless, she kept up a pleasant chatter with Tracey as they crossed the uneven parking lot.

The sun was high; noon had just passed. Light beat down on them, and it was warm. Mrs. Murdoch's car was an ordinary station wagon, the kind with panels on the sides. The windshield reflected the sunlight in a brilliant bar, as though it were a wall of light. For a moment, Tracey couldn't see as she walked around to the passenger side of the car.

"Sorry," Mrs. Murdoch called. "I should have parked in the shade. But I knew it would just be for a minute."

Tracey heard Mrs. Murdoch get in on the driver's side. Her hand fumbled on the passenger side door, found the handle, and opened it. Inside, the brilliant sun, though reflecting off the windshield, was also flooding through. She slid into the seat and closed the door, but she could not see at all for the brilliance of the light.

"Oh, I'm glad I brought my sunglasses," she heard Mrs. Murdoch say, and she felt the rumble as the car started up. "I'll get you out of this glare." They pulled away from the bus station, and Tracey's vision cleared.

Mrs. Murdoch wore enormous sunglasses. She turned on the air conditioner and continued to talk as she drove, telling Tracey about the school's history, the subjects the freshmen took, and the retirement home that was attached to the campus.

Tracey wanted to ask if it was a nice place. She hoped it was better than what the stories indicated. Mrs. Murdoch seemed to be an indication that it could be. She was certainly nice enough, and she said she would buy Tracey's lunch for her. Tracey thanked her.

They went into the McDonald's to eat since it had no drive-through window. Mrs. Murdoch removed the oversized sunglasses as they entered. They ordered and were quickly served. While Tracey ate, she was aware of Mrs. Murdoch's gaze resting on her. The woman's face was thoughtful.

"Did you go to the Sanctuary when you were in high school?" Tracey asked.

"Yes, dear, I did," she said.

"Did you like it?"

"I believe I liked it as well as I liked anything," she replied. "Do you enjoy schoolwork?"

"I never have," Tracey admitted. "I guess I'll learn to."

"I was a very good student," Mrs. Murdoch told her. "I mean, I worked very hard at my studies and took a lot of pride in them. But there were other things to learn—other items that we discussed now and again, and I was not very attentive of them. Spiritual things, I suppose you would call them."

Tracey abruptly changed the subject. "Did you get to play field hockey?" she asked. It was hockey season, and she had been pretty good at the game back at St. Anne's. But mostly she did not want this Catholic woman to start talking to her about the spiritual things the church had to offer. She didn't want to argue with someone who seemed so kind and beautiful. She didn't want to start the trouble she knew was coming, for she was perfectly aware that her father had told them why he was sending her away. She suspected Mrs. Murdoch had been coached to bring up the subject as quickly as possible.

"Yes," Mrs. Murdoch said. "I believe we all played field hockey in the autumn. Perhaps Sister Patricia Rose can get you on the team."

The talk remained on the safe subjects of field hockey and basketball, and Mrs. Murdoch did not bring up religion again.

It wasn't far from the McDonald's to the school. They kept up some conversation as they drove along, but as they passed through the ironwork gates of the school, they fell silent.

The Sanctuary of Mary and Joseph was a tall, gaunt huddle of brownstone buildings hemmed in by an ironwork fence. Statues of Mary and Joseph, and an unexplained one of Francis of Assisi, dotted the grounds that spread out behind the main buildings. One long strip of turf was bare of statues and of trees. That one patch of green grass looked pleasant and welcoming.

"I'll drive you to the hall," Mrs. Murdoch said. "Look, there is the gym over there, past the retirees' wing."

Tracey's eyes followed her nod, and she saw a long, low building with some type of figure painted on one of the glass doors. "What's that on the door?" she asked.

"The Valkyrie," Mrs. Murdoch said. "It's the school's mascot and emblem."

"Valkyrie," Tracey repeated, half to herself. "What's a Valkyrie?"

Mrs. Murdoch glanced at her. "It comes from Norse mythology," she said. "The Valkyries were the shield maidens who kept the halls of heaven. Odin used women warriors as his honor guard because if he'd used men, they might have been worshiped for their own strength and skill and cunning. He could glorify himself through women warriors because he was the source of their strength and power."

Even though it was a pagan story, the idea sent a thrill of hope into Tracey. She wondered if God—the real God, the Father of Jesus—did things like that. Probably not. It was probably one more mix of paganism and Christianity that had been blended into the Roman Catholic Church. But Mrs. Murdoch said, "I have found that God Himself does similar things. He transforms earthly creatures into heavenly beings. Nobody can stop Him from doing it, and nothing ever hinders Him from accomplishing it."

Her certainty caught Tracey's attention. Were her words a warning to Tracey to come back to the church, or just a straightforward testimony of the goodness of God? Tracey looked at her, but Mrs. Murdoch was intent on guiding the car to the center doors of the main hall, and the enormous sunglasses hid most of her face.

A sudden, loud rap on the roof of the car startled them. It made Tracey jump, but Mrs. Murdoch only grimaced. "I believe field hockey practice is now under way," she said. Something rolled off the car with two loud bangs and fell into the grass.

Tracey saw a tall blonde girl running toward them, field hockey stick in hand. "Liz Lukas," Mrs. Murdoch said. She pulled up in front of the doors to the hall and stopped the car. The blonde girl stopped long enough to scoop up the ball, then resumed jogging up to meet them.

Mrs. Murdoch rolled down the window. "Aye, Liz,"

she called in her Irish accent. "It was a grand shot—nearly a hole in one. Oh, excuse me! I thought it was golf you were playing, not hockey."

Still some distance away, the girl called out, "Sorry, Maddie! I didn't see you coming!"

"Come on, then, Tracey," Maddie Murdoch said to her. "Come on out and meet Liz. She would be a good friend to you, I think."

They got out of the car. Liz hurried up to them and said, "Sorry. I was just messing around. Didn't know anyone was coming."

"Well, for your penance, dear, you can help this young lady with her bags," Mrs. Murdoch said. "This is Tracey Jacamuzzi."

"Liz Lukas," the blonde girl said, and held out her hand.

Tracey shook hands. "Tracey Jacamuzzi," she said uncertainly.

Mrs. Murdoch opened the back of the station wagon, and they pulled out Tracey's bags. "Tracey, I've got to get back to work," Mrs. Murdoch said. "I'll let Liz look after you. It was nice meeting you." She took Tracey's hand again and said, very seriously, "I do hope to see you again. Take care, dear."

"Thank you," Tracey said. "And thank you for lunch." Neither she nor Liz Lukas said anything as Mrs. Murdoch got back into the car and drove away down the long lane. At last Liz broke the silence.

"You look like you been looking forward to this moment all your life," she said. She expertly flipped aside the ball and picked up Tracey's two suitcases. Tracey was glad she was so friendly. Liz was tall and athletic and sure of herself, and Tracey was grateful.

"This has been a big surprise," Tracey told her. "Two weeks ago I'd only heard rumors about this place."

"You pregnant?" Liz asked.

The question startled her. "No!" Tracey exclaimed.

Liz shrugged. "Better get used to that question, Jacamuzzi."

"I'm not Catholic anymore," Tracey told her.

"You mean they threw you out of the church too?" Liz asked. "What'd you do?"

"No, they didn't throw me out," Tracey said. "Back in July I started reading the Bible and—"

"Whoa." Liz Lukas stopped in her tracks and looked at Tracey like she knew what was coming and already didn't like it. "So you're the one everyone said was coming."

"Who said?" Tracey asked.

"Mary was telling Timbuktu about it, and some of the seniors overheard. They passed it around. Someone said you're a Jesus freak. You're out to save the world, right?"

Tracey shrugged. "Mary" would be Sister Mary, the acting principal. "Timbuktu" would be their name for one of the other nuns. "Look," Tracey began.

"Do yourself a favor and keep it to yourself," Liz Lukas said.

"I haven't even said anything about it yet," Tracey said.

"You must be nuts to let that make you leave home," she told her.

"Leave home?" Tracey exclaimed. "You mean get thrown out." For one vivid moment she recalled the episode on the stairs, and it sent a tremor of both rage and grief through her. But she said nothing about that.

"Why not?" Liz returned. "There are a lot of nutty people these days who see God every morning while they're shaving. You get your head on straight while you're here. Maybe it'll be a short stay."

"I hope it will be," Tracey said.

"Yeah, well, I gotta go now. Look, Tracey, I don't want to hear any of it, OK?" She set down the suitcases at the front doorway of what Tracey took to be the main building and walked away.

"Thanks for your help," Tracey said, and she tried to sound sincere.

"That's OK, just don't start preaching, or singing, or praying or anything. I can't stand that fake stuff." She walked away in a straight and determined line for the hockey field.

Tracey put her hand on the front knob to open the door, but it opened from the inside, and Tracey found herself looking at a short, slender woman who wore cat's-eye glasses. "Excuse me, Sister," Tracey said.

"Tracey Jacamuzzi?" she asked.

That was all she said, but Tracey felt the last of her courage failing her, oozing out through her shoes. "Yes, Sister," Tracey said.

"You'll need to get into your uniform first thing, and then I want to see you in my office right away."

"Yes, Sister. But where do I go? Upstairs?"

She gave a brisk nod. "Up the steps and to the left. Your dorm room will have a newcomer card on it. Room 214. Your uniform is already up there. Let me know if anything doesn't fit. I want you back downstairs in half an hour."

"Yes, Sister." Tracey struggled to pick up her things.

"Say, 'Thank you, Sister,'" she told her.

"Thank you, Sister." Tracey grabbed her bags and headed for the staircase. It was wide and wooden, with stained glass at the center landing. But it was a hard climb, loaded down as Tracey was. The halls above were less pleasant. The staircase that ascended beyond the second floor was narrow and steep. All facade of pleasant light and warm stained glass was quickly left behind.

The rooms on either side of the staircase landings were not numbered and had locks on the doorknobs. Tracey figured these rooms belonged to the nuns. Further down the hall, the shower room marked the division between clergy and laity. Past the showers were the dorm rooms. Tracey found hers, marked with a large white card on the door with her name and the word **NEWCOMER** in bold print.

The room held two sets of bunks, one a double and the other a triple. She had only ever seen a triple bunk bed in a Three Stooges film, and she looked at it with interest for a moment. The lower bed had no covers on it. A Mary and Joseph uniform hung on the upper bed frame. Tracey set down all her things and quickly pulled off her outer garments.

The uniform consisted of a gray skirt, wide and shot through with threads of maroon, green, and a subdued gold. But mostly it was gray. It was as ugly a uniform as anybody could want.

The blouse Tracey was to wear was green. A note printed on glossy paper was pinned to the inside of the collar. It depicted the proper colors for each class: Freshmen wore green, sophomores blue, juniors a shade of pink that was called maroon, and the seniors gold. The navy blue vest was a long thing called a bolero, with pockets on both sides at the waist and the Mary and Joseph insignia over one breast. The insignia matched the color of the blouse. The note also included instructions for wearing the uniform properly and caring for it.

The newcomer card informed her that pantyhose would not be permitted, nor would makeup, except for a little lipstick now and then. Tracey rummaged through her suitcase for blue knee socks and found a pair. She had brought the regulation blue saddle oxfords with her.

There was time only to brush her hair back quickly, force herself to be resolved into courage, and then run out again to find Sister Mary's office, where the acting principal waited for her.

# E L E V E N

Tracey found Sister Mary's office in a wide room under the landing. The rows of file cabinets cut a harsh contrast against the warm browns of the carpet and the dark trim around the ceiling and floors. Sister Mary's desk was metal, gleaming and spotless. It didn't match the wood tones of the room.

Sister Mary was seated when Tracey walked in, and Tracey stayed standing. In her grade school, manners, especially manners before the sisters, had been drilled into every student.

"Your parents have had several discussions with me," Sister Mary began.

"Yes, Sister," Tracey said.

"They regard this religious excursion of yours primarily as a discipline problem."

"It isn't, Sister," she said. She tried to sound humble.

The principal fixed Tracey with a look of doubt and contempt and fingered a pencil she'd picked up from the desk. It was long and pointed. "Let me be frank, Miss Jacamuzzi," she said. "You have not had a religious experience. You only want one. You're young and impressionable, and like most girls, you want more out of life than it has to offer. A religious experience comes at a culmination of years, not at the very beginning. You're looking for an easy out, but it's not there."

Tracey was a little surprised at how coolly the sister had told her off, and for a moment Sister Mary's skepticism made Tracey doubt herself. But Sister Mary seemed confused too. Tracey hadn't had a religious experience—she had only gotten saved. "I don't know what you mean by a religious experience," she said.

"I think you do. A sudden conversion. A bright light. Speaking in tongues."

"I never spoke in tongues," Tracey told her. "I don't believe in it."

"Are you picking an argument?" she asked. "Let us not split hairs. You believe that religion begins with an instant, a sudden revelation. Do you deny that?"

"No, Sister." But she wasn't sure. She hadn't thought about it in those terms. Getting saved had happened in an instant, but that was only because of a sacrifice deliberately acted out centuries ago, and even that had occurred because of a timeless plan and an eternal truth. It had never seemed like an instant, glamorous thing to Tracey. It was more like plugging into something that had always been there, waiting, watching. But for the first time she felt a doubt. Getting saved was a quick answer. One moment, and then all eternity was taken care of. Had she grabbed it because it was quick and easy?

Sister Mary paused for a moment, then said, "You will not be allowed to act out your fantasies here. The sooner you face real life, the better and happier you will be."

The doubt faded again. Maybe she'd been rash about a lot of things, but getting saved had involved more thought and inner struggle than she'd ever experienced. And being saved didn't go away just because things went wrong. The fight with Barbara had taught her that. For the first time in her life, she had felt impelled to ask God to forgive her. She'd been thoroughly ashamed and pained because of what was inside her. She hadn't made that up or acted it out.

Sister Mary stood and came around the desk. "Look at me. Yes, like that." She surveyed Tracey critically from foot to head. "This uniform is the uniform of Mary and Joseph. You will wear it at all times from breakfast until after supper in the halls and at all times on the front campus or in public. There are no exceptions except those approved from this office. Never appear in public in any garments other than the uniform. Is that clear?"

"Yes, Sister."

She returned to her inspection of Tracey and without comment made some improvements. With short twitches on the sleeves and waistband of the skirt, Sister Mary jerked and straightened the uniform until it looked presentable to her. It was the most impersonal way Tracey had ever been touched in her life, and the feeling of those efficient, quick fingers stayed with her long afterward as a sensation of stark loneliness and violation.

Her throat tightened, but Tracey felt she still had to answer in some way. Sister Mary had said it wasn't true, but it was true. She knew she was saved. So at last, as the acting principal finished twitching Tracey's bolero into place, Tracey said, "Jesus Christ has saved me. It is done, and I know it's done. If I said it wasn't done, it would still be done."

The principal's eyes darted to Tracey's, startled and offended, and Tracey flinched without thinking. Sister Mary did not strike her. But looking into her eyes for that one moment, Tracey realized she was good at breaking down girls. It was part of her job.

In the sudden silence, under the prolonged look from Sister Mary, Tracey felt color rush into her face in a burning wave, up her cheeks, to her forehead, even into her hairline. She met her eyes, though, until Sister Mary said, very softly, "You will not meet my eye like that. Look down."

Tracey did.

"I will give you time to adjust, and to think," she said. "Don't fancy yourself a martyr, miss. Great men and great women have been martyrs, but you aren't of that stock. Now look at me." Tracey obeyed her, and Sister Mary's steady eye held her gaze. "You are a troubled, disturbed young woman with delusions of sainthood," she said. "You think the world rests on your shoulders, but it doesn't. You may leave this office now. Return to your room and unpack. Appear for dinner at six o'clock."

"Yes, Sister."

"Say, 'Thank you, Sister.'"

"Thank you, Sister."

# TWELVE

Her roommates were in the room when Tracey returned. There were four of them: a freshman, two sophomores, and a junior. Tracey walked in and everybody looked at her.

"Hi," she said. She ducked her head and went to the pile of suitcases on her bed. Nobody said anything. Just in that short walk across the room, she could see that one of the sophomores was close with the junior. They both looked like they ran the room. That was to be expected. Upperclassmen and their favorites would run things.

She took one suitcase by the handle and started to pull it up, but a blue oxford shoe came down on it, and Tracey stopped.

The sophomore she'd picked out as the favorite had walked over. Tracey looked up at her. "We better make introductions first," the sophomore said, "and explain the ground rules."

Tracey let go of the suitcase and straightened up. She was the taller of the two when she stood. "OK."

"I'm Sue Clark. Scooter," the girl said. "You play basketball?"

"I'm Tracey Jacamuzzi."

"I asked you if you play basketball."

"No," Tracey said.

"Can you play?"

"No. I like field hockey better."

The girl in the pink blouse, the junior, came around the near set of bunk beds. "Field hockey?" She let out a laugh. "That stinks."

"We all play field hockey," Scooter told Tracey. "All the time. Till we're ready to throw it up. Basketball's the game here."

"You play basketball?" Tracey asked.

Scooter gave a careless nod and threw herself down on one of the other lower bunks. She looked at Tracey through the slats. "You might say that."

"Scooter was high scorer last game," the junior said.

"It was a scrimmage," Scooter said. "And that's the hardest game there is, 'cause there's nobody better than the MoJoes. So when we play each other, that's what counts."

Tracey turned back to unpack her things.

A hand grabbed her bolero and blouse from the back. Tracey turned her head. Scooter was holding her with the blouse and vest screwed up tight. A sudden tenseness went through Tracey's knees, and she felt and fought back the urge to swing her arm around and bring the older girl down. Remembering Barbara, she stayed still.

"No narcs in this room," Scooter said.

"OK."

"No playing games with us against Mary. It'll come home to you."

The warning sounded so unreal it was almost funny. "Do you mean Sister Mary?" Tracey exclaimed.

It was stunning to think that anyone would imagine that Sister Mary liked Tracey, or that Tracey would be ready to run and tell tales to her. But Scooter took the question the wrong way. "I mean Mary, Freshman. That's her name: Mary. You and she had a little meeting today. She's real keen on you. We can see that."

Scooter didn't seem quite ready to hit Tracey, so Tracey looked her in the eye and slowly relaxed. Scooter kept the grip tight on Tracey a little longer, and then, as the younger girl didn't answer, she relaxed it.

"Mary thinks I'm a 'deluded young woman,'" Tracey told them, imitating Mary's voice, "and that I've got emotional problems and a martyr complex." She cocked her head and raised her eyebrows. "And Mary's going to straighten me out. She said so."

Scooter dropped her hand and looked at Tracey, obviously surprised but trying not to show it.

"I don't think you need to worry about me and Mary having any little talks about anything else but what's wrong with me."

"Aren't you real straight? Real holy and everything?" Scooter demanded.

"I'm saved," Tracey said. "That means really a Christian and not a Catholic."

"Well, keep it to yourself and you won't get into trouble," she said.

Tracey had decided to be meek, but she'd had about enough. She looked up and dropped the suitcase lid back on the bed. The freshman girl and the other sophomore were hanging back, over by the far beds, but Scooter and the junior had come right up to her, bent on intimidating her.

"Look," Tracey said. "You keep it to yourself. What I don't know I can't say, OK? I won't look for trouble."

"Hey, Freshman," the junior began.

"The name is Tracey."

"All the freshmen answer to 'Freshman,'" Scooter said.

Tracey shrugged and went back to her suitcases. "Is there any free drawer space?"

"We're still talking to you," the junior said.

"No, you're not," Tracey told her. She nodded to the two in the background. "Nice meeting you too. Any of you guys play field hockey? It's my favorite game."

Scooter and her friend, whose name tag identified her as another Susan, stood there for a long moment while Tracey took stack after stack of folded clothes out of the suitcases and arranged them in piles on the nearest bed.

After an awkward wait, while Tracey tried to look relaxed but felt as tense as a spring, Scooter said, "Well, let's go. We can practice through dinner. Sister Rose said so." She strutted to the door, followed closely by Susan. "Get your stuff cleaned up and your suitcases out of sight, Jacamuzzi, or it's demerits."

Tracey didn't answer them. After the door closed, there was silence in the room for a moment. Then the other two girls came closer.

"Don't talk to her that way," the freshman said to Tracey.

"Oh, come on," Tracey told them. She kept her attention on unpacking. It seemed rude to address people by reading their tags, so she didn't look up as she asked, "What are your names?"

"I'm Amy," the freshman said, "and this is Lisa." Amy was a slight girl. Lisa was small too, smaller than Tracey and certainly smaller than Scooter and Susan. They both had a pale frailty that suggested bookishness and a talent for being bullied by their aggressive roommates.

"Listen," Amy said. "Freshmen do what they're told around here. A lot of people thought they were pretty tough when school started, but they don't think so anymore."

Tracey shrugged. "OK. I'm not a narc, anyway. Sister Mary can't stand me. They don't need to worry."

"What are you?" Amy asked. "I mean, what's your religion?"

"I don't have a religion, like being Catholic or Lutheran or anything. I got saved this past summer. I believe in the Bible, and I believe that Jesus died to save people's souls from hell."

"Everybody says you won't say the prayers or go to Mass," Amy told her, and Lisa nodded.

"Oh. Well, no, I don't. All that ceremonial stuff—it's all made up by men. None of it's in the Bible. Nothing. There's no purgatory, no saints—"

"There are too saints in the Bible," Lisa said. "Of course there are. St. Anne and St. Peter and St. Paul and all the apostles."

"OK, some of those people are in the Bible," Tracey agreed. "St. Anne isn't. And the Bible doesn't say they were perfect. It says they were sinners who were saved. They were just ordinary people."

"We'd better not talk about religion," Amy said. "My folks want me to be Catholic, and I think I should be. My whole family's Catholic."

"Anyway," Lisa added, "you can be any religion you want, Tracey. It's in the rules. The school takes girls of other religions and doesn't make them participate in Catholic things as long as they're respectful. You can be anything at all."

Tracey looked up in surprise. "Are you kidding?"

Lisa shook her head. "It's in the handbook. You'll probably have to read that tonight. You'll see."

Tracey shrugged. "Whatever the rules say, my folks sent me here to punish me and to convert me back to Catholicism. And Sister Mary wants to. She just ripped me apart—never even yelled or anything."

"She's like that," Lisa said. "She never hits people, though." Lisa wore the blue of a sophomore, so she should know, Tracey thought. "She pull out her box of Kleenex?" Lisa asked.

"No, why?"

"'Cause when she does that, you can bet you'll be crying before you leave. It never fails. Just give up and start crying right away, and maybe she'll let you go."

"What is this place?" Tracey asked. "Hell?"

"Freshman year is hell," Amy said with a nod. "Then you go up the ladder and get beatified as you go."

Tracey couldn't help but smile at that, and then she even laughed. "Why not?" she asked.

"Sure, why not?" Lisa asked. "But if it only lasts a year, it's purgatory. It just feels like hell."

Amy and Lisa explained the basics about the school to Tracey. The girls at the Sanctuary of Mary and Joseph called themselves MoJoes or MaryJoes. There was a proper way to wear the uniform, everything buttoned and in place, and then there was the slang way to wear it: the sleeves rolled up to the elbow, the bolero unbuttoned and loose, the skirt rolled up once at the waist or at least pulled up a little, and the knee socks down around the ankles. The students wore them slang when they had a chance to walk around the grounds, or as they studied in their rooms, or anytime they weren't subject to an inspection.

Sister Mary Mercy was the acting principal, and the girls called her Mary for short. There was a Sister Timothy who was called "Timbuktu." And Tracey heard a lot about Sister Patricia Rose, also known as CPR, even to her face. CPR was well spoken of by all the girls. She was the coach and phys ed teacher.

The retired nuns lived in a small, quiet wing off the

church building, a short walk across the lawn from the main building.

Amy and Lisa were a little nervous about being around somebody odd enough to get thrown out of her family over religion. Tracey got the idea that most of the girls had heard about her and believed she was a Hare Krishna or something else weird.

After a few minutes of talk, her two new roommates left. Tracey finished unpacking her things. It was just after five, and she realized that she didn't know where the dining room was. Something told her Mary would be watching to make sure she got there on time. She had to go find it, so she hurried and finished.

There wasn't any room in the closets for the suitcases, so Tracey crammed them under the beds. As she worked at this, she heard a swish of a gown and looked up, startled to see a black habit coming toward her among the beds. Already Tracey dreaded Sister Mary, and she wasn't ready for another interview.

But the sister who came around the bunk bed was much taller than Mary, and she was bent over a little at the waist. Her eyes were dark. They weren't just brown, but the skin around them was dark and pouchy. There were deep lines around her mouth and between her eyebrows, giving her a frowning, forbidding look. Tracey's heart told her that this was likely the disciplinarian. But the sister's next words instantly dispelled that impression. "Excuse me, dear. I wasn't expecting anyone up here. You must be the new student." Her voice was as quiet and kind as her looks were forbidding. Tracey straightened quickly.

"Excuse me, Sister," Tracey said. "Am I allowed up here now?"

"Oh, dear, yes." She laughed gently. "I didn't mean that it was against the rules. I was just afraid you might have been a mouse. Thank the Lord, you're not. Because if you were, I would have only screamed. I'm not much good against mice."

"Neither am I," Tracey said, and she smiled at her.

The sister reached out and put her hand on Tracey's shoulder. "I'm Sister James Anne," she said. "They used to call me Big Jim because I'm so tall. But you are too, aren't you, dear?"

"Yes, Sister, five feet eight," Tracey said. "My name is Tracey Jacamuzzi."

"They could call you Big Jack." She smiled again, and Tracey realized that Sister James Anne wasn't really seeing her—not well, anyway. She had sensed Tracey's height from the sound of her voice and the height of her shoulder.

"Can I help you, Sister?" Tracey asked.

"If you would, dear," she said. "I can see very well in the light, but the day is ending, and the lights aren't on yet. I wonder if you could take me down the stairs."

"Of course, my pleasure." Tracey exclaimed. "Is your room on the first floor?"

"No, I live in the outside wing," she told Tracey.

"Oh, I don't know the way."

"I can find it, dear. You be pilot, and I'll be navigator. It's best if you take my arm, like this." She showed Tracey how to let her put her arm through Tracey's. Tracey saw from the woman's hands that arthritis also had a claim on Sister James' health. Her fingers were bent from it.

"Did you used to teach here?" Tracey asked.

"For ten years, dear," she said as Tracey guided her

out of the room. "I cried all through my first year of retirement, and even now I sometimes come up here to remember, just to remember."

MoJoe had already taught Tracey to keep to herself around the nuns, perhaps even the retired ones. But she was so homesick and lonely, she was glad to talk to this first kind person. Tracey told some of her story as they walked across the grounds. She omitted the details of her last fight with Barbara and what her father had done to her on the stairs. She wasn't ready for anybody to know that yet.

Sister James Anne listened gravely and without interruption. When Tracey finished, the elderly woman said, "Yes, my dear. Maddie Murdoch stopped in on her way back to her office. She asked me if I might look you up."

The answer startled Tracey. "She did?" She remembered the Irish woman's gently probing comments about religion, the troubled gaze that she had rested on Tracey when Tracey had caught her in a few unguarded moments.

"Yes," Sister James Anne said. "She was in quite a hurry, but she said . . . she said you were hurt. Have you hurt yourself?"

So, the eye had betrayed her. "I fell," Tracey said. She hoped it wasn't a lie. She did fall, after she'd been hit. "It's almost better." She felt a slight pang at the thought that Mrs. Murdoch had sent one of the sisters after her. Who else might she tell? Tracey's mind flicked over to Sister Mary. The acting principal must have missed the signs of swelling visible under the makeup. What sorts of comments or questions would Mrs. Murdoch's statements open up in Sister Mary's

interrogations of her? Mary would blame her for caus-
ing him to hit her, or somehow Mary would say it was
an accident, that she'd been wrong to get so hysterical
over it . . . that anybody might accidentally hit his
daughter too hard once or twice in his life.

As they drew nearer to the doors of the retirees'
wing, another old, very plump nun came out to meet
the two of them.

"Here comes somebody," Tracey said.

"That will be Sister Lucy," Sister James told her.
The grounds were very dim by then, so Sister James
couldn't see. But her hand descended on Tracey's
shoulder again. "Come and visit me, dear. As often as
you like."

Tracey decided to face the religion issue head-on.
"You don't mind that I'm not Catholic?" she asked.

For a moment a shadow of doubt or trouble crossed
the sister's face, but then she said, "You seem like a
good girl. And I think that earnest religion is better
than no religion, or false religion. Maybe, in the end,
our differences won't be that great. Come and see me."

"Thank you, Sister."

The plump little nun hurried up, already talking
before they could hear her. "Oh, James Anne, I'm so
sorry. Was I supposed to go walking with you? Oh, the
girl was reading such a wonderful book to me, I forgot
all about our walk. Oh dear, I'm sorry."

Sister James assured her that it was all right, and
she introduced Tracey to Sister Lucy. Tracey said good
night to them, and they went in to the wing together,
the one sister very tall and thin, and the other short
and fat. They looked funny, but there was a kind of
aged and weary grace about them.

Sister James had pointed out the dining hall doors as they had passed them, and it was now ten to six. Tracey turned and walked back to meet the nuns, the other girls, and her fate.

# FOURTEEN

Dinner was a tasteless mess of white rolls and beef soup, bland and boiled to limpness. Lisa had told her they had beef soup or beef stew at least once a week, and likewise chicken soup or chicken potpie. The other evening meals were all casseroles, along with plates of the white rolls and sometimes a salad or vegetables. Lunch was usually better than dinner. On sandwich days they sometimes got tomatoes, and always pickles and lettuce, with processed luncheon meat and imitation cheese. Some days they had pizza, turkey salads, chicken salads, or an innovation called "beef salad."

Of course they had fish on Friday nights, incredibly bony fish like shad that made everybody talk about how the school was going to get sued as soon as somebody choked to death on a bone. Tracey thought that, in a way, all of them were kind of hoping somebody would choke to death one day just to show the nuns how unfair it was to serve shad.

One of the seniors led the two tables in the saying of

grace. Tracey kept silent, but nobody noticed her absti-
nence. She sat at a table with the other freshmen. She
didn't want to start out by getting them all nervous
about her, so she didn't say anything about why she'd
come. She just told them she was new and that Sister
Mary had given her a pretty rough welcome. Then
Tracey asked if any of them knew Sister James Anne.

"No. She must be one of the old ones in the wing,"
one of them told her. Tracey nodded.

"Mary gets an eye on some people," one of the other
girls said. "Watch out for her. That's what all the
sophomores told me. Don't let her get you into long
talks in her office. It doesn't look good, and she can
get you to say things."

"I think she can be nice," another, fatter girl said.
Her name tag had SANDRA KEAN on it. She was
pale and puffy and looked as nervous as a rabbit.

"You better watch out, Sandra," one of the other
girls warned her sternly. "Just keep quiet if you can't
get out of her way."

"I just said she was nice."

The other girls talked some more about Mary and
how rough she could be, but at last Tracey's curiosity
got the best of her. "Sandra, what does Mary call you
in for?"

Everybody looked at her. Then they all looked at
Sandra, as though Tracey had asked the very question
they all thought somebody should ask.

"We just talk," she said. Her lower lip trembled
slightly, and she tapped her fork on her plate a couple
of times, very lightly. "I just tell her about my home
and my parents."

Tracey shrugged. "Oh." It was hard to picture Mary

sympathetically listening to anybody about her home. But maybe she could. Maybe Tracey just happened to get on her nerves.

Nobody said anything after that except to ask for food to be passed. They ate supper family style. A food service set up the tables every night and ran the cafeteria every day. The service cleaned up after breakfast and lunch, and the boarding girls were on a roster to clean up after the evening meals.

Only the boarders ate supper, and there were six very long tables for them, the middle tables of the dining hall. During the day, the other twelve tables were used for the cafeteria workers and for the town girls who brown-bagged. They spread out more during the day meals, but at night they were all crowded together to eat. The sisters ate at a reserved table in the cafeteria during the day. For supper they ate a separate meal before the girls did. Afterward one of them would come down and check cleanup.

Food fights were strictly punished, so the evening meal was usually peaceful, whether one of the nuns checked or not.

Mary entered the dining room as they were finishing, and everybody stood.

"Good evening, girls," she said. "Be seated." As soon as the noise of chairs being pushed back in was finished, she said, reading from index cards, "Sister Patricia Rose wants to see all basketball prospects in the gym from seven until eight. The IPS lab will be open until eight-thirty tonight. Library books must go into the collection box tonight or be marked for re-stamping. We have a new student, Tracey Jacamuzzi. Stand, please, Tracey. Let the girls get a look at you."

Tracey stood, gave a brief nod, and sat down.

"No, dear, continue standing until I give you leave."

Tracey stood again. Probably, if she had waited the first time, Sister Mary would have told Tracey to sit right away. But instead, she went on giving announcements while Tracey stood there, to all appearances forgotten by her.

Tracey felt her face flame and her eyes get wet from the embarrassment, and the girls around her at the table looked down the whole time. Tracey picked out Scooter at the sophomore table. Scooter was watching Mary with a quiet, intense expression, maybe wondering why Mary would take such trouble to humiliate a freshman. Across the aisle, Susan gave Tracey a smirk.

Tracey also picked out Liz Lukas, who sat at the end of the sophomore table, only a few people away from Scooter. All the girls around her had a kind of athletic, clean look, with no forbidden makeup. It was the basketball team. Liz glanced at Tracey and then looked away. The other girls whispered among themselves while Mary explained the procedures for returning books by way of the book box and gave them a schedule for the next trip to the library.

At last she dismissed the girls. There was a general pushing back of chairs. Many of the girls looked back at her, but Tracey stayed where she was. Lisa, her sophomore roommate, passed by on her way out, and in the cover of the crowd—most of whom were taller than she—whispered, "Don't leave your place. Stay there."

That was what Tracey figured. She gave a slight nod and stayed put. Everyone cleared out of the room until Mary and Tracey were the only ones left in it—they and two girls who ran back to the kitchen to get aprons for clearing up.

Mary walked up to Tracey and handed her a slim paperback book. "Read this tonight, Miss Jacamuzzi. It should make your stay easier. I'll want to see you in my office at seven-thirty tomorrow to complete your registration. Return the book to me then."

"Yes, Sister. Thank you, Sister."

"You're welcome." She turned to go.

"Am I dismissed now, Sister?"

She looked back at Tracey without explanation and without a change of expression. "Yes, dear."

# FIFTEEN

Scooter was at the door when Tracey walked into their room after dinner. The sophomore was wearing sweatpants and a loose T-shirt with the word VALKYRIES scrawled across it.

"What's Mary's problem with you?" she demanded.

Tracey walked past her to the bed. "I told you. She's down on me because of this religion thing."

"That's crazy! That can't be it."

"Suit yourself," Tracey mumbled. She threw herself down on her bunk, opened the student handbook, and started to read. There it was, right in print on page 1: "The Sanctuary of Mary and Joseph welcomes girls of all faiths who are suited to work and learn together and become constructive participants in today's society."

"Hey, Jacamuzzi."

Tracey looked up. Scooter was right beside her, crouching over her. Tracey realized that she was not only down on her back; she had the wall beside her. She suddenly felt helpless and a little afraid.

"Be careful," Scooter whispered.

"You mean with Mary?" Tracey asked.

"I mean with me."

Tracey sat up on her elbow, but Scooter walked away.

Amy and Lisa came in later and immediately got out their textbooks. Tracey had no books yet, except for the student handbook. A bell rang at seven o'clock to signal the beginning of study time. Another bell at nine-thirty ended it. During study time, everyone had to stay in their rooms except for approved activities like practices, lab work, or tutoring. Conversation was frowned upon, even whispered conversation.

After study time, the students had thirty minutes to prepare for bed. A bell at ten gave them one minute to get into bed, and afterward one of the nuns came around to check the rooms. It wasn't their purpose to say good night. The bed check was strictly disciplinary in function. But some of the nuns handled it differently. Amy and Lisa told Tracey that on April Fool's night, Sister Patricia Rose would come around wearing a Groucho Marx mustache and glasses. She was the most likely one to make a joke here and there, or to wish someone a happy birthday. Sister Madeleine, the art teacher, rarely did bed check; but when she did, she always wished each room a good night and pleasant dreams. Sister Mary did bed check silently and quickly. Sister St. Gerard always swung the door wide open, looked at each bed, smiled at everyone whether they looked at her or not, and left again.

Amy's oldest sister had come to MoJoe. Back then, Sister James Anne had been on active staff. Amy told her that when James Anne had done bed check she had always gone to each bunk to wish the girls good night, sometimes to chat a brief moment with the homesick, the ill in health, or the restless. Bed check always took her so long that she was only allowed to do it about once a month.

"She told me to come see her as often as I want to," Tracey told Amy.

Amy nodded. "She's awfully nice. I think she would keep a secret, you know? I don't think she'd ever say anything to Mary about anything that one of the girls would say to her."

Tracey wondered if Maddie Murdoch had been counting on the same thing. Maybe Mrs. Murdoch did have the sense to protect Tracey's secrets.

The basketball practice was supposed to last only until seven-thirty or eight, but Scooter and Susan didn't come back in until the nine-thirty bell rang. Nobody asked why.

"How'd it go?" Lisa asked—mostly to be polite, Tracey thought.

"OK," Susan mumbled.

"We didn't get any good players this year," Scooter said. "All those freshmen really stink. It's awful."

"You didn't really need any new people, did you?" Lisa asked.

Scooter rummaged through a drawer to get her nightclothes and shower supplies. "We lost Betty from last year, but Liz Lukas and me have it all figured out. Karen Fisher and the Sharpe twins'll probably all be first-string with us. They're juniors, so everyone's played together before."

Tracey realized that Susan, although on the team, was not first-string. It looked like Scooter was the best player, with Liz Lukas as second best.

"Are you team captain?" Tracey asked.

"CPR hasn't picked captain yet," Scooter said. "I'm gonna grab a shower." She went out the door. Susan got her things together and followed.

"Liz Lukas will be captain," Lisa said in a low voice.

"How do you know?" Tracey asked, startled at her sudden candor.

Lisa sat down with her back against her bed, keeping one eye on the door. By this time Tracey was also sitting on the floor, just wrapping up the student handbook.

"Liz's the best player by a mile," Lisa said. "Everyone knows it except Scooter. And maybe Susan."

"I thought Scooter was high scorer in the scrimmage."

Amy, seated at one of the built-in desks in the room, gave up on trying to study now that the bell had rung. She joined her two roommates.

"Scooter was high scorer for her *team* in the scrimmage," Lisa corrected Tracey. "Liz was on the other team, and she was the high scorer for her team and for the game."

Tracey nodded.

"We were all freshmen last year," Lisa said. "But Scooter and Liz made the team and got put on first-string, and the Valkyries went right to the division play-offs."

"Oh, yeah?"

She nodded. "Basketball is big-time here. They said we took the district trophy every year for four years in the early sixties, and then there were a few years of slump. Last year we got up to division championships and then lost district in a close game."

"So basketball really is the game to play around here," Tracey said.

"You're almost as tall as Liz," Lisa observed. "You don't play?"

Tracey shook her head. "Messed around a little with my friends, but I don't even know the rules that well." In fact, she'd always done pretty well in the hoop-shooting contests, but Tracey knew she was nowhere near being a Scooter or a Liz Lukas. It looked like you had to come to MoJoe as a good player to make the team.

Tracey was exhausted by bedtime, and she was thankful just to crawl into bed at lights-out. Her homesickness and loneliness rushed her all of a sudden in the silent darkness, but Tracey forcibly pushed them away. First thing in the morning, she had to be back in that office, under the scourge of Mary's contempt, letting her take her apart into little pieces.

She felt that she should have prayed, but it was hard to understand why God had let all this happen to her. It was easier not to do anything than to ask Him. If Tracey should ask and plead and beg, and He never heard her, that would be worse than not asking. So she didn't ask.

I understand that you and some of the girls think I'm rough," Sister Mary said the next morning as Tracey stood before her desk. Mary's voice placed emphasis on that last word—a little show of triumph to quote Tracey's own words back at her. The statement startled Tracey, and her mind flicked back to Sandra Kean.

Tracey took a deep breath. As a Christian she should be absolutely honest. "Yes," she said, "I said that."

"So in addition to having your own corner on the truth, Miss Jacamuzzi, you also have a corner on judgment now." She picked up her sharpened pencil and fingered it.

*And you've got a corner on Sandra Kean,* Tracey thought. She didn't say it. Instead, she heard herself say, "It is what I believe about you, Sister."

Her frankness offended Sister Mary. "You have a very bad attitude, miss, along with several other problems. I don't know what to do about you. Already, you exhibit resentment about your treatment. What kind of special treatment do you want? Should I have rolled out the red carpet?"

Tracey said nothing.

"Answer me!" she exclaimed.

"No, Sister," Tracey said.

She raised her eyebrows over the rims of her cat's-eye glasses. "Oh? No red carpet? Well, what would you have liked?"

"Nothing, Sister."

"Come now, Miss Jacamuzzi. Something prompted your complaint."

"I can't think of anything, Sister."

She came around the desk and stood right up to Tracey. Fortunately, Tracey was taller, so the acting principal couldn't dominate her that way. But it was still intimidating to have her face in Tracey's face, her cold eyes right in front of Tracey's.

"I already told you that I think you're a very disturbed young woman, Miss Jacamuzzi. I am more sure of it now."

Tracey remained silent.

"Say, 'Yes, Sister.'"

"Yes, Sister."

For the first time, a tear stung at her eye, but Tracey fought it. No box of Kleenex. Not this time. Not ever. She would fight her. Tracey got so wrapped up in forcing back that tear that she missed most of the rest of what Sister Mary told her.

At last, Mary handed Tracey her class schedule and let her go, again making Tracey thank her before she left.

The hallway was like an oasis of freedom. She'd been betrayed, and Tracey felt it even more than she'd felt Mary's sarcasm and contempt. But at the moment, just being out of her presence was a tremendous relief.

Her first class was English, taught by Sister Madeleine. Madeleine was a short and energetic teacher. Her right eye was brown and the left was blue. That was always something to wonder about if class got dull.

Sister Madeleine had a strong Irish accent, much more thick and broad than Maddie Murdoch's. She smiled and laughed a lot. Sister Madeleine also taught art, and some of her pictures adorned the hallways.

When Tracey entered, Madeleine gave her some textbooks and pointed her to her seat. Tracey passed Sandra Kean as she went to sit down, and she shot her a look. "Thanks a lot," Tracey whispered.

Sandra kept her head down and pretended not to hear. Tracey slid into her desk and opened up to the assignment. It was going to take some work to catch up to everybody. School had been in session for two weeks already.

Tracey had never been much of a student. She thought her grade average from junior high would have been about a B- or a C+. But she wasn't going to add school troubles to all her other problems. Besides, diving into schoolwork was one great way to escape life as a freshman at MoJoe.

From a few rows over, Amy gave Tracey a glance of greeting, and then they began work on *Romeo and Juliet*. Madeleine was a thorough teacher, and Tracey learned more about Shakespeare's England in the next forty-five minutes than she thought she'd learn in a year. Not dull stuff, either, but good things—like the weird foods they ate (roasted chicken stuffed with grapes), and the politics, and the way people lived (no baths).

111

Sister Madeleine assigned outside readings to every-body, and Tracey picked an article about Shakespeare's treatment of the monk in *Romeo and Juliet*. The class was assigned to go to the public library the following Saturday.

During the class time Tracey forgot about Sandra's betrayal. But after the bell rang, Amy stopped her in the hall to ask what had happened in Mary's office.

"I get it now," Tracey told her. "I see why the sophomores and the others don't want people in Mary's office. She uses them as tattletales."

Amy nodded. "I've heard that. Some of the girls are kind of her pets."

"Yeah, well, Sandra Kean got me in a lot of trouble, and I didn't say anything that anybody else hasn't said around here."

"She's definitely a narc. Come on, Latin's next."

Tracey followed Amy out of the room and up the hall. "How did that happen?" Tracey asked. "Does Mary draft them or something?"

"She charms them." Amy rolled her eyes and gri-maced to show how frightful it would be to be charmed by Sister Mary. "Mary's got a whole squad of narcs who keep tabs on everybody."

"What in the world for?" Tracey demanded.

Amy shrugged. "I'm just glad she didn't single me out."

It was true that Amy walked around with the same half-frightened, half-nervous look Sandra Kean had. But Amy didn't need to get in good with anybody.

Amy stopped Tracey before they went into Latin class. "This one's a breeze," she said. "We're still on page 3 of the book. You can probably catch up this period. Just read the material. I'll help you tonight if I can."

"Thanks," Tracey said. Just then, Sandra Kean and a couple of other girls slid past them into the class-room.

"Hey, thanks, Sandra," Tracey said. "Thanks a lot. And you can tell Sister Mary that Tracey said that too."

"Tracey!" Amy hissed.

Everybody was changing classes just then, and some of the upperclassmen looked at Tracey. She was not only the new kid, she was also angry.

"I thought you were into forgiving people and all that," Amy whispered as she pulled Tracey into the classroom.

She was right. "I guess so," Tracey mumbled. "I just can't figure out why she had to pick me to tattle on."

Her remark to Sandra had been heard by some of the girls in the classroom, and as they set down their books and found their seats, Tracey heard them asking each other and asking Sandra what Tracey was talking about. They asked her in sarcastic voices for the most part. Apparently, it was already well-known that Sandra Kean was one of Mary's narcs.

Tracey saw her sitting alone in the back corner of the room and suddenly felt bad for her. No wonder Mary had picked her out. She was a prime candidate for Mary—overweight, unhappy, away from home. She had *outcast* written all over her.

Tracey's seat was close to Amy's. The class stood to say the Ave Maria. Tracey kept silent, not only from not knowing it but also out of conviction. After the Ave, they said the Pater. Tracey wouldn't even cross herself, and she felt several of the girls watching her out of puzzlement. While the others went through the Latin prayers, Tracey promised God she would forgive Sandra Kean and would try to befriend her. Sandra needed a real friend, not Sister Mary.

Some of the freshmen gathered around Tracey at lunch, asking what Sandra Kean had done. Tracey tried to sidestep their questions. She was sorry now she'd singled her out in front of the others.

They were insistent, until at last Tracey said, "Look, you guys, Mary's going to be after me whether anybody's reporting to her or not."

"What are you?" one of them asked, meaning what religion.

"I believe in the Bible," Tracey said. "I believe that when Jesus died for people, He really died for them. He didn't die so people could try to make it on their own."

"What's that mean?" another girl asked.

"I mean, if He died and rose for us, why are we supposed to go to Mass, take communion, be good, have faith, and all that?"

"Do you think we can do anything we want to? Boy, that's the religion for me!" somebody else exclaimed.

Everyone laughed, and Tracey felt annoyed. "Very funny," she said. "But no, that's not it. I believe that every person, on their own, has to come to Christ and become a Christian. The church can't do it because man can't do it. And then after you come to Jesus and are saved, you try to be good because you want to be good. Because He changes you."

Most of them shrugged. But one girl said, "Don't you believe that Jesus established the church?"

"Yeah, I do," Tracey said. "But He's the head of the church, not the pope."

"Well, the pope is His vicar," she said. "Like His spokesman."

Tracey piled lettuce and pickles on top of the salami and fake cheese in her sandwich. "If the pope's His vicar and representative and all that, then how come Christ never had a place to lay His head on this earth, and the pope lives in a castle? How come Catholics in South America starve to death and yet the pope doesn't help them? Why doesn't he sell all his goods and give the money to the poor, and then follow Christ? Wasn't that the commandment of Christ?"

The girls grouped closer. This must have been new stuff to some of them. If it wasn't, this was certainly the first time they'd ever heard somebody who dared to say it out loud.

Tracey started to explain to them what Christ meant when He called Peter a stone and then promised to build His church upon the rock of Christ, the Son of God. They really listened. But she suspected that not one of them was seriously thinking of being saved. Many of them were weighing out how far to follow her in this rebellion. If her challenge to their religion turned into anything like an outright rebellion, Sister Mary would be first in line to quell it and make an example of her.

Their discussion became more animated, and other girls came by, including upperclassmen, to hear what was going on. Liz Lukas stood just outside the knot of people, listening with a doubtful look on her face, her arms folded across her chest. She kept Tracey fixed with that look the whole time. Tracey couldn't help but wonder what Liz was thinking.

When the bell rang, everyone scurried to take their trays back to the kitchen. The upperclassmen got out first. None of them spoke to Tracey directly, but they'd been listening.

Religion class started right after lunch. It was called Salvation History, and it was a study of major Catholic doctrines. The room was filled with silent expectation as the bell rang. Obviously, a lot of the girls thought Tracey would speak right up in class. But it didn't work that way.

Sister St. Gerard, whom they all called Sister St. Bernard, was tall and energetic. Tracey liked her. She had a Ph.D. in philosophy, and her entrenchment in the church was firm. She could list what seemed like millions of reasons for being a Catholic, and she could rationalize away all the faults that anybody found in the church. But she didn't ignore or dismiss them. In fact, St. Bernard was very active in trying to make the local Catholic churches take active roles in caring for the poor and doing other things to serve humanity. She had a social conscience. She utterly disarmed Tracey in that first hour by letting her declare some of the faults she had found with the Catholic church. She even agreed with many of Tracey's objections and outlined the plans of concerned people in the church to right those wrongs.

Tracey had never met anybody like her, not even Sister Edward from St. Anne's. In fact, St. Bernard made Tracey wonder if she should rethink what she had done and reexamine the church.

She told Tracey to read the book of First Corinthians and then tell her what she thought of the church at that time. "I think," she added as she saw Tracey's surprise at being spoken to so earnestly, "you will find that the Corinthian church was much like the Catholic church today—broken into factions, confused, troubled by inner sin. But still a church, Tracey, and still the church of God."

"I'll read it, Sister," Tracey said.

Tracey kept her mouth shut through the rest of the class and realized that she might have been a little imperious about her new faith. Perhaps there were things she didn't know. Maybe—just maybe—she was a big mouth sometimes. St. Bernard made her feel all those things without a word of accusation.

But Tracey felt a little wary of Sister St. Bernard. In that first hour, the teacher gave the class her own spiritual history, a history of asking questions and reading voraciously. She seemed to expect thinkers and questioners to do what she'd done herself—ask a lot of serious questions, but come back in the end—after scholarship and years of study—as a thinking, new type of Catholic, the kind who would march for world peace and social justice and join the Peace Corps.

After religion class they had World History with Sister Timothy, an enormously fat nun whom the girls of some bygone era had christened Timbuktu. The name still stuck. She sat during class because she couldn't stand, but she kept order, and she did know her subject.

Tracey realized that the sisters at MoJoe were of a different sort than the nuns in parochial school. The only nun Tracey had in grade school who was college educated was Sister Edward. All the other teachers had earned only teaching certificates. At MoJoe, every sister had at least a four-year degree, and St. Bernard, Timbuktu, and several others had done graduate work.

The students didn't do the busywork they'd done in parochial grade school, like hunting through textbooks for terms they should know or making up their own test questions. Nearly every teacher assigned outside readings at the library, and right from the start, students at MoJoe stood up and gave class presentations.

It was a completely different setting, a different way of going to school. Tracey felt afraid at first because she'd never been a good student. But, oddly enough, where the teachers at St. Anne's had been hard on people who couldn't achieve, the teachers at MoJoe were sympathetic. Tutorials and private assistance schedules were posted in the hallways alongside the classroom doors—everything from organized help classes to weekly one-on-one sessions with nearly any teacher.

The day ended with gym class, and at last Tracey met the famous CPR. She was a tall, angular nun with a permanent tan. It was hard to tell her age. Her face had a few lines at the mouth and eyes, but she was as agile and limber as any of the students. Even in her cumbersome habit, she could get out on the hockey field and pass the ball back and forth with the first-string players.

Normally, CPR wore a dark running suit for phys ed activities, and she kept her hair neatly and tightly pinned back, except for her dark bangs. She had a lot of energy. She used her talents to drive the girls, and she drove them hard. On Tracey's first day, as soon as they were all dressed in their baggy gym suits, CPR sent them out to run two miles. The course was marked out around the grounds.

Tracey didn't know the way, but CPR told her to follow the crowd if she could keep up, and if she couldn't, just to do her best. Tracey easily kept up. She'd never jogged or run for health before, but she'd always enjoyed racing up the long, straight street on the way home from St. Anne's. That was exactly a quarter mile, only an eighth of the distance here. But she quickly realized that nobody ran as fast as they could to do the two miles. They paced themselves.

The second mile was easier than the first because by then Tracey was warmed up. Most of the girls had slowed to a walk and were about half a field behind those who were still running. The last half mile was hard. Tracey's feet ached, and a sharp stitch chewed at her side, but she kept at it. Finishing was a matter of pride. About a half dozen of the girls were still maintaining a good pace, and as they came into sight of the gym doors, the others sped up to a sprint. Tracey didn't have the strength to do that, but she did keep up her pace.

Once she'd crossed through the open door, Tracey slowed to a walk and swung her arms back and forth. She walked around the gym to slow her heartbeat and ease her breathing.

It wasn't until then that CPR said anything to her. She came up and walked the length of the gym with her. "You're new, aren't you?"

"Yes, Sister."

"Jacamuzzi, right?"

"Yes, Sister."

"You did well on that run. Do you play any sports?"

"Field hockey, Sister," Tracey told her. "But I guess you've already got the team picked, huh?"

She nodded. "I'm sorry, dear. The roster is full, and I couldn't take anybody off, no matter how good you are."

Though Tracey was tired and out of breath, she managed a laugh. "I'm not that good, Sister. I just like the game. It's all right."

"Do you play basketball?" she asked.

Tracey shook her head. "I don't even know the rules."

"Hmm. Well, you did well on the run, and I find that in most high school games, endurance is what wins in the end." She looked up with a sudden, un-expected smile. "Maybe after you get a look at MoJoe basketball you'll be inspired with a love for the game. We'll see. Thank you, dear."

She strode away to yell in the stragglers for calisthenics.

# E I G H T E E N

"What'd Sandra Kean do to you today?" Scooter asked Tracey as she came into the room that afternoon and threw her books on her bunk.

"Oh, it was no big deal," Tracey said. She flopped down onto her bed and flipped through the Latin I book. Three years of Latin lay ahead. She would have to get caught up fast.

"I asked you a question, Jacamuzzi," Scooter said. She came and stood over her.

Tracey sat up on her elbow and looked up at her from under the sheltering overhang of the upper bunk. "I gave you my answer," Tracey said. She was scared when she said it, but as soon as she did, she became convinced this was the only way to go. Standing up to the nuns about religion and then giving in to the older girls for everything else would be hypocritical. She would not tattle on Sandra Kean.

Tracey never knew what would have happened next because just then the other Susan burst into the room. "Hey, what'd CPR say to you today?" she demanded.

Tracey responded with a blank stare.

Scooter looked at Susan. "What's going on?"

"I heard CPR singled her out," the junior said. "You a jock or something?"

Tracey laughed. "No," she exclaimed. Susan relaxed a little. "I don't think she said anything special," Tracey told them. "Just checked my name and asked if I played sports."

"What'd she say about basketball?" Susan demanded. Scooter looked at Tracey.

Tracey shrugged. "Just what you said—that the team is really good and maybe I could try out for it someday."

"Well, I heard she told some of the girls to keep an eye on you," Susan said, "because you'd make a good player."

"She told me my endurance is good because I finished the run. That's all. She's never even seen me play anything. We just ran and did exercises." Tracey stood up and stepped away from them. "That's all that happened."

"We think maybe you're a narc," Scooter said suddenly.

"Well, I'm not," she said. "Mary's only use for me is to tell me I'm a mental case."

"Yeah, but you're into religion and all that. What're you gonna do when we want to do something on our own?" Scooter demanded.

Tracey knew "on our own" meant something against the rules. "I told you," she said. "Just stay out of my way and let me mind my own business."

"You've been preaching your stuff all day," Susan said. "Everybody heard you."

Tracey nodded. "But don't get me confused with the nuns. Believe me, we're completely different."

It was already clear to Tracey that the sisters were incapable of keeping students from breaking the rules. The girls easily picked out Mary's narcs and ostracized them. And there was really no protection Mary could offer to her narcs. After only two weeks of school, Sandra Kean was subject to all kinds of cruel comments and even stray pokes and cuffs the other girls dished out. Tracey knew it was impossible to win at MoJoe by siding with the nuns or helping them.

She walked out of the room and went downstairs to see Sister James Anne before supper. Liz Lukas passed her on the stairs, and Tracey went by without even thinking to say anything to her.

When Liz was above her on the stairs, she said, "Hey, Jacamuzzi."

Tracey looked up. "Yeah?"

"Can you run three miles?"

"I never ran two until today, and my legs are sore."

"CPR said you looked good. Run your feet more and your mouth less, and you might get along better."

"I'll keep that in mind," Tracey said. She went down the stairs and out to the wing.

Sister James Anne was in one of the parlors when Tracey came in. Though evening was coming, she looked up and was able to recognize her. "Tracey, have you come to visit?"

"Yes, Sister, unless you'd rather walk across the field," Tracey said. "I think there's some light left outside."

"Oh, I'd love to. I know the walkway well." Though she was bundled in her cumbersome habit, Sister James went to get a sweater. Tracey led her outside to a flagstone walkway around the border of the grounds by the retirees' wing. She told her all about her first day and listened while Sister James reminisced about the classes she had taught and the girls she'd known. For being a retired nun and half blind, she knew a lot more about what was going on than some of the nuns who were teachers. She begged Tracey that first day to promise she would never try that dreadful drug, marijuana. Tracey promised, and added that she neither drank nor smoked, two vices that were not taboo in the Catholic church. Tracey suspected the sister had personal objections to them, and her guess was correct.

"I thought you were a nice girl, dear, and I see that I was right," Sister James said. "Dear me, what is this world coming to when women with husbands and children are drinking and smoking just like coal miners?"

Because she was still feeling the sting of realizing that she could be a big mouth, Tracey was gentle with Sister James in introducing some of the ideas that had converted her.

All the elderly woman said as Tracey brought her back up the darkening walkway to the wing was, "Well, dear, we have a very forgiving God, a very forgiving Christ. That's the main thing." She thanked her for walking with her and told her to come again as soon as she could.

It was nearly six, so Tracey hurried back to the dining hall.

The days fell into a pattern of schoolwork and study. For a blessed week of freedom Tracey neither saw nor heard from Sister Mary. Amy helped her catch up with her Latin, but it was months before she felt comfortable with her position in the class. Latin seemed like something that could easily slip out of her grasp and turn into a jumbled confusion of words.

She was lonely nearly all the time. She missed Sister Edward dreadfully. But most of all, she missed Jean. Tracey knew she was suffering too. Dad wouldn't let even his favorite talk about Tracey now that he'd put his foot down. Tracey never heard from any of her aunts or uncles, but at the end of the first week, Jean did get a letter to her. She wrote it at school and mailed it from a friend's house. Even though it was a nice letter, with no reference to all that had happened, Tracey cried so hard when she got it that she couldn't even go out to see Sister James.

The only way she could think of to forget the pain was to throw herself into her studies. Amy, who had always been studious, had taught her to take one textbook at a time and plow through a neatly marked section of it. The more Tracey kept up with her studies, the more interested in them she became, and the more easily she could put off thinking and grieving over all that had happened.

Tracey worked just as hard at studying her Bible as she did at her schoolwork, but she hardly ever prayed.

She learned from the girls around her that a lot of the upperclassmen were keeping an eye on her. They weren't sure exactly how much she would side with the nuns against the girls should anything come down to outright conflict about keeping the rules.

Every morning at prayers in homeroom, Tracey stood with the rest but remained absolutely still. The two Jewish girls in the class at least bowed their heads for as long as their patience lasted, and then they shifted on their feet and looked around the room. Tracey stayed still but kept her head erect because there was a crucifix in the front of the room, and Tracey wouldn't bow her head in front of it.

An Episcopalian girl named Tina McCorkle declared herself a Catholic at the end of her first week because, she said, "People as good and as smart as Sister St. Gerard seem so much more right than anybody I've ever seen in the Episcopal church."

Tracey told Tina to her face that she was a traitor to every martyr ever burned by the Catholic church. Everybody else just called her a brownie. Tina was a town student, so nobody could figure out why she would take such pains to get in good with St. Bernard. Whatever the reason, it didn't really work. St. Bernard, who was as clear-sighted as the next person, said she approved of Tina's decision and wished her well. Tina turned her fawning attention to Timbuktu.

By the end of the first week Tracey felt a little better. She counted Sister James as a friend, and Amy and Lisa were helpful. Other administrative concerns had sidetracked Mary, and Tracey hoped she would forget about her. There seemed to be no indication that Mrs. Murdoch had said anything to the acting principal.

Tracey wondered about Mrs. Murdoch, and sometimes hoped she would see her again. The knowledge that the woman had seen her and somehow known what was under the makeup, somehow seen into her like the creature in the dream had, shamed Tracey. But, she reminded herself, Mrs. Murdoch had only seen what had been done to Tracey. At least she hadn't seen the things Tracey had done to others.

One night the fire alarm went off. It rang about twenty minutes after lights-out. Tracey was already asleep, so it took her a couple of seconds to wake up and realize what was going on. Lisa, Amy, Scooter, and Susan were already out of bed and scrambling into their robes and shoes.

She blinked and frowned at the continuing squall of the alarm.

"Come on, Tracey," Amy exclaimed. "Fire drill."

Tracey rolled out of bed and groped around for her shoes and robe. "Go on," she told Amy as the others hurried out. Tracey could see the other girls rushing down the hall, giggling and whispering. "I'll get down there. Don't wait for me." She pulled on her shoes and managed to get her robe tied. By then the hall was empty, and CPR was standing at the head of it, calling to see if anyone was left.

"Hurry up! Hurry up!" she exclaimed as Tracey came stumbling into the hall.

"Which way?" Tracey asked.

"Hurry! Hurry!" she yelled.

The girls from the floor above were milling down the stairs, and Tracey pushed herself into the line, desperate to get with her hall before anybody noticed she was late. She didn't want to give Mary another chance to rake her over the coals.

"Fall down these steps would be a shame," somebody above her said.

"Fat person going down the stairs would probably break right through the banister."

Something hit Tracey from behind, and she heard a girl scream. Sandra Kean hit her, but Tracey realized that somebody had given her a shove. She would have regained her footing without Tracey's help, but as she hit Tracey, another girl gave her another push, and a third girl smacked her on top of her head. Tracey turned and caught Sandra by the arm, and they both would have fallen if the banister hadn't caught them. Just as one of the girls hit Sandra's head again, Tracey reached over Sandra and backhanded the girl without even thinking. It was no joke to push someone on the stairs.

"Leave her alone!" Tracey exclaimed.

The push of girls put them almost on top of both Tracey and Sandra. Sandra regained her balance, and just as another one of the girls who had already pushed her once leaned forward to do it again, Tracey exclaimed, "I said to leave her alone!" and Tracey grabbed the girl by the front of her robe and pulled her down three steps to the landing.

That scared her. Sandra got away in the crowd, and several of the girls hooted after her. The girl she'd grabbed was a junior named Nancy Elkins.

"I said to leave her alone!" Tracey said again.

"Hey, Jacamuzzi, mind your own business!"

"Cool it, saint," someone said.

Most of them were angry. But Tracey was angry too. It was unfair to gang up on someone and hit her from behind. Nancy and Tracey exchanged glares but said nothing further, and Tracey went on downstairs.

The students' attitudes toward Tracey changed over-
night. There was no more slack, no more waiting
and watching, especially not from the upperclassmen.
If she went down the steps in a crowd, she was a likely
candidate for little pokes and pushes and remarks, just
loud enough for her to hear, about the things that
could be done to a narc with a big mouth.

Susan and Scooter stayed lined up with the attitudes of the other upperclassmen. Amy was too frightened to help Tracey study anymore, and Lisa usually
spent evenings in the study lounge. Tracey's loneliness
grew worse than any fear she felt.

After about two weeks of rigid, silent defiance,
Tracey felt as tense as a spring. But she kept up her
readings, and when St. Bernard asked her in religion
class if she had finished First Corinthians, she was
ready to talk about it.

"Yes," Tracey told her. "I finished it, Sister."

"What did you think?" St. Bernard asked. "Did you
see that Paul was appointed to exercise discipline over

the Christians, and that the church had serious problems with corruption?"

Tracey nodded. "But the point of the book is that salvation is an issue between a person and God. Paul could keep discipline in the church, but the church couldn't save souls."

"But salvation was an integral part of the church," Sister St. Bernard said.

Tracey nodded again, conscious for the first time in weeks that the attention of the class was directed on her again, everybody wondering what the new kid would say. "But Paul had no power to say who was saved and who wasn't," she told her teacher. "He never tried to, according to the book. He only told them how to discipline that one guy who was committing fornication."

St. Bernard flushed, and Tracey saw Amy shoot her a warning look. "I think you're interpreting the book in your own way," the sister said curtly.

Tracey shrugged. "Look, Peter was supposedly the pope. But First Corinthians proves that Paul had more authority than Peter. So I think this proves there was no pope. Paul preached at Corinth—"

"That's enough out of you," the teacher exclaimed. Tracey's heart went into her throat. St. Bernard was right on top of her. "You will be quiet! Quiet!"

Tracey froze.

"How dare you walk into this classroom and pull these stunts! How dare you brandish two weeks of study in my face! How dare you!"

After the first shock, Tracey suddenly realized that this class wasn't really an open, friendly discussion on First Corinthians after all. She wondered where she had misread St. Bernard in her invitation to read and discuss the passage. Her face went red and hot. She felt tears in her eyes but blinked them back.

"What do you know about church history?" St. Bernard exclaimed. "What? How can you say what the situation was? You don't know. You know nothing about these matters. I have a doctorate in these things!"

That boast saved Tracey. Deep as the stab of humiliation was, and as frightened as she felt, she picked up the challenge. Somehow she found the courage to speak. "Then answer me from Scripture," she said quietly.

"Quiet! I will not argue with a child. What are you? Some half-read child, somebody who has bumbled into an experience!"

Tracey's fear began to subside. She realized the teacher wasn't going to hit her. But she had liked St. Bernard, and now her words cut like a whip.

"You are out of control of your life. You've torn apart your own home and thrown away every good thing from God, and for what?"

Tracey couldn't stop the tears coming to her eyes then. Everybody in the room was frozen into silence. She didn't dare look away from St. Bernard's face while she was yelling at her. The sister saw the shock on Tracey's face and the tears that started in her eyes. Tracey didn't even dare to wipe the tears away.

St. Bernard stopped her tirade all of a sudden.

"You . . . you said it was OK to talk—" Tracey began, but a sob stopped her. She knew she had a big mouth, but she had believed her teacher when she'd told Tracey it was OK to talk about the book. It struck Tracey that she was guilty only of being perfectly frank with her teacher.

Tracey stopped and wouldn't say anything else. She just blinked and looked down.

"Tracey!" the sister exclaimed. She put her arms around Tracey, and it was unbearable.

"Get your hands off me!" she choked out. "Let me go!"

She didn't, and Tracey didn't have the courage to push her away.

"I'm sorry," St. Bernard said. "I am sorry."

"You don't know anything about my home," Tracey said slowly between clenched teeth. She caught her breath. "I want you to let me go." She could see that a lot of the girls in the room were on her side about this. They had heard St. Bernard praise her willingness to read up on things. They knew Tracey had only been honest.

But St. Bernard wouldn't let her go. Tracey's tears were replaced with a ball of rage in her stomach. St. Bernard had to come out of this at least looking like everything was all right. "Please forgive me, Tracey. I misunderstood you because you were so straightforward in your tone. I know you didn't mean it like it sounded."

Everybody looked at Tracey, expecting her to be swayed by the apology. After all, a Christian had to forgive. Everyone knew that. Tracey gave up. Sister St. Gerard was too deep and too subtle. She had hurt Tracey, but only because her temper had gotten the better of her. She tried to rebuild things in the way she thought best.

At last, because everybody was watching, Tracey choked out, "I forgive you." Mercifully, the bell rang.

She got up without another look at the teacher and rushed out of the room.

At supper the freshmen all sat together. After the scene with St. Bernard, Tracey sensed that some of them really admired her. She had stood up to a nun about religion and had held her own in the argument.

Sandra Kean wasn't at dinner that night. Tracey wasn't the only one to notice. "Wonder where the dough girl is tonight," one of the other freshmen said.

"She was at Latin," Amy reported.

"Sure not like her to miss dinner," another girl added, and everybody laughed.

Other remarks about Sandra went around the group—comments about the latest things she'd reported to Mary, and coarse laughs about who had recently short-sheeted her bed and stolen her underwear and hung it on the bushes out front. Tracey tuned them out. One thing was true at MoJoe—you had to stay on top, because once you went down, once your own classmates turned against you, there was no way out from under. Sandra Kean had already lost it all, before the first quarter was even finished.

The talk turned to the other narcs, some of whom were upperclassmen, and then to former narcs. Tracey discovered that Mary's special pets sometimes didn't want to retain their positions. They found out the cost was too high and spent a rocky school year not co-operating with her. Ultimately, they were freed, but not without some stern talks, Tracey thought, that ripped their psyches apart a little. Afterward they were tolerated, if not welcomed back, by their classmates. One or two even managed to beat the system by spilling back to the girls some of Mary's secrets and a few whispered stories about the nuns.

There were rumors that St. Bernard had been engaged to a man and had run away to the convent on her wedding day. And there was talk that one of the nuns had suffered a nervous breakdown years earlier. Somebody had reported that CPR had left the sisterhood for a good five years to reevaluate things before coming back. None of the girls could understand why she was a nun.

Talk turned fully to CPR. Most of the freshmen boarders were homesick, and talk of their favorite teacher gave them hope that someday she might like them, notice them, perhaps even befriend them. Nobody who was friends with CPR would have been called her pet, but then nobody was really friends with her, not even Scooter or Liz, the two star players of the basketball team.

# TWENTY-ONE

Whispers traveled from room to room that night that some of the girls had done something to Sandra Kean—beaten her up or hurt her somehow. She had not come out of her room since three-thirty, when classes had ended. Her roommates, normally as put out with her as anybody, were closed in with her. Somebody had seen them all huddled together, comforting her.

For the first time, the thought of all the girls who were against her scared Tracey a little, but she dismissed it from her mind. There was nothing she could do. She doubted that she was as bad in everybody's eyes as Sandra Kean was, and if they did come after her, she could fight back a lot better than Sandra could.

The next evening she went out for her nightly walk with Sister James Anne. Tracey always came for her at about five-fifteen and they walked until suppertime. The grounds were always dark as Tracey made her way to the dining hall, but MoJoe was fenced in, so there was no danger from outsiders.

That night, as she crossed the walk alongside the hedge, she heard somebody moving back behind the bushes. Before Tracey could say anything or yell, or even run away, she was tackled.

"Get her mouth first," someone hissed. "Don't let her scream!"

That cued Tracey to try, but three or four hands clapped over her face. The blows not only gagged her, they stunned her. She came to her senses quickly and rolled around with her attackers for a few seconds, trying to get an upper hand, but it was hopeless.

Her arms were pulled behind her back and held fast by two or three girls. Scooter herself had her hands over Tracey's mouth. She and Tracey looked at each other eye-to-eye for a split second before the girls dragged Tracey back into the bushes and forced her to the ground.

"Here it is," Susan's voice said. Scooter got into a better position behind Tracey, her hands pushing up so hard under Tracey's jaw that she choked and gagged. Tracey struggled to get a breath, but the hands tightened, and she gagged again.

"You've got this coming, Jacamuzzi," Scooter said into her ear. "You hate everyone, you know that? You'll do anything to cross people. You've got this whole religion thing and this whole narc thing. You ain't on nobody's side. You hate us all."

Tracey struggled to get away and got jabbed in the ribs.

"We're just gonna help you remember who you are."

She felt something like a rope or cord slip around her right arm, and she looked up at the ring of faces. She knew each one of them. Scooter, Susan, Missy,

138

Rita Jo, Tammy, and Lorraine—all upperclassmen. She wondered what the cord was for, unless it was to tie her up for some reason. Then Susan took out a straight stick and showed it to Tracey before it disappeared out of her line of vision. She felt the cord tighten and tried to get away, but they pushed her back. Two of them landed with their knees on top of her.

It knocked the wind out of Tracey, and she felt the rope getting tighter and tighter. In another minute the pain became harsh, then unbearable. She struggled and heard herself groan through the restraints of Scooter's hands.

"She's all right. Keep going."

"Let me try it, Susan."

"Come on, saint, pray. Let's hear you pray."

Tracey was praying. But her prayer became jumbled, lost in a wave of pain and the fear that they were breaking her arm. She heard one of them ask again to take the stick, and that was the last thing she heard before everything around her began to fade.

For some time, she still heard faint voices, though not words, as though they were at the end of a tunnel, a tunnel where Tracey's arm lay imprisoned in its cord of pain. The far-off voices were punctuated with shorter and shorter silences. At a great distance, she heard but did not feel someone pull the thong off her arm. At its release, one final great wave of fire rushed in tightening circles around her arm and then exploded in flames up her right side.

Tracey lay there for a while, neither awake nor unconscious, but in a stupor from pain and shock. At last the sound of footsteps coming along the hedge brought her fully back to her senses. She dug her heels into the soft earth and pushed herself further back into the hedge, closer to the wall. Through the curtain of twigs and leaves, the skirt of a MoJoe uniform and the blue of a sophomore's sleeve seemed to float above the dark ground and trunks of the hedge. Was it Scooter or one of the others coming to see if she was still where they'd left her?

For a split second she held her breath, hoping against hope that the intruder would miss her and go away. But the skirt pushed closer, and two big hands pushed aside some of the hedge branches.

Tracey had no idea how she would explain what she was doing in the hedge to a newcomer, and she wasn't about to tell the truth. MoJoe had to be her home, and it would be impossible to be a narc and survive. There would be other punishments worse than this if she told.

The stranger boldly stepped into the hedge and pushed aside two of the bushes at the top. Tracey watched the hands work through the branches, pushing them apart. The investigator would see her face in another second or two. Tracey's skirt and shoes were already in plain sight.

The branches above her separated. Tracey found herself looking at Liz Lukas. Liz started a little when she saw the younger girl's eyes fixed on hers, Tracey's face expressionless. Without a word she let the branches go and stepped back. Then she strode away, leaving Tracey there.

Tracey closed her eyes and relaxed. She didn't know what had prompted Liz to come looking through the hedge, but she'd been frightened off. She wasn't afraid of being the next victim. Liz feared nobody that way. She feared entanglements and emotional things. Tracey couldn't remember when she'd realized that truth about Liz; maybe it had come to her just then, when their eyes met.

She lay in the cold darkness and cried for a while. She had to go up to that room, caked with dirt and hurting. Somehow she had to find the strength to do it. And she had to go on living in front of Scooter and Susan without a word to Amy or Lisa about what had happened.

With her good left hand, she grabbed the trunk of one of the bushes and sat up. It had to be now. She had to do it before study time started and anybody came looking for her. With an effort, she stood. The whole garden swayed, but she got her footing. There was dirt in her eyes. She blinked and squinted out at the darkness, but her vision was still blurry. She tried to rub the dirt out and looked up again.

Down in the small parking lot by the retirees' wing, the single parking lot lamp was coming on, slowly brightening in the twilight. Tracey squinted at it and blinked several more times, unsure if the brightening effect was her own vision clearing or the light itself.

To her surprise, she saw an indistinct figure in the darkness under the lamp. As the light grew stronger, it began to take shape—something tall and slender, moving through the light with a sure, silent walk, almost floating. No sound of footsteps echoed back to her. The figure was so indistinct that it seemed to disappear and reappear, as though every shift of wind or light obscured it.

Her own eyes were still blurred by the dirt, but for a moment she watched the silent, arcane figure at the bottom of the hill. It moved in and out of the flimsy light, head erect and gaze outward, graceful yet strong, like an angel or some otherworldly visitor passing into and then out of this world. Then it disappeared in the darkness.

Nausea clutched Tracey's stomach, reminding her of where she was, and she made her way to her room.

# T W E N T Y - T W O

Tracey let Sister James Anne take her left arm for their walk the next day. Sister James talked for a while about what she had done that day, the volunteers who'd come in to read to the sisters and keep them company, the good lunch she'd eaten, the restful afternoon.

Tracey realized she was clinging to the older woman's arm much more than Sister James was clinging to her, and she forced herself to relax. As they came back toward the wing in the growing dimness, Sister James said softly, "What is it, dear? Why are you trembling?"

"I'm sorry," Tracey said. "I didn't know I was. I must be cold."

"You feel cold." She was silent for a couple of steps, and then said, "Can't you tell your friend what's wrong?"

Tracey cringed when she realized she'd given herself away, forgetting that James Anne's eyesight was almost normal in daylight. She would have known from the minute Tracey walked into the wing that she had been badly frightened by something.

"I can't tell you because you are my friend," Tracey said. "Don't ask me, Sister."

"Has your family hurt you, dear?"

"My family!" Tracey choked it out with a sob and then got hold of herself. "Please, Sister," she told her. "Don't ask me. Let it go for now."

Keen as her insight could be, Sister James Anne had no idea of the methods the girls were now using to ensure peace in the ranks. In her day there had been bullies, but nothing like this. Her far hand reached over to take hold of Tracey's left hand for guidance, and her near arm slipped around the girl's waist. The gesture of comfort brought tears to Tracey's eyes again.

"I love you, dear. I hope that can help you."

"It does," Tracey said. She didn't dare slow down because she knew the girls were watching her. It had to look like one of the regular walks. Tracey kept up their slow, steady pace.

"Sister Lucy said she would pick you up by the dining hall doors tonight," Tracey said. "You don't mind, do you?"

"Not at all, dear. Sister Lucy should get out more. She loves her books too much. A little walk now and then would keep her in better health."

"You're right," Tracey said, trying to smile.

"But I would miss this half hour with you," Sister James added gently. "You've brought me so much joy, dear."

This time the tears overflowed and trickled down Tracey's face, but she knew it was too dim now for Sister James to see them.

"You've helped my Latin," Tracey said, trying to make a joke out of it, but she couldn't. "And . . . and you've brought me joy." She bowed her head and cried. Sister James kept her arm tight around Tracey as they made their way up to the dining hall.

Sister Lucy met them there. Tracey said good night to them both and went in the side door.

At the sight of Liz Lukas, Tracey stopped short, and so did her tears. For one confused and jumbled moment, she wondered if it would mean another fight, more trouble—and here she was with a useless arm. Tracey's right arm was still a raging pain, and she wondered how damaged it really was. It was horribly swollen where the cord had been twisted in, and any bend of her elbow was excruciating.

"Don't you think that evening walk is a bad idea?" Liz asked. "The night air is bad for people."

"No," Tracey said.

Tracey didn't know whether Liz was giving her a warning or a threat, but she was so overwrought from the visit with James Anne that she just pushed past Liz and went to the dining hall. Liz couldn't have hurt her more than she was already hurt. She couldn't have driven despair home to her any more than it already had been driven.

Everybody had been playing field hockey in gym class, and as the end of the season approached, CPR announced an intervarsity scrimmage. It was held at four o'clock one sunny afternoon, sophomores against freshmen. Everybody divided up into squads, changed to their gym suits, and congregated outside the gym doors.

None of the girls were happy about the scrimmage because it was held after classes, and they would have preferred doing other things. But CPR brooked no complaints.

"OK, players, up the hill to the hockey field," she called. She had her habit on and couldn't keep up, but she ordered the squads to run ahead.

Field hockey sticks in hand, they obeyed. Tracey darted out to the front, ahead of the slower girls. By this time, her arm had healed enough to be useful, and she was eager for a chance to play.

A hockey stick poked between her legs in a failed attempt to trip her.

"Hey, watch it, saint. Lot of accidents out here," Scooter said from behind her as they jogged. Tracey glanced back, annoyed. Susan, a junior, was not there. But Tammy and Lorraine were sophomores. They ran alongside Scooter and grinned at Tracey. "How's that arm doing, Tracey?" Tammy asked.

"Let's go, you guys!" Liz yelled from the front. Tracey hurried to catch up, pretty sure that if she were racing with Liz, the others would leave her alone. But she was wrong. The stick snagged at her legs again, and she had to jump sideways while running to avoid getting hit. Liz glanced at her, and Tracey glanced back.

The rage of the past two weeks had built to its highest point, and the pokings of the stick kindled it even higher, but Tracey clamped down on it.

"Now or never," Liz called to her as Tracey clumsily tried to avoid the stick that Scooter rammed at her again.

Tracey took a chance. "Will you hold my stick?"

Liz gave a curt nod. "Go get 'em, kid."

Tracey threw the stick to her and turned abruptly. Scooter almost ran into her. She grabbed Scooter's stick by the curved end and brought it up quickly enough to pull it out of her hands with almost no effort. She turned to Tammy and Lorraine and pushed the stick against them, hard. Then she dived on Scooter.

The shock of those minor efforts drove fires up her right arm, but it didn't matter. The moment was bliss. She remembered Barbara and the horror she'd felt after that fight, so this time she forced herself to hold back. But she swung a right roundhouse at Scooter's jaw that knocked her down, right into the girls coming up behind them. They all screamed and separated, and then Tracey fell on top of Scooter. Maybe the others would kill her with their hockey sticks for this. Probably. She was going to make it worth it.

Tracey pummeled Scooter's ribs as hard and fast as she could, while Scooter, struggling to get to her feet, grabbed Tracey's hair and pulled until it felt like it would come out. When Scooter lifted her head, Tracey hit her on the jaw again, knocked her down, and finally got astride her.

She got a glimpse of raised sticks overhead, and suddenly Liz Lukas was in the way, yelling at Scooter's friends not to get into it. Some of the other girls were screaming for Tracey to get off, but she heard others—others, like music—and they were saying, "Get her, Tracey! Get her!"

Tracey got her. She knew better than to hit her in the face too much. The ribs were safer.

"Get off!" Scooter screamed. "Get off me!" Tracey couldn't even answer. Scooter tried to scratch Tracey's face, and Tracey forced her chin back and then hit her again.

A sudden, fierce, gripping pain on Tracey's ear

brought the fight to a halt. Pain flooded her eyes with tears, and for a moment she was forced upward onto her feet as the grip on her ear pulled her away from Scooter. Through the pain she got a glimpse of someone beside her. Tracey charged into her, intent on knocking her over.

She heard Liz yell, "No, don't!" But whoever it was who had Tracey kept the hold and neatly maneuvered around her clumsy charge. The twisting grip on her ear, which was already blinding her with pain, screwed tighter. "Stop it," a voice said. "Stop it right now, miss."

It was an adult voice, an Irish voice. Tracey did stop, horrified at the blunder she had made in fighting back. But all she said was, "Let go my ear!"

"Will you stop then?"

"Yes, I've stopped!" Tracey exclaimed. The hand mercifully let her ear go but took a strong grip on the collar of her gym suit. Tracey's eyes cleared. She was in the grip of Maddie Murdoch. Where she had come from was a mystery. But she was looking at Tracey with her jaw firmly set, disapproving and stern.

CPR was racing toward them, the skirts of her habit billowing behind her. She had one hand clapped down on her veil to keep it in place.

"Get that girl up! Get her up!" CPR exclaimed. She glared at Tracey and then glanced at the tall newcomer. "Thank you, Maddie," she said. She turned to Tracey, ready to reprimand her, but Liz Lukas exclaimed, "They were picking on the freshman, Coach! They started it! Hey, Maddie, they started it!"

Several of the sophomore girls were helping Scooter up. As they did, she suddenly sprang at Tracey, who was still imprisoned by the grip on her collar. Tracey

148

would have returned the attack, but Mrs. Murdoch nimbly got hold of Scooter's ear with her other hand and pulled her off, subjecting her to the same pain that had conquered Tracey so quickly.

"Oh, you're just as bad as this one!" the woman scolded Scooter as she twisted furiously on the ear. "The two of you aren't worth a heap of eggs in moonshine!" In spite of her anger, frustration, and embarrassment, Tracey felt shamed by Mrs. Murdoch's rebuke. She had genuinely liked this woman, in spite of some questions about how much she had reported to the sisters about Tracey. And yet the words angered her too. She did not deserve to be compared with Scooter. Mrs. Murdoch had no idea what Scooter had done to her.

"All right!" Scooter said, giving in. "I'm not doing anything."

"Both of you. At once. To the office!" CPR ordered. "Maddie, do you mind taking them?"

"Not a bit," Mrs. Murdoch assured her. "I was just walking one of the sisters over the grounds." She nodded toward the figure of one of the older nuns, standing by the fringe of trees that surrounded the field. "If you could have one of the other girls walk her back to her room, it will be all right." Tracey remembered that Mrs. Murdoch was one of the volunteers from town who helped at the retirees' wing. She looked like the sort of person who would do volunteer work—tall, capable, and attractive.

"One of you take the sister back," CPR said to the sophomores.

"Come on, then, you two," Mrs. Murdoch said sternly. "Oh, you've behaved like ruffians. I hope you're rightly ashamed of yourselves." She did not raise her voice; in fact, her words betrayed more shock then anger. But it was galling to be scolded.

Tracey tightened her lips. She shot a look at Liz, who was still between Tracey and the others. Liz's gaze met Tracey's, unreadable.

Oh, look at the two of you, all covered in dirt," Mrs. Murdoch scolded them as they walked. "And neither of you a bit ashamed for it, by the looks of you."

She still had each of them by the collar, even though Tracey had subsided into a silence of misery and frustration: frustration that her revenge on Scooter had not been finished, and misery at having been caught looking and behaving like a savage by the one person whose good opinion she had wanted. Scooter, ignoring Mrs. Murdoch, yelled, "You just wait, Jacamuzzi! You're going to pay for this!"

"That's enough, you!" Mrs. Murdoch told her. Tracey forced back tears and said evenly, "Make sure you bring all your friends, since you're so scared to come alone!"

It only got her in deeper. "Not a word, not another word!" the woman exclaimed, and she shifted her grip on Tracey's collar as though ready to grab for the ear again. Tracey remembered the fierce ear-twisting ordeal and was silent. Apparently Scooter got the warning too, because she maintained a stony silence.

Now, Tracey realized, Maddie Murdoch was going to march them into Mary's office and tell Mary the whole story—no doubt adding a great deal of shock to it. It was plain to see that the woman was shocked. And that was all that Mary would need. It was all going to come out. When you came right down to it, they were all alike. Maybe Mrs. Murdoch was beautiful and generous and all the rest, but she was just as inexorable as Sister Mary. She wanted punishment for this. She had been setting the nuns on Tracey from day one—all too eager to straighten her out, bring her into conformity with this place. First there'd been the little hints about spirituality and it being useless to resist and all that, and then she'd gone straight to Sister James and who knew which other nuns with her story about Tracey's concealed bruises.

Sister Mary's reaction was about as bad as anything Tracey had thought of.

"You've been fighting," Mary said as soon as the two girls were marched into the office. Only before Sister Mary's desk did Mrs. Murdoch release her two prisoners. They stepped away from her, straightening out their gym suits and eyeing both her and Sister Mary. They came up to the desk, and Tracey said, "Yes, Sister."

"She started it!" Scooter exclaimed.

Mary didn't like statements like that. She preferred the initial act of compliance, like saying, "Yes, Sister," and then the subservient wait for her to ask the questions. So in response to Scooter's rashness, Sister Mary acknowledged Tracey's look and said, "What happened, Miss Jacamuzzi, according to you?"

"Scooter and two of her friends kept trying to hit

me and trip me with their hockey sticks, so at last I turned around and knocked Scooter down, because she's the ringleader," Tracey said quietly. She kept her eyes down, but she could feel Mrs. Murdoch looking at her. She wouldn't look at Mrs. Murdoch. She had liked and trusted her at first—even hoped in her in some inexplicable way—and now she felt betrayed—twice betrayed.

"You knocked her down with your stick?" Sister Mary asked.

"No, Sister. I handed the stick to someone and punched her." Tracey rubbed her bruised knuckles and glanced at Scooter.

Sister Mary glanced at Mrs. Murdoch, who said, "I just saw them rolling around on the ground. I have no idea who started it."

Mary looked at Scooter. "Well? And what do you say?"

Scooter started to cry. "We were messing around, and she got mad. I didn't mean anything by it."

The statement startled Tracey out of her misery. "That's a lie!"

"Silence!" Mary exclaimed. Tracey heard Mrs. Murdoch's intake of breath, a sound of disapproval. Tracey's outburst had been a bad move that made a bad situation worse. Tracey wondered if she would ever learn to control herself.

"I'm sorry, Sister," she murmured.

"Hockey sticks are not toys, miss," Mary said to Scooter. "They are not provided for you to fling them carelessly about and endanger or anger other people. They are to be treated with respect and care. You are far too frivolous and heedless of others. I've noticed this about you lately. You're a thoughtless, self-willed girl."

"I'll go now," Mrs. Murdoch said, ready to leave the girls to their rebuke.

"Oh, please stay, Mrs. Murdoch," Sister Mary said. "I want to discuss this one with you." She nodded at Tracey.

Tracey glanced quickly from Sister Mary to Mrs. Murdoch, then down again. She wondered how much she had figured in any previous discussions between them.

"Did you hear what I said to you, miss?" Mary asked Scooter.

"Yes," Scooter said, eyes down.

"Say, 'Yes, Sister.'"

"Yes, Sister," Scooter whispered.

"You will go to your room now. You will abstain from supper, and during the supper hour you will go to the gym and personally account for every hockey stick in the bag. I want a list of what is chipped, nicked, or needs to be rewrapped."

"Yes, Sister."

"You are dismissed. Say, 'Thank you, Sister.'"

"Thank you, Sister."

Scooter didn't offer another glance at Tracey. She turned away and woodenly walked out. Tracey looked at Mary as the door closed.

"You will keep your eyes down," Mary said.

"Yes, Sister." Tracey looked down.

She came around the desk. "I am shocked this time," she said. "I knew you were troubled. I knew you were disturbed, perhaps, but to do this. To stoop to violence over a practical joke." Tracey's face burned at the insinuations, but she said nothing. It was pointless to argue that Scooter had meant to hurt her. And if she ever told what had been done in the bushes, she would become the narc they accused her of being.

"I have no idea what to do with you, Miss Jacamuzzi," Mary said. "I have never had a girl here like you. I am truly at my wits' end. I have reports from every teacher about your bad and disruptive behavior."

Tracey started without thinking. Mary's comment stunned her.

"Perhaps—" Mrs. Murdoch began, looking toward the door.

"Oh, no, please stay, Mrs. Murdoch," Sister Mary said. "Don't doubt me, Miss Jacamuzzi," she added. "I know of your confrontation with Sister St. Gerard and how she had to put you down in class. And then you fled to the refuge of tears and humiliated her."

Tracey's face flamed bright, hot scarlet. She felt betrayed by St. Bernard, but the feeling didn't last long. St. Bernard would never have carried that tale to Mary. One of the narcs had told her. The proud, self-assured nun was not one to run to Mary with every little thing.

However, for the moment the victory belonged to Mary. She stepped up to Tracey and Mrs. Murdoch. "Tell Mrs. Murdoch what you claim your religion to be, Tracey," she said.

Tracey raised her eyes to the woman. Mrs. Murdoch was taller than Sister Mary, taller than Tracey. She met Tracey's eyes with a serious, though somewhat questioning, glance, as though she herself were not sure where this conversation was leading. But her eyes were troubled.

155

"Do you not wish to tell her? You've been broadcasting it before the entire school. Why are you so silent now?" Sister Mary asked. She turned to Mrs. Murdoch. "She claims to be a Christian, Mrs. Murdoch. A true Christian, a real Christian, unlike the rest of the sisters and boarders here. What do you think of that?"

Mrs. Murdoch seemed at a loss to answer. Tracey felt the shame deeply. But why would Sister Mary think that shaming her for her religious beliefs was so especially appropriate in front of Mrs. Murdoch? The idea struck her that the two of them could be hand in glove, that all of Mrs. Murdoch's initial hospitality and soft-spoken kindness were simply a more cultivated exterior than Mary's blunt authority.

"Have you found your voice yet, Miss Jacamuzzi?" Sister Mary asked.

"I am a Christian," Tracey said, her eyes down. "I do believe the Bible."

"I doubt you would want to claim her," Sister Mary said to Mrs. Murdoch as she walked back to her desk. "She uses religion as an excuse to be disruptive. What should I do with her, Mrs. Murdoch?"

Tracey glanced at Mrs. Murdoch again. Under her roomy brown coat, which was a little like a cape and a little like a coat, Mrs. Murdoch wore tailored women's trousers and some sort of loose-fitting sweater. She sported tiny earrings in her ears, but there was no crucifix around her neck as some Catholic women wore. There was no indication of what rank or authority she held that would cause Sister Mary to appeal to her as an advisor or authority. But it raised Tracey's suspicions. She had assumed it was sheer bad luck that had made Mrs. Murdoch stumble into the fight. Now she wondered if the woman was some sort of agent who reported on the girls and brought them under the unquestioned authority of Sister Mary. There had been one or two women like that at St. Anne's—some teachers' aides and such who were always dragging kids into the principal's office for every suspected offense.

But even Mrs. Murdoch seemed puzzled at the question. Sister Mary nodded at her and said, "Thank you for bringing this matter to my attention. I won't detain you longer. Tracey and I will deal with this now."

"All right," Mrs. Murdoch said quietly. "Good day, then." She quietly walked to the door and went out.

The room was silent for a moment as the door closed behind her. "We have a special place for people like you," Sister Mary said. "People unable to control themselves and deal with real situations."

Tracey glanced at her.

"You will spend tonight and tomorrow night in meditation and reflection. Fourth floor. Take your clothes that you'll need for tomorrow, your books, and your bedclothes. The rules for meditation and reflection are posted on the room door. Abide by them."

Tracey didn't know what this punishment was, but she only said, "Yes, Sister."

"You are dismissed."

"Thank you, Sister."

Tracey walked out. She closed the door behind her, her mind still whirling from the confrontation, from Maddie Murdoch's unexpected appearance, from her own halting confession of her faith before the two women.

She looked up in time to see Maddie Murdoch waiting at the foot of the stairs. The sunset light came through the stained-glass window on the landing and threw many-colored lights over her. Tracey stopped by the shelter of the stairs. There was no way to get by her without being seen. She forced herself to go on.

"Tracey," Mrs. Murdoch said as she approached the landing. Tracey stopped, eyes down.

"I'm sure you're sorry for what you've done. I . . . I hope we can be friends," Mrs. Murdoch said.

Tracey was not sorry. And there was no answer to give her, nothing that she wouldn't run back to Mary with, or at least to James Anne, or to one of the sisters—and it could be any one of them. So Tracey said nothing.

"Won't you speak to me?" Mrs. Murdoch asked.

Tracey looked up at her and felt again all the resentment, frustration, and betrayal that this woman's actions could call forth. "What will I say to you that you won't say to them?" she asked.

"To who?"

"To any of them—Sister Mary, or Sister James, or any of the ones who are your friends."

The import of her words startled Mrs. Murdoch, and Tracey felt some pleasure at seeing her frozen for a moment with the sudden realization of Tracey's opinion. Tracey turned and started up the stairs.

Mrs. Murdoch stepped after her. "And was I supposed to leave you rolling around on the grass and fighting?" she asked. "Or leave you, a newcomer, without any friends here? I sent Sister James to help you."

But the rankling cuts of being scolded, of being blamed for starting the fight, of being forced to confess her faith and then derided for it were too fresh. "You don't know anything about this place," Tracey told her. "Or about me. I like Sister James a lot, but you didn't have to tell her—what you told her—" At the memory of that humiliating black eye, tears came to her eyes, and she resolutely turned away and went up the stairs. She was not going to cry in front of Mrs. Murdoch, and certainly not about that.

Reflection and meditation, according to the memo posted on the door of the fourth floor, was a provision seldom called upon at MoJoe. It was not exactly solitary confinement because you went to classes by day and had meals as usual. But all of your free time and study time and sleeping hours had to be spent in the narrow, chapel-like room.

The first thing Tracey did on entering the private room was to turn the crucifixes on the shelves to face the wall. Then she threw herself down on the bed and vividly replayed the fight in her mind. There was no doubt that revenge had been sweet, until the unaccounted-for Mrs. Murdoch had taken a hand.

She realized that James Anne would be told of what she'd done. And Sister James Anne would be at least as shocked as Mrs. Murdoch had been. What she'd done to Scooter had started out as something necessary in self-defense, but it had turned into something else: the sheer joy of beating up an enemy. Of course it would shock Sister James. It had been shocking.

Just like with Barbara, except this time Tracey had held back enough. And yet—it was the same sin. The memory of the fight with Barbara brought a flush of genuine shame to her face. Although the degree of violence in the two fights differed, she had wanted to hurt

Scooter. She still wanted to hurt her. Tracey hated her as she'd never hated anyone. Maybe there had been some room for Mrs. Murdoch to take such a strong hand and blame them both. But she didn't want to acknowledge this. She felt betrayed by this outsider laywoman who ran right to the sisters with every matter.

During her two days alone, she spent much time thinking about all that had happened, even when she tried not to. The girls called the two days of reflection and meditation "jug," or "being jugged." A person who was jugged was often treated warily by the other girls. Certainly, many of the nuns treated a girl in jug as though she were in serious disgrace. During Tracey's stint, she could count on not being called on in most of her classes. CPR ignored it, or never bothered to keep up with who was jugged. St. Bernard took a note from Tracey to James Anne to tell her she was jugged for a couple of days.

It was incredibly boring and lonely up there, with only the sisters' private prayer room across the hall from her and two bedrooms for a couple of the nuns way down the hall by the stairs. The rest of the rooms were used for storage or stood empty, reminders of a day when the dorm rooms had been filled all the way to the fourth floor.

Tracey probably would have yielded to the temptation to seek out company somehow, but it was impossible to leave the fourth floor without getting caught by nuns somewhere along the main stairs, and the fourth-floor door to the back stairs was locked and chained. Her only diversions came from using the bathroom and showers up there.

*What could I do?* she asked the Lord. *Where were*

*You when they had me in the bushes? If I'm not supposed to be violent, why didn't You save me?*

But then, she realized, she'd never asked Him until it was too late, until they were dragging her into the bushes.

She felt another rush of anger. It was unfair to be put through all this, without guidance and without help, and then to be treated as though she knew what she was doing. And that Maddie Murdoch, marching her in to Sister Mary, turning her right over to the acting principal, not even bothering to ask what had happened first. Yet Tracey did feel shame at Mrs. Murdoch's genuine horror at the fight.

*Look,* she prayed, *I don't know what I'm doing, but if You don't want me to fight, help me. If You want me to wait for You like Moses and Joshua did, then You've got to help me like You helped them. You've got to deliver me, Lord. O Lord, please deliver me from all of them. There's too many of them to fight.*

At her own words, she realized with a sinking heart that there were, indeed, far too many of them to fight. Scooter wasn't even the worst of the lot. The last bright gleams of her one battle faded quickly away. If it really came down to fighting each one of those six girls, then she would be fighting—and getting beaten—forever.

*Help me, Lord,* she prayed. *Don't let them get me again.*

## TWENTY-FOUR

On her first night in jug, Tracey studied the night away until she heard the bell from the halls below announcing half an hour until lights-out. Nobody came up even to tell her to go to bed, but she went anyway. The last hour of the evening was the bleakest. Bed and darkness were a welcome relief.

She tried some more prayer as she lay in bed, but it was hard to know where to begin with God. She'd already made more mistakes than she thought were acceptable, but she felt she was being put through one of the worst situations anybody could go through. In the end, she asked Him again to protect her and to keep her from making so many mistakes.

Without a sound or disturbance, the night slipped away. At rising bell, Tracey hurried to shower, dress, and get ready for breakfast and classes. But there was no need to rush. Because you didn't have to compete with people for showers or mirror space, you got ready in record time during jug.

She'd been pretty disgusted with herself during the night, but on the way back down the stairs, she could almost feel the waves of anger coming over her, like silent alarms. She dropped her shame and picked up her defiant, tough attitude. It came on like armor as she descended the stairs to the dining hall. She felt more than ready to take them on again, to fight harder, hit more often, and use harsher weapons than they could. Next time there would be no Mrs. Murdoch, and she would have to fight.

Most of the girls watched her as she passed them on the stairs and when she entered the dining hall. Nobody said anything to her except one or two individuals who liked to see someone buck the establishment, whether it was the establishment of the nuns over the students or of the cliques over the weaker girls.

Tracey sat with the freshmen and ate without a word. They said nothing. Nobody knew what to do. When Tracey looked up, she saw Scooter and Susan and some others come in together. Their eyes scanned the room and at last locked on her. She boldly met Scooter's eye. Scooter looked away first.

Classes were a welcome relief. The freshman girls were easier with Tracey when they were away from the scrutiny of the older girls.

St. Bernard stopped her in the hall after religion class. "I gave your note to Sister James Anne," she said soberly.

"Thank you, Sister." Tracey desperately wanted to ask her what James Anne had said, but she didn't want to show how concerned she was about it.

St. Bernard didn't make Tracey ask. "She was concerned," she told Tracey. "I didn't know the whole story, and I told her so. But I let her know that you felt some of the girls were bullying you."

Tracey nodded and would have thanked her again, but before she could, St. Bernard said, "Sister James Anne told me you've been badly shaken for several days."

"Well, I feel a lot of pressure," Tracey told her. "It's easier to show it when I'm with Sister James Anne."

St. Bernard was no fool. "Tracey, we do want to help you," she said. "Or, if you can't believe that, then let me tell you that I want to help you."

"Help me be a Catholic?" Tracey asked. "Or just help me?"

"Just help you," she said. But Tracey was silent. She didn't believe it.

St. Bernard said at last, "Well, I know you believe that Sister James Anne loves you and wants to help you."

Tracey nodded.

"But Sister James Anne can't do much," St. Bernard said. "Not in the way of intervening here in school."

"I think she might be able to do more than either of us think," Tracey told her. On sudden inspiration she said, "Because she's humble. God listens to humble people, doesn't He?"

The question took the sister by surprise. "Yes," she said after a moment. "Of course God and the saints listen to her, but there are other things people can do too."

Tracey left St. Bernard in the hall and hurried to class. Evening found her again ascending the stairs to jug. The loneliness was worse that night, but there was comfort in knowing that she would be returning the next day to her room. Scooter and her friends were waiting, of course. They weren't finished with her, and she knew it, but maybe things would go her way. Maybe somehow she could beat them.

## TWENTY - FIVE

After classes the next day, Tracey brought her things back to her room. Nothing had been disturbed in her absence, perhaps a mark of respect from Scooter for the types of punishment Mary could hand out. Only Amy was in the room when Tracey entered.

"You're back!" Amy exclaimed in a surprised whisper as they clasped hands. "I was so glad—" She stopped abruptly and turned to her desk as the door opened. Tracey threw her things onto her bottom bunk and glanced idly around. Scooter and Susan entered.

Tracey felt another stab of guilt when she looked at Scooter. Some of her remorse from the first night of jug returned to her.

"What're you staring at, ape?" Susan asked.

"Nothing much," Tracey shot back, and she resumed putting her things away. Her remorse ebbed.

Susan looked like she wanted to come right up to Tracey and egg her on some more, but for some reason, Scooter hung back. She and Susan murmured some comments back and forth, and Tracey could hear enough to understand that Scooter wanted to leave again. She was actually embarrassed, while Susan seemed to expect that Tracey's punishment had somehow cowed her. But it hadn't. Not outwardly, anyway.

After an angry, harshly whispered command from Scooter, and Susan's whining, sullen answer, the two of them left. Amy and Tracey looked at each other.

"You're in such big trouble," Amy breathed.

"Why?" Tracey asked.

"Them!" she said. "They say they're really going to get you for what you did. They said you jumped Scooter by surprise and it wasn't fair."

"I was right in front of her!"

"And they said you made her look bad in front of Maddie Murdoch," Amy added.

"Who is she, anyway?" Tracey demanded.

"She drives the team bus to the games sometimes," Amy told her. "All the girls like her a lot."

"She's a bus driver?" Tracey asked, incredulous. For a moment the memory of the elegant clothing, lilting accent, and perfect carriage came back full force. "A bus driver?"

"No, she just does that for volunteer work here," Amy said. "She does most of her volunteer stuff down in the retirees' area, keeping them busy and stuff. But the girls say she's really cool."

"She's had her nose in my business since my first day, and she really blew that fight up to Mary," Tracey said with a flare of both shame and resentment. "I know she thinks I started it. And I bet the whole basketball team tells her I did."

"That's just what they'll say. They'll do anything to

make you look bad." Amy hesitated, then suggested timidly, "Maybe you should go to Mary."

Tracey rolled her eyes. "No way! Are you kidding? That's all that old battle-ax needs." She sat down on her bunk. "Look, whatever I tell her, it's all going to come out to be my fault."

"What did they do to you that night?" Amy asked, coming to sit next to Tracey.

"Never mind."

"I know it was bad. They could do worse if you let them go on."

"Mary can't stop them," Tracey told her. "It would mean expelling them, and Mary doesn't expel people. No matter what she did, they'd figure out some way to outwit her or force me to be quiet." She hesitated, then said, "I prayed about it. God will help me."

"Oh, Tracey—"

"Come on, Amy. You never can know these things if you just figure they don't work."

"Well, why hasn't He helped you so far?" Amy demanded.

"I never asked Him," Tracey said. "That's the truth. I never did ask God to protect me."

"Don't you think somebody like God would know He could and should protect you?" Amy asked.

"Yeah, well," she looked down. "Maybe He had reasons not to help me until I asked Him."

"Like what?"

"Like maybe I have a big mouth. And maybe I'm too violent," Tracey said, her eyes still down. "There's a lot about me you don't know, and I just became a real Christian. Sometimes I don't feel like I'm saved. Sometimes I forget."

"Well, I would vote for you as a Christian," Amy told her. "But a lot of Christians got eaten by lions and killed by gladiators, you know."

"I know. But a lot got saved out of their troubles. David did."

"David who?" Amy asked.

"David, of David and Goliath," Tracey said. "You know, King David?"

"Oh, yeah. Didn't God help him when his son turned against him?" Amy asked. "Bathsheba?"

"Absalom," Tracey corrected. "Bathsheba was his wife, the mother of Solomon, the woman he killed the guy over."

Amy didn't know what she was talking about. But the reminder of David's sin against Uriah brought a sudden hope to Tracey. God hadn't deserted him after that. David had repented of it, and God had never left him. Her memory of the story was hazy; other subjects of Bible study crowded out the stories a lot of times. She decided to look it up and reread it.

"You sure know the Bible," Amy said.

"Because I know the difference between Absalom and Bathsheba?" Tracey asked, and she laughed.

Her walk that evening with James Anne was a pleasant one. Sister James asked no questions about her confinement. She only took hold of Tracey's arm with a tightness and sureness that welcomed her back. "I missed you, dear," she said.

They followed the flagstone path down to the green field below the retirement wing.

"I missed you too," Tracey told her. "I think you must be my only friend here."

"I can hardly believe that. You're such a sweet girl."

She glanced at Tracey and pressed her arm before returning her attention to their walk.

Sister James's serene confidence sent another needle of guilt into Tracey's heart. "There's a lot you don't know about me, Sister."

"Well, dear, you can tell me if you think I ought to know," Sister James said. Tracey glanced at her—the serene face, the eyes nearly blind in the waning twilight. Sister James had endured the pain of arthritis all her life, the emptiness of the early retirement it had forced her into, and then the slowly darkening blindness. In some ways, she had suffered more than Tracey had ever imagined.

But the suffering of the person within a person, the suffering of looking at the blackness within your own heart, of knowing you were unloved and unlovely, even to your own parents, were sufferings that Sister James would never know. And Tracey had the idea that if she confessed all her fears and griefs to the aging nun, James Anne would not be able to comprehend it all. In fact, it seemed likely that a person of James Anne's optimism and cheerfulness might even deny some of what Tracey had seen and done.

A new doubt entered her mind. Was James Anne really so serene, or was she merely sheltered? If all the temptations of Tracey's last three months had hit Sister James instead, would the sister have crumpled under them even worse than Tracey had?

There was no knowing, and Tracey decided not to try to figure it out. Right then she needed Sister James's comfort more than she needed her advice.

"It's enough just to have you," she said at last.

"You're a dear girl."

As was their new custom, they met Sister Lucy by the dining hall doors, and Tracey said good night to the two of them before leaving them to walk back to their wing.

If she had thought for a moment that the girls who had hurt her would also hurt Sister James or Sister Lucy, she would never have endangered them. But the sacrosanctity of a nun's person had been drilled into all of them from grade one. As long as she walked in the company of Sister James Anne, Tracey was perfectly safe. And because James Anne was one of the retired nuns, Tracey was also safe from being accused of being a narc or a pet.

Tracey had looked through some of the old yearbooks in the library, and she'd noticed that on certain years a girl would receive an award for faithful service in the retirees' wing. Some of the books even included pictures of the retired nuns coming out for lawn picnics with certain classes, usually home economics.

But no more. Few of the girls ever went over to help out, and so far Tracey had seen no requests for volunteers from the student body.

*It's just as well,* she told herself. *If we went over on a volunteer basis, we'd all get called pets or brownnosers or goody-goodies.*

Dinner was a more cheerful meal that night. Tracey deliberately sat next to Sandra Kean, as she'd been doing. She'd discovered that if she said nothing or very little, Sandra felt a lot less threatened. And at least Tracey's presence kept anybody else from sitting next to the other girl and bothering her.

Lately, all of the freshmen had been easing off on Sandra. Sister Madeleine had raked both of her English

classes over the coals for their treatment of the freshman outcasts. The freshmen, not yet strong enough to
be defiant and not hardened enough to be pitiless, had
lightened up.

There was talk that one of the town girls who had
enrolled as a freshman was pregnant, and some of the
girls were cautiously whispering about a secret outing
where everybody had smoked pot for the first time.
The girls talking about it kept their heads down and
voices lowered, and Tracey was glad. She didn't want
to know what they were talking about.

She noticed the people farther down the table were
being disrupted. Benches were rocking back slightly, and
heads were bobbing. Nobody at the other tables noticed.
She realized that somebody was slipping closer, squeez-
ing between the girls on their benches and the table itself, coming toward her with head low and knees bent.

As the girl got closer, Tracey recognized her as Peggy
Melsom, one of her classmates, and an exceptionally
uninteresting girl. Not the kind who pulled pranks.
Not even the kind who made fun of Sandra Kean.

Peggy squeezed herself between Tracey and Amy.
Sandra Kean, on Tracey's other side, looked a little
wary. But it was Tracey that Peggy wanted, not Sandra.

"What's up?" Tracey asked.

The other girls were giggling at Peggy's way of coming up the table. Peggy giggled back at them, but when
she looked at Tracey, she was serious. "I heard something," she said in a quiet voice.

"What's that?" Tracey whispered.

Peggy put her hand on Tracey's elbow, right over
the part of the sleeve that hid the last remaining traces
of the rope. "They got you here, right?" she asked.

Tracey's face flushed. "Yeah."

"I heard that the Deep Six are getting together tonight to pay you back. If they did this already, they'll go to step two next."

"What's that?" Tracey whispered. "What's next?"

"I don't know. They call it Step Two. I'm second-string on the basketball team, and I heard them in the locker room."

"When?"

"I don't know. Go right up with the rest of us and stay in your room," Peggy said. "They can't do it during study time." She glanced over her shoulder with an affected look of carelessness.

"They see you?" Tracey asked.

"No. Liz Lukas is telling them something about a ball game."

Peggy got up again and pushed her way back down the table, making the girls laugh again.

"What was that all about?" Sandra asked.

Tracey looked at her, surprised. "No big deal," she said after a minute. "Those upperclassmen—do they bother you anymore?"

Sandra's pale face turned whiter, and she shook her head—whether truthfully or not, Tracey didn't know. But she wasn't going to risk Peggy's safety on someone who wouldn't come through. She felt sorry for Sandra, but she knew she was as weak as water. You couldn't tell her anything that had to be kept secret.

They both finished their meals in silence.

The evening passed without incident. Study time ended, and Tracey stayed clear of the bathrooms, just to be safe. By lights-out, she was ready to believe that the "Deep Six," as Peggy had called them, had either been talking to sound big, or else they'd had to put off their plans to get her until they could be sure to catch her off guard. She prayed again and asked for protection.

For a while she lay awake, listening as the others in the room fell asleep one by one. Amy went first, with the sleep of the untroubled innocent. Then studious Lisa, worn out by a night of studying to the very last minute, began to snore softly. Even Susan and Scooter, who asserted themselves by whispering after lights-out, whispered for only a few minutes and then went to sleep. Tracey fell asleep soon after.

She dreamed she was back in her eighth-grade classroom, and Sister Ed was there. But Tracey was wearing the MoJoe uniform, and Sister Ed kept saying, "What is this? Where have you been? Tracey, where have you been?"

Every time Tracey answered her, Sister Ed would take hold of the bottom of Tracey's bolero as though it were some foreign, hideous object and ask the exact same question. "What is this? Where have you been? Tracey, where have you been?"

Her questions and Tracey's answers repeated countless times, until something grabbed Tracey's feet and began to pull her away, and Tracey yelled out, "The waves! The waves!" as they dragged her away from the classroom, Sister Ed, and everything that she loved.

"Shut her up!"

"Get that teddy bear, or use that slipper!"

Tracey woke up to find that she really was being dragged. It seemed that girls were all over her, ready to smother her.

"Get off!" she yelled. "Get off me!"

She was wound up in her sheet and blanket, but she got one hand free and hit aside the bedroom slipper that had been shoved against her mouth.

"Amy! Lisa!" she screamed, but now that she was awake, she realized her voice was still weak and shaky from sleep. It wasn't carrying.

The hands forced the slipper back, but Amy and Lisa woke up.

"What are you doing?" Amy cried.

"You two shut up," Rita Jo told them. "You shut up! And you don't tell anyone."

"Let her go!" Lisa yelled.

Susan rushed to Lisa's bunk and pulled Lisa half out of it. "Shut up! Are you going to shut up?"

Tracey knocked the hand away again. "Help me!" she yelled. They'd gotten her wound up better in the sheet, and it was nearly impossible to fight.

175

"Choke her, I don't care!" Scooter exclaimed. "Just shut her up."

"I'll shut her up," Susan said. She let Lisa go and grabbed Tracey by the hair. Tracey's strength came back to her all of a sudden. She leveraged herself against the floor and sprang up with the force of her hips and shoulders, butting her head right into Susan's face. Eyes flooded with tears, Susan fell back, but Scooter and Rita Jo fell onto Tracey and forced her back to the floor. They held her face into the carpet until she stopped struggling.

"We're going to the bathroom together," Scooter told her. "And you're going to shut up. Do you understand?"

The hopelessness of it all hit Tracey, and she let out a sob of grief and fear.

"She's done. Let's go," Scooter said to the others.

Just then the door swung open. As Tracey was released just enough to be dragged, she had one glimpse of a basketball coming right at her, and she shut her eyes. The ball caught Scooter full force on the side of her face and knocked her away. The other girls leaped up.

"Hi, guys," Liz Lukas said. "Anybody want to play a little ball?"

She stepped over Tracey and retrieved the ball before returning to the doorway. She switched on the light.

"Man, you almost killed my face!" Scooter said, sitting up from where she'd fallen. "What do you want?"

"Couldn't sleep," Liz said. "Wanted to play ball. But lo and behold, nobody was in their beds. So I came looking."

"Get out of here!" Rita Jo said.

"Sorry," Liz said. She put the ball under one arm and leaned against the doorway.

"You're not so tough that you can do anything to us," Scooter said.

"I guess I am," Liz said. "Anyway, once I start, the saint'll be freed up to help me. I bet we can take you guys on. What do you say, Jacamuzzi?"

For once, Tracey was too stunned to say anything. Liz looked her over. "You know, you guys are really pathetic. What'd the freshman ever do to you? She and I can kick your cans all over the floor."

"Would you shut up?" Rita Jo hissed. "And turn out the light. Mary'll be out here any minute."

Liz faked a throw at Rita Jo and then caught it back to herself. "Whatssamatter, Rita? You scared of Mary? Poor thing."

Tracey sat up and looked at Amy and Lisa. They looked scared, and Lisa had been crying. Liz glanced at them too. "Well," she said at last with a long sigh, "somehow, picking on freshmen doesn't put me to sleep like it does to you guys. But I still want that game of ball. So I tell you what: Little Bigmouth and I are going up to my room for some rounds of half-court. Get your stuff, Tracey."

Tracey stood up and looked at Liz, confused. "Come on, kid. We don't have all night—uh-oh." She gave the girls a mischievous smile. "Here comes da nun! Here comes da nun!"

Everybody scrambled under beds and into closets. The light went out. Tracey dived into her bed with her covers. Liz took a casual step inside the doorway and then behind the door, which was left half open.

In another moment it opened wider, and light from the hallway spilled into the room as Sister Madeleine, in her robe, looked inside. Her eyes fell on Tracey first.

"You were shouting in your sleep, dear. Are you all right?"

"Yes, Sister," Tracey said.

Sister Madeleine looked at Lisa, who had been caught with her eyes open. "You needn't yell back at her," she admonished Lisa. "Just get out of bed and wake her up."

Lisa, still stunned and frightened, hopped out of bed and walked over to Tracey. "Are you awake now?" she asked.

"Yeah, thanks," Tracey said. Lisa shot a nervous glance at Sister Madeleine and hopped back into bed. Liz Lukas, sheltered by the door, rolled her eyes.

"Good night, girls," Madeleine said, and she left.

"Good night, Sister," Tracey and Lisa called after her. "Good night, Sister," Liz called.

After another minute or two, Liz snapped the light on again. Everybody came out from hiding.

"Let's go," she said to Tracey.

Obediently, Tracey stood up and threw the disheveled covers back on her bed. "Bring them," Liz told her. "And bring your stuff for tomorrow. We'll see you guys later," she said to the Deep Six. She opened the door and stepped aside, giving them a clear path to leave.

The four girls who didn't belong walked out with many glances behind them. Scooter and Susan sat up in their beds.

"I'd shut up if I were you," Liz told them. "I would just shut up. Because the sides are even now. So just keep your mouths shut."

She put the basketball down and came around the beds to help Tracey. "We'll send some of my menservants and maidservants down to help get your stuff," she said. "We'll just take a load apiece for now."

Tracey followed her out, each of them carrying a load of Tracey's clothing, books, and bedclothes.

As Tracey followed Liz up the steps to the third floor, she asked, "What do you want me for?"

"Now you're talking to me like I'm a Klingon or something," Liz said. "What do I want with you?" she mimicked in a somber voice. "I just saved you from the dogs, right?"

"Thank you," Tracey said.

They got up to the landing. "You have got a big mouth," Liz said.

"I know."

"But you do practice what you preach." She started up the last flight. "What you really need," she added, "is to play ball. So I'll teach you, since you keep saying you don't know how."

"I don't like basketball," Tracey told her.

They reached the third floor, and Liz led her wordlessly into the room where she lived. There were two sets of double bunks, and all four beds were filled except Liz's.

Liz dropped her load onto the floor. "Look, Jacamuzzi, here's the deal," she said. "You can live in the hellhole down where I pulled you from and not learn basketball. Or, you can move in with me and learn basketball. But if you move in, I'm bound and determined to make you a useful citizen of the state."

Tracey couldn't help but smile at the way Liz talked. "Are you serious?" she asked.

"Yes," Liz told her. "Believe me, you need basketball in this place. It's the only way you're going to live through it, and it'll give you something to do other than talk too much."

"But you don't have room for me," Tracey said.

Liz switched on the light and snapped her fingers. Her three roommates sat up. They had their robes on, obviously waiting for Liz's return. All of them were freshmen. They smiled at Tracey. "Go down and get Tracey's stuff," Liz told them. "And don't make noise, because Madeleine's out there on patrol."

"End stairs, Liz?" one of them asked.

"Yeah, that's a good idea. Go on. We'll be down in a minute."

They hurried out on tiptoe, and Liz looked at Tracey. "We'll bring up your mattress, kid. Believe me, nobody'll say a word about it. You know why?"

"Why?" Tracey asked.

"Reason one is that you're a morale problem, and I've got the solution. So long as I get you to quit looking like you've seen a ghost, Mary'll look the other way, and so will Sister Madeleine. She's in charge of your hall." She sat on one of the desktops. "Reason number two is that CPR and me and Father Bing and, I bet, Mary herself all know that you're cut out for basketball. If I make a player out of you, then everybody's happy. Because everybody at MoJoe runs on basketball. Everybody wants to see you play. Everybody but Susan and Scooter, that is." She smiled.

"Why?" Tracey asked.

"Too late for you to make the team this year, child. But next year, you'll bump Susan for sure. And one of these days, if you work hard and say your prayers, you'll top Scooter. She knows it."

"I thought Scooter was second only to you," Tracey said.

"She is," Liz told her. "But I got a big lead on Scooter. Scooter's got twice the talent of Susan, but I'm Scooter squared. You wait and see. Let's go get your stuff."

"I don't know how to thank you," Tracey said as they went down the hall.

"Try shutting up for once."

I n a fairly short time, all of Tracey's things were brought up from her old room and stowed in various places in Liz's room. Her mattress had to go on the floor between the two double bunk beds, in the middle of where everybody walked by day. But there was no place else for it.

"We can rearrange tomorrow or this weekend if we have to," Liz said.

There was enough drawer space for her. All the rooms had the same number of drawers, but many of them supported five girls instead of four. As far as Tracey could see, the three freshmen in the room didn't mind her arrival at all. It didn't take long to realize why.

Liz was unique in being a sophomore in charge of a room. Such a position was usually held by seniors or juniors. But she was better than any senior or junior at managing things. For one thing, she didn't bully her roommates at all. And though she was the star player of the school's most important sport, she didn't try to impress them, either, or make them listen to her boasts.

Being awed by Liz came with being at MoJoe, and

the awe was doubled when Liz stooped to be nice to you, especially if you were a freshman. The girls in the room—Ingrid, Barbara, and Regina, (Ingy, Bingy, and Ringy, Liz called them)—knew that they'd landed on their feet. Their room was pleasant and was run like a tight ship—a yacht, to be specific.

So the arrival of a newcomer was without stress. All three of the freshmen seemed confident that Liz could handle any problems and keep things running smoothly. Tracey didn't want to do anything to change that opinion.

"There you go," Liz said as Tracey turned from putting the last of her things into a drawer. "Your mattress is made up."

"Thanks," Tracey said.

"And you don't have to worry," Liz told her. "No short-sheeting in here, and no midnight raids."

"Thanks," she said again. She sat down on the mattress. There was no way Liz would be pleased if she started to cry, and now that an hour had passed, Tracey could feel the shock and fear wearing off. They hadn't hurt her. God had really saved her. Through Liz.

"So, you're all right?" Liz asked.

She nodded. "I think so."

"Well, let's get to bed, then. It's almost one." She hopped up onto her bed, top of the double on Tracey's left, and nodded at Bingy, who switched off the light. Tracey slipped her feet under the covers, thankful that Liz had made up the bed with the covers tightly tucked in under the mattress. The tightness gave her a sense of safety. She was starting to feel a lot better.

"Tomorrow afternoon," Liz's voice said out of the darkness. "You meet me outside the gym, get it?"

"Sure," Tracey answered. "Good night."

"Good night, Jac."

She fell into a dreamless and heavy sleep. When the bell went off the next morning, she didn't know where she was for a second, and then she remembered. She wondered if Liz would really keep her.

"Let's go, kids," Liz said. The girls got up and scurried either for the showers or for their clothes. There wasn't much talk among them in the morning, and Tracey watched them from the corner of her eye, doing everything possible to fit in with their routine and keep out of everybody's way.

After they were dressed and the room was cleaned up for inspection, Peggy Melsom came by.

"Peggy!" Tracey exclaimed.

"Hey, what are you doing up here?" Peggy asked. She took Tracey by the hand.

"She moved in last night," Liz told her.

"Tracey, that's great," Peggy said. Tracey saw the brief look that shot from Peggy to Liz—sudden understanding on Peggy's part, acknowledgment from Liz.

"Her name's Jac now," Liz told Peggy. "It sounds better on the court."

"Let's go down to breakfast," Peggy told Tracey. "I'd like to hear about your move."

"You guys coming?" Tracey asked the other three freshmen.

There was a quick scuffling of papers as everybody scurried to get books and purses.

"Now, isn't that nice?" Liz asked. "All the kids playing so nicely together. Mind your manners, girls, and be sure to thank everybody."

Laughing at Liz, they hurried down the stairs. "I live right next door," Peggy told Tracey.

"Did you tell Liz what you told me?" Tracey asked.

"Hey, this is your turn to tell me something," Peggy said. "You tell me what happened last night."

"OK." She smiled, realizing that Peggy had worked pretty hard to save her. "The Deep Six jumped me when I was asleep and got me tangled in my blankets. They were taking me down to the bathroom when Liz came in. She bounced a basketball right off Scooter's face."

"Served her right."

"You ever find out what step two is?" Tracey asked.

"No," Peggy said. "I'm not sure I want to know."

"How'd you find out about step one?" Even that hint of what had been done to her made Tracey's face flame with the shame of the memory.

"No, you don't," Peggy said. "It's still your turn. What else did Liz do?"

Tracey told her the story in broken whispers as they went through the cafeteria and found their seats. The other girls wandered off to find their own friends, and for a few minutes, before the majority of the girls came down, the two of them had some privacy.

"Peggy," Tracey said when she'd told her everything, "what if I can't play basketball?"

"You're a natural, Tracey," Peggy told her. "Look, compared to Liz and Scooter, I can't play at all, and Scooter and Susan really harass me about it. But CPR knows her stuff, and she tells me I'll get there by next year. That's why she put me on the team. I trust her. You trust her too. Just do everything they tell you, and practice basketball until you do it in your sleep."

"I hope I can," Tracey said.

"I'll tell you one thing," Peggy said. "No matter how you look when you get out there, I will be one person who won't put you down. I'll help you all I can."

Tracey smiled. "Thanks."

"Liz would kill me if I didn't."

"Now, tell me how you knew about me and my arm and step two," Tracey said.

"Liz found you after step one; don't you remember?"

"Yeah, I remember."

"She told me about it, and she's the one who told me about step one." Peggy paused to rifle through the jelly packets on the table and find a grape-flavored one. "Anyway," she continued, "while you were jugged, some of the girls started talking about what they should do to you. Yesterday in the locker room when they thought nobody was around, three of them said it was time for step two. They said they were going to get you that night. I told Liz, and she told me to tell you at dinner, and she'd keep those three and their friends busy so they wouldn't know who told. That's when she named them the Deep Six."

"Liz doesn't know what they planned?" Tracey asked.

"She never said," Peggy told her. "But you said they were taking you down to the bathroom?"

"Yeah."

"Well, when they didn't do anything by light bell, I figured nothing would happen. But I guess Liz figured otherwise."

"It's a good thing," Tracey said.

# TWENTY-EIGHT

"Don't palm that ball that way, Jacamuzzi! You aren't catching it each time it comes up," Liz instructed.

"When I don't palm it, you say I'm beating it like a drum!" Tracey exclaimed.

"A happy medium, Jac! A happy medium. Like this," Liz walked alongside her, steadily dribbling the ball with her left hand. "Now, do it with me. Control the ball, but don't grab it like your hand is a Hoover."

Tracey copied her, and they walked up the gym floor. "Watch the stripe, watch the stripe and not the ball," Liz said. Looking straight ahead was too hard, so for the first week Liz let Tracey keep her eyes down, closer to where she was going and where the ball was.

Tracey had never spent a whole night at MoJoe without studying, but here they were. Nobody else was in the gym. The team's practice had ended a half hour ago, and Tracey had waited patiently in the locker room until Liz came to get her. Liz wore her new sweat suit, but all Tracey had was her clumsy blue gym suit. She looked and felt like a pathetic novice.

"We're gonna walk this ball all night," Liz told her, meaning until the end of study time. "Tomorrow we start running around with it and passing."

Liz showed her where the basketballs were kept. Liz was in charge of logging the balls in and out for practices, and she told Tracey to come get one whenever she had time to practice. "And make the time," she'd ordered. "If you can't shoot hoops, you dribble, dribble, dribble, and run, run, run. Fast moving is the name of the game."

Though she'd allowed Tracey some time to get used to the feel of a ball, before the night ended they tried a little half-court practice.

"Eyes up, eyes!" Liz yelled while Tracey tried fruitlessly to get around her. Tracey forced her eyes up from the ball and the floor, and Liz effortlessly took the ball from her with one short reach and a quick dribble. Liz dribbled away from her, shot, and sank the ball.

"Eyes up," she told Tracey again, "but watch my eyes or the hoop. Don't just force your eyes up."

"I can't watch you and think about the ball at the same time," Tracey said.

"You start that now, and by the time next season comes, you'll be able to do it." She brought the ball back and chest-passed it to Tracey. Tracey caught it without thinking.

"Good. You'll be good at getting passes. Go back out to the middle and bring it in again."

The last thirty minutes were a lot more interesting than the first hour and a half, but also more frustrating. Liz Lukas played with a deceptive smoothness and fluid motion that turned into sudden jerks and turns. She could get the ball away from Tracey and was even fast enough to get around her when it was Tracey's turn to guard the basket.

But even with the frustrations of a new sport, it felt good to run around, to simply play a game with someone. A stitch nagged at Tracey's side, and after only a few minutes of half-court, she felt like her arms were breaking from all the reaching she had to do to block Liz. But afterward, the wetness of her own sweat in her hair and down her back, the satisfaction of having gotten through the workout, all made that night her first really happy one at MoJoe.

Liz put the ball away and locked up the equipment closet. They walked back through the dark night to the rooms, and Tracey felt a sudden and even sweeter sensation. This walk through the darkness—forbidden to most of the girls at this time of night—was hers and Liz's alone. For Tracey, it was something even richer, because somehow, suddenly, she was friends with—and in a strange way, a junior partner to—the most sought-after girl at MoJoe. She remembered with another small shock of pleasure that she wasn't returning to her old room and its tensions, but to Liz's room, to new roommates from her own class, and to the friendliness of Peggy next door.

She glanced over at Liz, who walked along the dim path with her head down, breathing easily and deeply of the cold autumn air. Thanks would likely embarrass her, and Tracey didn't want to disturb this new bubble of happiness.

"Well, after two hours of coaching me, do you still think I'll be able to play someday?" she asked Liz instead.

"Huh? Oh, yeah, sure. Don't worry about that. Just concentrate on the game itself," Liz said.

"I will," Tracey promised. "I'm going to work hard on this. I really want to make the team next year."

"I told you it was a great game. It's lots better than field hockey."

Tracey only looked at her. It wasn't for the sake of the game. It was for Liz. She would do anything to keep Liz's friendship. Liz Lukas was the only girl at Mo-Joe strong enough to do as she liked without regard for what the others said. Tracey knew she needed her. And she was grateful to her.

They walked the rest of the way in silence. The bell to end study time was ringing just as they came in by the back door, and they took the back stairs up to their room.

"How was it?" Bingy asked as they came in.

"Oh, she'll do," Liz said carelessly.

"If I can just keep breathing," Tracey added, and Liz laughed her strong laugh.

"Any visitors?" she asked.

Regina shook her head. "No. I'm dying to go down there and ask Amy what happened after we got Tracey's stuff out last night."

"Shoot, I can tell you that," Liz said. "They made some threats and called Tracey a narc and said she was getting in good with me and that I'd get tired of her. And then they talked about what a jerk I am, and I guess Scooter dropped some hints that she's the better of the two of us at basketball."

"That's a laugh," Regina said.

"Now, now, girls. Let's be charitable."

"Do you think they'll come after me again?" Tracey asked.

Liz turned around with her usual grin. "Tracey,

child, I hope they do." She cracked her knuckles loudly. "But wishes like that just don't come true." She picked up her shower bucket and robe. "I'm gonna go get cleaned up, and hey—" she pointed to Tracey. "You better do it too, kid, because, not meaning to be offensive, you really smell."

All four freshmen laughed, and Tracey got her shower things together.

## TWENTY - NINE

November came with a whirl of rain that rattled the windows each night. By day, the clouds hung low and sullen over the green and brown fields around the school. Tracey lost track of days and of time. Life was a treadmill—a fast one—of basketball practice with Liz, hurried Latin sessions with Amy, studying at every spare moment, and certain quiet nights when she and her roommates stayed up and talked in whispers.

She prayed more often these days, when she could find time alone. On Sunday mornings she sat with the two Jewish girls and a couple of other nonparticipants during the morning Mass. Mass was held in the large chapel, and they sat in a small, unadorned room called the small chapel. The only things that made it seem like a chapel were its quietness and its blue walls that matched the blue carpet. The girls weren't allowed to talk during the hour that passed for Mass, so it was a good time to read the Bible and pray. The others most often did homework as they sat and waited in the few pews lined up in a wide row down the middle of the room.

But for the most part, Tracey's life was basketball—drills, dribbling, passes, and lessons in foot- and hand-work.

"Other hand! Other hand!" Liz yelled as she quickly closed with Tracey at the top of the key. "Other hand, Jac!" Even as she yelled it, Liz's own hand shot out and took the ball. She stopped, and the two of them straightened up. "Come on, Jac!" Liz never swore at Tracey or in front of her, but sometimes her patience got pushed to its limits when Tracey didn't catch on or was too slow to do what she wanted.

"I couldn't get it through my legs," Tracey told her. "Not without looking."

"Yes, you could. You had a whole stupid stride between your feet, and you were low. It was a perfect set-up. You should have passed the ball through your stride when I came up, and that would have kept it away from me." Liz passed the ball to her, and Tracey caught it. "Now, try it again. Go up to the middle and come down."

Tracey obeyed nearly everything Liz said, almost without noticing. Most of the people who obeyed Liz never thought much about it. Liz always told you why she was telling you to do something, whether it was directives for getting the room ready for inspection, orders about studying for an algebra test, or commands on the basketball court. When Liz was right, Liz was right, and she assumed people knew it. They usually did.

"Other hand, other hand!" she yelled as she closed with Tracey at the top of the key.

Tracey felt her hand tremble from the fear of ruining the play, but she bounced the ball down between her own feet and felt it come up to her other hand.

"Turn, turn, don't stop, don't stop! Agh! Traveling! Stop!"

Tracey straightened up and stopped. She caught the ball and cradled it in one arm, wiping the other arm across her face.

"Change hands through your stride," Liz told her, "but don't stop. Don't even hesitate, or they'll get you for traveling. You got to keep moving."

"I didn't think I stopped."

"You stopped enough. Let's try it again."

Liz came at her again, right up the key. Tracey passed the ball through her stride, cut a neat half turn, and got around Liz.

"Shoot! Shoot!" Liz screamed.

It was way too far to shoot. Tracey was on the outer edge of the key at the very top, but she took the shot and missed. It hit the backboard and sprang back. Liz ran up and got it.

"Okay, rebound time. Let's go."

Practicing rebounds always started as a nice diversion from the often frustrating work of bringing the ball down, but it was exhausting because Tracey could never drop her arms. Liz stood on one side of the hoop and shot for the rim. Tracey sprang to get the ball— sometimes caught it and sometimes didn't—and then threw for the rim too, trying to sink it.

She sometimes did sink it, but more often it bounced off the rim or backboard, and Liz rebounded it. They sometimes worked on straightforward shooting too. Liz advised her on arcing the ball up and down into the net and showed her how to line up her wrist and elbow with the hoop for a good shot. But for rebounding, it was speed they were working on, and Liz was interested more in Tracey's ability to save the ball from the enemy than to sink it herself.

"I made this team at the very bottom," she told Tracey one night as they stopped to rest a minute. "I was CPR's last choice. You know why?"

"Why?" Tracey asked.

"'Cause CPR's big goal was to get shooters. And I could do everything else but shoot."

"But you're high scorer," Tracey said.

"Sure. I worked my tail off last season and over the summer, learning to shoot. I could write a book on how to sink a ball. There's a whole science to it." She wiped sweat off her face. "But I'll tell you what: The Valkyries went into a bad slump for a while. They had great shooters on the team, but no one could play the game. The league just switched over from half-court rules, and it's still a passing game, but we couldn't pass. The Valkyries couldn't get the ball down the court because we were all playing man-on-man. That's when I started to shine for CPR. I'd played half-court in junior high, so I could play with a team. CPR put me up on first-string about halfway through the season. I didn't start right away, even though people say I did."

"And it worked?" Tracey asked.

Liz nodded. "Almost everyone passes off to Scooter or me to let us make the shots, but we win because we can control the ball." She let the ball drop down and caught it again. "That's really the name of the game. Control the ball. Get it back and keep control, and you can pick your shots. Come on. Let's bring it down together."

On one of their nights in the gym, Liz looked up from their drill to call out in welcome, "Hey, Father!"

"Whoa, boy," Tracey whispered.

"Cool it, Tracey, He's cool, even if he does say Mass."

A tall, slender man dressed in the black trousers and shirt of a priest walked across the gym floor, his shoes still on.

"Hi, girls," he said.

He had sandy blond hair and was clean-shaven. He looked a lot like Bing Crosby had looked in *The Bells of St. Mary*, Tracey thought. He grinned at her. "I know what you're thinking," he said. "I'm Father Williams, but they call me Father Crosby or Father Bing."

In spite of her reluctance to talk to the titular headmaster of the school, Tracey smiled.

"I know Liz, but who are you, dear?" he asked.

"Tracey Jacamuzzi, Father." She looked down.

"On the team?" he asked.

"No, too late to make it this year," she said. She glanced at Liz, hoping her friend would keep the subject on basketball.

"She's the one you asked me about," Liz prompted. "The one you said Sister Patricia Rose had mentioned to you."

"Ah, yes. Well." He looked thoughtful for a second and then glanced at Tracey with a smile. "Think you might join the team next year?"

"We're working on it," Tracey said.

"Sister Patricia Rose seemed very pleased with your abilities," he said.

The idea that some of the faculty had discussed her behind her back gave her an odd feeling. "I . . . I don't know how she could have been," Tracey stammered. "I've never played sports before."

"Never?" His sandy eyebrows went up. "Really? Well, I wouldn't have judged that from watching you and Miss Lukas drill just now. Lot of intensity. Good ball players all have that. And good confidence, strong and sure moves. I think you'll make it, Miss Jacamuzzi."

"Thank you, Father."

He nodded and shot Liz a smile. "You'll lock up, Coach Lukas?"

"Sure thing, Padre."

He laughed a short, sputtery laugh and sauntered away.

"Man, he sure does look like Bing Crosby," Tracey said.

"Well, you got ol' Bing on your side now," Liz said.

"What do you mean?"

"We aren't supposed to be in here. He was coming in to throw us out until he saw that I was coaching you. That's why he called me that."

"We aren't allowed in here?" Tracey asked. "You mean all these nights we've been down here, we weren't allowed?"

"Hey," Liz exclaimed. She put her hand on Tracey's shoulder. "Cool it, Jac. You think they don't know we're down here? CPR knows it, and St. Bernard knows it, and Bing Crosby knows it now. They've known all along. They just look the other way. I bet Mary even knows it."

"No way," Tracey said. "Not Mary. She believes in every rule she makes up, and besides, she doesn't have the imagination to think I'd make a good player."

"Well, maybe not Mary," Liz conceded.

"We better get out of here."

"Oh, cut it out, Jac! Father Crosby's a bigger wheel than Mary. He's headmaster. She's just acting principal. It's cool with him. Come on, let's play."

Reluctantly, Tracey fell back into step with Liz. After a few minutes of warming up again to their practice, thoughts of Mary, of the priest who looked like Bing Crosby, even of her own hopes of making the team, all fell away. She never felt that she was intense; it was the game that was intense, the orange ball that was intense. It drew her attention and her eyes and her mind, and its steady rhythm pulled her after it.

W hat are you brooding over, Jac?" Liz asked one afternoon as she came in and threw her books on her desk. Tracey sat alone in the room, cross-legged on her mattress on the floor, eyebrows together.

"You won't like it," Tracey said.

"It's about religion, right?"

"Yeah."

"Well, try me anyway. All I can do is yell."

"It's about something I read in the Bible. I don't understand it."

"What is it?"

"'Hear the word of the Lord, ye that tremble at his word; Your brethren that hated you, that cast you out for my name's sake, said, Let the Lord be glorified: but he shall appear to your joy, and they shall be ashamed.'"

"You think God appears to people?" Liz asked.

"No, not visibly," Tracey said absently.

"Well, it seems easy enough, for a Bible verse."

"I was wondering if it applied to me," Tracey confessed. "I wondered if it was kind of something to hang on to. It sure felt that way when I read it a few minutes ago—no, a half hour ago. It made me cry. It . . . it did a lot." She stopped, because she wasn't sure she wouldn't cry again. She couldn't understand what it was about the verse that had unearthed the deepest parts of her, made her feel that God had been watching her more closely than she'd been watching herself, even through all her mistakes. In a moment, the web of her mistakes had been brushed away by a hand that cared little about them for their own sakes, and was really interested in her. Her self. Her person.

That was a lot to dare to hope. Especially for a person who just went from one big problem to another.

"Look," Liz said, regaining her attention. "What's your story, anyway?" The tall blonde girl sat on the edge of one of the lower bunks. "I want to know. Your folks really kick you out?"

"Kind of," she said. "Only my dad. But the worst was what my mom did—is doing." She cocked her eyebrows at Liz. "What about you? What's your story?"

Liz shook her head. "I don't have a story. No big deal. I go to a private boarding school. The end. We're talking about you."

"I never told anybody about my mom, nobody except some old friends who never amounted to much and really didn't take it seriously."

"I take stuff seriously."

"I don't want to go back home," Tracey admitted. "Even here in this awful place, at least Mary and all of them are strangers. You can live with stuff when you know it's not your family."

"Tell me," Liz said.

And Tracey did—everything. The afternoon turned

to gray twilight, and she forgot about her walk with Sister James. She had never told anyone the whole story.

As she finished, the first supper bell rang below. Neither of them heeded it for a second, and then Liz swore under her breath. She caught herself. "Oh, sorry."

"What do you think?" Tracey asked.

"I'd still rather be there than here," Liz said. "I'd hunt that boyfriend of your mother's down and put a hanger up his nose if I were you."

"Liz!"

"I would," she insisted.

"He might not even know the truth about my mother," Tracey reminded her. "She lied to us. She might lie to him."

"You hate her?" Liz asked.

Tracey shook her head. "I can't hate her. She saved me from my dad a couple times. And right now she's the only one who sends me any money or any letters from home. Even my sister Jean won't write to me anymore."

"A lot of money?" Liz asked.

"Tons," Tracey told her. "Not that there's anyplace to spend it. I think she's kind of buying my allegiance, you know. For the big break. She's always been careful to let me know that all this is his doing, not mine."

"If they break," Liz said. "Your dad's a rich guy, isn't he?"

"Pretty rich." Liz's question and her own answer put the whole thing into a new light. Maybe her mom wouldn't leave her dad because of the money. Tracey had never thought of that. She couldn't picture her own mother marrying or staying married for money.

But it was possible. Anything was possible after the revelations of last summer.

"You hate him?"

"Sometimes. I try not to. I get mad. But the worst is my mom. I feel so deserted. Getting hit by my dad finished things off, but knowing about her and that guy— that's the worst. "

"Let's go to dinner," Liz said, a sign that she didn't know what to say.

As they went down the hall, Liz said, "Play basketball, Jac. Play real hard."

"Sure," Tracey said. "Why?"

"Because it helps," Liz told her. "It's always helped me."

## THIRTY - ONE

Tracey decided it was too much to expect of Liz to think seriously about what a Bible passage might mean. Liz had seemed oblivious to what had been a lance through Tracey's own emotions. The verse felt like it was for her, just for her, as though it had been put there in ages past as a marker that other people would pass over and find inscrutable until Tracey should find it.

But that was impossible, she realized. Other people had been thrown out, deserted, kicked around for their faith in God. In fact, judging from that passage, it had been a pretty common thing in Israel for people to gang up on the genuine believers and destroy them in the name of God. Posturing was nothing new to the twentieth century.

But her talk with Liz had raised other questions. Thanksgiving was just around the corner, and already the two hall bulletin boards were decorated with construction-paper leaves in brown and gold. Classes would be dismissed Thursday and Friday for the holiday. Most of the girls would be going home for the four-day week-end. In fact, a couple of the girls were going on cruises with their families.

Tracey doubted she'd be invited back home. Or, if she were allowed back, that she'd feel ready to go. The last two months had not faded her horror at all that had happened over the summer.

After Thanksgiving came the longer, more grip-ping holiday of Christmas. Thoughts about spending that vacation at MoJoe had started springing up every day, but Tracey kept pushing them back. She could only take one crisis at a time, and the crisis of a Christ-mas alone would not be faced until the absolute last minute.

That night at dinner, everybody was in good spirits. Amy sat by Tracey. She triumphantly held up nine fin-gers. "Nine more school days," she whispered, mouthing the words almost silently, like a prayer.

Peggy sat across from Tracey and next to Amy. "Hey, how's your room?" she whispered.

Amy rolled her eyes. "Take the elevator to purgatory and ask for the basement floor," she said. She looked at Tracey. "They say they want their mattress back."

"I go with the mattress," Tracey said.

"They might like to get you back," she warned. "They keep saying you can't stay up in Liz's room."

A twinge of apprehension went through Tracey. If they raised enough of a stink about her move and pointed out that she was sleeping on the floor, the nuns might acknowledge what was going on and make her go back to her assigned room.

Peggy shook her head. "I bet you they don't," she said. "If they get the basketball team messed up and fighting just as the season starts, CPR will have their hides. Scooter won't do anything to Liz right now to make Liz want to trip her up."

"I don't know," Amy said, shaking her head. "Besides, Susan's worse than Scooter about it. And she doesn't have to worry about keeping the team together. She's the lousiest player on it."

"Is she that bad?" Tracey asked.

Peggy, normally sensitive about criticizing people for things that couldn't be helped, gave Tracey a brief look and an equally brief nod.

"Why is she on the team?" Tracey asked.

"She's not *that* bad," Peggy said. "Just lazy, now that she's made it. She beat out a lot of girls to get where she is. But when you're talking about that part of the team, you're talking about kids who show promise and are supposed to develop skill. As soon as Susan made the team, she quit trying to make the team. Now, it's like she's scared to start trying again. I don't know."

"But she was always at the gym when I roomed with her," Tracey said.

"Oh, that." Peggy gave a contemptuous laugh. "Half the girls stand around and gossip. Liz and a few others are the only ones who really do anything at those practices. Unless CPR's there. Then everybody breaks a sweat."

"What about you?" Tracey asked.

"I do what Liz tells me," Peggy said evenly. "Anybody who's smart will do the same."

Tracey nodded. She planned to keep doing exactly as Liz told her. She and Liz were still having their practices after the regular team practices were over, two or three times a week.

"Hey, look at this," somebody said. "It's Mary." Everybody looked up to see Sister Mary enter the dining hall.

"Shoot," Tracey mumbled. Mary usually closed dinner only when she had to call somebody in for a chew-up, and the sight of her was enough for Tracey to recall her own vulnerability. Life at MoJoe had been too easy the last three weeks. It was about time for Mary to cut her to ribbons again. In fact, it was overdue.

Sure enough, after a few messages from the principal and a general lecture about silence during study time, Mary said, "I need to see Tracey Jacamuzzi in my office after dinner. You are dismissed, girls."

Every eye at Tracey's table turned to her. A second later, everybody got up and pushed in the chairs. Tracey stood up slowly as her stomach and knees turned to jelly. She tried to remind herself that this was one lone high school, and Mary was nothing but a nun, and she, Tracey, was nothing but a freshman. In years to come, she would look back on this and wonder at her own fears and at the pettiness of a woman like Mary.

Sometimes such visions helped put things in perspective. But not this time. The knowledge that she had once again captured Mary's full attention drove out her courage.

The quivering in Tracey's stomach and thighs grew worse as she shouldered her way through the crowd of girls to get to Mary's office. A long, heavy hand reached over the heads and backs of several girls and slapped her shoulder.

"Hang tough," Liz said. "Don't give in."

Tracey glanced at her, and Liz tapped her own head. "Play it in your mind. Basketball."

She found herself at Mary's office door and knocked. Maybe there would be no answer. Good. She could stand out here all night, listening to Liz in her mind: *Pass it when we cross the line. Pass it, pass it! Don't reach, don't crowd, don't hit the guy who's made a wall!*

"Come in."

It figured. Tracey entered. "You wanted me, Sister?"

"Come in, dear."

Tracey approached the vast and neatly arranged desk. Mary picked up a pencil. She was seated this time, but she did not offer Tracey a chair. Tracey wondered if this would be about what she'd said to Maddie

Murdoch. She had worried that Mrs. Murdoch would carry the tale of her brief, final conversation with Tracey back to Mary, but as the days had passed, it had seemed unlikely. Still, maybe Mary was wise enough to parcel out punishment in order to make it last longer.

*Elbow aligned with the target, wrist straight, body relaxed below the shoulder, feet loose,* Liz yelled. *Jump, jump!*

It wasn't working. She was still scared.

"I understand from Father Servitus that you have not been receiving Communion," Sister Mary said.

Father Servitus was the aged priest who bumbled through Mass every Sunday and once a year read a message to the girls on sexual purity. Tracey felt some surprise that the old man would have noticed her absence—or noticed anything, for that matter.

"No, I don't go to Mass," she said. Of course. He hadn't noticed. Mary had asked him, had perhaps been watching herself and had pointed Tracey's absence out to him so he could mention it back to her. The thought struck Tracey that perhaps Mary lied. Of course, everybody lied now and then, but the idea that Mary might consistently use deceit to get a grip on people and events suddenly seemed both unbelievable and yet very believable.

You didn't think about people like CPR or Sister Edward, and certainly never Sister James Anne, as being capable of lies. The idea seemed impossible whether you thought about them as nuns or as people. And yet, when you looked at Mary as a person, apart from that habit she wore, you suddenly found that you thought her capable of anything, any handling of truth. *The ends justify the means.* The Murphys had told her that the Jesuits themselves had coined that phrase. By its use, they had carried the Spanish Inquisition into the households and lives of men, women, and children.

But those facts of history were hazy at best to Tracey. She knew only what the Murphys had told her during those few weeks last summer. And they had been out of touch with her since her banishment.

Mary was silent during Tracey's musings. Her next question brought Tracey back. "I don't recall hearing you ask permission to miss Mass, dear," she said.

"I never did, Sister," Tracey said.

"Then what made you think you had the right to be truant from Mass?"

"The handbook says that nobody has to be Catholic here," Tracey told her.

Mary, smiling to herself as though foreseeing this objection, shook her head even before Tracey had finished the sentence. "No, Miss Jacamuzzi. The handbook merely opens a way for us to accept girls who are not Catholic. It does not give the girls carte blanche to be whatever religion they choose."

Tracey pursed her lips slightly and felt her fears begin to subside. She sensed what was coming—the very thing she had feared from the beginning—that Mary would try to bend her to her will. But though this had frightened her once, she now felt a hardening resolve within. The fears grew less as Mary spoke.

"I insist that you be in Mass on Sundays, Miss Jacamuzzi."

"If you want, Sister," she agreed.

Mary raised her thin, almost transparent, eyebrows. "I mean, Miss Jacamuzzi, that you will be a participant in the Mass. You will not disgrace that holy place by sitting inattentive."

"I can't do that," Tracey told her.

"I think you can."

"I'm sorry, Sister. Sorry to cause you trouble, I mean. But I cannot go into Mass and kneel. It's impossible."

Sister Mary stood, and Tracey noticed for the second time that she was taller than Sister Mary.

"This is direct disobedience," Mary said.

"I cannot disobey God," she said.

"You are not disobeying God by going to Mass," Mary said. "Am I disobeying God in the practice of my religion? Is Sister St. Gerard?"

Tracey only looked at her.

"Answer me."

"Yes," she said. The fear was still far away. Much closer at hand was the belief, as strong as strength itself, that she was right, that she could no more agree to kneel to the Eucharist, the statues, and all the rest than she could kneel to a Buddha.

"How dare you!" Mary exclaimed.

"You forced that out of me," Tracey replied, angry at Sister Mary for the first time.

"You will be silent! Look down!"

"I will not look down!" Tracey retorted. "I will look you right in the eyes and tell you that I will not kneel to anything material. I am not ashamed of that. I'm a Christian. A real Christian. I don't care what you do to me."

Her last words hung in the air between them, but she didn't flinch under Mary's stare.

"I was a fool to think that the first quarter here had done anything to abate your megalomania," Mary said. "I was an optimistic fool."

This was the posturing Tracey had thought about earlier. Her mind seized on her memory of the Bible with a sudden renewed vigor. "I will do anything you want," she promised. "I'll go to Mass; I'll even kneel there, if you can show me from the Bible that I should."

Mary almost jumped for the bait. Almost. Tracey saw it in her eyes: the sudden temptation to throw obedience to elders in Tracey's face. But then she drew back. They both knew, though Mary would have denied it, that if she had fought Tracey on Tracey's ground, the girl would have won the fight. Tracey had memorized verse after verse about the wrongness of idols, about grace over merit, about fools who prohibited marriage. No doubt Mary's narcs had reported to her that Tracey could talk well enough about purgatory, the worship of Mary, and the doctrines of the patron saints to hold her own against Sister Gerard.

"I will not argue religion with a girl," Mary told her. "Come back to me when you've grown up and seen life."

It was a resort to bluster, and Tracey knew it. She met Mary's eyes, letting her know that she knew it. Mary really was at a loss for the moment. She would not give in, and now she surely realized that Tracey would not—could not—give in, either.

*She'll expel me,* Tracey thought.

But instead, Sister Mary said, very slowly as though making an effort to control her tone, "I will give you until Sunday. If, at that time, you still prove recalcitrant, you will be assigned to reflection and meditation immediately after Sunday dinner."

"All right," Tracey said.

Mary's eyes flashed cold blue fire. "You will answer correctly."

"Yes, Sister," she corrected herself.

"Get out of my office." That last comment, intended to cut, only cheered Tracey. She wasn't sure how, but in some sense she had won against Mary this time.

T he next evening, Tracey and Sister James shuffled arm in arm through the brown leaves that blanketed the flagstone walk. The nights were becoming dark so early, the two of them had to wear jackets to be comfortable.

Tracey put her free hand on Sister James's arm, gently getting her attention.

"What is it, dear?" Sister James asked.

"I'm going to be jugged on Sunday."

"Oh, no." Sister James's face wrinkled in concern and dismay.

"Sister Mary says I have to participate in Mass."

"And you can't?"

"No, Sister."

Sister James nodded, and her serenity seemed to return. "Sister Mary spoke with me today."

Tracey's insides knotted. "About me?" she asked.

"She mentioned that you and she had a discussion in her office last night."

The remembrance of all that had passed sent a

sudden chill into Tracey. Mary had tricked her into indicting Sister James. A confusion of apology and excuses crowded her mind. How could she explain that she found Mass so abominable and yet did not find Sister James abominable?

"Sister—" she began.

"It's all right, dear," she said kindly. Her arm went around Tracey.

"I love you more than anybody else here," Tracey told her. "I don't want to hurt your feelings. Please—" She stopped, desperate to say something to elicit a word of forgiveness.

Sister James smiled. "Dear heart, I would rather have my fiery and free Tracey than all the Catholic girls in the world. I know it's been hard for you here."

"I never meant to say anything bad about you, but Mass is so against what I—"

"I don't expect you to be a Catholic for my sake, dear," Sister James said. "I don't expect you to approve of the Catholic church for my sake." She smiled. Her hand, bent and stiff from arthritis, found and then patted Tracey's cheek. "We ought to walk while we can. When you're kept indoors, I'm kept indoors too."

They linked arms again and resumed their walk in the dark evening. "When I was a girl," Sister James said, "long before I took my vows, I used to dream of the man I would marry. Dear me, how my mother would laugh at me when I told her of my romances. She told me that I was so fiery and ornery, I would never please any man."

"Is that why you became a nun?" Tracey asked.

Sister James laughed. "Oh, I gentled before I turned seventeen. I think I might have married, even though I was so tall for a girl. But not long after I turned seventeen, I found that all that I could give to God was my own self."

Her dark face became serious again. Tracey looked at her, alert for some indication that Sister James was trusting her convent to get her into heaven. But all Sister James said was, "I had no talent, and though some of the boys teased me about my long hair and the color of my eyes, I knew that I was no great beauty. Or if I was, that beauty wouldn't last. There was nothing to give God but my own self. So I did."

"At seventeen?" Tracey asked.

"Yes, dear. As soon as I graduated from high school."

"Was it worth it?" Tracey asked.

"I taught for ten years, and I loved it. Then, when my arthritis became too severe, I retired."

"You couldn't manage it part time?" Tracey asked.

"Oh, dear, the decision was final."

Tracey realized that the decision had not been made by Sister James. Someone else—a priest, the rector, a bishop, perhaps—had reviewed her health history and had retired her. A shaft of pity pierced her. She tried to count up the years, to calculate at what age the sister had been made to retire. Even if the order had trained Sister James with a four-year degree, that still would have meant that she'd been retired at thirty-one or thirty-two. She had lived longer in retirement than out of it.

"You've taught me a lot," Tracey said at last.

"And you've brought me joy, dear. The staff of my old age. That's what my grandfather used to call me when I was just a little girl." Again, Sister James smiled. "I didn't know what he meant. I was five and had studied piano, and the only staff I knew about was the musical staff. I used to think he was talking about my piano lessons." She laughed gently, but her hand squeezed Tracey's. "The staff of my old age."

A rush of sweetness went over Tracey, and her eyes suddenly became wet. She couldn't answer for a moment, and Sister James added in a softer voice, "Nobody could make me think ill of you, dear. Bear that in mind for my sake, as well as yours. I know you'll behave wisely."

"I will," Tracey promised.

Tracey walked Sister James back to the door of her wing. She no longer had any persistent fear that she would be ambushed again. Being Liz's friend had given her a certain immunity. As Sister Lucy and one of the attendants came to the wing door to get Sister James, Tracey surprised herself and her friend by throwing her arms around Sister James's neck and giving her a kiss. "Good night," she said, then ran back up to the dining hall for dinner.

H ey, you're late!" Liz yelled as she opened the locked
glass door for Tracey and let her into the gym.

"I got hung up," Tracey said.

"Dinner was an hour ago."

"I met Amy to get some notes on Latin, and then . . .
then I had to stop and pray."

Liz followed her into the gym, and Tracey hurriedly
threw off her jacket and hat, then pulled off her uniform skirt, bolero, and vest, revealing her blue gym suit
underneath.

"We gotta get you a real sweat suit, Jacamuzzi," Liz
said.

"Get me off this lousy campus, and I promise I'll
buy one," Tracey told her.

Liz retrieved the basketball from the middle of the
gym floor and slowly dribbled it up to Tracey as the
younger girl tied on her sneakers.

"What were you praying about?" Liz asked.

"Sister James."

"You never did finish telling me what Mary wanted you for yesterday," Liz reminded her.

"That's because you've been with the team the whole stupid day," Tracey replied, but she looked up and grinned when she said it. She could tell her friend was wound up over the season starting.

"Soon as Thanksgiving's over, baby, watch out for the wild Polack!" Liz let loose with a loud whoop. She kicked the ball up off the tip of her shoe.

"You figure out what to do about keeping me in your room yet?" Tracey asked.

"Yes, the wonder Polack has the answer," Liz told her. "Wait till Thanksgiving. I ain't going home—"

"You're not!" Tracey exclaimed, overjoyed.

"Cool it, kid. Show a little restraint. There's no point in going home when I could be practicing here. My folks don't understand about b-ball, not like Father Williams does, and CPR does." She grinned. "In other words, they won't let me play it all day long. So I figured to stay. And while I'm here, we'll settle this room thing on our own. You ready? Let's go."

Tracey leaped up, eager to play hard for Liz's sake, wanting to share in her joy of anticipating the basketball season.

"Hey, wait," Liz said. "What about Mary?"

"She's going to jug me Sunday," Tracey told her. "She says I have to be Catholic."

"That buzzard. Come on. Half-court tonight. I've had enough of drills."

After their practice and the trudge back to the rooms, Tracey sat and stared into space over her book. Sometimes she worried about keeping up her studies in this school where grades meant so much and yet basketball required so much. But her concerns took a backseat that night to a new fear: being deprived of the few joys she had at MoJoe. Jug would separate her again, take away time from basketball. Mary had already tried taking Sister James from her, but at least that had failed.

The memory of Sister James brought another prayer to Tracey's heart, a prayer of petition for the aging sister, and a prayer of thanks for her kindness. She wondered again if Sister James, a devout Catholic, could possibly be trusting Christ alone for her righteousness.

But Tracey's other worries soon crowded out thoughts of Sister James. For the first time, she felt the sharpness of the deprivation that jug meant. All of Sunday afternoon and night she would be isolated, not to mention Monday night and Tuesday morning. But Sunday was the killer, because Sunday was a free day, a day to talk with her roommates and joke around and relax.

Well, there was nothing to do about it. She sighed heavily.

Across the room, Liz sat at one of the two desks. She turned around. "What is it?"

"I got jug on my mind," Tracey said.

Liz came over to the mattress and sat down. "That jug stuff, huh?" Tracey nodded.

"You let me think about it a while," Liz said. "I'll find a plan."

"She's going to kill all my weekends," Tracey told her. "That's what she's up to. Soon she'll just ask me if I'll go to Mass, and when I say no, she'll put me in jug all weekend."

"Jug's limited to two days," Liz said thoughtfully.

"Liz, guess what? Weekends are limited to two days."

"Don't be so smart, Jacamuzzi Macaroni. There's a lot more to jug than you know about. You hang in there and let me see what's up with Bing Crosby."

Tracey felt her curiosity pique. "What else is there to jug?"

"Well, for one thing, it didn't start out as a punishment. But it didn't take Mary or some other dried-out old hag long to figure out it was a good way to get a kid to cool off and calm down."

"You mean people used to volunteer for it?" Tracey asked.

"I think so. Especially at Lent, you know? It was a real Lenten thing to do—cut yourself off and say a few beads for the Gipper. I get the idea from the old yearbooks and class meeting notes that running up to jug was the way to get ahead here, show the nuns you meant your stuff."

"Glad we're over that," Tracey mumbled.

"They have a roll book for jug," Liz told her. "Somebody keeps a ledger on it. So they can see who's been up there and how many times. And whether it was voluntary or disciplinary." She slapped Tracey's arm. "Jac, you just let me work on this a while."

She got up from the mattress and went back to her desk. Regina, Barbara, and Ingrid, who had looked up at the conversation, returned to their books.

On Sunday morning, Mary came into the small chapel and beckoned to Tracey. Tracey met her in the back. "I see that you are persisting in your stubbornness," Mary said. "Very well. Immediately after lunch, you will report to the prayer and meditation room."

"Yes, Sister. Thank you, Sister," Tracey said.

"I'm not finished with you, Miss Jacamuzzi," the principal said. "I want to see you next Friday, and I will then entreat you again to return to the normal practice of your religion."

It figured. As soon as Tracey refused, Sister Mary could jug her for the whole weekend.

"Yes, Sister," Tracey said.

Mary left her again, and Tracey watched the slight, small figure as it went out the doors in the back. She had battled Mary almost to a draw once, by not being afraid of her. That was the whole trick with Mary—not to fear her—or better—not even to pay attention to her. But Tracey doubted she could consistently act like Mary couldn't scare her. Mary could scare her, and usually did.

Tracey was jugged for the next few days, and she spent both Saturday and Sunday alone the next week. The week after that was Thanksgiving, and she wondered with a tinge almost of despair if she would again be incarcerated upstairs for two days of the holiday.

"I'm due to turn myself in to Mary tomorrow," she told Liz on Thanksgiving morning. All three of the other roommates had gone home for the long holiday. Peggy was gone too. Only about ten girls were left on their hall.

"Don't sweat it," Liz told her. "First problems first. Let's go scout the terrain."

They changed into holiday clothing—jeans and sweatshirts—and went out to see who was in the main building.

"No nuns in sight," Liz reported with satisfaction. "Let's go to work. We've got a lot to do."

"Like what?" Tracey asked.

"Like moving the double bunk from our room down to your old room and moving their triple bunk up to our room."

"Are you crazy?" Tracey asked. "Those things are huge, and they have metal frames!"

"Duh!" Liz exclaimed. "We take them apart first, genius. And it's not that hard."

"Well, it's a good thing we've got all day."

"Quit complaining and come on. We all have to make these little sacrifices."

Tracey remembered that Liz was doing this for her, so that Susan and Scooter couldn't get her back. "You're right," she said soberly. "Sorry I complained. I really want a bed again."

222

As it turned out, they didn't have nearly as much to do as they had feared. The metal frame beds were identical. All they really needed to do was take the top of the triple off of its frame, move it upstairs, and attach it to the double up there to make a new triple bunk.

Liz had a mini-set of wrenches. When they failed to work, she and Tracey went out to the toolshed and climbed through a window. They brought the custodian's tool chest up to Tracey's old room and set to work loosening bolts that had been tightened—as Liz reckoned—at least twenty years ago.

She swore profusely at the bed as she struggled to get the bolts loose, and Tracey finally prayed again and again for the bolts to come off. Finally, the first bolt gave way and turned.

"Dinner's in forty-five minutes," Tracey warned as they got the first bolt off.

"Blast dinner," Liz grunted.

They missed dinner. They also missed supper. At last, at eight o'clock that night, they got all the pieces of the bed up the stairs and put it back together again on top of one of the double bunks. At ten o'clock, they hoisted Tracey's mattress up on top of it and managed to smile at each other as they surveyed their work.

"We've had nothing but Hershey bars all day," Tracey said. "I feel kind of sick."

"Have no fear, Jac," Liz told her. "My mom sent me a Thanksgiving package. Let's get these tools back, and then we'll have our own feast."

Tracey nodded wearily. They picked up the tool chest between them and went back downstairs.

Later, Liz brought out her care package. Hot pots

were normally banned during school days because they put too much strain on the wiring. But without the load of endless blow dryers and electric curlers, Liz started one heating. They drank instant coffee with sugar and Cremora and shared cheeses and crackers, butter cookies, and a small canned ham. Tracey noticed the package was not a homemade assortment. It had come from a mail-order company.

"Nice of your mom to send all this," she said.

"Help yourself, Jac," Liz said. "Chocolates in there too."

"You and your mom close?" Tracey asked.

"No way."

Tracey didn't feel sure enough to ask any more about Liz's family. Liz never talked about her home, her childhood, anything at all that was that personal.

"You close to anyone?" Tracey asked.

"Sure, lots of people," Liz said. "Peggy, and Maureen on the team, and you."

"Yeah." But Tracey realized that Liz wasn't close to anybody. Not the kind of close that Tracey meant. Of course, Liz Lukas could hang around with anybody she chose. All the girls made room for Liz, and they were honored whenever she stopped to talk. Tracey's idea of close—like walking with Sister James and talking seriously about her own feelings, her life, and Sister James's feelings and life—those conversations didn't occur with Liz, not unless things were at an extreme. Even then, Liz listened and gave answers. She didn't open up.

"Now, about jug," Liz said, interrupting Tracey's thoughts.

"Yeah?"

"Tomorrow morning, you and me have to go see Bing Crosby."

Tracey's jaw dropped. Liz leaned forward and smiled. "Cool it, Jac. Trust Sister Liz. I have the care of your soul on my thin shoulders."

"Liz—" Tracey began. The idea of going to see the headmaster of the school was not her idea of getting out of jug.

"Trust me, I said. Trust me." She held Tracey's look with her own look, not unfriendly, but strong—willing the younger girl into submission until at last Tracey closed her mouth.

As soon as she did, Liz said, "You don't know the game, Jac. I had to teach you basketball. I'll teach you this game too."

"Sure," Tracey grumbled.

"Bing Crosby wants you and me and everyone else here to get out of this place not on drugs and not pregnant. He's been around, baby. He'll settle for nice kids who aren't Catholic. Just trust me."

Friday morning found Tracey and Liz at Father Williams's office. In contrast to Sister Mary's beautiful office, which had been uglified in Tracey's opinion, Father Williams occupied a smaller, plainer office that was enlivened (if not beautified) by cluttered walls filled with snapshots, framed pictures, old certificates and awards, and other odds and ends. His desk, a table, and two stuffed chairs were filled with stacks of papers, forms, and old trophies. His one bookcase held other stacks, a few books, and more trophies. A faint scent of pipe smoke hung about the room, and the sunlight peeped through worn old curtains that had been torn in several places.

"Welcome to my domain," he said as he noticed Tracey's eyes roving around the clutter of objects, souvenirs, and memorabilia. "I keep my office here in the rectory so Sister Mary won't drop dead on me. I have the hardest time keeping acting principals at this place. Something about the mess that they object to." He pulled out a pair of glasses, polished them with a white handkerchief, and added, "Women! Ah, well. What can I do for you, girls?"

"Tracey has come to request prayer and meditation," Liz said.

"Whoa-ho!" he exclaimed. "The very thing at the start of the season! Now, that's what I call putting a rookie to good use, Miss Lukas."

Tracey stared at Liz, aghast at the idea of requesting to be jugged, but Liz made a gesture for her to go along with it.

"I have the ledger right here," he said. He pulled an old black ledger up from the depths of one of his desk drawers.

Tracey wondered why such a disorganized man as Father Williams would keep such an unused book close by him. He opened it up. "Hmm, not many signees these days. Here's an entry from 1964." He looked up at them. "What'll it be, girls?"

"Every Thursday and Friday from now until . . . oh, March first," Liz said.

Tracey almost said something, but then suddenly she got it. Jug could only last for two days in a row. If she were up there on Thursday and Friday, then Mary couldn't put her back into it on Saturday and Sunday.

"Well, girls," he said. "I would like to oblige you, but I'm afraid the use of reflection and meditation is up to my discretion. Two days a week is far too much for a teenager. We'll say Thursdays and Fridays of every other week."

"That's fine," Liz said. Father Williams entered Tracey's name and dates in the ledger. "I see from this ledger that you've been up to the fourth floor several times this semester," he observed.

"Yes, Father," Tracey said.

"On Sister Mary's advice, I understand," he said.

"Yes."

"Hmm." He looked thoughtful. "Well, Sister Mary may want to override your requests here, girls. But I do maintain that reflection and meditation should never be put into the light of punishment, if it can be helped. Its primary purpose is to serve as spiritual refreshment for the needy."

"Could you please ask Sister Mary to let me not be Catholic?" Tracey asked suddenly.

Father Williams looked up at her. "Take the bull by the horns, eh?" he asked. He took off his glasses and chewed thoughtfully on one of the ends. Liz stepped on Tracey's foot, chiding her for her rashness. "I'll tell you," he said at last. "I'm an easygoing man, Miss Jacamuzzi. I feel that a young lady who has strong reasons to avoid tobacco, alcohol, and marijuana ought to be allowed to follow whatever path she's chosen." He leaned back in his chair. "But even my hands can be tied in some areas, such as the governing of young women when I—admittedly, and to my satisfaction— am a man. My position as headmaster is one that may change, should any complaints be leveled against me. You see, we figureheads—Queen Elizabeth and I—we rely much more on charm and intrigue, the subtleties of diplomacy."

"I see," Tracey said. Inwardly, she decided that he was a coward, or maybe too lazy to take on Sister Mary.

He seemed to read her thoughts, but instead of defending himself, he smiled at her. "Dear," he said, "win at basketball, stay away from drinking and drugs, and pretty soon, you'll find that you need no favors from the headmaster." He replaced his glasses on his nose and shot her a sharp glance. "I have the spiritual care of everybody here, and I will see to it that our schedule of prayer and meditation is not disturbed. But in the dormitory, and in the routine of this campus, you are in Sister Mary's charge. There's very little I can do, not during your first year, should she become displeased with your conduct."

"I understand," Tracey told him.

"And thank you," Liz added. "Getting out of jug on the weekends is good enough."

He smiled. "You put some prayers in for the team, Miss Jacamuzzi, and I'll call it a fair deal."

She decided she liked him after all. "Sure thing, Father."

Sister Mary never did challenge Tracey on the game-playing that she and Liz had used to get Tracey out of jug on the weekends. Tracey continued to refrain from Mass, but on every other Thursday, she went up to the fourth floor for two days of jug.

The first game of the season was on a Thursday afternoon, a home game, and Tracey worried that she would miss it because of jug. But she discovered that the game started at two-thirty, and all of the freshmen were required to attend in lieu of gym class. They were allowed to wear their uniforms instead of their gym suits.

On the morning of the game, Liz was more wound up than Tracey had yet seen her. Peggy was also uptight, with a tension that bordered on irritability.

"Will you cool it?" Liz demanded as the three of them went down to breakfast together.

"I can't help it," Peggy said. "How am I going to

229

make it to this afternoon? And what happens if I mess up?"

"You'll really have to mess up to look bad against St. Bede's," Liz told her. "We beat them every year by at least thirty points."

"Old rules or new rules?" Peggy asked.

"Bede's is still old rules," Liz told her. She glanced at Tracey. "We just switched over to new rules last year because that's how the public schools are going. But some of the Catholic schools are still using girls' rules. It looks a lot different. Wait and see."

"Old rules . . . six on a team, right?" Tracey asked.

Liz nodded. "Three forwards, three guards, and no crossing over from offense to defense. Rebounding's a lot harder, but there's no fast breaks. It's a passing game."

"And you'll win?" Tracey asked.

"We'll win. Bede's is always sending their graduates to Harvard and Yale and Cornell and places like that. They got a lot of brains over there but no brawn. You'll see for yourself. Their entire team is freshmen and sophomores. All the upperclassmen are too busy for sports."

Peggy let out a heavy sigh. "Six hours till we get dressed," she moaned.

Liz grinned and punched her arm. "Relax. This is cake today. Next week is chopped liver, when we play Villa Marie."

"If you say so," Peggy agreed, and Tracey felt a twinge of envy, wishing, as she'd never wished before, that she could be on the team.

Liz seemed to read her thoughts. She punched Tracey's arm. "You better give me a good report on this game, Jac. I'm counting on you."

230

Tracey found that MoJoe still had the power to surprise her. Everybody who could duck out of fifth-hour class had done so. It was odd how strict the nuns were about attendance until a game came up. Then, lame excuses for absences were somehow tolerated. Some of the sisters even handed out pass slips like awards for the most ingenious excuses invented. Everybody was in a clamor to get a good seat for the first game of the season.

Like the other inexperienced freshmen, Tracey sat through her entire class, went to her locker to leave her books, stopped at the candy machine outside the classroom building, and finally sauntered into the jammed gymnasium.

It was like a scene from a movie. Banners hung everywhere, and there was a clamor of war whoops, shrill whistles, and snatches of songs. A harsh bugle blast split the air. Blast after blast followed it. She stepped in, awed by the change.

Many of the girls carried red plastic bugles that

were four or five feet long. They couldn't be played for any musical quality, but they gave vent to the pent-up spirits of the MoJoes. One girl went by with a bundle of them under one arm and stopped at the sight of Tracey's admiration.

"Five bucks," she said. "Goes for new uniforms."

"You got it," Tracey told her. The girl wore the ribbon of a student council representative, so Tracey knew the offer was genuine. She didn't know the girl, but the girl knew her.

"Play like Gabriel," the older girl told Tracey, and she laughed as she walked away. Tracey found herself grinning in appreciation of the gentle ribbing.

"Trace, hey, Trace!"

She looked up at the sound of Liz's voice. Muffled in a beautiful black-and-white warm-up suit with black-and-white gym shoes, Liz motioned to her. "Come on."

"There's Liz!" someone screamed. A blast of the trumpets and a loud drumming on the old wooden bleachers filled their corner of the gym.

"Great," Liz said. "That's all CPR needs. She'll kill me for being out here."

"Do you need something?" Tracey asked anxiously.

"I need to get you a good seat. See that tall girl with the straight hair?"

"The senior?" Tracey asked.

"Yeah. Nina Korman. She said you could sit with her."

Tracey stared at Liz. "She did?"

"She's a real studious type, OK? Nobody likes to sit with her. But she promised me she'd get a good seat and would hold one for you. Go sit with her."

"Sure." She held out her hand to Liz. "Good luck, Liz."

"Quit shaking, Jac. It's a victory for sure. You won't see me or Scooter play much. See you later." Liz grasped her hand and then ducked away through the people, back to the locker room.

It took some nerve to push her way through all the upperclassmen just to reach Nina Korman. Tracey felt self-conscious. It seemed that at any minute she'd get yelled down to go sit with the freshmen and not butt to the front of the group. But nobody yelled at her, and Nina looked up with a smile on her acned face. She patted the seat beside her with a look of welcome that seemed a little overbearing. Tracey gingerly sat down.

"Ho!" some girls yelled, and immediately the cry was taken up.

> Ho! Ho! Where you gonna go?
> Whatcha got to show?
> Don't you know,
> Don't you know—

"What?" half the girls yelled back.

The answer was a thunderous drumming on the bleachers and a blast from every trumpet in the gym.

> We are the MoJoes,
> The mighty, mighty MoJoes!
> Everywhere we go,
> People wanna know
> Who we are,
> So we tell them—

"What!"

Ho! Ho! Everywhere we go
We make the center show
'Cause we know,
'Cause we know—

We are the MoJoes,
The mighty, mighty MoJoes!
Everywhere we go,
People wanna know
Who we are,
So we tell them—

The song went on for about five more stanzas. None of them were difficult to keep up with, and between choruses, Tracey figured out how to blow the trumpet. She let loose with a blast as soon as the first song was finished.

"Rowdy!" several people yelled. "Rowdy!"

"Rowdy!" the girls across the gym yelled back.

R-o-w-d-i-e!
That's the way we spell *rowdy!*
Rowdy! Let's get rowdy!

"Here they come!" the girls nearest the locker room yelled. "Here they come!" Some of the girls started a drumming tattoo on the bleachers. Tracey felt the rumbling deep inside her stomach.

The locker room's double doors burst open, and Liz and Scooter came running out together, each holding a papier-mâché spear. Between the spears was suspended a wide, white banner with the stencil of a woman warrior on a winged horse, and over her, the team name: Valkyries.

On the team's uniforms, the symbol was abbreviated to a shield emblazoned with a V. But at sight of the Valkyrie on the banner, Tracey felt, for the first time, an earnest wish to be wearing one of those uniforms, to have the honor of carrying one of those spears. And the desire had nothing to do with basketball.

The rest of the team streamed out the open doors and ran in a line across the gym floor. As each girl passed under the banner of the Valkyrie, Liz and Scooter shook their spears, and all the girls in the crowd cheered and blew their trumpets.

"This is great," Tracey exclaimed to Nina.

"You'll be out there someday too, Miss Jacamuzzi!" Nina said.

Tracey felt a blush at being talked to in such a little-kid way, but she managed a smile.

The girls from St. Bede's came out onto the floor in a line, and Tracey was surprised to see her classmates give them a cordial, if not wild, round of applause. The nuns still had some hold on the girls at basketball games, and there would be no rudeness—at least up front. Tracey had heard of the name-calling and even fights in the bathrooms after some of the games, all carried out by nonteam members.

Suddenly, everything fell dead silent. The captain of the other team was asked a question by the woman referee, and when the girl shook her head, the ref nodded at Sister Theresa, the chorus teacher. Sister Theresa came out from the sidelines. The players on both sides took their places on the court, a MoJoe girl by each Bede's girl. The MoJoes in the audience stood.

Sister Theresa put her pitch pipes to her lips and blew one note. Suddenly getting what was going on,

Tracey smiled. She had struggled through the school song for the first four weeks of chorus. It seemed to her an anthem of impossible tune—something like "The Star-Spangled Banner" in its range.

To her surprise, the school anthem of the Sanctuary of Mary and Joseph filled the gym with a loveliness and fullness of voice she would never have believed. On the court, Liz covered her heart with her hand, and everybody but the Bede's girls and the referees followed suit. There was no laughter, no drumming—nothing but the hard and heartfelt singing of 230 girls.

> For strength the black, for truth the white,
> Our colors we hold dear.
> Let strength and truth abide in us
> In every heart sincere.
>
> Pure Valkyries and maidens fair,
> We pledge our loyalty;
> The shield we love, nor can it fail
> As our hearts are true to thee.
>
> O Mary and Joseph, school we hail,
> Our bles't Sanctuary,
> The shield we carry in our hearts
> Is yours eternally.

Tracey was amazed to feel a rush of genuine emotion and love for her school. Not for Sister Mary, or for the imprisonment she felt, but for things like gym class, and Sister James Anne, and Liz. It was suddenly hard not to find something to love at MoJoe.

For a game of half-court rules, Liz, Scooter, and a

girl named Kathy Willis were the forwards. The team shucked their warm-up suits and returned to the court in black-and-white basketball uniforms. Liz jump-centered for the ball and hit it right to Scooter, who scored. Tracey realized with a slight disappointment that Liz's predictions seemed likely to come true. St. Bede's wasn't very good. But you wouldn't have known it from the way the MoJoe girls yelled and encouraged the team, as though the fate of the whole season hung on this game.

Tracey blasted on her trumpet and yelled too. But after a few minutes, she was engrossed in the mechanics of the game. Half-court rules were new to her. Liz and Scooter seemed comfortable enough with them, but the other four starters blundered offside a couple of times. Even so, the first-string retired after about four minutes, and the second-string came in to play. Tracey watched Peggy, who played guard.

She realized with some dismay that Peggy wasn't very good. She was barely managing to keep up with the guard from Bede's. Susan, Scooter's hanger-on, also played on the second-string. Her skill was cloaked with an aggressiveness that put off her opponents. But she was the worst for getting fouled offside.

Still, it was one thing to be a spectator and another thing to really be out there playing. Tracey tried to imagine making the team. To be out there, not so much playing as standing alongside Liz, holding up the spear, standing for something better than herself and yet being chosen to stand for that thing—these thoughts appealed to her. She vaguely remembered Mrs. Murdoch telling her about Valkyries. But now she wished she knew more about what the Valkyries were and why they had been chosen as the symbol for the school team.

The hurried half hour before study time was crammed with congratulations and visitors in Tracey's room. Even Scooter and Susan showed up, though they didn't speak to her. Liz, with her usual careless, half-defiant attitude, threw one arm around Tracey's shoulder and kept it there the whole time that Tracey's former roommates stayed in the room.

"There's next year's rising star," Peggy said, nodding at Tracey.

"You said it," Liz agreed.

"Maybe we better wait and see," Tracey said guardedly, conscious of Scooter's cold stare and Susan's sneer.

"Hey, I've seen you play, babe," Liz said. She held up her glass of ice water and lemon. "A toast—" she began boldly. She might just have toasted Tracey, even though Tracey desperately wanted her not to, but Peggy interrupted.

"To all good Valkyries and true," she said, holding up her own lemon water.

None of the players were allowed to have soft drinks or candy, so they drank water with lemons in it after the games. The other dozen or so girls crowded into the room had cans of soda pop. They lifted their drinks in solemn salute. Liz glanced at Tracey. "Right, kid?"

"To all good Valkyries," Tracey agreed. It was an odd hypocrisy at MoJoe that girls who would not touch sugar in snacks or drinks would nevertheless guzzle down beer and whiskey or drop speed. The girls who boarded at MoJoe were aware, even as they talked and joked, that the town girls who had made the team were getting drunk at somebody's house. One of the girls on the team had parents who kept a bar, and whenever there was a victory, the bar was open. Supposedly, the girls were entitled to only one easy drink apiece, but they had worked out ways of getting more with very little trouble.

"Ten minutes to the bell," Regina announced.

"I gotta go too," Tracey said, remembering guiltily that she was late for jug.

"Oh, that!" Liz exclaimed, half annoyed.

"It's not so bad," Tracey told her. She hurried to get her things together. There was a knock.

"Join the party," Liz yelled. Sister St. Bernard walked into the room.

At the sight of one of the nuns, Liz and Tracey exchanged quick glances. Mary must have had one of them watch to see if she got up to jug on time after the game.

"Well, girls, is this the victory party?" Sister Gerard asked.

"Have a Coke, Sister?" Liz asked.

"No, I wasn't expecting such a crowd. Tracey, I need to speak with you."

"I'm sorry I'm late—" Tracey began.

"You're not in trouble, dear."

"Oh." She looked at Sister Gerard and hesitated. "I'm supposed to be in jug tonight."

"I'll walk up with you to the prayer room."

The girls were mostly silent until Tracey had gathered her clothes and books together and walked out with St. Bernard.

"I'm sorry to take you away from your friends," the nun said.

"Well, I was supposed to go upstairs right after dinner," Tracey admitted. "So I guess you're keeping me on the straight and narrow."

The teacher actually laughed. But she didn't tell Tracey the purpose of her visit until they were upstairs in the privacy of the prayer and meditation room.

"Tracey," she began gravely, "your father has contacted the school."

Tracey felt a jolt of tension run through her like electricity. "Oh, yeah?"

"He made arrangements for you to stay here through the holidays," Sister Gerard told her.

Relief was her first response, but then Tracey realized what her father's action meant. She was still in disgrace at home. He still didn't want to see her. She would be incarcerated at the school for the best holiday of the year.

"I'm a new Christian," she said at last. "I believe that Christmas is a spiritual thing. Maybe . . . maybe it's better this way." She looked away.

"I am sorry, dear," Sister Gerard said.

"It's all right."

"Maybe somebody might invite you—"

"No," Tracey said quickly. "No." She looked up. "That would be worse, somehow."

"Not many people are here at Christmas," Sister Gerard warned.

"I'll get by," Tracey said. "What about the gym? Is it open?"

"Liz Lukas has a key," she reminded Tracey. "It would probably be best for you to use that without making any announcements about it aloud. Just be careful to keep the doors locked."

"Yes, Sister."

Sister Gerard didn't seem disposed to leave right away. In fact, there seemed to be something else on the sister's mind. Tracey stood awkwardly for a second or two. At last the woman said, "Dear, I hate to pry. I wouldn't want to interfere, but I wonder if there's more to your family situation than your conversion."

"Sure, there's more," Tracey said. "My dad knocked me around before I ever became a Chri—a Protestant. Sometimes I think he's just using that as his excuse." She shook her head. "I don't know. Life's so dark."

"I know he must love you, dear," Sister Gerard began.

"Tell me," Tracey began.

"Yes?"

"Did anybody tell you before I came here what happened—what he did? To me, I mean."

St. Bernard looked startled, almost frightened. "No, there was no indication from either parent of any trouble other than the question of your faith."

"Nobody else said anything?"

"No."

Tracey turned away and closed the curtains to shut out the dark and lonely night. "You and me seem to disagree on everything. But I can't help it on this. I don't know if he loves me or not. We're a lot alike in some ways, him and me. I wonder if that's part of the problem."

"Do you miss your family, dear?"

"Yes, Sister, but—I can't explain it. It's better when I don't think of them. I try to turn them off in my mind."

"You hear from your mother?" Sister Gerard asked.

"Sister," Tracey said suddenly. She turned back around, suddenly conscious that she'd been staring through that last crack between the curtains, her eyes lost in the vast darkness outside. She and the teacher looked at each other. "You won't say this stuff to Sister Mary, will you?"

Sister Gerard barely hesitated, but when she answered, she said clearly, "No, of course not."

"I don't ever want to have everybody know about it. But my folks are having a lot of problems right now. I was in the way."

Sister Gerard shook her head. "What do you mean?"

"My mom is seeing someone else," Tracey told her. "And I know about it."

"That's a serious thing to say!" Sister Gerard said with a gasp. But the look on Tracey's face must have convinced her. There were no arguments, no demands for proof.

"I am sorry," Sister Gerard said.

"I have to stay away," Tracey said. "I have to. She's

gone all the time—to him, whoever he is. And my dad's just a raging bull. He could have killed me before he even knew what he was doing." She looked down, and Sister Gerard said nothing. In the long silence, Tracey at last admitted, "I was hating him more and more each day. It was just impossible."

"Are you sure you want to be alone?" Sister Gerard asked with a glance at the room.

"I'm alone all the time," Tracey said. "I just don't notice it as much sometimes."

"I'll try to help you," Sister Gerard promised. "I'll try." She walked out quietly, and Tracey returned to unpacking her things. On sudden impulse, she pulled the curtains open again.

If it was all darkness, she wanted to see it, to face it. She stared out at the empty night. Down the hill opposite the retirees' wing, she saw that the gym lights had been left on. Perhaps not everybody was gone yet. She could see the silhouette of the Valkyrie painted on the glass door of the gym. To her surprise, it moved. And instead of being the painted, stilted, clumsily made figure, it moved with a sure grace. It came away from the door and walked up the hill, toward the hall—toward her. Then she realized that it was only somebody who had been standing in front of the glass double doors and who was now walking the footpath up the hill. Nevertheless, the light shining through the doors spread out behind the person like the brightness of wings.

Tracey thought it was one of the sisters, but the tall, dark figure turned away from the walk up to the main hall and stepped into the darkness of the unlighted grounds that lay between the school and the retirees' wing. After a moment or two, the figure emerged again into the indistinct light of the parking lot. It walked with an easy stride, but a long one, then paused and looked up at the main hall. It was certainly a woman, but not one of the sisters. Tracey could see the outline of full, shoulder-length hair.

The figure paused only a moment and then resumed its walk toward the cars. The momentary appearance that it had been searching for Tracey, seeing through the darkness and walls of the place and scanning for her, like some unknown messenger or otherworldly agent on a mission, unnerved her for a moment. The room was lonely and too quiet. It was easy to get eerie sensations and think of ghostly things. She drove her mind into familiar channels and spent a moment envying the freedom of being able to get into a car and drive away from this place. Then she turned to her books.

Tracey sat down heavily on the bed and put her head in her hands. No place to go at Christmas, no welcome from home.

She took out her algebra book, but even the neatly marked pages of study couldn't keep her mind off her troubles. For the first time in her life, Tracey was pulling A's—and not just one or two, either. Mostly A's, and two B's that were close to A's. She had never been much of a student. Yet MoJoe's misery had sent her diving into her books from the very beginning, and now there was a certain measure of happiness in knowing that she could get good grades when she tried.

But tonight, her careful rows of penciled algebra problems clouded over, and she shed a few tears before she rallied herself to go on. The night was endless, the assignment endless; her own life seemed endless. Not eternal, just endless.

She had no idea how long this dark mood lasted. By degrees she fell into a kind of doze, crowded with jumbled thoughts, neatly printed numbers, and tears. A soft sound at the door startled her awake.

She straightened in her chair. The dead silence all around her made her realize that she had missed the bell. Everybody was in bed. She jumped up. The sound at the door was repeated.

For an instant, Tracey wondered if her old enemies had come up for a visit. But then she realized that such a trip would be more dangerous for them than for her. Some of the nuns woke up instantly at any noise louder than a human voice.

She went to the door and silently opened it, ready to yell, just in case.

"Trick or treat," Liz whispered with a grin. She held a single lemon and a big plastic jug of water in her hands.

"What are you doing up here?" Tracey whispered back.

"Trick-or-treating."

Tracey stepped aside and let her in.

"St. Bernard told me to stop by," Liz said, handing her the jug. She pulled two cups from her robe pockets. "I got a knife in here somewhere," she mumbled. She looked up. "Cool it, Jac. You volunteered for this, remember. So one of the nuns thought it wise to have me check on you. No sweat."

"Even if Mary herself were standing guard up here, I don't think I could have turned you away," Tracey admitted.

"What did St. Bernard want?"

"Told me my folks don't want me back at Christmas."

"Shoot," Liz exclaimed in sympathy. "Your dad—"

"Don't," Tracey said. "It was a good day today. Let's not talk about that."

Liz nodded and started cutting the lemon into slices. Tracey set the jug down and, realizing she had forgotten her usual routine, walked around the room, turn-

ing all the statues to face the wall. She took the crucifix down and laid it on top of the chest of drawers.

Liz poured their water and swirled the lemons
around in the drinks. She held out a cup to Tracey.

"What time is it?" Tracey asked.

"Eleven-thirty. Here you go."

Tracey took it, and they looked at each other. "I
hope I make the team," Tracey said.

"To all good Valkyries," Liz saluted her. Then they
linked arms, tossed down the water, and laughed at
each other.

"What is a Valkyrie?" Tracey asked. "I mean, I've
seen the emblem of the woman on the horse with
wings. But tell me more about where it comes from."

"Oh, mythology somewhere—German or Norse or
something. The Valkyries are the royal guard of Valhalla. Valhalla's the halls of heaven."

"Like angels," Tracey said.

"Not really. Valkyries are strictly female. Only
ladies need apply; all others will be turned away." Liz
glanced at her to see if she understood.

"So more like an honor guard."

For once, Liz didn't make any jokes. "Whatever it
takes to maintain Valhalla, that's what Valkyries do.
They serve the food to everybody up there, and they
learn everything about the deeds of the brave, and
they're experts at war."

"So they do everything," Tracey said. "Heaven's
housekeepers and military elite."

"Everything that's strong and true. Like in the
song. We're supposed to want strength and truth to
abide in us because we're Valkyries." Then Liz corrected
herself. "Valkyries in training."

"Who picked them for the mascot?"

Liz shook her head. "We've always been the Valkyries. Why? Does it bug you because it's not Christian?"

"No. No, I like it. Valkyries are tall—like us, huh?"

Liz laughed. "Sure, I guess so. Tall. Like us." She turned to grab the jug and poured out another drink for each of them. "A little nightcap," she said, handing the cup to Tracey. "And then I better get back to the room. Hang in there."

"I'll be back Saturday morning."

"What will you do over Christmas?" Liz asked.

"Play ball if you'll leave me your key."

"Sure, you bet," Liz said. "Maybe I'll get back early."

"That'd be nice."

"Hey," Liz said.

"Yeah?"

"You see Mrs. Murdoch at the game?"

"That woman who dragged me to Sister Mary by the ear?" Tracey asked. "Why would I look for her?"

"You know, she's a graduate of this place," Liz said.

"Some people like it so much here, they never want to leave."

"She'd be a good person to have on your side, Jac," Liz told her. "You'd like her if you got to know her."

"Liz, she's the person who got me here in jug. And all the way up the field that day, she was telling me how rotten I'd been. Then Mary made me tell her I'm a Christian so Mary could show her I'm nuts or something—"

"But Mrs. Murdoch's like you in a lot of ways," Liz said. "Except she doesn't talk too much."

Tracey shot her a look but said nothing.

"I'll reintroduce you sometime. See you at breakfast."

# FORTY

The Sanctuary of Mary and Joseph became a waste-
land over Christmas. Even Mary was gone most of
the time.

Though packages arrived from Tracey's mother and
from Jean, the presents were of the useful sort—underwear, slips, and a purse. Nothing to eat and nothing to
read. She opened them right away, unable to wait until
Christmas. After the disappointment had worn off, she
was glad she hadn't waited. It would have been worse
on Christmas Day to be surrounded by the handiwork
of Carters, Inc.

After the first bleak day, she got a better hold of
herself. The last remaining boarders left the next
morning, and she went down to the gym.

At first it was hard to practice alone, in such a vast
silence. But it was necessary to concentrate, and she
made herself do it. She played scenes from the ball
games again and again in her mind, and as she ran
down the court with the ball, her work became easier.
She regained her interest in what she was doing and

paid greater attention to the way the coarse orange rubber felt in her hand, to how the ball angled away from her when she bounced it on the floor a certain way, to the perfect curve it made as she leaped for a layup and passed it underhand from left to right or over her head in an arc.

After a short while, she had broken a good sweat, and for the first time, she felt a distinct pleasure in it. It was a sign of hard work, and she was glad she had worked herself without Liz there to urge her on. The wetness of her clothing, the looseness of her muscles, now fully warmed up, suddenly came together in a new familiarity that told her she was improving, making herself a better player. This was the price of progress in basketball.

She varied her routine with shots from the top of the key and outside shots. She even tried a few from the middle-court zone. After that, she practiced rebounding for a while.

She rested and then spent about an hour exploring every corner of the gym. The storage room—or equipment room, as it was sometimes called—was a clutter of old odds and ends. There were floor mats, a horse, heavy climbing ropes with big knots in them, and racks of basketballs, volleyballs, softballs, and other equipment.

After her rest, she went back to the rooms, took a shower—a pleasant luxury in the middle of the day—and wandered over to the retirees' wing for lunch. During the vacation, she had the choice of either the small convent dining table, where the few remaining nuns ate, or the dining room with the older sisters. The main dining hall was closed.

Even Sister James was gone that week, taken for a short leave by a younger brother who was still in good health. But Sister Lucy was there, and Tracey spent her lunch with her. Without Sister James, Sister Lucy wasn't very happy.

"Won't you stay and read a while, dear?" she asked.

Staying with Sister Lucy was the last thing Tracey felt like doing, but the poor old woman asked the favor so plaintively that Tracey heard herself saying, "Of course I will. What can I read for you?"

"I used to teach third grade," Sister Lucy said. "I never have outgrown the books my children loved. Would you read this one for me? I've never read the series before, and one of the other sisters recommended it very highly."

Worse and worse. A little kids' book. Tracey glanced at the cover and guessed from the artwork that the author was British. *The Lion, the Witch, and the Wardrobe*," she said, and thought to herself, *Oh, sure. This should be good.*

Sister Lucy settled down happily to listen, and within a few pages, Tracey herself was captivated by the story. Halfway through the book, when the afternoon shadows were lengthening on the walls of the warm sitting room, she stopped and looked at Sister Lucy's rapt face.

"This is about the Lord," Tracey said.

"Oh, do you see that, dear?" Sister Lucy asked.

"Don't you?"

"The lion is much like the Lord. It makes me feel so inside out."

"Uh, yeah," Tracey said, and she went back to reading. She finished the book that day for Sister Lucy, and it was with some regret that she set it down on a coffee table. It had been a resting spell—a few hours of sweetness and new insights. She wished there were more.

"You read it with such feeling," Sister Lucy said. "Thank you so much, dear. Would you like to read the rest of the set?"

"Set?" Tracey asked.

"There are seven altogether: The Chronicles of Narnia. You may take them with you if you like."

"Don't you want me to read them to you?" Tracey asked.

Sister Lucy beamed. "I want to finish the set, but Linda will be back tomorrow, and she's reading to me from Charles Dickens." Linda, Tracey guessed, was a woman from town who came in to visit the sisters. There were three or four people who traded off reading books to Sister Lucy. The lonely little nun could read well enough on her own. But, Tracey guessed, it was the sharing of the book that was important to her. In that lonely place, the pleasures of companionship were few and scarce. For a guilty moment, Tracey wondered why she loved Sister James so much and Sister Lucy hardly at all.

Still, if Sister Lucy's only vice was that she wanted people to pay attention to her, that didn't seem so bad. Tracey thanked her for the loan of the books, took them, and went back up to the halls in the dimness.

She had some candy and peanut butter and crackers in the room, the latter two items left by Liz. She preferred the privacy of her room and the treasure of the books to the odd loneliness she felt in the company of the sisters at dinner, whom she didn't know.

The second book of the Chronicles didn't disappoint her. She knew they hadn't come to her by accident. Though her faith had failed often in this place, Tracey somehow knew, with a strong and sure knowledge, that the books were a gift to her that Christmas, a token from heaven that her loneliness hadn't been overlooked. They became her favorite books.

The following days repeated the pattern of the first one. Basketball in the mornings, with the workouts becoming longer as the days went by. A kind of desperation to practice seized her, a fear that she would lose her skill. She passed the hour after lunch with Sister Lucy. In the late afternoons and evenings, she stayed in her room and read.

There were a few interruptions. On one day, one of the sisters gave her permission to go into town with one of the volunteers from the retirees' wing. While the woman went to a doctor's appointment, Tracey had the presence of mind to use the hour and a half to run to the town's only department store. She purchased necessities like shampoo and soap and razors. But most of her time she spent picking out presents for Sister James, Liz, her other roommates, and Peggy. She still had money left, so she went to the book section and looked under L for C. S. Lewis, the author of the Chronicles, and purchased four other novels by him.

Loaded down with enough to satisfy herself, Tracey returned to the Sanctuary fortified against the attacks of loneliness and unhappiness.

The only really difficult times were Christmas Eve and Christmas Day. Tracey spent Christmas Eve making her empty room as cheerful as she could, with coffee on in Peggy's coffeepot and a paper plate arranged with Tastykakes from the store. The C. S. Lewis books cheered her a great deal. As long as she was reading, she was all right.

Her mother had given her permission to call collect from the pay phone in the hall. But that night, it seemed harder to call than to stay alone, so she neglected the phone call.

The next day was gray and cheerless. Neither rain nor snow fell, but it remained sullen outside, and Tracey couldn't work herself up to practicing. She passed the day in a sleepy, unhappy languor, and even the books didn't help much. She chose not to go down to the noon meal. The room became dimmer, with only one desk lamp lit, but Tracey neglected to get up and turn on the light switch. She lay half in a brown study and half in a doze until, well after seven, someone tapped on her door.

Tracey got up on her elbows. The knock repeated, and Sister James put her head inside the door. "Tracey?"

"On the bed," Tracey said.

No doubt Sister James could not see her, but she turned in Tracey's direction and smiled. "Merry Christmas, my dear."

Tracey got up, flipped on the light switch, and let Sister James greet her with a hug. "What are you doing back?" she asked.

"I told you it was only for a few days," Sister James said. "Besides, I knew that . . . that Sister Lucy would be unhappy."

"We were both unhappy," Tracey told her.

A brief, almost secret, look of regret crossed the older woman's face before she said, almost lightly, "I thought your parents might ask you home at the last minute."

"No," Tracey said. "But it's all right."

254

"You'll come down and spend Christmas night with two old women?" Sister James asked.

"With two old friends," Tracey said.

She had never been to Sister James's room before. Sister James was the only occupant, and for Christmas, she had persuaded some of the orderlies to bring in a table for her. It was filled with cheeses and baked goods from some of the volunteers. There was tea waiting for them when they arrived. The table was crowned with a spice cake.

"Oh, dear, what took you so long?" Sister Lucy asked when they came in.

"We had to turn out all the lights at the hall," Tracey said.

Sister James laughed. "I turned them all on while I was finding Tracey."

"Well, here we are at Christmas," Sister Lucy said gladly. "What a lovely party."

"And such a lovely guest to have," Sister James added. Though they were safe indoors where there was enough light, her arm was tight around Tracey's waist. Tracey knew her older friend was thinking of her separation from her family. It was never very far from Sister James's mind—a sorrowful, almost incomprehensible thing to this kind, naive old woman who had never had children but loved them. Tonight it weighed on her, and Tracey saw the dim eyes glance at her several times, felt the nun's arm slip around her, or the gnarled fingers take her own fingers in a quick grasp. She didn't know how to tell Sister James that being with her felt better than being with her own family. Even being at home would not have brought the sense of safety that comes with knowing your parents love you. She did not know it. She did not know how to find it out. It was better to be with someone who really did love her.

"Can I pour the tea for you, Sisters?" she asked.

"That would be lovely," Sister James said.

"Can you sing, child?" Sister Lucy asked.

"I'm afraid not," Tracey told her. "But I can read. What about the Christmas story from Luke 2?"

Sister James nodded, and Sister Lucy beamed. After their tea was served and the chapter from the Bible read, they sat close together and talked—Sister James in her worn armchair, and Sister Lucy in an overstuffed chair that had been brought in for her. Tracey sat on an ottoman near Sister James. The two women told stories of the old days, of their childhood Christmases.

Sister James had come from an Irish neighborhood. Her parents were immigrants, and she had entered the convent early, just out of high school. From all she said, Tracey gathered that she had been wild, funny, at times ungentle. Her parents had approved her decision to enter the convent.

Sister Lucy had some trouble remembering exactly when she had entered the order, but she did remember her novitiate clearly. She hedged on her stories about that, and Tracey guessed that, as a young sister, she had felt some strong religious doubts. It was odd to think of Sister Lucy, who seemed very simple even on her best days, putting in any hard thinking on anything.

The evening stretched out and became pleasant. Tracey told no stories of her own. She had only the present, and she was content to live in their pasts for a while, to feel Sister James's hand on her shoulder. If not a merry Christmas, it had at least turned into a happy one, her first at MoJoe.

Liz burst back into the room two days before vacation was over. "Look who's sleeping in my bed!" she
exclaimed, throwing a small, soft bag at Tracey.

Tracey dodged it and rolled off the bed, a grin on
her face. "You didn't expect me to climb all the way up
to the third bunk for two weeks, did you?"

"Not if you were a good girl and practiced while
Momma was away," Liz said.

"Practice?" Tracey asked. She flopped back onto
the bed. "That's just about all I did."

"Oh, I know you, Jacamuzzi. You lollygagged with
James Anne, didn't you?"

"Only in the afternoons. At night I was reading
C. S. Lewis."

"You mean you only practiced in the mornings?"
Liz asked.

"Four or five hours," Tracey said humbly.

The reply surprised Liz. "Oh. Long mornings.
Well, enough of this babble. What'd you get me for
Christmas?"

"Lucky for you, some nurse down at the retirees' wing took me to town," Tracey told her. "Or you'd have gotten sod in your stocking. Your presents are under the bed."

Liz scrambled under the bed. "There's boxes and boxes down here! Which one's mine?"

"All of 'em!" Tracey yelled.

Liz scrambled back out, one of the clumsily wrapped boxes in her hand. She tore off the wrapping. "Hey, Tastykakes! And they're Butterscotch Krimpets!"

"I'll relieve the suspense of opening the nine other boxes," Tracey told her. "They're all Butterscotch Krimpets. From me to you. I searched the whole town for them and bought every box I could find."

"How'd you know they're my favorites?" Liz asked.

Tracey shrugged. "Maybe it's the way you say, 'Man, I sure love Butterscotch Krimpets and coffee' every time we smell the coffee from the nuns' table."

"I see I gave myself away," Liz admitted. "Well?"

"Well what?"

"Aren't you going to ask for your present?"

"Did you get me one?" Tracey asked, feeling a little cautious. She had hoped that Liz would, and that it would be a present that might mean a little more than the underwear and purse from her family.

"Of course I did," Liz said. "But you'll be disappointed, because it's something you need, and it's clothes."

Tracey did feel a stab of disappointment. The only things you needed in a school that had a uniform code were socks and underclothes, or maybe long johns. "I won't be disappointed," she promised, but she forced herself to sound sure.

"Oh, I can see already that you are," Liz said. "Go on, it's not wrapped. It's in that bag I threw at you."

Tracey reached across to the foot of the bed and retrieved the bag. She pulled out the soft contents with a brave smile, but her smile became real as soon as she saw what was inside. "Real sweats," she exclaimed, jumping up. "And they're long enough!"

"As close to our colors as I could get," Liz told her. The running suit was black with white piping and white cuffs.

"It's beautiful!" Tracey said softly, almost reverently.

"I knew you'd be disappointed."

"Oh, cut it out." She would have hugged Liz for the consideration and time she had put into her gift. But a hug was the last thing anybody gave to Liz Lukas, so Tracey made a joke instead. "It really is a lousy present, but I know you did your best, and I really am grateful."

"Now, about those Krimpets—"

Tracey held up a warning finger. "They stay in the cupboard until after the season's over. You know what CPR says about junk food."

"You're nuts!" Liz yelled. She dived under the bed.

"Hey, get out of there!" Tracey yelled.

"Leave me alone, you Italian! Nobody gives me Tastykakes and then says I can't have one." She came out with an armful of boxes.

"You win," Tracey said.

"Let's have some after we practice," Liz suggested. "We've got two days with no classes. Let's make it count."

"That's fine by me," Tracey said.

"I got another surprise for you, *pisano*."

"What's that?"

Liz neatly stacked the boxes on the floor and sat on the other bottom bunk. "We're going to Maddie's house next week."

"Who?"

"Come on, ding-dong. Mrs. Murdoch. The Irish one."

"Are you nuts?" Tracey exclaimed.

"Would you quit it?" Liz asked. "I keep telling you, she's OK."

"She's one of Mary's special little pals."

"I never said that," Liz told her.

"She must be tight with Mary, Liz." Tracey let out her breath in a hard sigh of disgust. "You should have seen the two of them after she dragged me into Mary's office. 'What do you think, Mrs. Murdoch?'" she imitated Mary. "'What should we do with her, Mrs. Murdoch?'"

"There's a reason for Mary doing that," Liz retorted. "If you want to know the truth, I think Mary was trying to embarrass Maddie. Because Maddie's like you. That's what Maddie wants to see you about."

"No," Tracey said. "That's the woman who got me jugged! She never even asked me for my side of the story, Liz. She'll take anything I say right to Mary."

Liz sighed and, for the first time since they had become friends, looked genuinely exasperated with Tracey. "This was really hard for me to work out, Jac," she said through her teeth. "I had to go to Mary."

"And of course she said yes. This is just what Mary wants. Mrs. Murdoch and me, stuck in a room for an entire afternoon."

"We'll be doing housework over there. Sometimes girls can work on a Saturday, baby-sitting or cleaning in town to get money."

"This is a really bad idea," Tracey said. "Mary and Mrs. Murdoch are trying to convince me that I'm crazy. Or evil. Or both."

"That's the stupidest thing I ever heard," Liz told her. "Maddie's really cool. She won't ride your case."

"She dragged me by the ear over the hockey field," Tracey reminded her. "And told me the whole time what I wretch I was. Do you know how many hours I have spent staring at the walls in jug because of Maddie Murdoch?"

"Well, she did catch you fighting, Jac," Liz said. "What'd you want her to do, bet on the winner?"

"I just want to know why you did this," Tracey said. "Does she know I'm coming with you?"

"Yes, and I did it because if you get on the team, you need to get to know Maddie," Liz told her. "And like I keep saying, Maddie Murdoch is like you—with religion and the Bible and all that."

"Liz, no matter what religion she is, she's not the same as me. A person who believes in the Bible wouldn't be caught dead working in a Catholic school, hand in glove with Sister Mary."

"You're wrong, Jac. Look, I wish you'd quit blaming her for catching you in the middle of a fight. Of course it shocked her—"

"She's the one who got me jugged, Liz. Stuck in solitary confinement. It's her fault. And then she had the nerve to tell me that if I was sorry she might still be friends with me. Like she was doing me a favor!"

Liz pressed her lips together. She was, Tracey realized, becoming genuinely angry over Tracey's failure to come around to her point of view. "Maddie is really nice, Tracey, and really high-class. If we go to her house, she'll have us clean for a couple hours; she'll pay us ten dollars each, and she'll give us a nice lunch. While we're doing all that, you can show her you're a nice person too."

"She never even asked me why I was fighting." Tracey's voice sounded sulky, even to herself. She looked down, not willing to argue any more with her mentor, but in her head she repeated to herself that she was not going to prove anything to Maddie Murdoch. She wasn't going to care what Maddie Murdoch thought of her, and she didn't care what Maddie Murdoch believed about the Bible.

Liz took Tracey's silence as unwilling but submissive agreement. "I wish you'd get that brick out of your mouth and say something, like thank you."

"Thank you," Tracey gasped.

"Jacamuzzi, sometimes I wonder why I waste my time doing stuff for you."

Half defensive and half hurt, Tracey picked up the running suit and fingered it gently. "I'm grateful to you for a lot of things," she told Liz. "I'll go with you to her house. It would be worse if I said no after you volunteered me. Mary would never let me forget it. She'd probably engineer another three-way meeting in her office."

Liz looked exasperated for a moment, then confused. She shrugged. "Let's get dressed and go to the gym."

## FORTY - TWO

Tracey just couldn't feel good about going to Maddie Murdoch's house, and there was no way to hide her feelings. Liz became more and more exasperated with her and refused to talk about it. Liz would never risk being proved wrong.

"Just getting it over with seems best," Tracey told Peggy on the Saturday morning after the students returned.

There had been three away games, and Peggy knew who Mrs. Murdoch was. "She drove the team bus one time," Peggy said. "She seemed really nice—sang the cheers with us and wished us luck when we got off. CPR seems real good buddies with her."

"They're all like that," Tracey said glumly.

"Who?"

"You know, the goody-goody women who help out the nuns on school projects and stuff. Junior penguin patrol." The mockery made her feel a little better. Surely there was going to be a lecture, or worse, a thorough scolding once Tracey arrived. Or perhaps Maddie

Murdoch would seek to "help" Tracey, to slowly bleed her with question upon question. And it was all going to end up back in Mary's office.

Peggy laughed. Tracey had grown up calling nuns penguins. With their black-and-white habits and the way some of the fat ones waddled, it was a natural description. But Peggy had never heard them called that.

"You'll get by OK," she said. "Those types always pride themselves on being real patient. If you're as bad at housework as you say, she won't get mad at you."

"No, I guess not. But now Liz's in a bad mood. She bosses me around an awful lot," Tracey complained.

Peggy said nothing, and Tracey felt guilty. She glanced warily at Peggy, and Peggy nodded but still didn't answer.

Tracey sighed heavily. "Just get through it," she told herself out loud. "What a way to spend a Saturday."

"I'll say an Ave for you," Peggy teased.

Tracey gave her a rueful glance. "You believe all that about the statues representing the saints?"

Peggy shook her head. "No way, Jac. I'm not getting into it with you. You go on to Mrs. Murdoch's and leave me with the saints."

Liz looked half sullen and half ferocious that morning as she came up to the room to get Tracey. "Mary said we could go by nine," she said. "Maddie'll pick us up out by Joseph."

"Here I come."

They both had on their uniforms, as the rules dictated, but they carried their work clothes with them. They waited by the statue of Joseph out front. He had one hand raised in benediction, and Liz expertly rolled a fake cigarette, climbed up the base of the statue, and slipped the cigarette into a notch between his fingers.

"Every saint needs to be hip," she said as she got down and admired her handiwork. She glanced at Tracey. "Take the hint. Get loose."

"I'm loose," Tracey said.

"Must be why your fists are clenched."

"I'm loose except for being cold, OK? It's freezing out here."

They were both ready for an argument, but just then Maddie Murdoch pulled up in the station wagon. Liz and Tracey exchanged glances, and then Liz slid into the front seat. The backseats were both down, so Tracey squeezed in next to her.

"Good morning, girls," Mrs. Murdoch said. Her Irish accent was the first thing Tracey noticed again.

They both said good morning, then looked out the front window.

"I hope you had a good Christmas," Mrs. Murdoch said as they pulled out.

"Fine," Liz said.

"Yeah, fine," Tracey added.

"Yours wasn't fine," Liz contradicted her. "You spent it here!"

"It was fine enough," Tracey told her. She felt her face get hot. Liz did not know that Sister Mary had told Mrs. Murdoch that Tracey used religion only to be disruptive. This nitpicking of Liz's was making her out to be a liar now too.

Liz pursued it. "You told me it was boring."

"All right, it was boring!" Tracey leaned forward to look at Mrs. Murdoch. "Excuse me, I had a boring Christmas." She could just imagine the woman carrying this amazing conversation to Mary. The two of them would make capital out of it. "*So you thought it was a*

265

*boring Christmas, Miss Jacamuzzi?"* That's just how Mary would begin with her.

She looked out the window for the rest of the drive, while Liz carried on the conversation with Maddie Murdoch alone. Tracey didn't care. She wasn't going to talk if Liz was going to be arguing and contradicting her.

"Well," Mrs. Murdoch said as they pulled into the driveway of her house, "I thought we might do some general housecleaning today. As soon as you change, I'll get you both set up."

And she'll separate us, Tracey suddenly realized. Whatever was going on, whatever Liz's dumb reasons were for bringing her out on this trip, she knew that Liz hadn't done it to get her into trouble. But suddenly it seemed as though getting into trouble was very likely.

The house was small and pretty—three bedrooms downstairs, a big living room, a kitchen, and a dining room. The entire upstairs was an attic. At the top of the steps was a door of normal size, but it lay flat as part of the ceiling over the first floor. You had to reach up to turn the knob, open it like a trapdoor, and then walk up through it into the attic. Mrs. Murdoch noticed Tracey's glance at this curious bit of house design.

"Levitt designed these houses," she said. Tracey recognized the name. He was an architect and housing development planner. "The attic is made to be easily converted into upstairs rooms."

Tracey gave a dumb nod, and Liz shot her another look of annoyance, which Tracey returned with an annoyed look of her own. Maddie Murdoch hadn't said anything that needed an answer, had she? But it was obvious that she'd been watching Tracey, closely enough to see her curious look at the door.

266

"My friend must have been born in a test tube," Liz apologized. "You have a nice house."

"I never meant to say you didn't," Tracey began, but Maddie Murdoch interrupted her.

"It's all right, girls. Why not change first? Liz, you could do the vacuuming if you like, and, Tracey, would you do the bathroom, please? I'll be doing the laundry."

They both said yes and quickly changed into their work clothes. Without another word to Liz, Tracey went to the bathroom down the hall. She saw that there was another bathroom attached to the master bedroom. She would clean them both. If only Mrs. Murdoch would let her be.

She found the cleaning supplies under the sink in the first bathroom. First she wiped everything down, and then she started on the toilet. By that time, she was in such a bad mood that she didn't even care if Mrs. Murdoch thought she did a bad job. She'd do her best and then try to leave as soon as possible.

From out front, she heard the buzz of the vacuum cleaner, and, fainter and farther away, the rumble of a washing machine. The rhythm of her own cleaning helped her relax a little, and the sounds around her were familiar, almost homelike, at least in her imagination. She finished the inside of the toilet and started on the outside, crouching in front of the bowl and working away with the sponge and cleanser.

"There's a hard worker," Mrs. Murdoch said. Tracey nearly jumped out of her skin. She looked up. Of course, Liz had to stay with the vacuum, but Mrs. Murdoch would be free to do other things while the laundry ran.

"Thanks," Tracey said. She looked back at the toilet, willing in her mind for the woman to go away.

Instead, Maddie Murdoch took a step into the bathroom. Tracey ignored her, but she could see her at the edge of her vision. Mrs. Murdoch was a tall woman, taller than Tracey, but not with the same kind of tallness. Where Tracey had little skill and grace in walking and carrying herself, Maddie Murdoch had lots of it. She stood easily, walked easily, even picked up laundry with a certain grace that only tall people can possess, though few of them do.

It set Tracey even more on edge. She was used to the rough-and-ready friendliness of Liz, and there was a way the nuns carried themselves that she under-stood. But the mix of bigness—long hands, long legs, even broad shoulders and a face with high cheekbones and a strong jaw—combined with slimness, grace, and a kind of big-eyed prettiness—these were an odd com-bination to Tracey.

Maddie Murdoch awakened another feeling in Tracey, a new feeling of shame about herself. Her mother's sin was not the grand darkness Tracey had sometimes thought, but only the cheap sin of a cheap woman. And Tracey had done cheap, vulgar things—nothing involving sex, but the fights, the cigarettes, the lies. It was all cheapness and vulgarity. Maddie Murdoch had seen the worst of Tracey's bad behavior. And she had seen to it that Tracey should be sent away: locked up, kept in jug.

Tracey pushed her bitter shame away, not compre-hending why she could not keep it back. She pumped her hand energetically back and forth on the outside of the toilet bowl, but it was no good. Maddie Mur-doch was still standing in the bathroom. If she came a step closer, Tracey knew she would have to jump up.

She didn't want this stranger near her. The questions would be coming any minute now.

"Your friend Liz must have gotten up on the wrong side of the bed this morning." Another step closer.

Tracey jumped up. "Liz's all right," she said without looking at Mrs. Murdoch.

"She tells me that you've had quite a time at the Sanctuary."

"It doesn't matter," Tracey said.

To her surprise, chagrin, and alarm, Mrs. Murdoch stepped even closer. Tracey backed up, still not looking her in the eye, and Mrs. Murdoch stopped, as though surprised that Tracey would retreat. She hesitated and then tried another tack. "The sophomores used to boss us freshmen around too."

"Liz's OK," Tracey said again.

"I was sorry to hear that you stayed at the school over Christmas, dear. I might have had you over if I had known. I wish she had called me sooner."

Something inside Tracey broke. "Would you please leave Liz alone?" she said, and this time she looked the woman in the eye. "She never hurt you."

Her rough answer startled Mrs. Murdoch, and Tracey felt a rush of relief. She would do anything to stop the questions, to stop this person from interrogating her. She would get in trouble from this anyway, so she might as well make sure Maddie Murdoch never asked her back.

"Dear, I didn't mean—"

"Don't call me that!" Tracey exclaimed. This was another surprise to the woman. While she was speechless, Tracey followed up on it. "I know full well you wanted me here today. What do you want?"

"Why are you so angry with me?" Mrs. Murdoch asked.

That was a prime question. It would force Tracey to accuse her—no, not force—coax Tracey into saying it all, into committing to words her grievances. Mary had worked that strategy on her once and nearly succeeded. If Tracey named anything, she could be held to it and punished for it, told she was a megalomaniac again.

She decided not to confront Mrs. Murdoch about her talebearing to the sisters. Tracey suspected that she had told more of them about her black eye, but only Sister James had ever said anything about it. Instead, Tracey talked about what could not be hidden, denied, or left unmentioned. "I know what you saw me do, and I know what Mary said, but there was more that you never saw," she began. She had no intention of giving Mrs. Murdoch the details, but perhaps she could give her some idea that other things were going on at the school, without naming anybody.

"And did that justify striking another person?" Mrs. Murdoch asked softly.

Tracey saw that the shamefulness of it was still very real to Mrs. Murdoch. For a moment she remembered the horrible night in the bushes, when the thong had slipped off and pain had exploded in her arm. She was lost in the ring of faces over her. She didn't know what to say. Nobody should ever hurt a person the way they had hurt her. Wasn't fighting against that necessary?

"Did it?" Mrs. Murdoch asked again.

"Yes," Tracey said clearly. "Yes, it did."

"Tell me why," Mrs. Murdoch said.

Tracey looked at her, unexpectedly drawn by her request, surprised at how much she did want to tell what they had done to her. It was an unexpected, wrenching desire: *Pour it all out.* But she couldn't, and she knew she couldn't. For a moment she was torn between her grief and her resolution.

"Do you have no answer?" Mrs. Murdoch asked. There was a hint of satisfaction in her voice.

"Yes, I do," Tracey exclaimed suddenly. Sudden anger replaced the longing she had felt for a moment. This woman, a hundred times more subtle than Sister Mary, a hundred times more engaging, had nearly gotten it out of her, made her commit it all into words. Being beaten. Being trash. It was a story Mrs. Murdoch would carry to the sisters with that same blind sense of doing the right thing. She was so satisfied that she was good and right. "I have an answer," Tracey said, "but not for you. You saw what you saw. You got me in trouble. You got me jugged. What more do you want? I will answer to God for what I did, but I won't answer to you again for it!"

"Tracey—"

The shame of that walk across the field rushed over Tracey, just as fresh as it had been on that day, and it was followed by furious anger. "You saw me fight, and you've punished me more than I deserved. Sitting in jug, and I'll have to keep going there for as long as I'm here. What does it take to satisfy you? Isn't what you've done to me enough?"

Her eyes were suddenly wet, and a horror that she might cry stopped her instantly. For a moment she was frozen as she willed back the unexpected tears. Maddie Murdoch was also stopped cold.

Tracey finally regained control of herself. She had

to stop pouring out her anger and grief. "I want to go back," she said. "Back to the hall."

Mrs. Murdoch hesitated. Tracey could see pity in her face, the pity that any do-gooder would feel for a wayward student. But there was also a hint of sternness, as though Mrs. Murdoch felt some duty to rebuke her for this latest rudeness, and there was confusion, as though she wasn't sure what to do.

"I didn't want to come," Tracey said. "Liz made me. I know you told her to bring me." Sudden fear took hold of her as she realized how alone she was in this strange place. What if Mrs. Murdoch refused to take her back right away? What if she continued to confront her over all that she had done and said?

"I did ask her," Mrs. Murdoch said.

"Take me back," Tracey repeated.

"All right, then," Mrs. Murdoch said quietly.

Out front, the vacuum stopped, and Tracey heard Liz whistling. Mrs. Murdoch went to get her keys. Tracey let out her breath and realized that a cold film of sweat had rushed over her. She stayed where she was until Mrs. Murdoch appeared again in the doorway, keys in hand.

"I'm sorry," the woman said in a very low voice. "I didn't mean to frighten or offend you."

Tracey still didn't dare say anything that would pull her into a conversation. "Just take me back," she said.

"I only meant to help you—" Mrs. Murdoch began again.

"Please," Tracey exclaimed.

"All right," she said quietly. "We'll go now."

# FORTY-THREE

The brown and green of the ground passed under her feet in a blur. Her own huffing blocked out the sound of the evening crows and the distant drone of a chain saw. Nothing seemed real but the ground beneath her, the loveliness of her black-and-white running suit, and the cold burning of the air in her lungs.

Over the sound of her breathing, she heard Liz's voice, faint and high, calling for her to stop. But Tracey didn't stop. She just wanted to run. Why did Liz bring her there? Normally sensible Liz—

"Jac, you stop or I'll knock your head off!"

Tracey glanced back and quickened her pace. Liz was closing the distance between them in the afternoon twilight.

"I said, slow down!"

Tracey pushed harder, but she'd been running a mile and a half, and Liz had just come out.

Tracey felt the tackle take her at the waist and heard Liz's grunt as the big girl brought her down. They fell to the ground and rolled apart.

"What's gotten into you?" Liz yelled. "Why didn't you stop?"

"Couldn't," Tracey gasped, panting.

"You're an idiot sometimes, Jacamuzzi!"

"Liz!" Tracey said. "Maybe you ought to go give your orders to someone else. I didn't slow down because I didn't feel like slowing down." She stood up to start running again.

"Well, what if I asked?" Liz said suddenly.

Tracey, huffing and puffing, caught herself and looked back down at Liz. For once the older girl showed some indication of hurt feelings, and Tracey remembered again all that she owed her.

"What did you want from Maddie Murdoch?" Tracey exclaimed, hands out in desperation, as though she would have grabbed the answer from Liz if she could.

"What happened?" Liz asked. "I thought it was a great morning. And then suddenly we're back in the car." Her puzzlement seemed sincere. "Didn't you like her?"

"No, I didn't like her," Tracey said. "For starters, she had enough to say about you."

"What'd she say about me?" Liz asked.

"Said you boss me around—"

"I do boss you around."

"Well, quit bossing me around!" Tracey yelled. Her own anger took her by surprise. She had never imagined that she would yell at Liz.

Liz looked surprised too, but all she said was, "I'll try, OK?" And then she added, "But you need some bossing to be a good player."

"You can still do it, just not so much." Tracey slowed her breathing. "I'm sorry I yelled," she said.

"What else happened with Maddie?"

"I just told her to cool it," Tracey said. "To leave me alone. That's all I want."

"Tracey!" Liz exclaimed, genuinely shocked. Tracey had never seen Liz reveal shock to anyone. The sense that she'd done something dreadful hit her, but she forced it away.

"What?" Tracey asked.

"You told Maddie Murdoch that? Were you rude to her?"

"What do you care about being rude?" Tracey asked.

"You were, weren't you?" Liz asked. "Man, what were you thinking?"

"Oh, Liz! I was in trouble all over again the minute I walked into that house. There was no getting away from it. I wanted her to leave me alone."

Liz stood up. "Tracey, she's one of you! She's a what-you-call-it."

"Italian?" Tracey asked, puzzled.

"No. You know, the Bible and all of that."

"She graduated from here," Tracey said. "And whatever nutty cult or religious movement she's into, it's not like what I believe. She is still serving the Roman Catholic Church."

"And in four years you'll graduate from here," Liz said. "Tracey, she converted about five years ago."

"To Baptist?"

"I don't know. Something like you. She used to have a Bible study with some of the girls once a week down in the little chapel, but Mary told Father Bing to put a stop to it."

"She goes around this campus telling the nuns

275

about the girls—about me, anyway," Tracey objected. "Liz, she's the one who got me jugged."

"One time, she told one sister one thing about you, Tracey!" Liz exclaimed. "For all you know, that's the only person she ever told." She threw up her hands. "I could see you had a black eye under all that makeup. Anybody could see it. It wasn't like Maddie was telling a big secret. She went and told Sister James something everybody else on the campus could see and asked her to go make you feel welcome."

"You don't know that it was just James Anne," Tracey said, but she felt shocked at this version of the story—shocked, and dismayed to realize that the makeup had not fooled most people.

"Well, why didn't you just ask Maddie who she told?" Liz asked. "And for crying out loud—she comes on you in the field punching the daylights out of Scooter. What did you expect her to do?"

"She blamed me for it," Tracey said, lowering her head. "She wouldn't listen to me."

"No, Tracey, Mary blamed you for it while Maddie just stood there," Liz said. "OK, Maddie was shocked, and maybe she was disgusted, but I was there when she marched you off. You were still yelling at Scooter. You didn't try to calm down and talk to Maddie. You didn't ask her to hear your side. You just wanted to hit Scooter some more. Everybody could see that. So what was Maddie supposed to think?"

Tracey had not considered this way of looking at it. Liz pushed the point. "When Mary started on all that stuff about religion, it would have just embarrassed Maddie. That's what Mary was trying to do, getting her little digs on Maddie because Maddie's the same religion as you are."

"No, Liz, that can't be right," Tracey said.

"What did Maddie say when Mary was making fun of you?" Liz asked.

"Nothing." With a sharp pang, Tracey remembered Mrs. Murdoch's curious silence when Mary had asked her advice. Had the mockery really been coming just from Mary? Would Sister Mary really be that arrogant? If so, then no wonder Mrs. Murdoch had seemed embarrassed. Mary had paraded Tracey in front of her as a failure of Mrs. Murdoch's religion.

Tracey began to feel in earnest that she had done something dreadful.

"Look, it was Maddie that asked me to watch out for you," Liz said. "And don't start that stuff about Maddie telling other people about you. Whatever happened in Mary's office, it upset Maddie. She came back to the field to find me. She was really shaken up. For you."

"Maddie Murdoch did that?" Tracey asked.

"Sure. That's why I decided to take you on," Liz said. "I'd already decided I liked you when I saw you fight Scooter. Then Mrs. Murdoch asked me—you know."

"Asked you what? To make friends with me?" Tracey's face started to burn. "That's why you made me your roommate?"

"I'd already decided to make friends with you. As soon as you started punching Scooter, I knew there was more to you than all that religion stuff. But yes, that's what Maddie asked me."

"You never told me that," Tracey said. "Liz, why didn't you tell me that?"

Liz looked sheepish. "I didn't want you to think I was just being nice to you because somebody asked me to," she said. "I really liked you once I got to know you better. I thought it would hurt your feelings if I ever told you about her asking me."

"But when she came out on the field and asked you, did she tell you what I'd said to her?"

"Jacamuzzi, you idiot!" Liz exclaimed. "No. She didn't. She wasn't telling on you, she was trying to help you. Why can't you be grateful to her?"

"Is she really Protestant?" Tracey asked.

"She believes the Bible, and she's always talking about the Resurrection and how there's room at the cross for you and all that. Just like you," Liz told her. "Only, Maddie's got more tact."

"I thought she was in good with Mary."

Liz put a patronizing hand on her shoulder. "She is in good with Mary. She has to be to do anything here."

Tracey shook her off. "Leave me alone." She took a step away. "I don't understand. We're not supposed to have ties with Roman Catholicism. What's she doing here, volunteering at a Catholic school?"

"Good," Liz said. "She's doing good. Jac, this is the dumbest thing you've done. Even I like Maddie Murdoch!"

"I wish you'd leave me alone," Tracey said. She shook her head. First the torture, then the fight, then Mary's accusations—now this. And somehow Maddie Murdoch was seeing it all—seeing right through Tracey. Sudden shame sent a red flush over her face.

"Hey," Liz said and took her arm.

"Please, Liz—"

"Don't send me away," Liz said. "I'm sorry I yelled at you. Come on back. We'll give her a call."

"No," Tracey said. "I said too much to her."

"What did you say?" Liz asked.

"Never mind. And there's other things. She's still mad about the fight, Liz. She's never going to understand that. You know she's not. She wants reasons. Explanations. That fight really disgusted her."

Liz gave a slight nod, forced to agree. "It's true that she doesn't know what goes on here."

"I really told her off," Tracey said. "First the fight, and then I tell her off. Twice."

"Maybe you could work that out," Liz said.

"Maybe." She remembered coming so close to telling Mrs. Murdoch all of it—the pain, the ring of faces. And behind that, the other pain: falling down the stairs. She closed it off abruptly in her mind. "No," she said. "It's like the Murphys. If she started out being nice to me and then got tired of it, or disgusted, or moved away, I don't think I could go through that again."

Liz didn't answer, but Tracey realized the older girl wasn't angry with her anymore. "I don't think Maddie would treat you like those Murphy people did," she said after a moment.

"Maddie must have children of her own," Tracey said. "I can never matter very much to somebody who has her own children. Good, well-behaved kids, I mean. And I know one thing about church people: Kids like me embarrass them. They start out trying to help us, and then they find out it doesn't work the way it does on TV. They give up after a while."

Head down, Liz remained silent, heeding Tracey's analysis yet not entirely convinced.

"What would you do," Tracey asked her, "if Mrs. Murdoch came along and wanted to know everything about you? And I mean everything. You never even tell me what you're thinking, and you're my best friend."

"I'd put her off," Liz admitted. "Maybe." She looked up at Tracey. "I forgot about what they did. The Deep Six. I forgot a lot. I thought everything would be OK if you two just talked. But you're right. You can't tell her everything. And she would want to know."

They were silent, and then Liz said, "Let's go have some coffee or something." They walked back in the cold twilight, both silent and regretful.

# PART THREE

SOPHOMORE YEAR

The first concern as the school year drew to its close was the May procession. Tracey was already familiar with all of the ritual and celebration associated with May, the Blessed Virgin's month, as it was called. At St. Anne's she had been among the dutiful congregation of singers who stood by and watched, then knelt when the May queen came up the center aisle with the flower crown for the statue of Mary, the mother of Jesus.

May queens at St. Anne's had usually been the prettiest girls, or girls who possessed a combination of beauty and good grades. Of course, the rank of May queen had always gone to an eighth-grader. At MoJoe, the sisters selected a senior whose moral character was above reproach. Anyway, that was what they said they based their judgments on.

"Seems like whoever grades papers for Madeleine gets it most of the time," Liz had observed one morning when they'd been getting ready for class. "And," she'd added with a glance at Tracey that was part grimace, "I ain't never seen an ugly May queen."

Neither had Tracey. But she hardly cared. She felt sure that Sister Mary would be watching her. Everyone at MoJoe had to at least walk with the May procession, an obligation Tracey could not find an objection to. It wasn't sinful to walk around the school grounds. But she was adamant that she would not sing, she would not say the rosary, and she would not kneel to the statue when it was crowned.

For once, St. Bernard actually pleaded with her. "Don't give Sister Mary grist for her mill," St. Bernard had begged, shocking Tracey with both her tone and her frankness. She saw the shock on Tracey's face. "See there," she added hurriedly, "look at what you drive me to say. Dear, I hate to see you in trouble, and think of what Sister James will go through if you stay so stubborn." She lowered her voice to a whisper. "Sister Mary was furious over how you got out of prayer and meditation, Tracey."

"Serves her right," Tracey said with a flare of anger and equal frankness.

"Listen to me, Tracey. You will never top Sister Mary," St. Bernard told her. "Please. I'm not asking you to worship what you won't worship, or even to kneel down if you don't think you can. Just carry the rosary in your hand, walk with the procession, and keep your head down. Behave yourself."

In the end, St. Bernard's earnestness moved Tracey to agree. She had doubts about carrying the rosary, and she probably would have refused if St. Bernard had tried to force her into carrying it. But—for that year's May procession, anyway—she carried the rosary given to her and walked in line with the girls.

When it came time to kneel to the larger-than-life-size statue of Mary on the grounds, Tracey didn't kneel. She did flop to a sitting position to stay out of Sister Mary's sight. Her sullenness in doing it sent waves of giggles through the crowd of freshmen around her. Few of them took the May procession seriously, and speculation had been high as to what Tracey would do for the religious celebration that—at MoJoe, anyway—was more important than Easter or any other holy day.

But the day ended safely, and it marked only another week until graduation.

Some girls stayed for summer school at MoJoe, but Tracey was the only one who would board through the entire summer. It was made clear to her that she would be expected to work: six hours a day making the gymnasium spotless, even down to stripping and polishing the floor.

"What are you doing this summer?" she asked Liz a few days before commencement.

Liz was busy cramming for an English exam, but she looked up and said, "Oh, Mommy and Daddy and little Lizzy are taking off for three months' imprisonment in New England, up in the mountains."

"Sounds great," Tracey said wistfully. Inwardly, she wished her older friend would invite her along, at least for a week or two. But Liz had not shown the slightest inclination to do so.

"Oh, sure," Liz said sarcastically. "Us and a cabin and a lake, and nothing else."

"It's better than this," Tracey pointed out.

"Hardly. They'll want me to go to dances in town once a week, and Mom'll try to drag me off to stupid teas and luncheons until I manage to get her mad enough and tired enough to quit it and leave me alone."

"You don't like teas and lunches?" Tracey asked, but even as she asked it, she realized how stupid she herself would feel at a tea or luncheon. It would be about as bad as being at Maddie Murdoch's. The same feeling, in fact. Out of place.

Liz read her thoughts and gave a grim nod. "Somehow, small-and-lovely Mommy and small-and-lovely Daddy gave birth to big-and-homely Liz, the last of the Polish peasants."

"Come on, Liz," Tracey began.

"I mean it, Jac. I don't know how it happened, but I'm a throwback. Both my parents are gorgeous and short, and here I am. They can't deal with it any more than I can. They just try to pretend I'm beautiful for vacations and holidays, and then they let me go back here and do what I like—basketball and sports." She turned back to her book. "Now, come on, kid. I gotta study."

"Will you write to me?" Tracey asked.

Liz turned around and gave her a grin that was, for once, not entirely put on. "Sure, I'll write. I'm good at that. And you better write back."

"Sure," Tracey said.

Most of the students left immediately after graduation, and everybody else was gone by the afternoon of the next day. One pleasant surprise was that most of the sisters left too. Even many of the retirees went away, at least for short vacations or retreats. Sister Mary completely disappeared: four weeks for a visit to her family, a two-week administrator's seminar, a two-week yearbook seminar, and two weeks for a retreat.

She wouldn't return until just before school started again.

Tracey had known before her tasks in the gym started that nobody could clean like Catholic nuns. That was because nobody could work like Catholic nuns. She had learned the Catholic work ethic in St. Anne's, where endless drills, drills, drills had not been superseded by tricks like audiovisual aids, filmstrips, and field trips until Tracey's eighth-grade year. MoJoe's spotlessly clean hallways, bathrooms, and cafeteria; the immaculate grounds; and the daily, weekly, and monthly inspections in the boarders' rooms all reinforced the work ethic.

One of Tracey's first jobs in the gym was cleaning the Peg-Boards in the equipment room with cotton swabs. And one of her worst jobs was cleaning the toilets in the gym because she had to clean every inch thoroughly, even under the rims. Sister St. Gerard kindly provided her with a box of toothbrushes for this job.

She knew that complaint was useless. Besides, while she worked and sweated in the hot gym, she knew that St. Bernard herself—Ph.D. and all—was sweating and toiling in the huge garden behind the main buildings. St. Bernard usually worked in her habit until afternoon. Her order was a conservative one that didn't approve of changing out of the habit. CPR was the only sister at MoJoe who spent any length of time in ordinary clothing.

The other nuns, all of them, had chores to do over the summer. And they spent a full day working, whereas Tracey only had to put in six hours and could put in any six she chose. She usually got up at five and worked from six until noon, trying to avoid the awful heat of the afternoon. Every day one of the sisters came in several times to check on her.

After her work for the day was over, she took a shower, usually in the gym locker room, and changed into clean clothes to join Sister James Anne for lunch in the retirees' wing by twelve-thirty. During the summer, Tracey's uniform was not mandatory, and it was nice to wear what she liked for meals. She usually spent an hour or two with her older friend, reading to her or talking, and sometimes walking if the weather wasn't too hot.

Then it was time to practice. Even the hot outside court was often cooler than the gym in the afternoons. After supper and a walk with James Anne, Tracey returned for her harder, longer practice session that lasted from about seven o'clock until dark.

If the summer wasn't a lot of fun, it was at least peaceful. She could sleep late on Saturdays and Sundays, and she had plenty of time to read.

One day in July, during the hardest part of cleaning the gym—the weeks of stripping the ancient floor by hand—Tracey came walking by the retirees' wing to tell Sister James that she was too tired to stop for lunch. It had been a hot, sticky job all morning, and she only wanted to take a nap. Liz had left peanut butter and crackers in her room, and that would suffice if she got hungry.

Tracey was directed by one of the nurses to the screened-in porch at the back of the wing. Tracey went out back and stepped onto the wide porch. Sister James was the only one there. In spite of the rising heat, she sat, composed and without a sign of discomfort, in her habit and veil. Many of the older sisters, especially the infirm ones, didn't wear their habits most of the time. But Sister James did. Tracey had never seen her in anything else.

She sat gazing out across the grounds, as though she could see the grass and flowers. Tracey doubted that she could. The screens on the porch were probably enough to close in Sister James's poor vision. But the breezes were alive that hot day, and they carried the fresh, hot smell of drying grass. The noise of a chain saw came whirring over the faint wind. Sister James loved life and the outdoors. Even when she couldn't see much, she was still able to appreciate it.

"Sister," Tracey said softly.

Sister James turned. "Tracey? Is it lunchtime, dear?"

"No, I was coming to beg off," Tracey said. She stepped closer. "I'm wiped out from that gym floor." When Sister James held up a gnarled hand to find her, Tracey reached out and took it.

"Can you sit beside me a minute?" Sister James asked.

"Sure." Tracey flopped into a porch chair alongside her. "I was afraid I might be intruding on you."

"You, dear? Never. Oh, my, you've been sweating."

"Uh-oh, do I smell?" Tracey nearly stood up. Her T-shirt was wet with sweat down the front and back.

"No, no, sit down. I only felt it on your arm."

Tracey settled back and looked at Sister James's dark eyes as the old woman serenely gazed out at the screens.

"I'll come down for supper," Tracey said. "And we can walk tonight. I'm just all worn out right now."

"I understand. You can take a night off if you like."

"No way. I have to have my walk." Tracey laughed.

Though Sister James, like most of the nuns, was not often demonstrative, she put her nearest hand up on Tracey's shoulder.

Tracey looked at her again. "Can I ask you something?"

"Anything, dear."

"Do Sister St. Gerard and Sister Mary not like each other?"

The question obviously startled Sister James. She was silent for a minute. At last she said, "You know, dear, that Sister Mary has asked me about you several times."

"Yeah, I know," Tracey said.

"And I felt that I could not discuss you with her. We approach you from two different avenues. I felt that I had your confidence."

"You do," Tracey said.

Sister James nodded and turned to Tracey. "And so, dear, I must play fairly. It would be gossip to discuss Sister St. Gerard's relationship to Sister Mary."

Tracey blushed a little under the gentle rebuke. "You're right," she said. "I'm sorry."

Sister James patted her shoulder. "It's all right. I know that you don't ever want to use the enemy's weapons, dear."

Tracey sat with her a minute or two longer, then went up to her room and the shower. But the memory of that mild lesson stayed with her.

The gym was finished by early August, but there was nobody around to tell Tracey what to do next. She wandered around the halls for a while, offering to help the two or three remaining sisters with whatever they needed. There was not much work for anyone to do.

Her duty satisfied, she spent her mornings in the gym, practicing. For most of the summer she had practiced outside in the evenings when the daytime heat had abated somewhat. But "out of sight, out of mind" seemed the best policy, even during the summer at MoJoe, and she realized that staying in the gym was probably her wisest course of action. Mary would be back any day, and Tracey dreaded the idea of being the only person around to undergo Mary's scrutiny.

Her morning practices were hard and earnest, for the days were running out on her. By this time, the ball came easily to her hand, either left or right, and she was jumping better. Her shooting was the least promising thing about her skills, but she felt confident about moving around with the ball. Days and days of practicing, either alone or with only one other person, had made her emphasize dexterity. She already knew how to roll around a player, either to make a quick pass or to receive one. And she understood the concept of making herself a shield in front of an opponent to allow one of her teammates a quick, unhampered shot.

But the best feeling, the one she thought would be most valuable, was her familiarity with the ball itself. It was like an extension of her hand, and when it went from hand to floor and back again, her hand always seemed to know where it was and how it would come up again. She could dribble without thinking about it, and her mind and eyes were free to look up the court, make plans, and pass.

She continued to take her lunches with Sister James Anne. Now that the hottest part of the summer was ending, they had many walks together after the supper hour, before Tracey went back to the outside court to practice shooting before bed.

The books in the retirees' wing tended to be more interesting than what could be found in the school's library. Tracey read several that were new to her. Already, her supplies of C. S. Lewis were exhausted. But she discovered the allegorical fantasies of George Macdonald: *Phantastes* and *Lilith*. These books were hard to understand, but there were moments when she felt as though a window to greater and lovelier things had been briefly opened by them, then closed before her slower wits could comprehend what she was seeing.

Sister James could make nothing of MacDonald, and Tracey gave up reading him to her. The older sister was unable to illuminate her about his messages. After only a few chapters of one of the books, Sister Lucy commented, "He is talking, dear, about something more alive than we are—those worlds that are good as opposed to our world—our shadowy world."

"Yes, I think that's it," Sister James said.

"Holiness," Sister Lucy said after a moment of thought.

"I think so, Lucy," Sister James said. "Something brighter and better and bigger somehow. Oh my, all B's. Well, I was clever and didn't know it."

Tracey didn't understand what they were saying, but she asked no more questions.

Alone in her room, she thought about it more. To her, holiness had been the dimness in the Catholic church sanctuaries. The idealized plaques of the Stations of the Cross, standing out in relief from the walls, the kneeling and the murmuring and the long tapers. In fact, since her conversion, she had thought very much about God being good, but not at all about Him being holy. The rituals of the Mass were now repulsive to her, and because she had equated those things with holiness, it also had become repulsive.

Now, it seemed, her equation was wrong. Holiness spelled out something bigger and better and more alive than what was here. Something that made this world, by contrast, a shadowy region.

These were strange new thoughts, and her only resort was to turn to her Bible, which had a small concordance in the back, and to find out exactly what holiness meant. She had linked it to silence and rigidity and things forbidden to humans—generally dull or unpleasant in its scope. Well, she would search and see.

Aside from her questions about holiness, Tracey made very little progress in her Bible reading over the summer. It was easy to do at least a chapter a day, but she was intimidated by books like Leviticus and Numbers. She had the idea that Ezekiel was supposed to ring with grandeur, but it made no sense to her. In the end, she stayed with the New Testament and reread the Epistles.

Liz's letters had come steadily, one a week. But by the tenth day of August, Tracey had gone a week and a half without hearing anything from her. Instead of making her impatient or increasing her loneliness, the silence raised her hopes. Sure enough, as she practiced in the gym the next day, she heard a thunderous rattling of the locked glass doors. She ran to let Liz in.

Even Liz couldn't complain when Tracey threw one arm around her quickly and yelled, "You're back! I knew you'd be coming!"

"Aw, shucks, pilgrim." She was in street clothes with her gym bag over her shoulder.

"Hurry up and get dressed," Tracey said.

"Well, I was going to," Liz told her. "But then I did some figuring, and I realized that you probably haven't been out of this place all summer."

"I wish," Tracey said.

"So I'll get changed, but we'll skip campus a while." She headed toward the dressing room.

"Are we allowed to?" Tracey asked. "Out of uniform?"

"Those rules apply only during terms," Liz said. "I guess we could ask permission to go bike riding, but there's no one around to ask. We won't get in trouble. Mary won't be back for three more days."

Tracey followed her. "You been gone all summer and you already know when Mary's getting back?"

"I saw the school secretary up at the main hall and asked her. She gave me the key to the bike barn."

Every now and then, select groups of seniors went biking on field trips in the autumn and spring. Tracey had never wondered where the boarders got the bikes from.

After Liz changed, she led Tracey up the small hill to the main hall, then out back to where several old sheds stood locked. She opened the door to one, throwing it wide open to reveal a dozen bicycles in various states of repair.

"The blue one's in good shape. That one with the rusted frame doesn't look like much, but it won't lose its chain, anyway."

"Where will we go?" Tracey asked.

"Town's five miles. How about that?"

"Sounds great. Let's attach baskets and find some locks."

They collected their money from the dorm room, where Liz had also stashed her luggage. Then they found the baskets, bicycle locks, and chains in one of the other sheds and peddled out together, with Tracey on a blue three-speed and Liz on the rusted boy's bike.

"I hate to sound disloyal," Tracey called over the sound of the breeze, "but this sure beats basketball."

"For now," Liz called back.

That trip became the first of many. Liz was well acquainted with the local flora and fauna, having stayed in town for a few days at various intervals when her parents had picked her up for vacations. Tracey learned something else about the Sanctuary of Mary and Joseph: It was situated in beautiful countryside. The town was small and old, and on the west side of it lay farmlands and tall, narrow houses that came right up to the narrow roads.

Already in mid-August, some of the trees had lost their fresh greenery and showed touches of scarlet and gold. Tracey realized that her second year at MoJoe was approaching fast. The knowledge came down on her like a weight, but then she glanced over at Liz. A new year meant new chances at everything.

Jacamuzzi, in for Willis."

CPR blasted one shrill note on the whistle. "Willis out, Jacamuzzi in. Go on, go on," she ordered. Tracey came to the line with a confused look around to see who Willis was and what position she'd been playing. The coach nodded to Scooter. "Bring it in."

"Sure, come on in, Jacamuzzi," Scooter said with a sneer, the ball poised in her hand to pass in.

"No, you come in," Liz called out. "We ain't got all day. Bring it in."

Tracey still wasn't sure of her position, but she stepped onto the court. Scooter passed to one of her own teammates, and Tracey sailed between the girl and the ball, caught the pass, and passed off to Liz. Scooter bumped into her and jostled her.

The petty revenge drove a flush of anger across Tracey's cheeks, but she smothered the feelings as she tore down the court after Liz.

"Get to your zones!" CPR yelled as the knot of girls ran in disarray after the ball.

Liz got to the basket first and did a layup that missed. Tracey came down in time to jump for the rebound, caught it on the tips of her fingers, and inexpertly pushed it up to the basket. It bounced off the bottom of the rim. Liz swung in front of her to rebound it and put it in. "Arc, baby," she said briefly as she passed off to Scooter again.

"Nice try, Jacamuzzi," Scooter said.

*Well, I got it away from you, anyway,* Tracey thought. But she didn't say anything.

CPR's whistle blasted again. "Willis, in for Lukas."

Even after months of running and practices, Tracey felt hopelessly outmaneuvered and awkward in a real game. Scooter, Liz, even Peggy and Susan, seemed to move with sureness and a sense of direction. Tracey was having a hard time just keeping up with the ball.

As if in agreement with her thoughts, Liz yelled from the sidelines, "Jac! Watch the ball!"

"That's enough, Lukas," CPR yelled.

Scooter came up the center of the court, right into the key. Tracey planted just in time to get hit by her. CPR blasted on the whistle and pointed at Scooter. "Foul on you, Junior."

"She was moving, Coach!" Scooter yelled back. She turned to Tracey. "Don't mess me up on the court."

"Then quit tripping over yourself," Tracey said.

"Girls, you'll both get benched if I don't see some action," CPR yelled at them. "Scooter, you bring that ball up again, right through the key. I want to see some good plays here from you old players."

Scooter brought the ball up the middle again, and this time she neatly maneuvered around Tracey, passed to Susan, and dived around the two guards to get open under the basket. Susan passed back to her.

Tracey was playing forward, but as Scooter jumped to make the shot, Tracey jumped out of her zone and caught the rebound.

"Tracey! Tracey!" Peggy yelled from the top of the key, and Tracey flung a long pass that overshot her. Everybody tore after the ball, but Peggy got to it first. Barely in control, she got it down the court. CPR was shaking her head as Tracey dashed by her.

All of a sudden, another burst of strength filled Tracey's lungs. She caught up to the knot of girls and maneuvered to the side of the key opposite to where she belonged. "Here! Here!" she yelled, and Peggy, almost thankfully, pushed the ball back to her in a bounce pass. Tracey scooped it up with a high jump and put it in the basket.

"Nice work," Liz yelled.

"Yeah, for a lucky shot," Scooter added.

Tracey said nothing. Scooter didn't know how lucky it was. Tracey was no shooter, not even for layups. For some reason, shooting from the forward position, when she was alongside the basket, was hardest for Tracey. Being right in front of it was also hard. She did better either from a few paces in front of the free throw line or, best of all, from either of the two places about forty-five degrees in front of the basket and within a few feet of the key's border. Good luck alone had placed her in her good shooting spot just in time to catch the ball and make the shot.

CPR blasted on the whistle. "Get some water. Jaca-muzzi! I want to see you."

Tracey jogged up to Sister Patricia Rose.

"Look, I see you can play," she greeted Tracey. "But you have to play with the team."

Her comments—both of them—took Tracey by surprise. "I . . . I don't see what you mean," she said.

"Play your zone. I have to see that you know your zone, the strategies, and the way this game is played. It can't be four quarters of one-on-one, Jacamuzzi." CPR's gray eyes were fixed on Tracey with an intentness that was not anger. She seemed to be trying to read right through her.

Tracey decided to tell CPR the awful truth right away. "I don't know any strategies, Coach," she said. "I only know how to get the ball around and shoot."

"Oh," CPR said, sounding mollified. Tracey realized that frankness would always be the best policy with CPR. She felt a secret relief that the coach could settle for the plain truth. "Well," CPR said after a moment's thought, "we'll have to start going over the strategies soon. Just try to stay in your zone and work with the other players. The time will come when you can take shots and make moves that look right. But for right now, I want you to try to be part of the team."

Tracey nodded. "I'll do my best." She trotted off to get water and found Liz at her elbow.

"Don't get thrown," Liz told her. "CPR likes you. You're doing great."

"I don't know the strategies. I never knew there were any."

"You'll learn them easy enough. And don't let Scooter throw you, either."

Tracey ducked her head to drink from the fountain. The other girls were milling around, talking. Most of them headed for the bleachers, where one or two of the benches were pulled out and looked inviting.

"Scooter's running scared," Liz added as Tracey drank.

Tracey straightened and moved aside for Liz to drink. "I can hardly shoot, Liz."

"You'll learn," Liz said before resuming her drink. At last she straightened up. "It's gonna be you and me and Scooter this year, the whole way. She's going to have to get used to that."

"If you say so. Maybe I'll make second-string. But look how I messed up that rebounding."

"This is only the start of practices, Jac. Give yourself at least until the next one before you pass judgment on yourself. Come on." They made their way over to the bleachers. Tracey was aware of Susan's glance as she and Liz found places to sit by Peggy.

Susan was a senior now. If she only made second-string, it would be more worthwhile for CPR to replace her with a younger girl of equal or even slightly less ability. There were several girls who seemed to play better than Susan. But Tracey had no doubt that if Susan were dropped and she were picked, Scooter and Susan and their friends would only add that to their grudge. And Liz would think it all very funny.

Tracey closed her eyes and pushed her wet hair back. The summer had been nice in that it had been free of enemies. No Mary, no Scooter, no Susan, no Masses, no May processions. She wished it were summer again.

"You all right?" Liz asked.

"Yeah," Tracey said without opening her eyes.

Still, wearing the blue of a sophomore had its rewards, not the least of which was knowing the ropes better this year. She and Liz were roommates again, a situation they had ensured simply by moving in together before the start of the school year. They had two freshman roommates, both of whom appreciated the fact that Liz was the school's star basketball player. Liz had convinced them that Tracey was the rising star of the team. They had very wisely become basketball enthusiasts.

Tracey was not quite as devoted to the sport as Liz was, but even she knew that freshmen at MoJoe usually went nowhere their first year. Being Liz's roommate and friend could open doors later, if only by giving the girls a certain notice from the other students. And Liz was good at including her younger roommates in secrets, jokes, and celebrations. Tracey followed her lead.

Later, up in the room, Liz dug out the last of the Tastykakes.

"I thought we swore off those," Tracey whispered while Nikki and Toni looked longingly at the waxed paper-wrapped packages.

"Season ain't started yet," Liz said. "Toni, will you get some water for us?"

With a nod, Toni went out, taking Liz's and Tracey's plastic cups. After she returned, Liz gestured at the small array of cakes. "Dig in, one and all," she said, letting the freshmen go first. Tracey took one of the cakes for herself. The four girls sat on the floor with their backs against the bunk beds.

Liz stretched out her long legs. Outside, they heard the swish of a gown as a nun went by. Toni and Nikki froze guiltily. It was study time, and eating in the room was banned. Tracey hardly noticed rules like that anymore. If one of the sisters should come in, she would most likely pretend not to see the small feast spread out on the floor. It was much simpler to overlook minor infractions than to prosecute them. Usually, only things like noisemaking and horseplay attracted the attention of the sister on hall duty. If you kept quiet and didn't bother anybody, you could pretty much do what you pleased.

The gown swished by, out of earshot.

"How do your legs feel?" Liz asked.

"Real tight," Tracey told her.

"It ain't the distance we run, it's the turns and stops. Better get a hot shower tonight if you can get in."

"OK."

"And quit worrying!" Liz started to throw the last Butterscotch Krimpet at Tracey, then thought better of it and put half of it in her mouth. "You're doing great."

Two weeks after practices had begun, the first cuts
list came out. It was posted outside the gym doors
immediately after breakfast. Most of the girls trying
out stopped for only a quick bite. Liz had warned
Tracey that if CPR caught anybody hanging around
the gym before seven-fifteen, she would postpone the
list's appearance until after lunch. Everybody was supposed to attend and eat breakfast, and CPR would not
allow them any excuse to miss it.

They congregated around the cafeteria doors, and
as soon as the minute hand on the cafeteria clock
turned to the quarter mark, all the girls burst out the
doors and ran down the hill toward the gym.

"Slow down, Jac," Liz called as Tracey ran with the
group.

Tracey didn't answer, and—for once—Liz gave in
and hurried to catch up.

The girls arrived at the double doors in a huddle and
pushed close in the eager search for names. Twenty people had survived first cuts. Liz's name topped the list, of

course. Tracey began her search from the bottom up, but Liz impatiently tapped her shoulder. "There you are, Jac. There you are. Come on. Let's go get our books."

"Where? Where?" Tracey asked.

"Right there, under me. Just look, will you?"

Tracey raised her eyes and saw her name directly under Liz's. Right below her name was Susan Clark's. So Scooter had come third in first cuts.

"We're not listed in any special order, Jacamuzzi," Scooter said, as a look of stunned realization passed across Tracey's face.

"Just the order of CPR's assurance," Liz said.

It was true. CPR thoroughly knew each girl who tried out: her abilities, her experience, her likelihood of being able to play with the team. Topping the list was not an indication of how good a person really was, only an indication of the order in which the players who survived cuts had occurred to CPR.

Tracey tried to look humble as she followed Liz back up the hill, away from the knot of girls. Liz studied the ground as they walked, apparently involved in her own thoughts. Tracey willed her sense of exultation to shrink to more acceptable levels. It was no big deal. There were still second cuts ahead. And hours and hours of practice, more than any talent, had given her the edge in first cuts.

But then Liz glanced over and shot her a smile. A knowing, conspiratorial, congratulating smile.

Tracey jumped up in the air. "Yahoo!" she yelled.

Liz slapped her on the back and let out a whoop. "Watch out, world, here comes the dynamic duo!"

"It's Wonder Polack and the Italian Miracle!" Tracey yelled.

They got it out of their systems before class time. There was a brief, noisy announcement in their room to Nikki and Toni, and then it was time for class. Throughout that long day, Tracey dared betray none of her elation.

Peggy, who had also gotten through cuts, shot her one look of happiness for both of them, and Tracey returned it. But otherwise Tracey kept a low profile. Second cuts would draw blood from a lot of people. People who had made last year's team would be eliminated.

There were other reasons for forcing herself to pay attention in class that day. Wearing the blue of a sophomore didn't guarantee all the pleasure one might expect. Sophomores were almost universally expected to be big mouths and bullies. Tracey was surprised in the first month of school to see how many times she and her classmates were rebuked by teachers.

They had begun readings in Latin II, and the English course was American Literature. They also had grammar, of course. Tracey's math course was geometry, and the religion course was a study of church history from the Council of Nicea to the Council of Trent.

Basketball practice came right after classes. For the first several weeks of school, that was Tracey's most important subject. Now that first cuts had been announced, she was already aware of a decrease in whatever hard feelings still lingered against her among some of the older students. Many of them seemed genuinely surprised and pleased to see the outspoken idealist make good.

It was true, she realized later as she laced up her sneakers in the locker room, that she had run afoul of some of the toughest girls at MoJoe. There were gentler ones—town students, mostly. Yet even among the boarders, not every girl was a juvenile delinquent in the making. Peggy and Liz, for instance, had been in boarding schools for years, and both of them were nice, though in different ways. And both were clean of beer and pot, a rare thing at MoJoe.

Out in the gym, CPR's whistle sounded its warning blast. Tracey and the last stragglers hurried out. Liz was already in the gym. She gave Tracey a curt nod and rolled her eyes upward. "We got company."

Tracey looked up. There was a single, narrow balcony at one end of the gym, reached by a private stair whose door had remained locked all summer. It was the only door in the gym that Tracey had not been through. Sister Mary, St. Bernard, Madeleine, and several other nuns were taking their seats on folding chairs up on the balcony.

CPR passed out red flags and white flags for the girls to tie on. "Scrimmage today," she announced. "Team captains are Lukas, red, and Scooter Clark, white. I'll assign the positions and players. Full court."

To her dismay, Tracey found herself on Scooter's team. She would be playing forward, under the basket, and Scooter was center. Tracey shot a look at Liz, but Liz grinned and winked.

They came to center and took their positions. Liz and Scooter jumped for the ball. Liz slapped it to one of her own forwards, but Tracey jumped and caught the ball, then ran down the court.

"Pass! Pass!" Scooter yelled from her right. Tracey caught a glimpse of somebody's hand on her left, trying to get the ball. She passed to the right, to Scooter. The

307

ball almost surprised Scooter, who apparently hadn't expected Tracey to obey her.

The older girl leaped and shot from too far away. The ball hit the backboard and bounced high. Tracey jumped and caught it and passed back to Scooter, even though her other teammates were yelling for her to shoot. She still wasn't confident in her shooting ability. Scooter shot and sank it.

The white team whooped congratulations and returned back up the court. Scooter did not acknowledge the assist from Tracey. The two guards from the red team brought the ball up. Liz weaved expertly in and out of the key, and Tracey saw how well the red team's offense maneuvered into place for a passing strategy that would free up Liz for a good center shot from the top of the key.

Tracey admired their smoothness and coordination and then caught herself admiring more than concentrating. She jumped into the key just as one of the red guards rolled around a white guard and passed to Liz, who had gotten clear of Scooter. Tracey jumped as Liz jumped, and the ball brushed her fingers as she awkwardly tried to push it away from the basket.

"Dumb Italian," Liz murmured and ran for the rebound. Both teams went after the ball. Tracey found herself back in her zone almost more by accident than skill. She jumped again to block the red forward's shot. The ball bounced off the rim. Liz caught it and tried again to come up for a shot. This time Scooter was on her. CPR blew the whistle for the three-second violation.

"Nuts!" Liz exclaimed as she threw the ball to one of the white forwards. Tracey just looked at her. A sense of guilt rushed over her, but Liz gave her a grin.

"Play hard, little Italian Miracle. The Wonder Polack's got your number."

"Let's go, Jacamuzzi!" CPR yelled. Tracey ran after her team.

"Watcha doin', making up with your mama?" Scooter asked.

"Shut up, number three," Tracey told her without any remorse for the cut she knew had to dig deep.

"I don't see you sinking any baskets," Scooter returned.

"I don't see you catching any rebounds, either. Or stopping anybody else from doing anything."

"Come on, you guys," one of the others said.

That was all they had time for as the guards came down. The brief squabble had blown their intensity. Scooter caught a pass, shot, and missed. Tracey missed the rebound. The ball went out of bounds.

"Shape up, white team, shape up," CPR yelled as they ran back down the court. Tracey and Scooter traded looks. By silent consent, the war had to be postponed. They both knew they had to play well.

The game was Tracey's introduction to real playing, with an audience watching that was not entirely friendly. For ten minutes she played with all her intensity and concentration. She assisted Scooter and the other forward several times and made some successful blocks on defense, including some neat turnarounds that could have been fast breaks if her team had been more tightly knit. But she didn't sink anything. She tried only a couple of times, and all her shots bounced off the rim or the backboard.

At last, CPR's whistle shrilled at them. They cleared the court quickly. Tracey assumed the sisters had seen enough. But when she looked up, they were still seated in the balcony. They all looked just as intense as she had felt during the game.

"Jacamuzzi," CPR said, "you'll go red after the break. Willis, take white. No water, girls. Let's get the other squads out."

The other squads, presumably the lesser ten people, went out onto the court. Liz flopped down on the bench and patted it. Tracey sat down.

"Good playing," the blonde girl said.

"No points," Tracey answered.

"You hardly tried."

"I'm glad CPR finally put me on your team."

Liz nodded. "Just relax, Jac. Relax, and when I pass to you under the basket, take your shot. I'll pass off on easy shots."

Tracey shook her head. "You're taking a risk."

"I'm not worried. You sink plenty of shots when you practice."

"It's different when people are running after you."

Liz smiled. "I'll pick your shots."

The eight-minute break seemed to fly by. CPR's whistle shrilled again, and they went back out on the court.

This time, Liz slapped the ball right to Tracey. She raced down the court ahead of the white forward, jumped for a layup, and made it.

"Just like that," Liz called to her as they went down to the other basket for defense.

It was a lot harder to play the second eight minutes. Tracey's body didn't want to obey her commands, and the sharp edginess that had helped in the first eight minutes was dulled. She could not jump as spontaneously, nor as high. But she was still playing, and she

310

saw that three or four of the girls were badly winded by this time. Sweat streaked her lovely, polished gym floor.

This quarter had more fast breaks. Tracey and Liz had the strength to set them up and carry them out for the red team, and Scooter managed to pull off a few for the white team. Tracey did score on some more layups, and she even sank two baskets from the key. But she missed several too.

By the end of the quarter, her vision was hazy at the edges, and she had a knot in her middle and a dull cramp in her left calf. Scooter looked tired, and even Liz's face was red, though her eyes still followed the ball as keenly. CPR was right. Just being able to endure an entire game would give you an incredible edge over most high school teams.

At last the quarter ended, and the other squads went in for another quarter. Tracey glanced up at the nuns on the balcony. Several of them were making their way to the back stairway. She glanced at Liz.

"It's us they want to know about," Liz said. "First-string types."

"How'd we do?" Tracey asked.

Liz shook her head. "You and me did good. But I don't know how the team looks this year. We'll see."

Dinner was an unusually happy meal that night. Peggy sat by Tracey, and talk was brisk about prospects for making the team. Tracey sensed more than ever the subtle change in the attitudes of her classmates. They liked her more now, that was for sure.

"I'm grading papers for Sister Madeleine tomorrow," Amy told Tracey happily. "I know I can get her to tell me what she thought of your playing."

"I may not want to know," Tracey teased. "What if she thinks I stink?"

"Her eyes may be two different colors, but they see just fine," Peggy chided. "You did great out there, Jac."

Tracey started at the nickname. So far, Liz had been the only one to call her Jac, but it tripped easily off Peggy's tongue.

"You did good too," she told Peggy.

Peggy smiled ruefully. "For second-string."

"You did better than Susan."

Peggy shrugged. Then she said, trying to sound off-hand, "CPR talked to me after practice tonight. She said she thinks I've come along well." She looked directly at Tracey. "I think I'll get through cuts, Jac."

"That's good, isn't it?" Tracey asked. Peggy looked almost disappointed.

"Maybe. I guess I'm just tapped out. I don't think I'll get better than this. I wish there was more time to practice."

Tracey looked down at her plate for a moment. "What about Susan?"

Peggy shook her head. "Never. I don't see how she got through first cuts."

"CPR's got a soft heart, that's why," Tracey said.

Peggy's belief that she would make the team made Tracey feel sure of making it too. She was glad—if not for the sake of basketball itself than because it at least would purchase some peace for her.

That night after dinner, she ran over to the retirees' wing to see Sister James. Basketball practices had interrupted their walks, but the half hour between dinner and study time was enough for a short visit.

Afterward, she hurried back to the halls. The first floor was full of its after-dinner silence, and the stairs were dim. Because their room was closer to the end staircase than the center one, Tracey took the end stairs. Everything seemed peaceful and still, and she wondered if she had missed the bell. She sauntered up the steps carelessly, with her head down, at peace with herself and the world.

A body like a wall suddenly cut her off. She looked up and saw Susan and Rita Jo. Rita Jo had not even tried out for the team that year. She had put on weight.

Tracey sensed that this meeting was an accident. The two of them had been sneaking off somewhere, and she had happened along. But Susan was quick to assume her usual hard, belligerent expression.

Tracey met the implied threat of their stance with her usual bluntness. "You take a lot of chances, getting in a person's way like that."

"Jacamuzzi," Susan said, "you think you're something now that you're trying out for the team."

"You got your cord tonight?" Tracey retorted.

"We don't need it," Rita Jo said. She stood behind Susan, and neither of them made a move. Two against one wasn't good enough odds, considering Tracey's strength and new standing as an up-and-coming ballplayer.

Tracey had no idea what to do. She was sick of her own violence, but backing down might bring on the trouble all over again. And now that they had made a point of blocking her way, they wouldn't back down either.

The only thing to do was be bold. Take the bull by the horns—or Susan by the bolero.

Without another word, Tracey grabbed Susan by the front of her uniform and pulled the shorter girl down the steps with her. They both might easily have lost their footing, but they didn't. She didn't let Susan fall. She just pulled her down, heard with some satisfaction Susan's gasp of horror, and twirled her around as they swung down the steps toward the ground floor. She ended by slamming Susan against the wall.

Quick as a flash, she looked up to check what Rita Jo was doing. The older girl looked stunned and had come only one step closer.

"Stay where you are," Tracey said. There was no reason that Rita Jo should, but she did, apparently at a loss. Tracey looked back at Susan, who looked pale after her quick dance down the steps. "Next time pick on someone your own size, Susan," Tracey said. She climbed the steps and boldly pushed past Rita Jo.

Rita Jo swore at her. "You're lucky you're on that team, Jacamuzzi."

Tracey stopped and looked down at them. "Well, cheer up. Maybe I won't make it and we can all do this again sometime. But you better bring the rest of your friends."

The bell rang, and she went up the steps to the room. Liz and Nikki were there. Liz looked up when Tracey entered. "That's trimming it close."

Tracey flopped down on the bed. "Cool it, Liz."

Nikki looked up. Liz came over to the bed and sat down. "What's wrong?"

Tracey shook her head. "Just had a little scene on the steps with Rita Jo and Susan." She sat up.

"Who came out on top?" Liz asked.

"I guess I did."

"I heard some of the girls saying that Susan won't make it," Nikki told them.

Liz shook her head. "Won't know until the list is out, kid. Everybody thinks they know ahead of time, but there's no telling."

"Oh, come on, Liz," Tracey said. "Susan knows she'll never do it." She knew that she sounded on edge, but Liz didn't get mad.

"Maybe not," she agreed. "But you don't need to worry about her. You make that team, and you're immune. They're just trying to get their last licks in on you."

Tracey should have studied, but instead she flopped back on her bed and lay still.

Liz looked down at her, a frown on her broad face. "What's wrong?"

Tracey shook her head. She was quiet for so long that Nikki returned to her books. But Liz stayed where she was.

"If I make the team," Tracey said, "I'll be seeing a lot of Maddie Murdoch."

"Maddie doesn't hate you," Liz said.

"I almost wish she did," Tracey said. "It'd be easier."

"Why?"

She looked at Liz. "I feel dirty, Liz."

"What about that stuff about redemption and atonement and all that?" Liz asked.

"I don't feel dirty because of what I've done. Not right now, anyway," Tracey said. "Sometimes I feel dirty because I feel cheap."

"Cheap how?"

"Cheap 'cause my dad's some two-bit guy who makes good money but—you know, he's a drinks-hard, bets-hard, fights-hard type of guy. And my mom's . . ." She looked down.

"Lots of women have done that," Liz reminded her.

"Sure." But she didn't feel any better. The more Tracey remembered her family and home, the cheaper it all looked: the empty wine bottles on Sunday mornings, her mother's bingo games, the casino nights in the church basement, the Saturday poker games when her uncles came over, her mother's visits to the dark motel off the interstate. In some ways, even people like Sister Mary were above that kind of stuff.

"Nobody made you cheap or dirty," Liz said. "You play hard, and you play clean, and you've got a lot of heart out on the court."

Tracey let out a laugh. "Are those my virtues?"

"When you ain't got nothing else, that's something," Liz told her. She got up and went back to her desk.

The second cuts list was posted a day early, catching everybody by surprise. The freshmen in gym class saw CPR posting it, and they ran to tell everybody else. Before Tracey could get down to the gym, she'd heard the news from at least a dozen different people. She was on the team. Liz was captain again, with Scooter as alternate. Peggy had also made it, and Susan had been cut.

That night at dinner, Tracey and Peggy were toasted by the other sophomores at the table. Across the aisle, Liz and Scooter were being congratulated by their classmates. Snatches of school cheers and the school song went up here and there. The girls drummed on the tables and whooped, and for once nobody came in to make them be quiet.

Tracey turned once to catch Liz's eye, and Liz held up two fingers. Not "V" for "victory" as many of her friends supposed, but two for "dynamic duo."

Basketball practice began in earnest the next day. Their first game was a week away. The practice was moved to after dinner, and by the time everybody had congregated, their hilarity had worn off. The first game was against a good team, St. Anthony's. It was a private school with many black students. Tracey wondered if it was only a stereotyped image that made the Valkyries wonder at the skills of this team. It didn't really matter. Every year, MoJoe and St. Anthony's had a close game. MoJoe had won for the last three years, but the games had always been later in the season. This early, the huge turnover in their team might work against them.

Before practice, CPR gathered them in a loose huddle on the gym floor, everyone looking serious. "You've got to keep your skills sharp and practice on your own," she said. "For team practices, I want to emphasize the plays that have worked for us in the past. It may be a new way of playing basketball for many of you, but don't get discouraged if things don't go well at first. Just work hard."

Tracey felt almost desperate. Losing the first game would be a terrible blow to the spirit of the school.

"Sister?" Peggy said.

"Yes, Melsom?"

"Can we pray before we start?"

The request caught CPR by surprise, but she quickly said, "Of course. Would you like to pray for us? Or would you like to have everybody pray?" She meant all of them saying a prayer together, like an "Our Father," in petition for the team.

"I didn't mean a set prayer," Peggy said.

"Let Jac pray," Liz said. "She knows how."

Several of the girls nodded. Tracey's sense of desperation increased, but she looked at CPR. If the sister permitted her, she would do it.

CPR nodded at her. "Will you, Tracey?"

"Sure, Sister." She set her basketball down and bowed her head. "Lord, I . . . I thank You for being saved. And that Jesus died to save us. And now we—I mean, I ask that You'll help us to do well in practice and to learn the new plays. In Jesus' name, amen."

"Amen," several of the girls said. Tracey's voice, higher than usual from nervousness, had sounded loud in the big gym. As the team looked up, Liz nudged her. St. Bernard, Mary, and another nun named Sister Francis were up on the narrow balcony in their folding chairs. The gym lights reflected off Mary's pointed glasses, obscuring her eyes, but Tracey guessed that she was not happy at what she had just seen.

CPR's blast on the whistle made her push these thoughts away. It was time to practice.

The next day, Nikki came up to the room, looking important. "You know where I saw CPR?" she asked her three roommates. Toni barely glanced at her, but Tracey and Liz looked up quickly, as though expecting trouble.

"Where?" the blonde girl asked.

"Coming out of Mary's office, the one downstairs," Nikki said. "Kind of mad-looking. She slammed the door. She didn't know I was on the stairs." Nikki had been on kitchen duty, cleaning up after supper. Kitchen duty was a thankless job except for the moments when a person managed to observe things after hours, unnoticed.

"Wonder what she's upset about?" Toni murmured absently, scanning her vocabulary list.

"I bet I know," Tracey mumbled.

"You don't know that," Liz corrected her.

"Not until Mary calls me in," Tracey said.

As if on cue, there was a knock on the door, and St. Bernard walked in. "Sister Mary is asking for you in her office, Tracey," she said.

Tracey sighed and stood up. Luckily, she still had her uniform on. She tucked in her blouse, pulled up her socks, and fastened the bolero. Liz looked long and hard at St. Bernard, and the tall sister looked away as Tracey went out the door.

So far that year, Tracey had gone unnoticed by Mary, a circumstance the acting principal quickly explained. "I had hoped, Miss Jacamuzzi, to be spared any more trouble from you," she said as Tracey stood mute before her desk. Sister Mary picked up one of her pencils and turned it over in her hands. It was perfectly sharpened.

"Yes, Sister," Tracey said.

"But now I receive a complaint from Sister Patricia Rose that you are seeking to use basketball to win converts to yourself."

"No, Sister," she said quietly.

"No?"

"No."

"Am I to understand that you did not persuade the girls to allow you to say a few words at practice and lead them in prayer?"

"They asked me, Sister. So did Sister Patricia Rose."

"You've misinterpreted the facts to suit yourself," Sister Mary said. Her eyes were as hard as diamonds. Before Tracey could answer, she added, "This is a Catholic school, miss. We will conduct ourselves publicly as good Catholics."

Tracey didn't answer, and for once Sister Mary didn't seem to notice.

"But I know," she said, standing, "that if I punish you for your insubordination to your teacher and your coach, you and Miss Lukas might just go running to Father Williams as you did last year."

Tracey chose again not to answer. She looked at Mary with a new coolness that had nothing to do with having made the team. But Sister Mary interpreted it that way.

"You will look down," Mary said. Tracey did. "Don't think that I won't pull you right off that team, miss. Right off. Do you understand me?"

"Yes, Sister."

"Do you want that?"

Tracey didn't want that, and she almost gave in and said so. But something stopped her.

"Do you want that?" Mary asked again, her voice more urgent, her face close to Tracey's.

"You'll have to do what you think best, Sister," Tracey said.

Mary looked as though water had been thrown in her face. "What did you say to me?"

"You'll have to do what you think best, Sister," Tracey said again.

"Now you mock me!" She had a lot more to say after that, but Tracey was so surprised that she'd really gotten to Mary, she forgot to listen to the tirade. She remained dumb with wonder, not sure if Mary was really out of control of the situation or if it only seemed that way. She had half suspected that Mary would pull her from the team, but now Tracey realized the sister couldn't do that. The story about CPR's complaint was a distortion of the truth to start with.

CPR had probably been raked over the coals first for letting Tracey pray for the team. Maybe that had been what Nikki had seen the tail end of. But CPR wouldn't want Tracey off the team. Even Mary would hesitate to brashly pull Tracey, against CPR's wishes.

Tracey held her breath and waited. Finally, Mary dismissed her. When she walked out of the office, she realized that she was still on the team and in full control of herself.

# FIFTY

The day of the first game passed by in a kind of blur, and Tracey was surprised to be excused from participating as much in class as was usually expected. It was a home game, and Tracey's biggest hope that day was not so much for a victory as for Sister James to be brought up to watch.

Sister Madeleine promised to bring up the elderly nun in time to get a good seat.

"Not on the balcony where the rest of you sit," Tracey pleaded. "She can't see from up there."

"All right, Miss Jacamuzzi," Sister Madeleine said. "I'll get her onto the first row of the bleachers. Just concentrate on your game, and maybe the Lord will answer your prayers." She turned to gather her books for the next class, unaware of letting it slip that all the nuns knew about Tracey's prayer in the gym.

The sense of suspense that was mingled with both fear and pleasure heightened after fifth hour as Tracey went down to the locker room to change. The black-and-white team warm-up suit had never looked so striking as it did when she pulled it on over her uniform and looked at herself in the bathroom mirror. Liz slapped her on the back.

"You praying anyway?" she asked with a grin.

Tracey nodded. "All morning."

They could hear the noises in the gym slowly getting louder as people drifted in. Tracey let out her breath in a hard sigh. "Got a knot in my gut."

"Take it easy," Liz said. "And if you start, pace yourself. Don't blow it all in the first quarter."

The other team had to dress in the same locker room, and they came bursting in a few minutes later, five white girls and seven black girls. Both teams eyed each other. Tracey noticed that the black players and white players for St. Anthony's did not mix freely with each other, either. The team was in two cliques—not hostile maybe, but definite.

"What you staring at, MoJoe?" one of the black girls asked her. Tracey felt all eyes on both teams turn to her. Liz looked ready to speak up if necessary.

"You guys," Tracey said. Her voice sounded high.

"What for?" the girl asked her.

"I was wondering who your forwards are," she said.

The opposing team relaxed a little.

"Forwards," the girl said. "Why? You a forward?"

"Me?" Tracey asked. "No, I'm a guard." She glanced at Liz, who looked startled at this bold-faced lie. "And Liz here is a guard. Our forwards are a lot taller than this." Some of the MoJoe girls smiled at her joke.

"Well, where are they?" the girl from St. Anthony's asked.

"They gotta change outside; they don't fit in here," Tracey told her.

"Oh, get lost!" Liz exclaimed, and she pushed Tracey. Tracey laughed. Most of the girls from the other school relaxed and laughed too.

"She's a forward and I'm a center," Liz told them. She pointed at Scooter. "And she's our other starting forward."

"Hope you guys are good," the other girl said.

"We think we are," Scooter said evenly.

"And when we don't think so, we get our little preacher to pray for us," Liz said, dropping a hand on Tracey's shoulder. "She's our token Protestant."

"Protestant, huh?" For the first time the newcomer showed a glimmer of a smile. Tracey smiled back. The other St. Anthony's girls came closer as they changed, and for a few minutes the talk was courteous enough.

In spite of all of their toughness, the MoJoe team had a lot of school spirit, and part of that spirit involved sportsmanship. For CPR's sake, they usually made an effort to be friendly to the other team before the game. Other MoJoe girls were not so noble.

CPR came to the door. "Let's go, Valkyries, warm-up."

They started for the door. Tracey turned around. "Hey," she said to the black girl, "what's your name?"

"Theresa," the girl said.

"I'm Tracey." She ran after Liz.

The gym was bright and hot. A drumming on the bleachers started as they went out for layups. They ran up and down the court, passing to each other while the audience clapped and whistled. Under the glare of the lights, sweat trickled down Tracey's neck. As she ran, she scanned the crowd until she saw Sister James seated happily on the front row of the bleachers, smiling in blind contentment at the court, probably unable to pick out which player was Tracey.

CPR's whistle shrilled again, and the team ran back into one of the hallways to make their grand appearance. There was a confusion of paper and spear staffs as the banner was unfurled. Liz took one spear and Scooter the other. Peggy and another second-string girl took hold of the double doors. In unison, Liz and Scooter burst out of the doors, shaking their spears and holding the banner high. As they reached center court, Tracey ran through the open doors and passed under the banner. The wave of applause and cheering startled her. She had wanted this moment, but when it came it scared her.

She ran to the far corner of the court. The other players were behind her in an even line, all wearing their matching warm-up suits.

The St. Anthony's Saints came out, declined their school song, and stayed standing as the MoJoes stood to sing.

This time, Tracey's heart was in her throat. MoJoe was a different place when you played on the team. The full and lovely singing filled the gym, and she saw that Sister James's lips trembled a little as the girls sang.

For strength the black, for truth the white,
Our colors we hold dear.
Let strength and truth abide in us
In every heart sincere.

Pure Valkyries and maidens fair,
We pledge our loyalty;
The shield we love, nor can it fail
As our hearts are true to thee.

O Mary and Joseph, school we hail,
Our bles't Sanctuary.
The shield we carry in our hearts
Is yours eternally.

The quietness lasted a moment longer than the song, and then the referee's whistle blasted. CPR had already tapped Tracey to start, and she took her position as Liz centered up with one of the girls from St. Anthony's.

Liz took the jump and slapped the ball right to Tracey, but it fumbled on her fingers, and one of the Saints got it away from her. They tore down the court after her. Scooter got under the basket first, blocked the shot, and jumped high for the rebound. She had never looked so good in practice. The first game had wired her.

Tracey was not yet in position, and the ball came sailing toward her. She jumped and caught it, then looked wildly in every direction before she realized Liz was screaming at her to pass. She did, a barely controlled pass that Liz managed to catch and dribble for a layup that went in.

The MoJoes roared and drummed on the bleachers. A sense of self-control returned to Tracey, and the hysteria from the opening of the game subsided.

She got under the basket and managed some good blocks before rebounding a shot and passing off to a Valkyrie guard. But the pass was intercepted by Theresa from the Saints, and she shot and sank a basket.

The game was almost frightening in some ways. For every basket the Valkyries scored, the Saints also scored. CPR called a time-out and yelled at them.

"You play man-to-man," she said, "and you lose with this team! We didn't learn those plays for our health."

"Coach, they intercept too well," Liz gasped.

"Then fake them out. They've got good shooters. You keep them out of the key, do you hear me? And don't you let them put any moves on you. I want plays. I want teamwork and strategy. You girls just calm down and think, and quit taking every free shot you think you have."

They went back to it. Tracey felt completely unable to do any better as far as thinking and using plays. But to her surprise, she found the ball being passed to her more often. They ran the Saints around a little more, and Liz and Scooter managed to slip into the key unguarded a couple of times and sink baskets.

On defense, they got better as the game went on. The Saints apparently weren't used to getting called for three seconds in the key, and the Valkyrie defense managed to tie them up a few times until the whistle blew to indicate time was up.

By the end of the first quarter, the Valkyries were ahead by only four points, the widest margin of the game so far.

"Jacamuzzi out, Willis in," CPR said as they came to the bench. "Just that way, girls. Strategy."

Tracey shot a helpless look at Liz. It would have sounded too conceited to say, but she didn't think anybody on second-string could hold out long against the Saints' hard-driving game. CPR switched out one of the guards and put Peggy in.

For all her worries, Tracey didn't stay out long. The Saints pulled the score up to a tie again, and she was sent back in.

At halftime, the score was tied again after seesawing back and forth. CPR allowed the players some lemon water. The girls on the bleachers behind the team lent a hand by rubbing their shoulders as they leaned back on the benches.

"That's the way, Jac," one of them told her. "You seem to know what's going on all over the court."

"Oh, sure," Tracey said with half a laugh. The thought of losing was almost unbearable at this point. She wondered if she was going to go through this at every game. And the fear that maybe they weren't that good this year, that maybe this would be the first of many defeats, suddenly struck her.

She saw Sister James way down on the bleachers and abruptly got up to go see her.

"Sister," she called as she approached her. Sister James turned around. At this short range, she easily recognized Tracey.

"Look at how sweaty you are. Oh, dear, it's such an exciting game! You've got to win for me."

"I want to," Tracey said, kneeling in front of her and putting Sister James's hand on her own shoulder. "Can you follow it OK?"

"Oh, my, yes. And some of the girls behind me were explaining it. They went to get something to drink. They're all so proud of you, dear."

Tracey smiled at her older friend's guilelessness. She would not disillusion Sister James. She looked up and saw Maddie Murdoch down the row of bleachers, only three or four people away. The tall woman had been keeping an eye on the spears during the first half, and she now stood up with them in her hand, ready to go put them someplace—probably back in the storeroom.

Mrs. Murdoch glanced up at the clock, spears in hand, then noticed Tracey.

"I better get back," Tracey said to Sister James. As though in agreement, she heard CPR bawl out, "Jacamuzzi, get back here!"

"Do well, dear," Sister James called after her.

It was during the second half that weariness hit like a wall. But if it took a toll on the Valkyries, the toll seemed much worse on the Saints. Their shots became wilder, and they took more chances to get points. Every now and then the fast breaks went out of control, and there were some skirmishes for the ball. Slowly, the Valkyries tipped the scales in their own favor. Their lead increased to eight points. All of the Saints' first-string came back in.

Though the cheering was wild in the bleachers, Tracey felt the harsh intentness of her teammates as they struggled to hang onto this slim lead in their first game. They had started play with loud encouragement to each other, but now they played in a kind of dead-earnest silence, so much so that Tracey could hear Liz's hard breathing as Liz rolled around the Saints center in the key and passed off to Tracey.

Tracey was on defense when tragedy struck. The Saints guard took a long shot from near the top of the key, and Tracey and the Saints forward both jumped for the rebound. They rammed into each other in a tangle of arms. Both of them tried to land upright, and the other girl's ankle caught Tracey's.

Tracey yelled and went down, the other girl on top of her. There was a scurry of feet after the ball, and the girl quickly rolled off her and stopped long enough to say, "You OK?"

The whistle blew as the ball went out-of-bounds.

"You OK?" the ref called.

The fall had sent a sickening shaft of pain through Tracey's ankle, but her head cleared as she sat up. "Yeah," she said and tried to stand.

Another shaft went through the ankle. She fell back and grabbed her ankle, gasping.

"You can't get up?" the ref asked.

Tracey felt a sudden wave of nausea. Liz caught her as she went faint for a moment.

"Jac," Liz exclaimed, "what is it?"

"It's my ankle," Tracey said. "Oh, no, Liz. Not now."

"Can you stand?" the ref asked.

Tracey shook her head. "I don't think I can."

"This is all Mary needs," Liz murmured.

"Quiet, Liz. Be quiet."

CPR came out onto the court. The audience fell silent.

"How bad is it?" CPR asked, kneeling by her and pulling off her shoe. "Nothing broken," she answered herself.

Her probing fingers sent jabs of pain shooting up Tracey's shin, but Tracey said, "It's not so bad, Coach. Just give me five minutes or so. Just to rest it."

CPR looked up at her. "It's already swelling, Jacamuzzi."

"No, Coach. It's not that bad," Tracey pleaded. "I can play."

"Get her off the court," CPR said to Liz and Scooter.

Without a word, they got under her arms and helped her up.

Tracey began to cry.

"You better act like it's nothing," Liz whispered. "Don't let anyone see if it hurts."

Tracey forced back the tears.

Play resumed. Tracey could hardly follow the game; her mind was too filled with worry. If her sprain were bad enough, she would surely be pulled from the team. A bad sprain would keep her out of play for several weeks, and she would have to be careful for a couple of months. Tracey pushed these thoughts away and quickly, almost viciously, wrapped the swelling ankle in an Ace bandage.

She forced herself to stand up on it, and she sensed the color going out of her face. But she had the benefit of the injury being new and her body still being in shock from it.

"I can play," she insisted to CPR. "At least for a few seconds, Coach. At least a little."

Something passed between them as they looked at each other. Tracey felt it, but later she could never be sure if CPR had or had not at that moment consented to assist her in hiding how bad it was from the rest of the school.

She returned to the court for the last minute of play. The Valkyries had only a six-point lead. Every footstep sent arrows of pain up her leg, but the ankle did not give way under her, and she even succeeded in a fairly long-distance shot from outside the key.

But the buzzer that ended the game found her in a cold sweat. MoJoe girls were practically hurling themselves off the bleachers in ecstasy over the victory. Without a word, Liz got under Tracey's right arm and helped her off the floor. Tracey allowed herself to relax enough to feel the rush of sweat and wave after wave of nausea.

"I'm going to throw up," she said.

"Just hold it in a minute."

Liz dragged her through the double doors, into the locker room, and into a stall. Tracey threw up over Liz's arm, barely missing it, and then subsided into dry heaves. She could hear the clamor of the other girls coming in.

"Hey, I'm sorry about what happened," the Saints forward called.

"S'okay," Tracey gasped.

"She'll be all right," Liz told the girl. "She only throws up when she's happy."

Theresa came up to the stall door. "You better quit playing a while, girl," she said. "Give your foot a chance to come back."

"No way," Tracey told her before she threw up again.

"She's got to play," Liz said tersely. "No breaks in this school unless you're on the team. You all right? You done?"

"I think so," Tracey said. She looked up at Liz. "Mary'll want me off the team."

"I'll help you," Liz told her. "And CPR might let you fake it through a couple games. Come on. Let's get your clothes together."

# FIFTY-ONE

T he room was jammed with visitors after the game: Amy and Lisa had come up by invitation, as well as Ingy, Bingy, and Ringy. Even Scooter put in a showing, and Tracey was surprised when the older girl asked how the ankle was.

"Hurting a little," Tracey told her. She had been reclining back on her bed, resting the foot up on the bed frame of the bunk. But at the intrusion of so many people, she sat up.

Peggy came up with one of her friends, a girl named Debbie, who had tried out for the team and been cut. The other team members who were boarders soon came crowding in with their friends. Liz mixed up lemons and water in a huge bucket she kept reserved just for that purpose, though she called it the scrub bucket. The nonplayers drank soft drinks from the machine.

"Well, here goes," Peggy said as Liz passed out the cups. Tracey saw the wink that passed between them. Peggy held out her cup toward Tracey, and Tracey raised her cup.

"To all good Valkyries and true," Peggy said. Her eyes and smile met Tracey's, and Tracey smiled back.

"*Salut,*" she replied, and they drank.

"You scored twelve points, Jac," Peggy observed.

"Third on the roster," Liz agreed. Liz had scored most, followed by Scooter and then Tracey.

"Boy, you really get wired in a game," Tracey said. "Suddenly you can do things you never thought you could do."

Scooter nodded. "That's why I like it so much. You're more alive when you play than at any other time," she said.

Tracey was surprised at this new frankness from Scooter. Was the older girl changing, or simply giving in to the inevitable? Not so long ago, she had been civil to Liz's face and sneering about her behind her back. Was all this an act?

Tracey thoughtfully turned to her water and took a long sip. She wondered where Susan and Rita Jo were that night. Eating their hearts out, wherever they were. For the first time, she felt sorry for them. *Fortune is fleeting, fame is fleeting.* She remembered the line from an Old English poem. She realized that the best thing anybody could do was make good and true friends through the best times in life. That way you'd have them through the worst times too.

The study-time bell drove everybody out of the room. As Nikki picked up the clutter of cups left behind, Liz came over to the bed and sat on the edge of it. Tracey sighed and stretched her foot out onto the bed frame again.

"What are we going to do?" she asked Liz.

Liz unwrapped the ankle. Tracey winced from the

pain of the blood flowing into the constricted vessels around the injured joint.

"This does look bad, Jac," Liz said. "You really did it proper. I'll give you that." She frowned in thought.

"Mary would love to pull me from that team," Tracey said. "I told you what she—"

"Yeah, yeah, calm down," Liz told her. "We'll do what it takes. There's ways to treat athletic injuries. They just came out with that new aspirin substitute—what's it called?"

"Acetaminophen," Tracey told her.

"Duh, I meant the brand name," Liz replied, laughing. "Tylenol. Somebody told me it's better for swelling and stuff. I'll see who has any. And then it's hot and cold treatments."

"What about practice tomorrow?" Tracey asked. Already, the ankle was stiff and much more painful than it had been several hours ago.

"CPR might go easy on you if she thinks it's not that bad. Let's just worry about tonight first, OK?"

"OK," Tracey said.

Already, both she and Liz had impressed upon Toni and Nikki the absolute necessity for Tracey to make the team. From their own experiences and from Tracey's testimony, they were quite ready to believe that union against Sister Mary was crucial to the well-being of the room. They were ready to do what was needed to help Tracey's ankle heal.

That night, two hours after lights-out, Liz got up and woke Toni and Nikki. Then she woke Tracey. By this time, the ankle felt almost immovable. The three of them got Tracey out into the hallway and down to the bathroom.

Each bathroom had five showers and one tub, with rubber curtains for privacy. With Liz's help, Tracey sat on the edge of the tub. Nikki and Toni went back to the room, one to bed and the other to keep watch.

"Okay, ten minutes hot and ten minutes cold," Liz told her. They turned on the water, and it came crashing down over Tracey's foot and ankle in steamy torrents. Her ankle turned red, then almost purple. The veins stood out on her instep. Liz at last moderated the temperature. They let the foot soak, and after ten minutes Liz drained out the water and turned on the cold tap. That was much worse than the hot. Tracey hated extremes of cold, and keeping her foot in frigid water for ten minutes was about the hardest thing she'd ever done.

They repeated this simple treatment for an hour and a half, talking in whispers every now and then, until Nikki came back for her shift. Liz went to keep watch while Toni went to bed. Tracey couldn't help but fall into a doze every now and then, and her partner at the tub was hard put to keep her from falling over.

Liz came back out at four and added short massages to the treatment, as vigorous as Tracey could stand, for about two minutes at a time.

"I've got to sleep, Liz," Tracey told her a half hour later.

"All right. Let's walk you back to the room. How does it feel?" she asked as they managed to stand up together.

"Hurts," Tracey said.

"As much?" Liz asked.

"No, not as much. It's not stiff anymore."

337

"Come on. Keep it up on the bed frame for the rest of the night."

She slept for two and a half more hours, and then the bell went off.

All four of them were groggy, but Liz's first question was about the condition of her foot.

"I still can't put weight on it," Tracey told her.

"Well, you're putting more on it than you were last night," Liz said. "Wrap it tight, and let's go."

Tracey got through that day by staying seated all the time. She hopped around on her good foot when she had to go from class to class. But she discovered that if you start a day by vowing not to walk, you can get by without a lot of movement. Peggy helped by wordlessly and nonchalantly carrying her books for her between bells.

It was a Friday, and the afternoon practice would be the last one until the next week. To Tracey's relief, CPR announced that they would be watching a basketball film that day to emphasize the importance of good strategy and passing techniques.

"We can all be thankful," Liz whispered, but Tracey shot a glance at Sister Patricia Rose. Was this a coincidence? Or was CPR shielding her from watchful eyes? Even the rest of the team had no idea how much the ankle was paining her. Nobody but her own roommates and CPR, who understood injuries and had examined the ankle, knew how bad it was.

But despite the risk of Sister Mary finding out, other people had to be let in on the secret. Tracey and her roommates could not last long on four hours of sleep a night. Amy was sworn into the fellowship, and so was Peggy. Peggy's friend Debbie, whom everybody called

Dibbles, also came into it, at Peggy's recommendation and against Tracey's better judgment.

"We hardly know her, Liz," she said on Sunday night as Peggy went to bring Dibbles down for an explanation.

"If Peggy says she's cool, then she's cool," Liz insisted. "And you wait, Jac. She'll be a guard next year for sure. I can't believe CPR cut her."

Dibbles was remarkably short and plain. Her voice was a singsong that verged on whining. That, combined with her small stature, gave her a comic air, rather like a living cartoon. She was matter-of-fact about Tracey's injury, and she readily agreed to keep the secret and help out with tub duty.

"Anything for the cause," she told them.

"What cause?" Peggy asked.

"Any cause," Dibbles said. "Well, come to think of it, any good cause. I wouldn't want to be vague. So, when's surgery?"

"The nurse will get you at midnight," Liz said.

"Oooh. The witching hour."

"We'd need Sister Mary for that," Tracey quipped.

"Shame on you. When life throws you lemons, become a nun. OK, girls. See you at midnight. Whooo." She left, waving her arms and fingers to impersonate a witch, then blessing herself.

"The danger," Peggy said, "is that sometimes I understand Dibbles' train of thought. That's what really scares me."

By Sunday night, Tracey couldn't stay awake for her ankle therapy, so it took two people to make sure she didn't fall into the tub or onto the floor. They gave up posting a watch. Nobody could warn them of a nun in time to avoid her if she heard the water, so they decided they might as well get caught gracefully if it came to that.

The next week was a long, tired routine of classes by day and therapy at night for Tracey, who was semi-conscious most of the time. The only thing she thought about during that time was how much she wanted to sleep, undisturbed and in a bed.

"I know it's better tonight," Liz said the next Friday night as Tracey woke up from a doze on Liz's shoulder.

"Yeah, sure," Tracey mumbled.

"It is, Trace," Amy told her.

Tracey woke up more and looked at her red foot and ankle. "OK."

"See," Liz said. "Florence Nightenpolack has done it again."

"Well, CPR says I have to get in some practice Monday if I want to play at that away game on Tuesday," Tracey told her. "So it's do or die. I can't put it off anymore. Mary's been snooping around, wondering if I can play OK."

"You'll play on Tuesday," Liz said. "And Mrs. Murdoch's driving the team bus. Maybe it's time to make your peace."

"Oh, come on, Liz, not that again."

"Have it your way. You sure don't know a friend when you see one, Jac."

"I got you. I got lots of friends." She threw one arm around Amy's thin shoulders and looked defiantly at Liz.

"Suit yourself."

# FIFTY - TWO

The second game was an away game at St. Bede's. There was always the chance that somehow the worst school in the league had improved since the previous school year. If not, then Tracey could count on being pulled out of the game early for the second-string to go in and get some practice.

As it turned out, she started and played for less than half a minute before Kathy Willis went in for her. Her brief time on the court was enough to show her that the foot was in no shape for play yet. She'd gotten through a practice by working mostly on free throws and long shots, hobbling around while CPR industriously looked the other way.

But a game—even a game against St. Bede's—was the real thing, and each step cost her a lot of pain. She spent the rest of the game on the bench with only one brief intermission near the end of the first half when CPR told her to go back in. But the buzzer went off before she got a chance to trade with Kathy again.

The Valkyries won the game against Bede's, even

without Tracey's help. She felt as though she'd been put into the shadows a little by the victory in which she'd played no part. But there was nobody to be jealous of. Scooter already outshone her, and she liked her other teammates too much to want to steal away their glory.

"One more game," Liz mumbled as they went out to the bus together afterwards, with Tracey leaning on Liz's arm. "Then you can rest over Christmas vacation."

"Sounds good to me."

Maddie Murdoch had driven the bus to the game, and Tracey had managed to avoid her, sitting in the back with her foot propped across the aisle. But as Liz helped her up the front steps of the bus, Tracey saw that Mrs. Murdoch was already in place behind the wheel. She smiled at the two of them.

"Top o' the morning, Mrs. Murdoch," Liz said in a broad Irish accent. Tracey's face flamed scarlet.

"Go on with you, now," the Irish woman answered Liz, purposely increasing her accent. "You know it's evening, scamp."

Tracey nudged Liz to tell her to hurry up, but Liz said, "Well, we won our game tonight. Did you watch?"

"Aye, I did. You played smartly—when you played."

"Talk it up big to the second-string," Liz advised her. "I mean, that they played well. They don't play much after Bede's."

"All right, then. And how are you, Tracey?"

Tracey's face was still red, and the familiar sense of shame increased as she met Mrs. Murdoch's eyes. "Fine," she said.

Liz and she went down the aisle. "Talkative," Liz whispered sarcastically. Tracey didn't answer. Somehow, just looking into Mrs. Murdoch's clear gaze brought back the deep humiliation of her foolishness on the hockey field and again at Mrs. Murdoch's house. Sister Mary had told Mrs. Murdoch that Tracey used religion as an excuse to be disruptive, and so far, that was all Tracey had done whenever Mrs. Murdoch was around.

Here's to Peggy and the way she does the Hula-Hop,
Here's to Peggy and the way she does the Hula-Hop,
Here's to Peggy and the way she does the Hula-Hop,
Hula-Hop!

Kathy Willis sang as Peggy came dancing and "Hula-Hopping" onto the bus. Then Liz took up the song:

Here's to Willis and the way she does the Hula-Hop,
Here's to Willis and the way she does the Hula-Hop,
Here's to Willis and the way she does the Hula-Hop,
Hula-Hop!

Kathy Willis danced into a seat. More girls came clamoring onto the bus, and Liz and Peggy and Kathy sang them on, one by one. After a while, Tracey joined in. Hula-Hopping was not so much dancing as it was clowning around while coming down the bus aisle. At last they all sang:

Here's to Sister and the way she does the Hula-Hop,
Here's to Sister and the way she does the Hula-Hop,
Here's to Sister and the way she does the Hula-Hop,
Hula Hop!

"No, you don't!" CPR exclaimed, laughing at them but looking a little stern.

"Hey, Mrs. Murdoch!" Liz called as the bus pulled out, and everybody sang to her. Maddie Murdoch looked up at them in her rearview mirror, smiled, and waved her hand around in time to their song. They cheered. Before she looked back down, she glanced at Tracey, and for once Tracey didn't look away. What did it take, she wondered, to fit in with people who had always been Christians? She lived in a netherworld—not fit for her old ways, and certainly not fit for the better world of Christians who knew what they were doing.

There was talk on the bus that the classrooms at MoJoe would be renovated over Christmas, and real lockers put in.

"Get me on this, girls," Liz told them as they discussed it over the seats. "Lockers mean locker raids. Mary can put us on the hook more easily. She's going to be looking for pot."

"Who'd be dumb enough to bring pot to school?" Peggy asked.

"People who sell it, that's who," Liz said.

"Nobody sells pot at MoJoe. They'd have to be nuts."

Tracey looked at Peggy in wonder. Could she really be that naive?

Liz tossed a towel at Peggy in disgust. "Wake up, sleeping beauty."

"Well what's it matter, anyway?" Tracey asked. "You don't smoke pot, Liz. I don't. Peggy doesn't."

Liz rolled her eyes. "Look, why don't they just be up front about pot? Why put in the lockers just to catch people? Mary won't bust anybody. Just use 'em. *Talk* to them." She rolled her eyes as she stretched out the last phrase. They all knew what she meant. Getting busted by the police in their businesslike way would be a lot easier than having to sit through Sister Mary's interrogations.

"Boy," Peggy said, throwing herself back on her seat and stretching out her legs, "it's not like *The Trouble with Angels*, is it?"

They nodded. They had all seen the idealized and yet funny movie about a Catholic school, where the strictness of the strictest sister had hidden a heart of wisdom, and the badness of the baddest girl had been only foolishness, not real wickedness.

Tracey wondered if—assuming she survived MoJoe —she would find in a Baptist church, or any Protestant church, the power, the deeper life, that they were all missing here. Maybe they were all chasing rainbows. Or maybe the power of God, the power to make situations change and to help people worship Him, was bestowed only upon individuals. Maybe if she ever got good enough, God would give it to her, and she could help people. She would help all the people who were just like her in her badness. She would love loveless people, as soon as she knew how to do it.

Tracey soon was able to join in the practices again. The pain in her ankle subsided to a dull ache that she became used to. She had to play. She ran with a slight limp, but she learned to accommodate it, and after a week or so CPR forgot to ask about it and to talk about resting the foot longer.

Just after the Thanksgiving holiday, the workmen came and started installing lockers in the school hallways. It didn't take long. Students were assigned lockers as they became available. The sections slated for the seniors and juniors were installed first, so Liz got hers before Tracey got one.

Two days after Liz had the locker, she met Tracey after breakfast and said, "Come with me to the school office."

"What for?" Tracey asked.

"What for?" Liz echoed. She held out her big hand and opened it. Tracey saw two black lumps on her palm.

"That's mouse droppings," Liz told her. "There's a mouse in my locker."

"Liz—" Tracey began.

"Come on. They say I got to have a locker, well, they better get the mice out of it."

Tracey fell into step beside her. "Mice don't get into lockers."

"Jacamuzzi, the mouse droppings were in the locker. Hey!" she called as they entered the office doorway. "Mrs. Sladern!"

The part-time school secretary was a heavy woman with hair piled high on top of her head in a vintage sixties style. She turned and glanced at them. Sister Mary bustled into the front office from the duplicating room in the back.

"There's a mouse in my locker!" Liz exclaimed.

Sister Mary hardly looked up, and Mrs. Sladern seemed at a loss.

"Come on, I mean it," Liz said. "Check for yourself. It left its calling card." She dropped her cargo onto the counter. Mrs. Sladern drew back, and Sister Mary looked alarmed.

"Put those dirty things in the trash, Miss Lukas," Mary said. "And don't worry about the locker. Likely as not, the droppings were brought in it from the manufacturer."

"Well, maybe the mouse came, too."

"If a mouse did come, it's likely dead by now," she said. "Or gone, anyway. It wouldn't stay in your locker."

"I don't know—" Liz began.

"Come on, Liz," Tracey interrupted. "There's the bell. I gotta go."

"Sure. It's not your locker that's got the mouse."

Tracey rolled her eyes and left for class. She didn't

know what Liz was up to, but she was almost certain there was no mouse in her locker.

Liz had been right about locker raids, though. A week after all the lockers were installed, Tracey heard a rattling in the hallway while she was in geometry. She glanced out the open classroom door and saw Sister Mary and a police officer going through the lockers, one at a time. Well, she had nothing to hide and little sympathy for people who sold pot. But she also knew that her locker would be searched even though everybody knew she didn't use or sell pot. She made a mental note to leave a gospel tract in her locker for the police officer, and a booklet on what was wrong with the Catholic church for Mary.

Liz was uptight about the locker searches, but Tracey had other things to think about. Christmas wasn't far off. Her time with Sister James had been cut short by practices and games, and the two of them had plans to visit a lot over the holiday.

During the last week of school, when many of the girls exchanged presents and the workload was eased, Liz once again brought up the problem of the mouse in her locker. "Look," she said one morning, and held out her hand.

"What is it, more mouse doo-doo?" Tracey asked.

"No, see."

Tracey looked and saw the remains of a five-dollar bill.

"Chewed to bits!" Liz exclaimed. "Half of it, anyway. Look at it. Some little ball of fur is really feathering his nest in luxury. That's five bucks ruined. I'm going to go see Mary."

Tracey was curious to see what Mary would do. She

hung around the school office and looked through the glass while Mrs. Sladern paged Mary. Tracey had just enough time to duck into the girls' room before Mary arrived. After a minute or two, she slipped out again and returned to the glass. Mary was in the front office, listening with tight-lipped patience while Liz gesticulated wildly at the ruined bill in her hand.

Maybe there really was a mouse. Tracey could hardly imagine anyone blowing five bucks over a mouse story. She could tell from Mary's expression that the acting principal was giving Liz some cool and slightly sarcastic reply. Liz at last came away, steamed and unsatisfied.

"I'm emptying that locker," she said under her breath as she stomped off to class.

If it was an act, it was convincing. Liz fumed about the mouse in her locker for the rest of the day.

There were no more games until after Christmas. The Valkyries had three victories to their name, and talk had already turned to the championships. CPR took little part in these discussions, and Tracey wondered if their coach was reluctant to put hope in something that was still so far away, or if she really doubted they could get that far this year. It didn't matter much to Tracey. She had what she needed: a place on the team and all the benefits that it brought.

Her church history class was so full of new ideas that she had little time to challenge what she was taught. But as she read the textbook and listened carefully to her teacher's lectures, she did get the idea that all of this was one-sided. Maybe not lies, but not the whole truth. Things like the Great Schism were touched upon very lightly—not the events themselves but the reasonings and the details. She had heard that during the time of the papacy at Avignon, the two popes had waged wars on each other, slaughtered peasants, employed torture, and used assassins against rulers. Her textbook did not give any specifics about these events.

Tracey knew that she needed to study church history for herself. On one of her class's monthly trips to the town library, she had checked out an abridged version of *Foxe's Book of Martyrs*, half expecting from its woodcut illustrations, stilted figures, and sentimental wording that it would be a Roman Catholic account. She quickly saw that she had been wrong. The book was eye-opening. But between practices and term papers, she hardly had time for any reading at all. She read only a few snatches in the two weeks before the book had to go back to the town library. She wrote down the Dewey decimal number so she could look through that whole section the next time. There would be no more library visits until after Christmas.

"Are you and your folks doing anything special for Christmas?" she asked Liz on the morning before vacation started.

"Going to see my rich older brother," Liz said carelessly.

"Is he a lot older?"

"Fifteen years. Any other questions?"

Tracey glanced away. "No," she said and changed the subject to something else. Liz often became testy as vacations approached. Maybe it was harder for Liz. At least Tracey knew the score with her parents: Her father didn't love her and her mother loved somebody else more. But Liz's parents played it both ways. They had her home for vacations and did things together, then packed her up and shipped her back to school for another semester. Did they or didn't they love her? That was the question.

Maybe everybody wondered those things. Maybe family life never was the sunshiny existence she'd always supposed it could be. It was hard to know. In some things, like family and love, you only knew your own story, not anybody else's.

Christmas vacation was not as hard to handle this year. For one thing, Sister James was staying home. For another, Tracey knew her way around much better now that she was a sophomore. It wasn't hard to beg rides to town from some of the aides at the retirees' wing who had to go pick up prescriptions or do shopping.

A couple of the days were fair enough for Tracey to do some unchaperoned bicycle riding along the narrow farm roads outside of the Sanctuary. She peddled past the cemetery where the sisters were buried when they died, those who had spent long years in the convent and had no place else to go. There were old tombstones there; some of them so old that they really were just stones: big, flat rocks on which early homesteaders had either frescoed or scratched the names of deceased loved ones. Tracey loved wandering through the rolling grounds and searching out the oldest stones to decipher and ponder.

Returning from one of her forays out into the real world, she saw Maddie Murdoch's old but very clean station wagon pulling onto the grounds of the Sanctuary. She wondered what Mrs. Murdoch would be doing at the school with all the girls gone. Maybe she was visiting the retired nuns.

Tracey rode the bike up to the bike shed and hung around there until she was satisfied that the way back to her room was clear.

The days were so mild throughout the holidays that she could have practiced basketball outside. But she wanted to be left alone, so she used Liz's key to let herself into the gym and practice.

During one of her morning sessions, Father Williams came sauntering in with another priest at his side. Tracey would have kept practicing; she knew Father Bing was too easygoing to insist on all the tokens of respect normally paid headmasters by students. But she saw from the corner of her eye that they apparently wanted to talk to her. She stopped, wiped the sweat from her forehead with the back of her hand, and carried the basketball as she walked across the floor to meet them.

"Tracey Jacamuzzi!" Father Bing greeted her. "I haven't seen you all semester, except here."

She smiled. It was impossible for her to feel as at ease with a priest as Liz did, but she knew she owed him a lot. "Sorry to disappoint you, Father," she said. "I guess I've been a good girl this year."

"Or maybe other people are just giving up, eh?" He turned to the other priest. "Father Matt, this is Tracey Jacamuzzi, the girl I've told you so much about. Tracey, Father Matt is from Villa Marie." His smile broadened. "Our chief rivals."

Tracey held out her hand to the new priest. "Father," she said.

"Miss Jacamuzzi." He smiled a little ruefully. "Father Bing tells me the Valkyries will sweep us up."

"I hope so," she said frankly, laughing. But it was a laugh with a needle of pain in it. Villa Marie had been the only school to defeat MoJoe for two consecutive years. Two years ago, the Villa Marie Villains and the MoJoe Valkyries had battled it out for the district championship. The MoJoes had beaten the Villains once, and after both teams had won their division championships, they had played each other again. The Valkyries lost the district championship to the Villains in a game so close that even now Liz could hardly talk about it. Then, during Tracey's freshman year, the MoJoes had lost both to the Villains and to Lady of the Valley, barring the Valkyries from both the division and district titles.

The Lady of the Valley loss had been an upset, but Villa Marie was a team to be reckoned with, and always had been.

Father Matt talked with her about basketball strategies and the top players in the league, while Tracey wondered what the two of them were leading up to. At last Father Williams put a hand on his friend's arm and said, "Well, Tracey, we ought to leave you to your workout. I see that your foot is doing better these days."

"I didn't know the sprain was that obvious," she said guardedly.

He smiled and winked. "When I see a Valkyrie on the bench, I know something is wrong, even if the other team isn't all that good. Now that it's rested again, I hope to see great things from you."

"I'll do my best," she promised.

They said good-bye and left her.

Tracey thoughtfully dropped the ball to the floor and let it come back up to her hand. Could Father Bing have been showing her off to a rival?

Tracey still wasn't used to basketball—especially girls' basketball—meaning that much to an adult. From her own perspective, each game was tremendously important during the game itself. And when she practiced, she practiced with a seriousness and intensity that she knew separated her from most of the other players, except Liz and Scooter. But after-hours, she was just plain old Tracey, and MoJoe was plain old, lonely MoJoe.

She switched hands and dribbled with the left. One thing about basketball was true: You could let yourself be lost in the rush of practice, of running, of gradual improvement, of victories. For some people, like Scooter and Susan, making the team had been a means of getting what they wanted: popularity. But for other people, like Liz, the game was not the means but the end. No wonder Liz had pushed her into it. In the game itself, everything else dropped away: guilt and shame and anguished memories. There was nothing but you in the black-and-white uniform, a shield across your back, the number emblazoned on your chest, the action of the game carrying you away like a drug.

She shook away these thoughts and returned to her practice, but not before she acknowledged to herself that even in practice she was drinking oblivion. When she practiced she forgot the rest of the world.

She ran down the court, dribbling the ball, and came up for an almost-dunk. One hand's length was all that separated her from that particular glory. As the ball went in, she realized that these sessions were not much different from the old nighttime vigils out on the roof, with her cigarettes in her pocket.

She wondered where the sense of wonder about her new religion had gone, and whether her flame of belief was merely waning or had gone out. She observed her faith in Christ now almost as mechanically as the nuns observed their Roman Catholicism.

It takes two to make religion, she told herself. I can't do it all myself. I can't hold out against Mass and statues and confession, and be singled out all the time, and beat up, and still not see anything. God has to do something for once; He's got to be my God if I'm going to be His Christian. She involuntarily glanced up at the roof. *I hope You heard that. I wish you would show me something—anything. I wish I could see something of Your glory.*

A movement at the door caught her eye and interrupted her prayer, but it was just Mrs. Murdoch walking by with one of the retired sisters. They did not look in.

With a tremendous act of will, Tracey forced her thoughts away and went back to her game. If she started on her regrets about this true religion that she no longer enjoyed but could not leave, she'd get nothing done all day.

After a moment it was back to the game, back to running and jumping and making that last stretch to control the ball into the hoop.

356

Oh, dear, it's so nice to have you here all to myself,"
Sister James said on Christmas Eve as she and
Tracey sat together in one of the worn, old parlors of
the retirees' wing.

Tracey could stay in the wing until ten; all that required was a breathless run across the dark grounds
and then another run up the dark steps to the sanctum
of her room. She hated the nervousness that bordered
on fear as she ran through the dark outdoors, and the
darkness of the main building was even worse. But it
seemed a price she should pay to spend time with her
friend.

The small Christmas tree twinkled at them, and
Sister Lucy nodded in the rocking chair. It was a little
difficult for Sister Lucy to share Sister James these
days. During the previous semester, Tracey had sensed
that Sister James was having to slip out for her occa-
sional walks with Tracey. Not that Sister Lucy would
prevent them, but she spoke often of joining them,
and it was clear that Sister James not only cherished

her privacy with Tracey but also respected it. Somehow this childless old woman understood that Tracey needed her all to herself sometimes.

After another moment, Sister Lucy sank into sleep. Tracey looked up at Sister James and cautiously slid closer for Sister James to put an arm around her. Sister James smiled.

"Has it been a merry Christmas so far, dear?"

"Happy enough, Sister."

"I think you'll be able to use the scarf and gloves."

Tracey smiled. "I guess so. Where did you find black-and-white gloves and a scarf to match?" She cast an involuntary glance at Sister Lucy, who was slumbering peacefully.

"I had no idea of what color to get you, dear, but there's a dear lady who runs errands for us if we need her to. She picked them out, and I agreed with her. You wouldn't like anything so much as the team colors."

"She had good taste," Tracey agreed.

"She knows you," Sister James told her. "It was Maddie Murdoch."

"Oh," Tracey said. Questions flooded her mind. She desperately wanted to know if Maddie had gone back to Sister James with any stories of her troubles with Tracey. But all she said was, "Yeah, she drives the bus for the team. Sister Patricia Rose used to, but now she has to have her hands free to pull her hair out before and after the games."

Sister James laughed gently.

After a moment, Tracey became serious. "Is Sister Lucy . . . all right?"

"Shhh, dear. She'll hear you."

"She can't hear me, Sister. She never wakes up."

Sister James looked at her gravely. "Sister Lucy and I have been friends for many years. Dear me, it's so hard to see her failing. But yes, dear. She is not doing well."

"Can the doctor help her?"

"Oh, my, she takes so many medicines now that I can't keep up with them. One of the girls here has to keep track of them for her and make sure she takes them all."

By "one of the girls," Sister James meant a nurse. Tracey prayed a secret prayer of thanks that Sister James was still mentally keen. The old nun had too much delicacy to speak candidly of her friend's increasing feebleness of mind and body. And Tracey, remembering the respect that Sister James had taught her the previous summer, pried no further.

After a moment, Sister James began, "At Christmas when I was a girl—"

Almost on cue, Tracey leaned her head against the old woman's shoulder. It was a familiarity she had never allowed herself before with Sister James. There was something about the habit, and the vows it implied, that repelled the images of grandmothers and great-aunts that Sister James's person could call up in Tracey. But on Christmas night she had to feel close to someone. She had to belong to somebody. And she was right in assuming that Sister James would accept her.

"We used to have a wire corn popper," Sister James continued. "It sat mounted alongside the fireplace most of the time. It was black and long-handled, like a collection basket."

Tracey closed her eyes and breathed in the faint scent of plain Ivory soap mingled with the fainter scent of starch that was, in fact, the way most of the sisters smelled. They did not wear perfume. It was a homey and safe smell to her by now. She let Sister James talk on, and in the dim twinkle of the lighted tree, she fell into a doze, at peace and satisfied.

The next day, Christmas, was cheerier. Tracey joined the retired nuns for their Christmas dinner. As one of the boarders, she was entitled to simply eat and not serve or clean up. But her face was familiar to nearly all of the retirees, and she was young and dressed up for Christmas in one of the dresses she had brought from home. Many of the older women, who lived most of their days as prisoners of fading minds, probably thought she was their own niece or younger sister. And she played her parts for them, carrying food around to the tables, talking, making jokes, and teasing back and forth with those sisters who were able to.

She had never realized how one outsider's face could brighten up the day for so many of them. More than once a sister reached out to pat her face or put a lingering hand on her hair. She felt a little ashamed for having spent so much of her time exclusively with Sister James when there were so many lonely old women here. They were all well taken care of, and the attendants in the nursing wing were concerned and dedicated. But even a nice nursing home was still a nursing home, and isolation from youth was still isolation.

Apparently Tracey wasn't the only one who had realized these things. She had finally sat down next to Sister James to eat when a new outbreak of laughter and greetings made her look up. Maddie Murdoch, tall and elegant with that unconscious elegance of hers, was in the entryway of the dining room. She had a wide satchel on one arm and a stack of cards in her hand.

Tracey swallowed. A desperation to leave seized her, but there was no graceful way to go. Luckily, she was at the end of a table, with Sister James on one side and two very fat nuns across from her. Surrounded, as it were.

But Mrs. Murdoch, unaware of Tracey's presence, was already at one of the smaller tables, talking with three of the women and handing them cards and small wrapped gifts.

"Who is the woman in the dress, dear?" Sister James asked her.

"Maddie Murdoch," Tracey said.

"Oh, isn't that nice of her to come visit today?"

"Yeah," Tracey said.

"She's a Protestant, you know," Sister James added.

"I know. We . . . uh . . . had a misunderstanding a while ago."

Sister James turned her full attention to her. "You did, dear? I'm so surprised. Both of you are so kind-hearted."

"Sister James," Tracey began. "There's a lot you don't know about me—I mean, about my worse side. I . . . I talk too much, for one thing."

Sister James looked puzzled and concerned. Tracey didn't even know how to start telling her about all that had passed. There were some things Sister James had never felt and would never understand. Tracey wasn't eager to have the naive, kind old woman see the darkness in her past. With a small shock at her own forgetfulness, Tracey recalled that Mrs. Murdoch had been the one to send Sister James after her, and Tracey had distrusted even that action at first.

361

"I'll tell you about it sometime," she said lamely.

"And how are you, Sister James Anne?" Maddie Murdoch asked. Tracey started.

"Well, just fine, dear, and a merry Christmas to you," Sister James said, kissing Maddie Murdoch's cheek. "This is my dear friend, Tracey," she said.

Tracey glanced up at Mrs. Murdoch. "Hi," she said.

"Well, Tracey, and how are you, then?" Mrs. Murdoch asked.

"Pretty good. How about you?" Tracey asked, trying to sound at ease, and failing.

"Have you had a merry Christmas?"

The question caught her off guard. She hadn't had a merry Christmas, not really, only a peaceful one. But she said, "Yeah," and then shrugged so as not to be guilty of lying.

"Tracey let me tell her stories last night," Sister James said with a laugh, "and then complimented me by falling asleep."

"Well—" Tracey began.

"That is a compliment!" Maddie exclaimed lightly, turning her attention to one of the older sisters who was reaching to say hello to her. "I used to beg my daughters to go to sleep with stories, and they never would drop off. Good day, and a merry Christmas to you both."

"Thank you, dear," Sister James said. She returned to her meal while Tracey breathed a sigh of relief.

Tracey talked about other things as they ate: basketball, upcoming games, how much better her foot felt.

Dessert was little squares of pumpkin pie. A lot of the sisters offered theirs to Tracey, and she accepted them gladly. The food in the retirees' wing was pretty good, especially at Christmas. Sister Lucy, on Sister James's other side, was fussing about not being allowed to finish her main course properly, and while Sister James attended to her, Tracey happily went to work on all of her pie.

"Dear, you ought to make your peace with Maddie Murdoch," Sister James said suddenly, turning back to her.

Tracey looked up.

"You of all people ought to be at ease with Mrs. Murdoch," Sister James said.

"Sister," Tracey said gently, "don't you see how different I am?"

"No, dear," Sister James said.

"We're all different here," Tracey reminded her. "The boarders, anyway. You only get sent away here for one reason. Because somebody either couldn't handle you or didn't want to." She put down her fork. "How am I going to fit in with Mrs. Murdoch?"

"You fit with me, don't you, dear?"

"Because you don't mind," Tracey said. "And," she added after a guilty pause, "because you don't know about some things. I have to be tough sometimes. I said some terrible things to Mrs. Murdoch once— twice."

"I see," Sister James said quietly.

"It made me feel ashamed later," Tracey confessed. "I just couldn't face her. She knows things about me that I wish she didn't know. I think she's only ever seen the worst things in me."

"Dear heart," Sister James said, suddenly very serious, almost urgent. "Don't ever do anything that makes you feel ashamed later. Don't ever give in to shameful things."

"Sister, they did shameful things to me. Mrs. Murdoch never saw that."

"Let the crime be on them, then, not on yourself. Don't ever shame your own self."

Tracey hesitated. Sister James's age was not lost on her. The old nun had seen many young girls who had shamed themselves in any number of ways. Her own life of restraint and forbearance gave her the grounds to urge Tracey to restrain herself, and Tracey knew it.

"All right, Sister," she said at last. "I won't."

Satisfied with this submission, Sister James looked at her a moment longer and then said, "Make peace with Mrs. Murdoch, dear. Whatever was done can at least be settled. You need not be good friends, only at ease with each other. It's easier afterward to have everything cleared up than to carry around the dread of running into somebody or having to speak to them."

"You're right, Sister," Tracey said at last. "I'll talk to her after dinner if I can catch her alone."

# FIFTY-SIX

Bedtime came early that night for the retired sisters. It had been a big day for them, with an early morning Mass to celebrate the Nativity. Sister Lucy began to nod immediately after dessert was cleared away, and though an urn of coffee had been set out with paper Christmas cups, Sister James also looked weary. Rather than stay and visit, Tracey told her older friend that she would be going back up to the hall.

"So early, dear?" Sister James asked, but she looked relieved, as though she hadn't expected to be allowed to go to bed so soon.

"I'll be down tomorrow first thing," Tracey promised, and she kissed Sister James's cheek.

"All right, then. See you tomorrow, Big Jac."

"You too, Big Jim." Tracey laughed. Calling Sister James such a disrespectful nickname was a familiarity she wouldn't normally have permitted herself. But Sister James had talked so much about her old nickname, Tracey realized the lonely old woman had enjoyed knowing that her students had made her a topic of conversation and had christened her behind her back.

One of the nurses came to help Sister James off to bed. In the winter she was often stiff in the ankles and knees from arthritis. For a fleeting moment, Tracey wondered if Sister James would still be able to enjoy their walks when the basketball season ended and Tracey had more time. There was always the possibility that arthritis would win its slow but inevitable fight to confine the sister to a wheelchair.

These were bleak thoughts for a Christmas afternoon. Tracey hurried into her wraps and decided to go up to her room and read some Lewis. There were some contraband Tastykakes up there, and she could make coffee.

Rather than go out the front door, she took a shortcut through the kitchen. The service door was closer to her hall. She went through the area Sister James called the scullery, then past a big steel sink, then out the door, which had been propped open to let out some of the heat.

Another figure stooped outside the door, wrapped in a dark coat. For a moment Tracey wondered what one of the nuns was doing out there, but when the figure straightened and turned, she saw it was Mrs. Murdoch.

"Tracey," she said with a smile.

"Oh," Tracey said stupidly.

"I told the ladies I would drop some of this garbage out here on my way out. It was getting too crowded in the kitchen."

"Yeah," Tracey said.

"Well, I trust you had a good Christmas," Mrs. Murdoch said with another smile. She would have left, but Tracey said, "Mrs. Murdoch."

"Yes?" Mrs. Murdoch looked at Tracey with that clear, kind look that Tracey both desired and feared. Tracey steeled herself.

"I want to apologize to you for how I acted—that time," she said.

Maddie Murdoch only looked at her, and Tracey didn't know what else to say. Even if she thoroughly abased herself and called herself the cheap daughter of an adulteress and a violent man, she would sound like she was making excuses. And if she tried to explain to Mrs. Murdoch about how everything between them had seemed like another ploy from Sister Mary, that would be another excuse. So after a long and awkward pause, Tracey said, "It wasn't right to talk to you the way I did, and I'm sorry I was too chicken to apologize to you for so long."

Still, Mrs. Murdoch didn't answer her, only fixed her with a puzzled, though not angry, look.

Tracey said again, "I'm sorry."

"I didn't mean to offend you," Mrs. Murdoch said at last.

"I know, and I'm sorry," Tracey replied.

Maddie Murdoch seemed to check herself at Tracey's answer, perhaps realizing that Tracey would just keep apologizing if she tried to reason out what had happened last time.

"They tell me you're not Catholic," Mrs. Murdoch said.

"Who told you?" Tracey asked.

"Liz, for one, and Sister St. Gerard."

"I went to a tent meeting at a Baptist church one day, and pretty soon after, I got saved. About two years ago," Tracey said. "Do you know what that means?"

Mrs. Murdoch nodded. "The Bible says that the Lord died to make an atonement for us—"

"Yes," Tracey said.

"And God, by His sovereign grace and mercy, calls His people to repentance, to be saved."

"I know about to repent and be saved," Tracey agreed. "I don't know what that first part means."

"It means that salvation is all of grace and not of works, dear," Mrs. Murdoch told her.

Tracey remembered that she had once told Mrs. Murdoch not to call her dear. She hoped Mrs. Murdoch didn't remember that and wasn't embarrassed about letting the word slip. It seemed like Irish people always called girls "dear." Or maybe all Catholics and former Catholics did it.

"I believe that," Tracey told her. "All of grace and not of works—Ephesians chapter two, verse eight, right?"

Maddie Murdoch smiled as though with sudden recognition. Certain verses always drew converted Catholics.

"Is your family Catholic?" she asked Tracey.

"Yes, but I have to go now," Tracey said. "I'll see you on the bus at the next game, OK?" She held out her hand to Mrs. Murdoch. She wanted to be polite, but more than anything, she wanted to get away before her story spilled out or was drawn out. She didn't want Mrs. Murdoch to know the rest; there were too many bad parts. She didn't know how to face those eyes again and talk about how she had lived her Christian life. Mrs. Murdoch had not understood the fight, could not understand the way things were at MoJoe.

A little surprised, Maddie Murdoch nonetheless shook hands with her. Tracey hopped off the step and ran up to the hall, her room, the shelter of C. S. Lewis, and the security of Tastykakes.

T he first game after Christmas was against Lady of
the Valley. It was an away game. Tracey had purposely not told Liz about her apology to Maddie Murdoch. She was still a little angry that Liz had been so
cavalier in dictating what sort of friends Tracey should
make. But she also just wanted to shock Liz for once.
She lived too much in suspense about what Liz would
do next. It was time for Liz to be taken aback by something Tracey did.

On the Friday of the big game, there was a pep rally
in the gym, and sixth hour was canceled. Pep rallies at
the Sanctuary usually happened only once or twice a
season, mostly because they were so unnecessary. The
girls stayed wound up over basketball from game to
game without any help. But the Lady of the Valley
game was big, and this year it seemed more certain
that the MoJoes could win it. They were undefeated
after three games. Certain school rituals were appropriate to anticipate an event that would be almost as
big as a championship.

Tracey knew all the cheers, of course, and part of the routine of a pep rally was for the team to come out and cheer too. She didn't like to yell and scream so much before a game, when she would need her voice and her wind so desperately, but Liz had taught her to mouth the words almost silently, opening her mouth wide on every yell. The volume was usually up enough for nobody to notice.

The final cheer was the "MoJoe Ho Ho." The team linked arms and swayed to its rhythm, then went out in a line, arms still linked, to get on the bus.

Maddie Murdoch greeted them as they clambered aboard.

"Hey, hey, Mrs. Murdoch," Liz said. Tracey came up the steps behind her.

"Hey, Mrs. Murdoch," Tracey exclaimed easily.

"There's our forward!" Mrs. Murdoch replied.

"Gimme five for luck!" Tracey held out her hand, and Maddie inexpertly slapped it. It was a custom the Irish woman had obviously never practiced much.

Liz stopped and turned at this exchange of pleasantries. "Hey," she said to Tracey.

"Hey yourself," Tracey returned. "Come on, Wonder Polack. You're blocking the aisle."

Liz flopped into a seat, and Tracey took the one behind it.

"You and Murdoch friends?" Liz asked.

"I been giving her investment advice, that's all."

Liz threw her gym bag at Tracey. "Get real."

"We're cool," Tracey told her, tossing the bag back over the back of the seat.

"Well, isn't that nice. When did it happen?"

"We had a chat over Christmas."

"See, I told you she was OK."

"Yeah, she's OK."

"And Protestant."

"And Protestant. For a Catholic who says you don't believe anything, you're sure concerned about who's Protestant and who's not."

"I hang around in bad company." Liz jumped up and clapped her hands. "R-o-w-d-i-e, that's the way we spell *rowdy!* Rowdy! Let's get rowdy!"

Everybody whooped as loud as they could. Peggy and some of the others began their drumming tattoo on the sides of the bus and the backs of the seats.

> R-o-w-d-i-e!
> That's the way we spell *rowdy!*
> Rowdy! Let's get rowdy!
> Whoo!

Lady of the Valley's gym was nice, though small. The game was so far away from the Sanctuary that not many MoJoe spectators had been able to come. The bus pulled up for the game in the dimness of early evening, and the team hustled out to get dressed and warmed up.

Away from the pep rally and the good wishes of their schoolmates, they all felt a little more on edge, less confident. Lady of the Valley was one of the few schools whose spirit for basketball was as high as MoJoe's. They had their own opening ritual with a school song and mascot, a girl dressed up like a bird. Everybody called it the Chicken of the Valley, though it was supposed to be a ptarmigan.

"I read about ptarmigans in *White Fang*," Tracey

whispered to Liz before they ran onto the court to sing their own school song. "And you know what, they're really stupid birds."

Liz snickered, but then it was time to go. Tracey quickly learned that you might laugh at the team's choice of mascots, but there was no way to laugh at the way they played.

Tracey's ankle was strong enough to withstand a lot of punishment and give back only a few twinges. She used it that night. The Ptarmigans had developed a good half-court press, a strategy that Tracey had learned in practice but had never used or played against. Time after time, the Ptarmigans took the ball from the Valkyries and passed it back down to their own basket. CPR called two time-outs in four minutes.

In spite of her frantic instructions, the first quarter ended with things looking bad. The Valkyries were down by twelve points.

"Skip this junk," Tracey whispered to Liz as they walked off the court to where an agitated CPR waited. "My man's passing off a lot while I'm playing zone. Get clear when they have the ball, and I'll pass off to you. Trash the zone stuff."

Liz gave a brief nod, and they went to hear what CPR had to say.

The Ptarmigans started with the ball in the second quarter. Tracey managed to interrupt their passing strategy by hanging back and jumping to intercept their forward's pass.

"Liz!" she yelled.

"Here!" Liz barked. Tracey hurled the ball as hard as she could back to Liz, who was back almost at the half-court line. Liz caught it unhampered and ran for the basket. Tracey followed, but Liz sank it on the first try. Loud cheers came from the MoJoe crowd, and the Valley girls added a few yells of their own.

"They're calling us JDs," Liz yelled to Tracey as the Ptarmigans took the ball to bring it in again.

"What's a JD?"

"Duh, juvenile delinquent."

"Yeah, practicing faith without a license. Look me up." Inwardly, though, she cringed. *Man, if they only knew some of what I've done.* Being a MoJoe girl meant catching some flak from other schools. But it was OK; as long as they were winning, they could stand to smile at all their foes. *Hey, that's a line from a hymn. Which one?*

Tracey covered her man. The other forward tried to pass; Tracey caught the ball on the edge of her hand, and they both dived for it. The ref's whistle blew.

"Jump ball," she called.

"Let's go, Tracey," Liz said as the two teams circled for the jump.

Both girls leaped, but Tracey was the better jumper. She hit the ball to Liz, who was closest to the MoJoe basket. Liz passed back to her as she sped up and got ahead.

"Over here!" Scooter yelled.

Scooter had somehow managed to sprint even farther ahead. Tracey passed to her, and Scooter put it in.

"Man-to-man," Tracey whispered to her as they jogged back down the court. Scooter nodded.

The whistle shrilled for a time-out. "You can't keep up man-to-man through a whole game," CPR told them.

"We lose every other way," Liz said.

"All right. Stay on your man, but watch out on offense. They want to foul you if they can."

The man-to-man defense worked for the rest of the quarter, and the score crept closer. The Valkyries were down by only four points at the half. But they were exhausted.

Liz griped as they drank their water. Tracey began to realize that this was a losing game. Maybe they could have pulled it off at home, with the whole school yelling and screaming for them. But here, in this small gym, with only a few friends and some jeers from the other kids, they weren't likely to make up for Valley's superior half-court press.

All the same, the game had its highlights. She brought the ball down on one of the first plays, and this time, when the opposing forward stayed on her, Tracey didn't pass off to Scooter. They kept losing possession that way. She bent and pivoted as she came, but she didn't shrink back, and she didn't pay too much attention to her hands. It was almost like it had been when she'd started playing with Liz: *Look ahead, look ahead, keep the ball controlled and close—*

Something hit her arm, and the ref's whistle blew.

"Reaching!"

Tracey smiled at her opponent.

"Pass off," Scooter hissed at her after the other forward's foul had been logged.

"Cool it," Tracey hissed back. She brought the ball all the way down to the key and nodded at Liz to play the crisscross under the basket with Scooter. They did, and Tracey passed a quick, short pass to Scooter, who took the shot and missed. Tracey rebounded and put it in.

She found a moment to explain to Scooter that too much passing had been their problem, but she realized after a few more lost possessions that Scooter wasn't as agile as she was. The other Valley forward could get the ball from her. That, or Scooter lost control of the ball, and everyone went for it in a free-for-all.

CPR called another time-out. "Lukas and Jacamuzzi, bring it down," she ordered. "Scooter, top of the key."

They all nodded. Scooter might easily assume she was at the center because her shooting had been good this game. But Tracey realized that she and Liz played alike. They could both move with the ball and with each other.

After that, the score seesawed back and forth a few times. Tracey stopped caring. It was great to be playing this way with Liz. They each seemed to know where the other would go, how the ball should best be handled, when to pass, when to fake, when to pivot. They tried a pick-and-roll at the top of the key, and Tracey made the shot.

As the game's focus shifted to the top of the key, the Valley defense came out more. Then it was time for quick passes to Scooter or to the guards.

The end of the third quarter saw the Valkyries ahead by six points. When the two teams returned to the court, the Valley kids began a steady drumming on the bleachers.

Tracey had played the entire game except for a few minutes, as had the rest of the first-string. It was harder to concentrate and harder to keep up. Several times the ball was lost because she was slow to catch it or got distracted by the player who dogged her when she brought it down. The score tipped back to a four-point Valley lead, and the Valkyries never regained it. The final score was a disappointing 96 to 92, in favor of the Ptarmigans.

"Shoot," Liz said as the buzzer went off. The Ptarmigan kids had been counting down the seconds, and they came spilling out onto the floor.

Tracey was just glad it was over. She looked back at the small MoJoe cheering section. Maddie Murdoch offered a sympathetic smile and a shrug. CPR looked tight-lipped. The other spectators were milling around, looking for the quickest way out for the long drive home.

"Ptarmigans are undefeated now," Liz said glumly, "and we're one down."

"Then we might meet them again," Tracey said.

"They have to lose to someone to play us again," Liz reminded her. "If not, they get the division title. And who's going to beat them? All the other teams are a joke."

Tracey sighed. She had not come to MoJoe hoping to win a championship. Even though she keenly felt the disappointment of this first loss, she was unable to grieve over not getting a championship that she'd never even heard of before being sent to MoJoe. She had never felt cut out for greatness. Just making the team had been a high enough peak for her life.

Liz would never understand that, so Tracey tried to look grim too. But inside, she had something to exult over. She had outscored Scooter.

# FIFTY-EIGHT

Even the saddest of defeats and the closest of close games could be comforted by a stop at McDonald's and a break from the monotonous dinners at MoJoe. Each girl who was a boarder, as she sat swigging down a milk shake with extra-large fries and one or two hamburgers, ate knowing she was enjoying this privilege whether she won or lost, whether she was first-string or second, whether she had a lot of talent or none at all.

Tracey had all the money she wanted, supplied by her mother. Lately, in her letters, she had been confiding in Tracey about how unhappy she was and how violent and uncaring Don Jacamuzzi could be. These complaints somehow called up both disgust and rage in Tracey, though she knew her own situation was a confirmation of everything her mother said. In her careful replies, she never alluded to these comments. With a kind of desperation to appear normal, she hoped to put off the inevitable.

But the money came in handy for the stops at McDonald's. Peggy seldom had money, and Tracey liked to treat her when they stopped for dinner after a game. Peggy usually protested before giving in to a chocolate milk shake and absolutely nothing else; then Tracey ordered for her whatever she ordered for herself. She knew it was genuinely humiliating to Peggy to be so poor, but Tracey could think of nothing worse than having to sit forlorn and hungry while everybody else ate McDonald's.

"Hey," Liz said to her as they dug into their French fries. Tracey and Liz always ate their hamburgers first and then worked on the French fries separately. Liz called it "keeping kosher," but Tracey didn't know what she meant.

"What?" Tracey asked.

"Come up front. Let's keep Mrs. Murdoch company."

"You want me too?"

"Yes, hotshot. Come on."

Tracey gave in and followed her. She really wanted to be left in peace to doze once she finished eating, but Liz liked to talk in front of an audience. They both slid into the front seat behind the driver.

"Come for a visit, girls?" Mrs. Murdoch asked.

"Want a French fry?" Tracey asked.

"No, thank you, dear."

That took care of Tracey's obligation to the conversation. She returned to the big cardboard holster of fries.

"You know what?" Liz said. "I got a mouse in my locker at school."

"A pet?" Mrs. Murdoch asked.

"Oh, come on, Liz!" Tracey exclaimed. "Would you quit that mouse bit?"

"Hey, shut up!" Liz yelled back. Then she said,

nicely, to Mrs. Murdoch, "No, a vermin mouse. I can't catch it, but he's been leaving his calling card. Or, they've been leaving their calling cards. It might be one, it might be more."

Tracey sighed and rolled her eyes.

"Liz Lukas," Sister Madeleine exclaimed from the seat across the aisle. "I thought you gave up on that at Christmas."

"I didn't give up on it, Sister," Liz said. "I just took my stuff out of my locker. It's not fair. I asked for a new locker, but they won't give me one."

"We don't have any spares," CPR told her.

"Well, it's still not fair. I brought back some mouse poison after Christmas. So nobody better eat in my locker."

"Nobody eats in a locker," Tracey said.

"Miss Lukas, poisons of any kind are a serious thing," CPR said. "You ought not to be storing it anywhere at all."

"Oh, come on, Sister. It was only about a half ounce. A few pellets, that's all," Liz assured her.

"It's still dangerous. Accidents happen."

"All right. I'll put up notices on the locker. If the mice can read them, well, I'll let them keep the old locker."

"You don't have any more poison in your room?" CPR demanded.

"No, Sister, I just brought enough to put in the locker and prove to everyone that I've got mice."

CPR seemed satisfied, and Maddie Murdoch looked amused. Tracey still didn't know what Liz was getting at with this mouse business. Maybe there really was one. She certainly had been carrying on about it.

379

"I hope that's the sum of your troubles, Lizzie," Mrs. Murdoch said, glancing at her in the rearview mirror. Tracey finished her fries and put her trash in the big garbage can that sat wedged between the front seat and one of the crash bars.

"If you had a mouse anywhere in your house or garage, you'd probably be pretty uptight about it too," Liz said.

"I'd purchase myself a cat."

She smiled at Liz and turned her eyes back to the quiet road. Tracey looked at her in the rearview mirror. It was a long and wide mirror, as big as a sun visor. There was no doubt that Mrs. Murdoch was an attractive woman, tall like a basketball player, with clearly defined cheekbones, chin, and shoulders, and long, slim arms. She looked almost athletic, but she had a grace that Tracey had seen in very few women, and never in a tall woman.

"Did you play basketball ever?" she asked suddenly.

"In high school," Mrs. Murdoch told her.

"At MoJoe."

"Yes, dear. But back then, everybody played basketball who wanted to. Dear me, I think we had at least twenty girls on the team."

"Did you start?" Tracey asked.

"I don't really know," Mrs. Murdoch said. "We took turns, I believe."

Liz let out a slight laugh.

"Aye, we had horseback riding back then, and fencing too," Mrs. Murdoch said. Both Liz and Tracey perked up.

"Wow," Liz said.

Mrs. Murdoch kept her attention on the road but

added, "I never lost my love for equestrian sports. I still belong to a stable and have the use of some horses there."

"You don't own a horse?" Liz asked.

"No, but I own two saddles that I keep there."

"Does your husband ride?" Tracey asked.

Mrs. Murdoch glanced up at her in the mirror. "I'm divorced, dear."

Liz gave Tracey a sharp dig with her elbow. Tracey felt her face flame with embarrassment.

"I'm sorry," she stammered.

Mrs. Murdoch gave her another glance and a quick smile. "It was what brought me to the Lord, dear. He works all things to His good purpose."

"Me too," Tracey heard herself say.

"You too, what?" Liz asked. "Work all things out to your good purpose?"

"No, I got saved because of . . . of things . . . like that. I don't know, forget I said it." Her face got hotter. There it was, being drawn out of her again. She turned away from Liz and saw out of the corner of her eye that Mrs. Murdoch was looking at her again.

CPR glanced over, probably disapproving of this talk of conversions. But she said nothing to stop them.

"Anyway," Mrs. Murdoch said, "I fenced and rode and played basketball and volleyball."

"Did you go to college?" Liz asked.

"No, dear. I married immediately out of high school. I was seventeen."

Liz let out a gasp of horror so loud that Tracey forgot her own shock at the idea of someone marrying so young and laughed.

Maddie Murdoch laughed too. "I would be shocked

now if one of my own daughters should announce such a thing, though both of them are past seventeen."

"How old are they?" Liz asked.

"My oldest, Patsy, is twenty, and Beth Ann is eighteen."

"Are they married?" Liz asked.

"Neither one, dear. Patsy is in Ireland, in school. And Beth Ann is at Stanford University in California."

"Man, they really commuted," Liz said. She shot a glance at Tracey. The girls, indeed, had gone far away.

Mrs. Murdoch nodded but didn't look up. After a moment, she said, "Patsy is going to save the world, or save Ireland, at least. I don't think Beth Ann has quite made up her mind what she wants to do."

"Are they . . . are they saved too?" Tracey asked.

"Saved from what?" Liz demanded, irritated at Tracey's religious terminology.

Maddie answered Liz. "Saved from the power and judgment of sin, dear. No, Tracey, they aren't. I believe that Patsy was an agnostic last we spoke. Beth Ann told me she was 'searching.'"

Talk waned. The bus rumbled on, and Tracey moved to the next seat back so she could stretch out her legs. Liz also stretched out, leaning her back against the side of the bus. After a few minutes, she began to doze, her head propped on her hand. CPR was also dozing.

Tracey looked up at the rearview mirror and thought about this woman who had divorced and yet was a Christian, who spoke more freely of the Lord than Tracey did and yet had daughters who had apparently rejected her beliefs and—perhaps—her. Why would a Protestant do all this volunteer work at a Catholic

382

school, especially now that Mary had put the kibosh on her Bible study? Tracey knew that a couple of girls went to Mrs. Murdoch's to do housework every week. No doubt she influenced them as much as she could. And Tracey had noticed that she had freedom to bring Bibles to the retirees and often read to them and talked with them.

She had a dignity that never put itself forward. And yet she also had a kind of sureness. She walked with long, graceful strides, and she wore carefully tailored women's trousers more often than skirts. Her clothes were tasteful and modest, but just a little more elegant and perfectly accented than Tracey had ever seen. So there was nothing retiring about her, either. She wasn't like Mrs. Murphy, Tracey realized. Maddie Murdoch was much more a doer; she'd certainly proved that when she had snatched Tracey and Scooter apart by the ears.

Tracey felt that certain obligations existed for them to be friends. But even with all that Mrs. Murdoch had seen and done, Tracey's life and person would be a real shock for her.

Tracey frowned as she thought of this. Just then Mrs. Murdoch looked up in the rearview mirror to check the traffic and saw Tracey watching her. It happened so quickly that Tracey didn't have time to look surprised or to look away. They traded glances before Mrs. Murdoch turned her eyes back to the road.

For a week, Liz's locker remained decorated with her hand-drawn sketches of mice and warning signs in large letters.

DANGER! DO NOT ENTER.
MOUSE!
MOUSE POISON INSIDE.

The warnings failed to prevent a search of her locker during fifth hour. As nearly as Tracey could tell, all the searches took place at about the same time of day. She always heard the voices of the police officer and Sister Mary, along with the creak and slam of locker doors, during her geometry class.

"You'd think that cop would get sick of looking through our lockers," Peggy said that afternoon after the search. As usual, nobody had been caught with anything. Whoever was selling the stuff was either too smart to leave it lying around, or somehow was able to figure out when the police were coming.

"I wonder if the sellers know when the police are coming out," Tracey said.

Liz, who was at her desk busily drawing another mouse warning, looked up. "Mary doesn't have to have a cop here to conduct a search. She can do it herself, because the lockers are school property. He's just been coming around to show her the ropes."

"That means we can count on a lot more searches," Peggy guessed.

"Looks that way. I told you," Liz reminded them.

Tracey felt exasperated. "OK, Liz, you told us. What are we supposed to do, boycott the lockers? They can search mine as much as they want. I don't have anything to hide."

"They're not catching anybody anyway," Liz said. "This is just another way for Mary to keep tabs on all of us. She's using pot as an excuse."

"Oh, who cares?" Tracey said. She was tired of Liz's unending complaints about lockers, privacy, and mice.

"Well, I have a mouse in my locker," Liz said. "And it's cost me five bucks so far, not to mention the pages of my notebooks that it chewed. I can't open that locker without having my heart in my throat."

"I thought you weren't keeping your stuff in it," Peggy said.

"I'm getting too lazy to carry all my books around with me all the time. Besides, it looks so stupid. Nobody else does."

"Since when do you care what other people do?" Tracey asked.

"I care about being the only person in the room with a two-foot stack of books."

"Well, don't keep your basketball uniform in there," Tracey said. "We don't want that ruined."

"No, not before we take on Chickens of the Valley again."

They had played two more games since their first loss and had won them both. It looked certain that they would play Lady of the Valley for the division title. The winner of that game would play Villa Marie for the district championship.

"How many more games we got?" Liz asked Peggy.

"Two more. If we win them both, we go up against Lady of the Valley on February 23," Peggy said.

"Not that you're counting."

"Who's counting?"

The next game was an easy one. Tracey doubted that they would be defeated again before semifinals. But even when they were sure of victory, games were a pleasant diversion. Even an easy victory was more challenging than a hard practice, and after a game there was nothing as satisfying as the hot shower, the relaxing jet of warm air from her hair dryer that made her feel drowsy even as she used it, and then the comfort of her bunk bed.

After the victory that night, she was glad to get cleaned up and patiently wait for lights-out. Nikki and Toni, rowdy from the game, kept giggling and whispering, tossing stuffed animals back and forth between their two upper bunks. But Liz was tired too. She fell asleep first, and then Tracey dropped off.

Her sleep was deep and dreamless. It seemed a long time later that she awoke, disoriented. Gradually she realized that a strong hand was gripping her arm, and a voice, intense yet gentle, was repeating, "Tracey. Tracey, wake up. Wake up."

With difficulty, she opened her eyes. It took her a second to recognize St. Bernard.

"What's wrong?" she asked.

"Shh. Keep your voice down." St. Bernard looked across to the other bottom bunk. Liz was sitting up, sleepily thrusting her feet into her slippers. Her face wore a fixed expression, grim and a little surprised.

"Come downstairs," St. Bernard said. "Get your robe."

The clock read four. Tracey grabbed Nikki's robe, which was too small for her, and hurried out. Liz came too, and put her arm across Tracey's shoulders.

"We in trouble?" Tracey asked. Liz mutely shook her head.

They went down the center stairs to the upholstered chairs that served as a small waiting area for guests and visitors.

"Sit down," St. Bernard said, not unkindly. Tracey sat, but Liz stood behind her.

"I didn't know how to go about this," St. Bernard began, taking a box of Kleenex, presumably the one from Mary's office, and putting it in Tracey's lap. Tracey glanced up sharply, instantly awake.

St. Bernard glanced at Liz and then abruptly dropped into the chair across from Tracey.

"Tell me what's wrong," Tracey said.

"Sister James Anne . . . died a short while ago."

In her mind, Tracey leaped to her feet and exclaimed, "What?" But in reality, she only sat there.

"Dead all the way?" she asked.

St. Bernard seemed caught off guard, and then she said, "Dead, Tracey."

"Sister Lucy or Sister James Anne?"

"Sister James Anne, dear."

"Sister, I saw her before the game. She was fine."

"I know, dear." Sister St. Gerard watched as Liz dropped her hands to Tracey's shoulders. Tracey started at the hands on her shoulders and came back to the reality of what she was hearing.

"She had a slight seizure at about three and asked for you, but she was gone a minute or so later," St. Bernard said. "I am very sorry."

"Sorry?" Tracey echoed.

"She was unafraid, if that's any help to you, Tracey. And she didn't seem to suffer." St. Bernard hesitated. "I didn't want to pull you out of bed to tell you. But I didn't want to tell you at breakfast, either, in front of all the girls. I hope I did the right thing."

It was unusual for St. Bernard to confess to uncertainty. Tracey looked at her silently. Liz spoke up. "You did the right thing, Sister."

Tracey looked up at Liz. "How do you know what the right thing is all of a sudden?"

"Come back up to bed," Liz said.

"I want to see Sister James," Tracey said. She looked at Sister St. Gerard.

"They've taken her away, Tracey."

"Where?"

"To the undertaker's parlor, dear."

"But she'll be alone there. Alone in his basement. It's dark down there."

Liz leaned down. "She's in heaven. She's not in a basement. She's in heaven."

Tracey looked at her. "Come up to bed," Liz said again.

"I don't want to be alone," Tracey said.

"I'll sit by you a while. Come on." Liz helped her up, using the same grip she'd used when Tracey had sprained her ankle. "You get in bed, and I'll sit by you a while."

On the way up the steps, Tracey suddenly leaned her head against Liz and looked at her friend for a moment in speechless grief and shock. It was impossible to cry right then. But she knew she would be crying more—a lot more—in the days to come.

Hear, O Lord, the sound of my call,
Hear, O Lord, and have mercy.
My soul is longing for the glory of you.
O hear, O Lord, and answer me.

The well-known Catholic school hymn echoed through Tracey's mind, half a song and half a prayer. Protestant hymns had no equivalent for the grief that it expressed.

If only God would grant her one request, this one last time. She could bear the exile at MoJoe, the stark loneliness, the knowledge of what was going on at home, if He would only show her that she would see Sister James again. If He would show her that there was a resurrection of the just, for real and not just make-believe. And, if there really were such a thing, that Sister James would have her part in it.

She'd never known that she didn't really believe in the resurrection. Not until she had seen Sister James in the coffin. All her life, she had heard people say they could tell that the soul was gone from dead people, that the dead body was just a shell. She couldn't say that. It was Sister James Anne in the coffin, the coffin that now sat alone and unattended about three pews ahead of her, soon to be taken away in preparation for the burial the next morning.

The kneeler under her was padded, but Tracey, unused to kneeling for so long, was uncomfortable. She leaned back against the pew. Already, she had been up to the coffin twice to look for a sign that the soul was a separate thing from the body and that Sister James's soul was gone, really gone, to live in some other place. But she couldn't see the separation of body and spirit. It seemed that if she knew the right words to say, Sister James would open her eyes and look at her.

She set aside prayers and tears and worries for a moment to glance at her watch. Two more hours, and then they would take her away. Take her away and put her into the ground. That was the worst: the idea of Sister James being under the ground on a hill somewhere, where the snow would cover her and the rain would fall down on her. Who had come up with the idea of burial for the dead?

But then, what else could you do with them? Science, if not religion, had proved that dead bodies were dead bodies. They decomposed. Like it or not, as unbelievable as it seemed when looking at Sister James, she really was dead. She no longer had the power to hold her body together. It would return to the earth like any dead animal's body you might find on the roadside or in the woods.

The fact that a part of a person could be completely invisible defied Tracey's comprehension, but it was still true, and she knew it. Whatever had made Sister James Anne a distinct person was either dead or someplace else. And that problem opened up a whole new set of questions and fears.

"O God, I'll never bother You again, just tell me she's in heaven," Tracey begged, half in her mind and half in a whisper. "You wouldn't hold it against somebody for being ignorant, would You? She seemed to love You. She was better than I am. She loved me for Your sake." This last part reminded her of her own loss, and she stopped and began to cry again.

"Tracey, I had no idea that you spent time praying for the dead."

Tracey jerked her head up and looked around. It was Sister Mary. How long had she been standing there?

"I don't pray for the dead," she said angrily. "This is a sanctuary, isn't it? Why don't you leave me alone for once?"

"I didn't come to disturb you," Sister Mary said coldly. "James Anne was my friend too. And I didn't expect to find you here, where you would never come when she was alive."

Tracey stood up. "I came to see her," she said woodenly. She made her face a mask so Mary wouldn't see her grief and confusion. "It will probably be a long time before I see her again."

"She died as she lived, a Roman Catholic sister," Sister Mary reminded her. "Now are you willing to see that you Baptists don't have a corner on heaven?"

Tracey began to sidle out of the pew. "I'm not a Baptist, Sister," she replied. "I went to a Baptist church when I was allowed to, and I'd probably go again."

"Then what are you, dear?"

"I'm a Christian," Tracey said. She walked up to the coffin again but turned to look at Sister Mary. "Don't tell me that Sister James died in the same faith that Lucrezia Borgia and the Mafia kings die in." She stopped at the open coffin and glanced at her friend's body. There was a black rosary wrapped around Sister James's gnarled fingers, and a crucifix lay on the white wimple at her throat. "No," Tracey said. She turned back to Sister Mary. "It was a different faith. She didn't trust in these things for forgiveness, and I know that."

"She died a Roman Catholic," Sister Mary reminded her. Mary's smugness lit a fire in Tracey, and for one instant, her anger drove her back into certainty.

"Well, she's not one now," Tracey said. "Now, she's as free of that stuff as I am. More free, because she's in Christ and Christ alone."

She started to walk out of the sanctuary, and Sister Mary called after her, "She died in the church, Miss Jacamuzzi."

Tracey stopped and turned. "Then why didn't she ask for a priest? Why did she ask for me instead?" It was a point she had not thought of until then. "She had peace with God, Sister Mary."

Then she turned and walked out.

One good thing about anger was that it drove out the grief, at least for a while. Out in the windy afternoon, Tracey stopped and surveyed the grounds before starting her solitary walk. Anything to be free of the confines of that place.

Unexpectedly, Sister St. Gerard, wrapped in a black sweater, was already out on the grassy hill that overlooked the retirees' wing. Seeing Tracey, she came over.

"I was wondering if you were all right," Sister St. Gerard called over the wind.

"I'm OK," Tracey said.

"You look angry."

"Sister Mary had to come and crow," Tracey snapped. "Thank God that Sister James is free of her at last. I sure wish I was."

St. Bernard seemed startled to hear that Mary had gone in to visit Sister James. She glanced at the chapel.

"Yeah, she's there," Tracey said. "She says that she was a friend of Sister James's too. I don't remember them ever getting together, except when Sister Mary wanted to pump a poor old lady for information."

"We're all members of the community," St. Bernard reminded Tracey.

"Oh, right," Tracey said. "How could I forget that, when I was the only one who ever gave any of those little old ladies down there any of my time at all. You'd almost think I was a member of the community, wouldn't you, and you guys were the Protestants."

"I was always glad that you spent time with some of the retirees," St. Gerard said in a mild tone, so mild that Tracey felt ashamed of her outburst. "And you were precious to Sister James Anne."

"I was the staff of her old age," Tracey said without thinking. How long ago had they had that conversation? And yet the words had tripped off her tongue as though hidden under it for just that moment.

Sister St. Gerard smiled. "Did Sister James tell you that?"

Tracey nodded. With Sister James Anne, she had always been a better person, and she had always attributed that to the Lord's making her a genuine help and comfort to the lonely old woman. Would the same God who had stooped to give comfort to an old woman, really forget her in the hour of her death? Was Tracey herself the sign that Sister James had the favor of God?

She saw the irony in such a thing. And yet it might have been so. But if Sister James had truly been saved, why hadn't she rejected the Masses, the candles, the patron saints, and all the rest? That was the mystery.

Sister St. Gerard was still talking, and Tracey realized that she hadn't been listening. At that moment, St. Bernard realized the same thing, but she smiled gently. "Well, there I am, burbling away, and you've got a lot on your mind." She put a hand on Tracey's shoulder. "Try to maintain some peace of mind, Tracey. Remember a few things that we both believe. God is good, and God is merciful. Not a soul on this campus can point a finger at Sister James Anne to find fault with her. Just you remember that, all right?"

Tracey nodded and went back to the hall.

Cold sleet, whipped by the wind, whacked against the outside walls and windows of the hall. The trees, weighted with ice, creaked as they bent under the force of the wind. Loud reports like rifle shots echoed across the grounds as branches snapped off. Ice and sleet whirled, rattled against the roof and walls, and slammed into the building again.

Tracey jumped upright in bed. "No!" she yelled. "No!"

Liz leaped out of her own bed and onto Tracey's.

"Get her out of there!" Tracey yelled.

"Tracey, wake up," Liz exclaimed. Nikki and Toni sat up on the upper bunks. Out in the hall, the light clicked on, sending a golden sliver under the door. Footsteps came padding up the hallway.

"She's under the ice. She's out there, Liz."

"She's in heaven, Tracey," Liz said. "She's up in heaven now. She can't feel the snow and ice. She doesn't feel the cold."

Tracey shivered and pulled her knees up. The door opened.

"Everybody all right?" CPR asked.

"Everybody's OK," Liz said.

"You all right, Tracey?" CPR asked.

"I'm OK. Don't tell Sister Mary."

"I'm sure that Sister Mary heard you," CPR said. She went back out into the hallway.

Liz and Tracey looked at each other in the darkness.

"Who cares about Mary?" Liz asked. "You have all the bad dreams you want. I'll settle that vulture's hash."

"Maybe if she had let me go to the burial it wouldn't be like this," Tracey said after a moment. "But I don't know. I don't know what I would have done when they lowered it—"

"It wasn't Mary's decision!" Liz snapped, but not at Tracey. "I'd have gone with you."

"You always get embarrassed if I cry," Tracey reminded her.

"Not at a burial, for crying out loud. That's the only time I can cry, when everybody else is doing it too." Liz patted Tracey's back and then got back into her own bed. "You all right?"

"I just hate this storm," Tracey said.

"You know, Jac, it's kind of weird that I'm just a heedless heathen, but I don't have any problem believing you'll see her again—in the spirit world somewhere."

"The Bible teaches a resurrection," Tracey said. "There's no point in being a Christian if you don't believe in the resurrection of the body."

"So, you still going to be a Christian?" Liz asked.

Tracey stayed upright, her knees drawn up. "Sometimes I would leave it, but it won't let me go. I'm not a very good one, but it won't let me go."

Liz said nothing for a moment, but she rearranged her

pillow and lay on her side so she could talk more comfortably. "I think you're a good enough Christian," she said at last. "A whole lot better than Mary and the rest of them. Hey, isn't suffering and doubt a part of the game?"

"Suffering," Tracey confirmed. "But not doubt, I don't think. The Lord never doubted. I don't think Paul ever doubted."

"Seemed to me that Peter did a few times," Liz suggested.

"Peter?"

"Yeah, like when he sank instead of walked on the water. And when he told Jesus that Jesus couldn't die on the cross, he got in trouble for that."

"Yeah—" Tracey agreed.

"But not kicked out," Liz added. "And then there was the big one when he cussed out that maid at the fire and said he wasn't an apostle and didn't know Christ."

"Oh, yeah," Tracey said.

Both of them were silent. Then Liz said, "You've been right about one thing, Jac. The guy was not a pope—but then, I never believed that anyway. Still, he was an apostle. He never lost his title."

"I guess not," Tracey agreed. She could feel sleep coming back over her in waves.

"Don't get bugged by how smug Mary is because she knows you're having doubts," Liz told her. "At least you have a faith that can have some doubts. That old battle-ax hasn't got any more religion than I do." She stretched out onto her back. "All she's got is a program, and she follows it."

"Sure," Tracey said.

"And you wait. She's gonna get her dues someday."

"OK," Tracey said. She slowly stretched out again.

Peter never lost his title, Liz had said. He not only stayed a Christian, he stayed an apostle.

*Have I got a title?* she wondered. *And do I get to keep it?* She drifted toward sleep and dreams, her mind a muddle of images: the cemetery where Sister James lay, the ice and sleet, and one upright figure in the darkness with two bright doors behind it, spread out like wings of light.

The rumble of the bus on the trip to the game the next afternoon had a lulling effect on Tracey. In the past week she had slept very badly and with many night-mares. She had a seat to herself, and she began to doze.

"Jacamuzzi, don't fall asleep before the game!" CPR snapped, and Tracey jerked awake.

"She's had a rough week, Coach—" Liz protested.

"Lukas, you stay out of this," CPR ordered. "The trip is less than an hour, and I want everyone awake and alert to play."

"It's all right," Tracey said to Liz. "I'll stay awake, Sister."

Maddie Murdoch glanced up in the rearview mirror. "Come up and keep me company, Tracey," she invited.

Tracey nodded and went up front. She had avoided Maddie's eyes upon entering the bus, knowing that Maddie knew about Sister James's death. It wasn't Mrs. Murdoch's consolation she feared—what she feared was that the look on her own face would betray her doubts about the resurrection.

She flopped into the seat right behind the driver's seat. "It's not like this is Chickens of the Valley," she mumbled. "It's only St. Agnes. I probably won't play for more than the first quarter."

"Well, you know how it is with semifinals so near," Maddie said sympathetically.

399

"Oh, sure. I'll stay awake. I know CPR gets her beads in a knot when we get this close."

Maddie Murdoch couldn't resist smiling at Tracey's slang. The gentle Irish woman wasn't used to the slang peculiar to Catholic high school girls of the seventies. In her day, nobody had really had the courage or irreverence to talk about a nun flipping her veil or getting her wimple into a flap. Liz was much better than Tracey was at coming up with new phrases to use, but whatever Liz and Tracey said was usually imitated first by the team, then by everyone else in the school.

After a moment, Maddie said, "I missed you at the burial service for Sister James Anne."

"Mary told me I couldn't go," Tracey said. She glanced at Maddie by way of the mirror. "Did you go to the funeral?"

"Not to the Mass, dear, but I went to the cemetery."

The question Tracey desperately wanted to ask—whether a Catholic could possibly be trusting in Christ alone and not in works—hung up on her tongue. She was too afraid of what Maddie Murdoch would say. Instead, Tracey said, "Sister James was always good to me. I sure loved her."

They were in traffic, so Maddie didn't glance away from the road. But she said, "Sister James was very kind, I know. She used to come to the Bible studies I had in the retirees' wing. I gave her a Bible of her own once."

Tracey's hopes flared, then dropped. A lot of Catholic people liked to own a Bible. Her own family had owned several. It didn't mean anything unless it was used and read. She could count on the fingers of one hand how many times Sister James had specifically referred to a passage from the Bible, though she had often talked about the parables and sermons of the Lord.

"You must miss her dreadfully, dear," Maddie said.

"I do." Tracey couldn't say anymore.

"Jacamuzzi," CPR called from several rows back, "are you staying awake?"

Tracey turned around to show that she was wide-eyed. "Yes, Sister," she said with an edge to her voice.

"We've been chatting, Sister Patricia," Maddie said.

"All right. You keep her awake."

"It's time for the cattle prod if you don't," Tracey added to Mrs. Murdoch.

Liz came up front.

"CPR send you?" Tracey demanded.

"I don't do jobs for any nun," Liz retorted, angry at Tracey's insinuation.

"I'm sorry," Tracey said.

Liz cooled down. "Don't let her upset your game, Jac. She gets uptight when we get close to play-offs."

"Man," Tracey exclaimed, "what's her angle, anyway? We beat St. Agnes every year."

"They've had one defeat, just like us," Liz told her.

"Oh, yeah?"

"They've improved a lot. Got a big center, I hear, and they've learned a couple good plays." She shrugged. "I think we'll take them OK. But don't get overconfident."

"OK."

Liz changed the subject. "Anyway, tonight you'll sleep good. Right?"

"Yeah." Tracey shot a nervous look at Maddie, not wanting her to guess that Tracey was so afraid of death. But Mrs. Murdoch was intent on making a left turn, and Liz's comment passed her unnoticed.

The gym at St. Agnes was small and not very clean. St. Agnes had a great reputation for academics, but its buildings were old and in disrepair. A busload of MoJoes was going to come up as soon as classes at MoJoe dismissed. The team could count on playing the first quarter without much of a cheering section.

But cheering wasn't a big deal at St. Agnes. Not many St. Agnes kids showed up to cheer for the game. Their team was made up of a few girls fiercely devoted to basketball.

The St. Agnes coach started things by asking to play by half-court rules. Sister Patricia Rose looked startled at this request.

From the bench, Liz guessed what was happening before CPR even walked over to tell them. "They want half-court," she said.

"Uh-oh," Tracey said.

Liz looked at her. "I taught you half-court, Jac!"

"Sure, a year ago," Tracey exclaimed. "I don't know if I can do it."

"CPR's never turned down half-court," Scooter told her. "Just remember to stay on either offense or defense. Don't cross over. And don't try to dribble up the court. Take only three steps at a time."

"What, are you kidding?" Now that Scooter reviewed it for her, she could remember Liz's teaching her these rules, but that had been long before Tracey was any good, and the rules had not seemed all that different. Now, after a season of playing, the realization that she couldn't pass down the court or dribble around the other team's defense dismayed her. She, Liz, and Scooter had all engineered some good fast breaks that season.

CPR came up to the bench. "Half-court rules," she said.

"Sister," Tracey began, "I don't think—"

"Just don't get offside, Jacamuzzi," CPR said. "Watch your feet! They're big enough to see, aren't they?"

Tracey's face flamed, and she felt her eyes fill. She fiercely blinked back the tears, too angry to cry at this sudden outburst. "Have it your way, Coach."

If CPR was ashamed of her words, she didn't show it. "Lukas, Scooter, and Jacamuzzi are forwards, and Melsom, you go in as the third guard. Keep that center of theirs out of the key. Are there any questions?"

"Do we have to play half-court?" Liz asked.

"Lukas, we've practiced girls' rules ever since you made this team."

"But we're better at full-court rules," Liz argued, undaunted by CPR's edginess.

"It's already been settled. You concentrate on this game, and you'll do fine."

The girls looked at each other as they took their balls from the bag.

It felt better out on the court, under the glare of the gym lights. They warmed up with a better sense of camaraderie than they'd had yet that season, united in the face of CPR's bad mood.

"Don't let her bug you," Scooter said as she passed off to Tracey in their passing drill. "You were speaking for all of us. Don't take it personal."

"I swear," Liz mumbled as they went into the girls' locker room together. "Sometimes I think they're all like Mary underneath the surface. Hang tight, Jac."

The team clustered in the locker room, and then Liz and Scooter burst out with the banner. Tracey followed them, and the rest of the team followed her. The opening ritual was a little difficult with nobody but Maddie Murdoch and CPR to cheer them on, but the Valkyries behaved like the Valkyries no matter what. They sang the school anthem alone, and then the game started.

The girls' rules came back to Tracey as the game progressed. By the middle of the first quarter, she and Scooter and Liz had tacitly arranged how they would get the ball into the key and up to the basket. The St. Agnes defense wasn't that good, so the MoJoes usually scored when the ball came into the offense zones. Tracey was fouled twice for traveling because she took too many steps without passing. That passing rule was the hardest one to remember. Liz and Scooter each fouled on it once.

One of Liz's favorite plays was to get in the forward position on either side, catch the ball and jump up as if to sink it, then pass it off to Tracey or Scooter and have her jump and sink it. The play never failed because as soon as Liz got the ball under the basket, the St. Agnes defense would swarm to her like bees to honey. Whoever caught Liz's sideways pass would most likely score two points on the first try. The play wasn't new to Scooter, but it was to Tracey, and the first time she went for the pass, she was fouled for three seconds in the key.

But they all scored well. The Valkyries' problem was that their defense, like the St. Agnes defense, was not very good. And they were up against a very good offense. The St. Agnes center was tall and fast, and she made most of the shots for them. At the end of the first quarter, the score was 32-30, with MoJoe in the lead.

CPR fussed and fumed. There was no sign of the MoJoe bus yet.

The second quarter shouldn't have been harder, but it was for Tracey. She completely missed a pass from Liz, and she fouled again for three seconds in the key. With three minutes left in the quarter, CPR called a time-out.

"You're on the bench," she told Tracey as the team came off the floor. Tracey sat down without a word. "Willis, you go in there and see if you can play today," CPR barked.

Tracey kept her eyes on the floor. She was mad. She sensed Maddie Murdoch's eyes on her, and that put more pressure on her temper. Here she was again, in trouble in front of the only Christian woman she knew. But CPR didn't bother her anymore as play resumed. She stayed standing on the sidelines, her eyes glued to the game.

The MoJoe cheering section—twenty-five or thirty girls—showed up at last, late but cheerful. They giggled and whispered to each other when they saw that MoJoe was up by four points.

As soon as they were seated on the MoJoe side of the bleachers, they began the "MoJoe Ho Ho" chant. It looked to Tracey like the team's spirits picked up immediately. She knew that if she had been playing, the presence of a crowd would have energized her.

"Hey, Jac," Amy whispered, coming up behind the team's bench. Tracey turned around. "Why are you here?"

"Messed up one time too many," Tracey said. "CPR's mad."

"Uh-oh." Amy looked sympathetic. "Maybe, with everything that's happened, you know . . ."

"Sure," Tracey said. She wished CPR would remember that her best friend had died a week ago. But she wasn't about to go begging off with CPR. Not now.

The team was still four points ahead at halftime. CPR called them back to the locker room.

"You did all right," Liz told Tracey as they went through the doors together. "Don't get phased. You'll play second half."

"I'm seeing some pretty shoddy defense out there," CPR said as they congregated around the benches. "Defense doesn't change. It's zones. Now, you play your zones. Don't start following your man. Play your zone! Just concentrate on the principles of winning, and we'll win!" The defense girls nodded soberly. "And you, Jacamuzzi!"

Tracey looked up, startled.

"Listen to me, prima donna, you play this game with the team. I've had enough of your one-man show."

"Coach!" Liz exclaimed. Even Scooter looked aghast.

"Jac doesn't have a one-man show!" Peggy said.

"I swear, I'll pull you from this team if I can't depend on you, Jacamuzzi!"

Again, her tears were replaced by anger. "Well, you say the word, Coach. You just say the word," Tracey told her.

"Don't push me, miss. You can turn in that jersey tonight if you can't play with your team."

Rather than answer the accusation, Tracey straightened and put her hands on the bottom of her jersey, ready to pull it off. "You want it now, or after we get back to school?"

For a moment, everybody was silent. Tracey began to pull the jersey off. She meant it too. Suddenly it was hateful to her. Having any part of MoJoe was hateful. No matter how much you got ahead in that place, it was still a prison. A place of suffering.

"I didn't say to take it off!" CPR exclaimed. Her voice was shocked.

Tracey looked at her, the jersey around her neck.

"For crying out loud, Jac, put it back on," Liz said.

"I'm not a prima donna!" Tracey yelled. "And she knows it."

"We all know it," Scooter said.

Tracey ripped the jersey off and threw it down. "That's what I think of your team and your cracks about me!" she yelled at CPR. "You just leave me alone. I quit—or you can throw me off. I don't care. I'm getting out of here."

She went to the bench where their sweat suits were thrown and struggled into hers.

"Jac, nobody thinks you're a—"

"Tracey Jacamuzzi, you are not excused from this team," CPR said.

"You leave me alone!" Tracey yelled, and this time she felt the hot tears start down her face.

"Where are you going?" Liz demanded.

"I don't know! I don't care!"

"Stop that girl!" CPR exclaimed, suddenly struck with the fear that Tracey really would run away. Tracey darted out the door. As the door swung shut behind her, she heard Liz say, "Don't chase her. Somebody get Maddie Murdoch and tell her to come to the parking lot." And then to CPR, "Man, I really hate you." The door slammed open and Liz burst out of it. Tracey heard her coming, and she yelled back to her, "Just leave me alone!" She ran down the unfamiliar hall, found a door at the end of it, and gave it a push. It opened into the parking lot. The cold air hit her face, and Tracey began to cry again. That was when Liz caught her.

"It's just me," Liz told her. "It's just me."

"Leave me alone," Tracey said. "Let me go!"

"You're my best friend," Liz exclaimed. "I can't leave you alone, not now. Not after all that."

"I won't play basketball," Tracey said.

"Look, Jac, basketball's not my life!" Liz said. "Just stop a minute." She grabbed Tracey, and Tracey stopped. "The whole game, the whole team, and the whole championship can go on without me. I don't give a rip. I know CPR was wrong in there, OK? I know that. They can play without me and without you and lose tonight. Because I don't play by those rules. Nobody hurts my friends and expects me to go along with things."

"You're the team captain," Tracey reminded her.

Liz shook her head. "I'm a Valkyrie," she said. The shiver that went through both of them had nothing to do with the cold.

"You mean that?" Tracey asked.

"Yeah. Strength and truth and all that," Liz said. "I hated bullies before I ever started on this team, and I still hate them. Wearing a habit or wearing a letter doesn't mean a person can be a bully."

Just then, Mrs. Murdoch came out of one of the gym doors and hurriedly crossed the parking lot toward them. She had her spacious coat wrapped tightly around herself, but Tracey wore only her warm-up suit, and Liz was in the team's shorts and jersey.

"Oh, you both must be freezing," Maddie exclaimed.

"Watch out," Tracey said as CPR came out the other gym doors.

The sister approached with some caution, but she said sternly, "Are you playing, Miss Lukas?"

"Play, Liz," Tracey said. "We can talk about it at the room."

Liz glanced at her and then at Maddie Murdoch, who nodded.

"Here I come," Liz said.

"And what about you, Miss Jacamuzzi?"

"I told you," Tracey said. "I'm off the team."

CPR looked like she wanted to stay and argue, but Maddie Murdoch said, "Halftime is almost over, isn't it? I'll watch out for Tracey."

After a reluctant pause, CPR went back inside. Tracey looked at Mrs. Murdoch, and more unwilling tears forced themselves out of her eyes, onto her numb cheeks.

"You must be freezing," Maddie said again, kindly. "Come onto the bus a minute, and we'll see about getting you put back together."

Tracey couldn't argue. She didn't want to go back inside.

"Would you like to tell me what happened?" Maddie asked as she started the bus and turned on the heat.

"CPR kept yelling at me," Tracey said. She sat down on one of the seats, and she began to cry again, a hiccuping kind of cry that sounded—to her ears—childish. "She said I had big feet, and then she said I was a prima donna. And I don't know why she said those things. I was doing my best. I really was!" In spite of the heater, the cold came penetrating through the walls of the bus. It chilled the sweat on her. She shivered uncontrollably.

Maddie sat down next to her. "Poor dear. Come here," Maddie said. She opened her voluminous coat and took Tracey into her arms, wrapping the coat around them both. The sudden warmth made Tracey shiver harder for a moment before she stopped. She felt that she should not cry. She wanted to be angry and strong. She wanted to demand that CPR apologize. She wanted to be too right to cry. But she cried anyway. There was nothing to do but sit there and cry onto Maddie Murdoch's neck and shoulder, remembering the whole while that it wouldn't do any good. Because Sister James was gone. They were all gone—the Murphys, her father, her mother, Jean.

"Tracey, dear, the Bible tells us that there's a time to cast away stones, and a time to gather stones together," Maddie said.

"What does that mean?" Tracey asked. She hiccuped and sobbed again.

"In regards to Sister James's death, the time has come for her to be flung away from you, and for things to go wrong on the team. To lose everything. But the day comes when the stones are gathered back together."

Tracey shook her head and looked up at Maddie. "I've lost everything," she said. "My family, my friends, my home, and now this. I hate this place, and I hate this team too. But I can't go home, and if I did it would be worse than this."

Maddie Murdoch said nothing for a few minutes. She put Tracey's head back onto her shoulder and rocked back and forth with her. This startled Tracey. It had been a long time since an adult had simply comforted her. She didn't resist. In fact, part of her hoped Maddie would not stop.

As she relaxed, Maddie said at last, "Do you really hate the team, Tracey?"

"Why did CPR say that?" Tracey asked in her turn. "Why did she say those things?"

"To make you angry," Maddie said suddenly. "So that you would forget Sister James and play hard. So that you would prove yourself to CPR."

Tracey looked up. "I swear, I never try to prove myself to anybody. I never have. I never will."

"Don't swear, dear, it isn't right," Maddie said gently.

"It's okay for a Valkyrie to swear, because we mean what we say," Tracey said fiercely.

A light of surprise lit up Maddie's eyes and a smile suddenly pulled at her lips, but she smothered both. "Well, we may have to discuss that again sometime. In the meanwhile, I really suppose that she meant to anger you but overdid it."

"I don't play games like that, Maddie," Tracey exclaimed. "I play straight and fair with people." Then she remembered the fight Maddie had witnessed. "I know it doesn't seem that way to you," she whispered, "but she can't treat me like that."

Maddie smoothed back Tracey's sweaty hair and said with a smile, "I imagine, dear, that if Sister Patricia Rose can only get you on that team again, she will always play straight and fair with you." She put her eyes close to Tracey's in a conspiratorial look, as though inviting her to share a funny joke that only the two of them knew.

Tracey suddenly saw the humor in it, from Maddie's perspective. CPR had meant to strike sparks and had made an explosion instead. No doubt she was, at this moment, dealing with an unhappy and emotionally upset team, wondering what in the world to do to get her forward back again. Tracey managed a brief smile. But she knew she was being unfair to her own teammates. She had to go back inside, at least so they would know she was all right. She didn't want them to throw the game because of her.

"Don't go yet," Maddie whispered. "It's still half-time." Tracey glanced up. For a moment Maddie only looked at her, her eyes solemn and kind. Then she lifted her hand, and with the back of it, she stroked Tracey's cheek. "Oh, your hair is so wet, Tracey. You'll catch your death of cold." She rested her hand on Tracey's head, as though in a benediction, or a prayer to heal the sick. But Maddie didn't say anything.

Without a word, Tracey hesitantly came into her

arms again, and Maddie wrapped the coat around her. She pulled her soft scarf loose from the collar of the coat and draped it around Tracey's head like a shawl. "There, that will keep the cold out," she whispered. "Stay here with me for a few minutes."

With no other prompting, and without thinking, Tracey buried her face into Maddie, and after a moment she began to cry again. But these were not tears of anger. She didn't know where they came from. They were just suddenly there, and she was crying.

"I'm here with you," Maddie whispered. She stroked her hand over the shawl and kept the side of her face at rest against Tracey's head, her breathing calm.

"I'm sorry," Tracey gasped when she could speak. She was surprised at herself.

"I'm sorry about Sister James. Is Liz looking after you?" Maddie asked. Maddie, Tracey realized, would think it very important that she and Sister James had been friends. Those things did matter to Maddie. Of course, Tracey thought, Maddie understood the progress of friendship and aging and death and grief. And with her voice so soft and reasonable, and her eyes so concerned, Maddie suddenly seemed very wise and yet very accessible.

"Do you think Sister James is in heaven?" Tracey asked. Her voice was small.

"I once asked Sister James Anne what would take her to heaven, and she told me that belonging to the fold of Jesus the Good Shepherd was the only way for anyone to get there," Maddie said. "When I asked her what she meant, she quoted John 3:16 for me. It's hard to say, when someone is a member and participant in a religion that violates the simplicity of the Gospel.

And yet, Sister James gave me a good enough answer, and her life showed many fruits of the spirit: love, joy, peace, long-suffering, gentleness, goodness, and the rest. We have to leave the matter in God's hands."

She looked down at Tracey. Her eyes were large and serious, yet kind. This closeness to a person was a rare thing for Tracey, and Maddie's calm voice had soothed her. In the soft shelter of the coat, looking at Maddie's face, she forgot all her fears for a moment.

"I've been thinking about the Resurrection," Tracey began, almost in a whisper, ready to ask that hardest question. "Have you ever doubted—"

But she was interrupted. The bus doors suddenly popped open, and CPR came up onto the step. Tracey quickly straightened up and turned to face CPR, pulling herself out of the coat and turning her back to Maddie. She whisked the scarf away.

"Will you come back inside?" Sister Patricia Rose asked.

"Isn't Mrs. Murdoch an approved chaperone?" Tracey asked. "We're talking. About important things."

"Tracey," Maddie said, a tone of gentle reproof in her voice.

"I didn't mean to upset you so much, Tracey," CPR told her.

"Not so much, but you did it to upset me," Tracey said. Maddie put a hand of restraint on her shoulder, but Tracey ignored it. "You know I'm not a prima donna."

"Then I'm sorry, and I'm asking you to come back inside."

"OK," Tracey said, and she stood up.

"Your uniform is in the locker room on the bench," CPR told her.

"I don't need it because I'm off the team," Tracey said. She brushed past CPR and got out of the bus.

CPR hurried after her. "You don't need me," Tracey told her. "And I don't need being called names and made to feel stupid."

"The team needs you," CPR replied.

"The team didn't call me names and make me feel bad. They knew my best friend just died. They were helping me. Not like you. That was really mean." She stopped and looked at CPR. "Shame on you."

"I've apologized to you once already, Miss Jaca-muzzi," CPR reminded her.

"Out here," Tracey agreed. "But you called me names in front of the team."

"And you expect me to apologize in front of the team?" CPR demanded, a little angry at the idea.

Tracey, who had started to walk back to the building, turned to her. "No, because I quit the team. You gave me the option, and I took it."

When she got back to the gym, the score had changed. The Valkyries were down by eight. It was still the third quarter because several time-outs had been called. Liz and Scooter and Kathy Willis were passing back and forth to get a good shot in the key, but one look at their faces showed Tracey just how bad team spirit was at that moment. There was some comfort in the confirmation that nobody thought she was a prima donna. Any accusation, no matter how baseless, always made Tracey feel a little wary. There was always the chance that you had some fault you had never even suspected, but that everybody else knew about. Being a big mouth had been like that.

CPR called a time-out at the first opportunity. The players and the second-string huddled together.

"Girls, I would like to apologize for any comments that I made in the locker room," CPR said with Tracey standing by her. "I regard you one and all as valuable players. I regret that Miss Jacamuzzi has chosen to leave the team, and I wish she would reconsider." She glanced at Tracey, who looked annoyed at this ploy. "I apologize for my temper."

"Next time you say something like that, I quit too," Liz said, her fair cheeks red from exertion and anger. The rest of the first-string looked at CPR, not verbally agreeing with Liz, but they all looked mad.

CPR herself flushed at this threat, but she didn't say anything. She looked from Liz to Tracey, very deliberately. The ref's whistle blew.

"Come on, Jac," Liz begged, and then they went back out on the floor.

"Whoever plays for this school is a slave," Tracey yelled after her.

"Or a Valkyrie," Liz yelled back. Play started, but she glanced at Tracey. "It just depends on what it takes to bend you, baby."

"They need you," CPR said in a low and urgent voice. "Quit if you have to, Jacamuzzi, but finish the game!"

"All right," Tracey said. "I'll be right back."

The audience had no comprehension of what had been enacted during halftime and during the third quarter. But when Tracey reappeared at the start of the fourth quarter, the applause was loud. Her own team-mates greeted her with a shout.

They were down by ten, but CPR put Liz on defense to slow down the other team's center. Tracey, Scooter, and Willis played offense. Inch by inch, the score nudged up again until the Valkyries were leading, 82-76, with thirty seconds left to play. CPR switched Tracey off to defense, and Liz came back to offense. The game ended 86-76 in favor of the Valkyries.

Liz's rough hug and the scrape of her forearm across Tracey's head gave Tracey her first taste of their chance at the semifinals.

"You got to stay with us now," Liz told her as the MoJoe crowd came spilling onto the floor, squealing and yelling and congratulating them.

Scooter crowded in next. "Stay on the team?" she

asked Tracey. What it cost for her to ask that, Tracey never knew.

"I will, Scooter," she said.

"See how things change," Liz said, with a glance at Scooter.

"I guess."

The team quickly got through the handshaking with the St. Agnes girls and hurried into the locker room to put on their sweat suits and coats.

"We're a team, right?" Peggy asked her.

"Right," Tracey said.

"Right!" Liz yelled.

"Right!" Scooter yelled back.

"We are the MoJoes, the mighty, mighty MoJoes," Liz yelled, swinging her fist in the air. "Everywhere we go, people wanna know—"

"Who we are," the rest of the girls joined in, "so we tell them, we are the MoJoes—"

"The mighty, mighty MoJoes," Tracey joined her voice to theirs. They lined up, front to back, their hands on the shoulders in front of them, and went out in a conga line.

> Everywhere we go,
> People wanna know
> Who we are,
> So we tell them—
> We are the MoJoes,
> The mighty, mighty MoJoes—

They went out to the bus that way, with CPR bringing up the rear. Once aboard the bus, they sat as far away from her as possible. She took the front seat to make it easy for them. Tracey felt bad for her. CPR had shown a side of herself under pressure that Tracey would never have guessed, but Tracey was in no position to judge her anyway. She spent most of her time avoiding people or situations that she couldn't cope with. If Maddie Murdoch had known half the things Tracey had done, that scene on the bus tonight would never have happened. Maddie would have kept her distance.

They went through a McDonald's drive-through, and still nobody would say anything to CPR. None of them asked her to come and eat with them. But the coach ate quickly, and as the girls were finishing, she stood up in the bus and addressed the team. This was not unusual. CPR often gave them a pep talk after a loss or some constructive criticism after a win.

"Girls," she began. Liz groaned loudly. Nobody looked very friendly.

CPR continued, undaunted. "I feel good about our win tonight. In two weeks we'll enter the semifinals against Lady of the Valley, and I feel after tonight's game, we have to get back to the basics. Our zone defense is weak."

"Oh, that again," Scooter said.

"We have to play as a team, and with a good defense, we as a team can lock another team out of the key and reduce their scoring."

"You know all about playing as a team," Liz said, not loud enough for CPR to hear, but from the snickers of the girls, she could probably guess Liz's comment.

Tracey stood up. "I have something to say," she said and turned red up to her hairline. CPR looked at her, startled, but Tracey waited for permission to speak. At last, somewhat reluctantly, CPR gave her a nod.

"You guys don't know this," she said, looking down. "And even Sister doesn't know that Liz and I know this, but, well, I think we're all a little mad tonight, and I wanted to tell you something."

"What do we know?" Liz asked her.

"About when CPR got in trouble because she let me pray. You guys remember that time before our first game. Well, Liz and I found out later that CPR got in a lot of trouble—because I'm not a Catholic, I mean. But she's never told me that I can't pray. And she never yelled at us for it, even though my guess is that she was instructed to."

She glanced at CPR, who seemed mortified that Tracey would mention such a thing. "I didn't mean to embarrass you," Tracey said. "But ever since then I've really been grateful because you gave me a chance on the team. And besides that, I owe you and the team an apology for what I said tonight. I really am very sorry, Sister, and you guys. I was mad, but I shouldn't have run out in the middle of a game like that. I don't think I ever acted like a prima donna until tonight, when I said I was quitting. And I said some other things that weren't nice. So I'm sorry for those things too. And if I can stay on the team, I'd like to." She sat down.

Her face was red and hot, and she looked away to let it cool off. Maddie gave her a glance in the rear-view mirror.

The team looked from her to CPR.

"I think we may all regret things that were said and done tonight," CPR conceded. "Forgive and forget is probably the wisest course."

Liz spoke up. "On top of that," she said, "I think we should all keep this to ourselves." She looked at CPR.

"No offense, but why stir up a hornets' nest now that everybody's apologized? Forgive and forget, and keep your mouth shut, is really the wisest policy."

Scooter nodded vigorously and added, "We don't want to blow our chances with Lady of the Valley. We don't want anyone getting into trouble."

The team agreed, and the tension seemed to ease after that. Tracey, suddenly weary again, stretched her legs out on the seat and propped her back against the wall of the bus. She had meant to go keep Maddie company, but now that everything was all right, she only wanted to sleep, which she did, for the last twenty minutes of the bus ride.

When they arrived at MoJoe and were getting off the bus, Maddie Murdoch stopped her. "I'm very proud of you, dear," she said. Tracey turned to her.

"For apologizing?" she asked.

"Yes, and for doing it so well. I'm glad you have a tender heart."

"Tender heart?" She almost couldn't believe her ears. "If I were tenderhearted, I wouldn't get mad in the first place."

"No, dear, you've got a heart that wants to do God's will," Maddie said. "I can see it plain as plain."

To her own surprise, Tracey's eyes filled up with tears. "There's a lot that you don't know about me, Mrs. Murdoch," she said. She wanted to go on, but she found that she had no voice. "I really am a Christian, but I haven't lived a very good Christian life," she choked out at last.

"The power of the Resurrection begins here," Maddie Murdoch said, tapping the front of Tracey's sweat suit where the emblem of the Valkyrie lay across her heart. "It does not begin at death, Tracey, but now. To live in Christ, you must live in His resurrection. And then you will have a godly life: *His* life, living in you. The power that gives you His righteousness in this life is the power that raises you from the dead."

"Let's go, Jac!" Liz yelled from the doorway to the hall.

Maddie Murdoch had her full attention, but Tracey didn't know what to say. She didn't even know what to ask. For a long moment Tracey looked into those eyes that seemed to know—that revealed a life that was all she had wanted and expected when she had first claimed to be saved.

She reluctantly turned to follow the others into the building. "Good night," Tracey said over her shoulder, almost as an afterthought.

Liz and Tracey excluded all visitors from the room that night except for team members. Nikki and Toni took the hint and went down to the library to study.

With the pressure of playing in the semifinals so close upon them, nobody was cheating on the training diet. All they had to celebrate were water and lemons, which Liz mixed up in the scrub bucket.

"I hope the town girls keep quiet about tonight's game," Peggy said, referring to the five team members who lived in town with their parents.

"They'll keep quiet," Liz said. "We all agreed, and besides, who are they going to tell? Mommy and Daddy? That's not likely. Nobody wants to see CPR get in trouble. Nor Jac. I think we all want Mary kept out of it."

"Hey," Scooter said, changing the subject, "they passed the movie list around today. You guys see it? Here it is."

They all crowded around Liz as she took the movie list and read it. Once a year at MoJoe, each girl was allowed to donate one dollar to the school and cast a vote to see an old black-and-white movie on Color Day. There were usually three to choose from: a romance, an adventure, or a horror movie.

"Here goes," Liz said. *"Romeo and Juliet—"*

Everybody booed or groaned.

*"Dracula* with Bela Lugosi, or *Dragnet* with Jack Webb."

"I vote for *Dracula,*" Tracey said right away. Peggy and Scooter frowned at her.

"We watched *The Fly* last year, and that was bad enough," Peggy said. "I couldn't sleep for a week."

"That's 'cause you're a sissy," Liz said, and she dodged as Peggy flung a pillow at her.

"I want *Romeo and Juliet;* I'm sick of horror movies," Scooter said.

Liz made a gagging noise, and most of the other girls laughed.

"We always get horror movies, you guys," Scooter complained.

"Scooter," Liz told her, "the vote is always overwhelming for the horror movie. You might as well accept it and vote with the rest of us."

"I want Jack Webb," Peggy said. "That's action and no horror. That's for me."

"Jack Webb couldn't make an exciting show if his life depended on it," Liz said.

"Oh," Tracey groaned, "who cares? When is the stupid Color Day?" She had slept through last year's showing of *The Fly.*

"The day after we play Chickens of the Valley," Liz

423

said. "Now, who's going to sit still for a romance after a big game like that?"

"I know we'll get another horror movie," Scooter said, disgusted. "This place has no class." She stood up to go.

"We got tons of class," Tracey yelled.

"Why, we reek of class," Liz added.

The other girls filed out after her. Tracey, who was sprawled across her lower bunk, glanced at Liz, seated on the floor next to her.

"You all right?" Liz asked.

"Yeah, I'm OK. I'll sleep OK tonight," she said. "Because we played so hard, and I guess I already took one kind of beating. I don't think I'll have any bad dreams."

"What'd you and Maddie talk about on the bus?"

"Oh, you know, what happened with CPR in the locker room. I was mad because she embarrassed me so much. Maddie helped."

"Was she the one that told you to apologize to CPR?"

Tracey shook her head. "No, I think the Holy Spirit made it kind of weigh on me. That's called being under conviction—when He shows you your sins and how to get them taken care of."

"Been a long time since I've heard you talk about God," Liz said. "Up here, I mean. You talk about Him all the time to the nuns."

"Maddie says she thinks Sister James went to heaven."

"See, I told you. Did you talk to her about the Resurrection?"

"No," Tracey admitted. "But she said something about it to me. It wasn't what I expected."

They were silent for a long time. Suddenly Tracey said, "I gotta go see Sister Lucy tomorrow, Liz."

"Yeah?" Liz had been getting up to find her chemistry book, but she stopped and looked down at her.

"She's not all right," Tracey said. "I think Sister James's death really undid her."

"They were good friends," Liz said. Liz knew about Sister Lucy through Tracey. Liz never went to the retirees' wing. Old people, especially senile ones, scared Liz. Even though the retirees who stayed at the wing were in fairly good shape, it was still a place where Liz felt ill at ease.

"Remind me to get Maddie to go see her too," Tracey said. "I think Sister Lucy is going to need a lot of help."

Tracey was a little surprised the next day at lunchtime to find out that Sister Lucy was not yet ready for any visitors. Sister Lucy had always been regular in her waking and bedtime hours, following the discipline of her order and attending the morning services and vigils conducted in the retirees' wing.

As she hurried from the retirees' wing to get to the cafeteria, Tracey wondered at the old woman's increasing feebleness. She felt guilty too. She had gone during lunch hour in order to have an excuse to get away from the old sister before her next class started. Now it turned out that Sister Lucy wasn't even able to detain her or beg her into reading several chapters from one of those long, old books.

"What're you doing here?" Liz asked as Tracey joined her at the lunch table with a tray.

"Sister Lucy got up too late this morning," Tracey said. "She wasn't washed and dressed yet."

Liz, oblivious to the implications of Tracey's statement, passed her the salt and pepper. "Well, I went to the office and told Mrs. Sladern I still have that mouse," she said. "Mrs. Sladern got mad and told me to quit nagging them about it."

"Oh, yeah?" Tracey asked, only half listening.

"I mean, Jac, what's the big deal? They could have the janitor come take a look at the locker," Liz complained. Her voice was loud enough for girls up and down the table to hear her. Guarded smiles went back and forth. Liz's obsession with the mouse in her locker had become a standing joke among the students.

Tracey knew that if Liz had some joke to play, she would do it alone, without help—a Liz Lukas masterpiece, like her good plays on the court. It was impossible to believe that Liz would really be this concerned about a mouse or that—if there were one—she would be unable to get rid of it herself.

"Well, I told Sladern that if she wouldn't get Szymansky to look at it, I would just have to do it myself," Liz said. "And Mary heard me say it, even if she pretended that she didn't."

"Sure Liz, sure," Tracey said.

There wasn't time to speculate on what Liz was up to and also worry about Sister Lucy. Through her next class, Tracey sat more quietly than usual, wondering what was going to happen to the old sister. Was it possible that you could love someone so much that when she died, parts of you began to die? It had felt that way for Tracey herself. With the loss of Sister James, she had lost sleep, she had lost peace in her dreams, and she had struggled in her classes and in her game. Even now, with her grades and her basketball skills back up to what they had been, she found it hard to concentrate at times. Only Liz knew about her sudden midnight awakenings.

And even Liz didn't know about the other moments—the moments when it wasn't nighttime terrors that disturbed her rest, but sudden memories that cut through her sleep and woke her quietly. Then, all she could do was remember that her only adult friend was gone. She was alone. Even with Liz's friendship, she knew that she was alone. Because she and Liz were both floating along; neither one of them could really tie onto the other. Life had thrown them together in a cataract of changes. They could hang onto each other only as long as circumstances kept them together.

Liz had no idea of some of the things that went through Tracey's mind, but Tracey also realized that she didn't know half of what went through Liz's mind. It was remarkable how two girls that everybody looked at as a matched set could be so lonely and isolated from each other.

A familiar noise out in the hallway interrupted her brooding. Mary was checking the lockers again, this time without the police along to help.

Tracey had noticed that the locker checks usually fell on Thursdays at one o'clock. They didn't happen every week, but when they did, it was always on that day and at that time. Mary would never find the drugs she was supposedly looking for. She had reduced the surprise raids to a routine.

Tracey forced herself to return to the class lecture. She was not good enough at geometry to let her mind be wandering all over creation. Half the class was already on academic probation in this subject, and if Tracey were put on it, she could kiss basketball good-bye.

Sister Aquinas was working out a theorem on the blackboard, and Tracey scribbled the notes down in her

428

notebook, momentarily lost as to what the theorem was proving. Liz would have to go over it with her later.

The opening and closing of the lockers was getting closer, a background noise to Aquinas's lecture about the uses of this particular theorem.

Aquinas had promised them that they would have to memorize only six theorems for the whole year, and surely anybody could do that. But now Tracey wasn't so sure. It took a lot just to understand these theorems, and then you had to apply them on the tests. The class was already hard, and they were only up to the fourth theorem.

A sudden report like the shot of a small pistol jerked everybody's head up and stopped Aquinas in the middle of a sentence. A stifled cry came from the hallway, unmistakably the voice of Sister Mary. The girls heard a strangled gasp or two, and several of them ran to the front door of the classroom. Tracey went to the back door and looked out.

Sister Mary stood at Liz's locker, her face a study of surprise and pain. She wrenched at her hand with a second gasp and pulled a mousetrap off her fingers.

She saw the faces at the doorways and snapped, "Get back to your studies this instant!"

The girls ducked back inside and scurried to their seats, shooting guilty looks at Sister Aquinas.

Aquinas was a scientific and thorough teacher, not much given to prejudices. She had gone to the door herself. "Let's resume, girls," she said briskly. Too briskly. Though scientific and thorough, Aquinas also had a sense of humor and a sense of adventure. Tracey had always gotten along with her. And Liz had been a special favorite of the math teacher.

The PA system interrupted them. "Liz Lukas," Mrs. Sladern said over the loudspeaker. "Report to this office immediately."

The girls looked at each other. Sister Aquinas glanced at them.

"Well, girls," she began. She seemed to have an inspiration. "I believe I left my roll back in my office. I'll be right back. I want it silent in here, young ladies. Silent."

"Yes, Sister," they chorused. She hurried out, and the room exploded into laughter. Liz walked by, stuck her head in the back door, and shrugged at Tracey. "Now what?" she asked in a loud whisper.

Liz wasn't at practice that afternoon. Neither was Sister Patricia Rose.

Scooter, as alternate captain, took over the practice. They were too close to the big game to be loose in their discipline, so they obeyed her better than they might have otherwise. Conversation was brisk as they warmed up and practiced their shots.

"Why did she have to pull this now?" Peggy asked as she chest-passed to the target on the wall and Tracey caught any ricochets.

"Shoot, I don't know," Tracey said. "But it was the greatest thing you ever saw, Peggy. I'll never forget the look on Mary's face as long as I live."

"Mary'll never let her play," Peggy insisted.

"You just watch," Tracey told her. "They might flay the skin off her after the game, but Father Bing is not going to let Liz get pulled." She switched off with Peggy and started shooting at the target. "I bet that's why Liz did do it now—she can get away with it."

"She's crazy, but she's got guts," Peggy said after a moment or two.

"I sure would like to know what's going on," Tracey said.

Scooter, who was going by just then, stopped. "They're all in a huddle in Mary's office, raking Lukas over the coals," she said. "They got to make it look good—like she's in big trouble, you know?"

"But you think she'll play?" Tracey asked.

Scooter nodded. She added, as though stating the obvious, "I mean, Liz's been after Sladern and Mary both to get rid of the mouse for her. They told her it was her problem, and they told her she couldn't use poison. She did have signs posted all over her locker warning people to be careful because of the mouse. I mean—" Scooter shot them a look of startled innocence, "how was Liz supposed to know that Mary would be going through her locker?"

All three of them laughed.

Scooter walked away to check the other players, and Peggy and Tracey looked at each other. "Scooter's cooled off a lot," Peggy said.

"Yeah, I guess so," Tracey said.

"Come on, Jac. She fell in with bad company, OK? But she's seeing the light. She doesn't play quite as rough as she used to."

"I guess not," Tracey agreed reluctantly. It was true that as the year had progressed, Scooter had relaxed her dislike for Tracey enormously. Part of the reason for the change Tracey had attributed to CPR's vigorous insistence that all of the girls on the team get along with each other. But the team itself had changed faces. Liz and Tracey and Peggy were believers in democracy.

Liz's policies carried a great deal of weight, and Tracey was enough of a rising star to give support to the team captain.

Tracey didn't see Liz until after supper. The tall blonde girl entered the room just before study time and exclaimed, "Well, they certainly didn't like the mousetrap idea!"

Nikki and Toni burst out laughing.

"No, I guess not," Tracey agreed wryly. When she and Liz looked at each other, their eyes both revealed their glee, their absolute revelry in the memory of Sister Mary caught in a mousetrap. Such glee was not something they would show to their younger roommates, though.

"You gonna be allowed to play?" Tracey asked.

Liz flopped down on the floor with her back against Tracey's bunk. "Oh, sure. That never even came up. Conspicuous by its absence, I guess you might say. Once Mary got done giving me grief, she called in Father Bing. He really looked mad too. I got kind of scared then. But as soon as Mary went out to get CPR, Bing dropped the act. He told me that it was a silly thing to do, putting that trap in the locker. And I told him that everybody in the whole school knew I was trying to get rid of a mouse."

"You mean you're still sticking with that story?" Tracey demanded.

"Sure. It's the truth!" Liz's look quieted Tracey from further protests. "Anyway, then CPR came in and got into the act, yelling at me and saying I was irresponsible and careless and on and on. It lasted from fifth hour until supper. So you'll understand if I can't remember all of it. I missed sixth-hour class—which was only religion—and I have to make it up. So that means that St. Bernard will be under instruction to give me a piece of her mind about it tomorrow too."

Tracey shook her head. "Mary bosses St. Bernard gently or not at all, Liz. Ain't you figured that out yet?"

Liz glanced at her. "No, I haven't."

"Just you wait. She might tell St. Bernard exactly what to say to you. But St. Bernard won't do it. The more Mary tells her, the more St. Bernard will do the exact opposite." Tracey smiled, pleased that for once she could tell Liz the way things were.

Liz nodded, looking thoughtful.

"But you really scared the team," Tracey said in a quieter voice. "If they'd suspended you from play, we wouldn't have a chance against Chickens of the Valley."

"Baby," Liz said, suddenly serious, "we won't win against Chickens of the Valley."

Tracey glanced at her sharply.

"We ain't got it," Liz told her. "Too many close shaves with too many teams. Maybe next year. We'll be in third this year, which, in this division, means nothing. No trophy at all."

"Kind of early to be throwing in the towel," Tracey said.

"I play hard—win or lose," Liz said. "Nobody but you will ever know I'm going into this not believing in us. But I don't. Not this year."

Liz's prophecy proved true. Though the Valkyries played hard, and as well as they were able, they ended the division championship game down by seventeen points, their worst defeat of the season.

Against a better team, Tracey could see more clearly where the Valkyries were weak. The strategies they used were good enough, but most of their plays depended on the forwards or the center making the shots. The guards might as well have been invisible once the ball was brought up. She remembered Liz's comment that Debbie Dibbley ought never to have been cut from the team, and she wondered if Liz had foreseen this weakness much earlier. Dibbles was a good shooter, though she had little knowledge of the rules of basketball and had never played before. Her entire experience of basketball was playing "PIG" with her brothers and other neighborhood kids. And since she had always won, everybody had told her all her life that she should play basketball when she got to high school.

Every girl at MoJoe learned the rules of basketball in gym class, and they had some pretty good intramural games in the autumn while CPR was scouting for possibilities. Maybe next year Dibbles would make the team.

The girls left the game feeling dejected. It was hard to come back as losers, and it was hard to know that the season was over. No more fun until next year. No more feeling as alive as you felt on the court—until next year's cuts were over with.

"At least we got Color Day tomorrow," Peggy observed that night before the lights-out bell. "And then it's only seven more weeks until summer."

"Yeah, summer. Yippee," Tracey said dryly. A summer here without Sister James Anne. With every blade of grass and every flower echoing back her memory. She wasn't ready to look that loneliness in the face. Life was quickly returning to a one-day-at-a-time process. She couldn't handle it in chunks anymore.

"What's the movie?" she asked, to change the subject. Like Liz, she had not bothered to keep up with Color Day preparations while there had been basketball to think of.

"*Dracula* and *Romeo and Juliet* tied," Peggy said. "And only two people voted for *Dragnet*."

"Yeah, I know who they were," Tracey told her. "You and your friend Dibbles."

Peggy nodded. "But Debbie said she's seen *Romeo and Juliet* a million times already. So she's going to vote for *Dracula,* and I'm going with *Romeo and Juliet*."

"So you both cancel each other out."

"I guess."

"When's the next vote?"

"Tomorrow." Peggy looked as humble as she could. "Won't you switch to *Romeo and Juliet*, Jac? For me?"

"Peg, I hate romances," Tracey protested.

"Oh, come on. You slept through the movie last year anyway."

"Oh, all right. For you, Peggy, because we're teammates. OK?"

"OK," Peggy agreed, and she smiled.

The vote was taken the next morning in homeroom, and the winner was announced during sixth hour. Another tie.

Everybody groaned as the announcement came over the PA in each classroom.

Mary herself made the announcement, and the groans were quickly cut short as she concluded, "We cannot have bickering over the selection of an appropriate film, girls. Therefore, the entertainment committee will select a film that is neither *Dracula* nor *Romeo and Juliet*, and we hope that all of you will be pleased with the selection."

"Who's the entertainment committee?" Amy whispered to Tracey. Tracey shrugged, but one of the other girls whispered back, "Sister Theresa, Mary, St. Bernard, and Timbuktu."

"Oh, they ought to pick a real winner," Tracey mumbled.

Amy shrugged. "We always do get really good movies."

During homeroom the next day, the announcement was made: The movie of choice was *Green Dolphin Street*.

"*Green Dolphin Street?*" Tracey asked. "What's that about?"

None of the girls knew. But when they asked Sister

St. Bernard, she told them it was a movie about a love triangle.

"What's a love triangle?" Tracey asked. By this time, Tracey was the acknowledged spokesperson for any questions that the class might share—about anything.

"It means that two women love the same man, or two men love the same woman," St. Bernard said. "There are many famous stories of love triangles."

"Like *Gone With the Wind*," Amy suggested. "Somebody always has to lose out, like Scarlett O'Hara did over that first guy she fell in love with."

St. Bernard nodded, pleased that they had caught on.

"That means it's a romance," Tracey said with a groan, and many of the other girls groaned too. Romances were not fast-paced enough, especially for the boarders. Love stories like *Casablanca* could hold their attention because they had the threat of Nazis and Gestapo and spies. *Green Dolphin Street* didn't sound like it promised many thrills. However, all of the nuns seemed to have seen *Green Dolphin Street*.

At lunch that day, Liz's report on the movie matched Tracey's. "Timbuktu says it's about a love triangle between two sisters," she said. "Both after the same guy."

When Tracey went to visit Sister Lucy later, even she was lucid enough to recognize the movie's title. "Oh, dear, yes, how I enjoyed that film when I saw it— so long ago now," she said. "I must ask James how she liked it. I haven't seen it in years."

Tracey's visits to Sister Lucy were as one-sided as ever, with Tracey doing most of the talking for the first part of the visit while Sister Lucy tried to remember who she was. Although Sister Lucy remembered Sister James clearly enough, she had almost no memory of Tracey. And most often, Sister James's death was also a thing forgotten by the old woman. She seemed to regard Sister James as a dear friend who kept getting misplaced all over the retirees' wing, rather like an odd set of keys.

Tracey never tried to correct the sister's memory, though occasionally one of the nurses said, "Sister Lucy, Sister James Anne is no longer with us. Don't you remember?" Then Sister Lucy would agree very pleasantly with the attendant, and Tracey saw that she had no idea what the attendant was talking about but was too kind to argue. The few times that reality did sink in, Sister Lucy's look of grief was just as sharp as it must have been that first morning when they had told her.

Tracey could imagine no fate more cruel than having to be told your best friend was dead—and always hearing the news as though for the first time all over again. It was a punishment right out of Greek mythology, as cruel as the vines of fruit and waters that forever tortured Tantalus.

Sister Lucy was better at remembering things distant than things up close. Once she decided upon Tracey's identity, she would take up the conversation and talk on and on until Tracey said it was time to leave. Sometimes Tracey could read to her, but the old woman's attention span was diminishing with the rest of her. Being read to was no longer her favorite pastime.

Tracey managed to visit Sister Lucy once a week, though it was a battle every time. If she had decided to go on a Thursday, then on Thursday she would excuse herself for having too much homework. On Friday she would excuse herself because the basketball team members were getting together for a game of half-court now that the days were warmer. She usually ended up going on Saturday afternoons, when it was hardest of all to get away from Sister Lucy. For all her mental decline, the sister understood what going away meant, and she always begged Tracey to stay longer. Assailed by guilt and pity, Tracey usually ended up staying for nearly three hours.

She knew she should go more often. If she would go three or four times a week, she needn't stay more than forty-five minutes or so each time. And she knew it was her own selfishness that kept her from being truly concerned for Sister Lucy. Each trip cost her pain, showing her the decline of this poor, lonely old woman—a decline that could never be reversed or even eased. Each look at Sister Lucy, who would die as witlessly and as gracelessly as any animal, cut again into her belief in the Resurrection. She wasn't sure anymore if man himself, man the created being, really possessed those mystical things called soul and spirit. Old age, drugs, fear, pain—any of these was strong enough to tear away his dignity. And what about sins like lust and greed? She remembered with a knife thrust of memory the day she had realized that the grand darkness of her mother's sin was nothing more than a facade. Prostitutes did the same thing several times a night on bare mattresses or urine-stained cots for a few dollars, another fix, a bit of food, a bottle of whiskey.

What was that resurrected life that Maddie Murdoch had spoken of? Tracey probably wouldn't see Maddie for months, now that basketball season was over.

After one of her torturous visits with Sister Lucy, she came back to the room and threw herself onto her bed. Liz looked up and said, "Why not give it up, Jac?"

"I'm all she's got left," Tracey said.

"Give her three days, and she'll never remember you at all."

There was no answer to that—no answer except for that thing deep inside of Tracey that wouldn't let her go. Tracey could not explain it to Liz. Her belief in God's love was more uncertain now that she was a Christian than before she had become one. The idea that man was nothing more than a highly evolved primate had risen to torment her. But she could not leave Sister Lucy for the simple reason that such an act would be the worst of sins—desertion in a time of need.

"You aren't doing her any good," Liz would point out.

"Nobody knows that," Tracey would say. "Sister James's death has done her a lot of harm, even though she can't remember that Sister James is dead. Maybe she won't remember that I'm not visiting her anymore. But it still might hurt her." This argument was the only thing that gave her hope about the existence of a soul or spirit. Maybe some unseen, unremarked part of a person knew about things like death and life and companionship—and dictated the response of the body and emotions.

The worst realization was that if God was real, and if God was as good as the Bible said, then Tracey's faint-hearted attempts at visiting Sister Lucy weren't doing much to please Him, anyway. She knew she ought to be more consistent, more patient, and less unwilling.

If Liz had once suggested calling Maddie Murdoch, Tracey would have done so. Even though Liz seemed to have dropped her campaign to personally supervise a friendship between Tracey and Mrs. Murdoch, Tracey's mind went back to the Irish woman several times. She bitterly regretted that she had not confided her fears about the Resurrection to Maddie.

She wanted to believe the Resurrection, and she wanted some hope that God could someday forgive her for all of the mistakes, all of the anger, all of the sins, and all of the doubts. Once she got to heaven, where all of her doubts would be exposed for everyone to see, and then all the sins she'd committed since getting saved were put on display, there wouldn't be any reward for her. And there'd probably be as much censure as you could get in heaven. Maybe she'd be one of the dishwashers or something.

Tracey knew she wasn't even consistent in her doubts. Sometimes she didn't believe in a resurrection or even an afterlife, and then two minutes later she contradicted herself by picturing the trouble she would be in once she got to heaven.

When her doubts and worries pressed her hardest, she was only a heartbeat away from calling Maddie Murdoch. But she never went through with it. The moment to confess her doubts had passed that night on the bus when CPR had interrupted them, and now it was gone. She would not recall it.

Color Day made a nice change from routine. You could pay a dollar to get a Color Day tag, and that entitled you to wear regular clothes instead of the uniform. Everybody tried to wear black and white, except for a few girls so into their studies that they didn't understand what Color Day was for, and a few other girls so into money that they wore the most lavish things they owned.

Classes lasted only through the morning, and then it was time for skits and games in the auditorium, followed by a mock ceremony in which the seniors gave awards to underclassmen who had gotten their attention. Her freshman year, Liz Lukas—who even then had been the high scorer for the basketball team—had won a pair of glasses so she could improve her shooting and make the team the next year. Tracey had come close as a freshman to being voted the girl most likely to take holy orders. Sister St. Gerard had vetoed that award on the grounds that it was in bad taste.

Some of the awards, especially toward the end of

the ceremony, were more serious. The senior class occasionally took great pains during the second semester either to make something or save up for something to present to the school. The senior class of 1968 had given the team its banner and spears to carry into the games, and the remarkable senior class of 1971 had presented an electronic scoreboard to the school. That presentation likely would never be duplicated.

After the skits, games, and awards, everybody would settle down for the movie and refreshments.

The ceremonies that day were no disappointment. One of the seniors was an accomplished gymnast, and she gave a demonstration that impressed everybody. Memories of Olga Korbet were still fresh in everyone's mind, and they responded enthusiastically There were other skits, songs, and then a few rounds of "Simon Says," led by CPR. She was good and hard to keep up with. It was easy to see, when she was clowning with them and they were responding as willingly as little children, that CPR's place was not in the convent, nor even at MoJoe. She could have done anything.

After CPR had retired to the applause of the school, it was time for the awards. Sister Aquinas, the math teacher, was given a calculator, and Sister Theresa was awarded a book on singing for beginners. Tracey had nearly forgotten that MoJoe's small chorale had placed first in a competition in New York the previous autumn. Sister Theresa, instead of being amused at the gift, was so touched that she left the stage dabbing her eyes. The students gave her a loud round of applause.

Even Sister Mary was called to the stage. Her award was odd and unexplained: two Popsicle sticks. She held them up and looked at Karen Fisher, the

444

president of the senior class, who was making the awards. Karen shrugged. This time, applause was scattered because nobody knew what the gift was for.

Liz was called next.

"We thought," Karen said, "that we would replace something for you that you lost earlier this year." She handed Liz a mock-up of a road sign that said "DO NOT ENTER," and then passed a mousetrap over to her. The auditorium erupted into applause and cheers, and several people started yelling, "Splints! Splints!" indicating that they'd realized what Mary's gift had meant.

Tracey was aghast at this boldness in recalling Mary's humiliation. This was one award that had not been approved by St. Bernard, she was sure. But for the moment it went unchallenged and unrebuked.

Snickers kept rippling through the audience as the rest of the awards were passed out. Tracey was shocked to hear her own name called at the end. She glanced at Liz and then went up to the stage.

"The senior class," Karen Fisher said as she reached into the recesses of the speaker's stand, "has asked Sister Madeleine for her assistance in making something that we could leave the school. The Valkyries had a great season this year, and we look forward to a championship next year, though we won't be able to see it. But we want you to remember us. First, we would like to announce the donation of two hundred dollars in the name of the class of '75 for the founding of a pep band to accompany the Valkyries."

The audience applauded and cheered, and Tracey wondered why in the world Liz had not been called up, or even Scooter, to give thanks on behalf of the team.

But then she realized that Karen did not mean for this to be Tracey's gift.

"And," Karen added, "just in case it takes more money and time to establish the pep band, we also took our art classes to work on one major project for the team, and this is what we would like to present now."

She cleared her throat. The mystery gift, apparently, was something serious. Tracey felt very hot and conspicuous on the stage, and she wished this part was over.

"We would like to add to the Valkyrie equipment given to the team by previous senior classes," Karen said. "And we feel in this presentation that it is only fair to call upon that player who, aside from the captain, best exemplifies the qualities of the Valkyrie: strength and a love of truth. The senior class asks that Tracey Jacamuzzi be appointed to keep these things in her possession, either until she is appointed team captain herself, or until she leaves the team. In either event, we ask that she appoint a successor to wear the armor of the Valkyrie, and that this armor be passed down from girl to girl, not based on skill, but based upon the two principles of moral strength and love of truth."

Karen finished with a nod to Tracey. Then she handed her a shield that was metal but felt very light, and a sword with no scabbard. The applause was thunderous. For a moment, feeling the shock of the applause and the heat of the lights, Tracey thought she might faint or be sick. But the moment passed, and she was left standing on the stage with the sword and shield, unsure what to do. She heard Liz's piercing whistle of approval, and it brought her mind back to the image of the team.

Whatever she felt at the moment, she had to appear both thankful and willing to live up to a charge she knew she could never live up to.

She slipped the shield onto her forearm and clashed it against the sword in token of victory, like the soldiers she had read about in the *Iliad*. Everybody applauded again, and she hurried off the stage.

Liz grabbed her as she came back to her seat.

"Man, are you shaking!" Liz exclaimed. "Look at that sword and shield! They're beautiful!"

Tracey slipped off the shield and handed both to Liz to admire, while up front, Karen ended the ceremony and called for a stanza of the school song.

After the song, everybody felt ready to get some popcorn and give *Green Dolphin Street* a try. Tracey, still trembly and nervous, was glad to sit down and rest while Liz went for popcorn.

As soon as everybody settled back down, the lights went out and the whir and click of the projector was the only noise in the auditorium. The big screen was let down above the stage.

*Green Dolphin Street*, to judge from its warbling music and white streaks of splicing, was an old movie. Tracey was able to follow the first ten minutes of the picture, which consisted of two girls who kept putting on hats and gloves, either to go visit people or to go shopping—Tracey couldn't tell which, because all the houses looked like shops on the outside, and all the shops looked like houses on the inside.

"What year is this supposed to be going on in?" she whispered to Liz.

"You got me," Liz whispered back. "*Romeo and Juliet* would have been better than this."

Tracey didn't care. After the shock of getting a real award, she was willing to let her mind wander. Pretty soon she was dozing.

She woke up once to see that the scene had entirely changed. There was some sort of island on the screen, maybe the Philippines or somewhere in the Caribbean. Everybody was dressed like a thirties film version of a "native." And there were rubber palm trees all over the place. Then someone in the film screamed, and the ground started to shake.

No, she decided, the ground wasn't shaking. It was billowing up and down in waves like a muslin sheet. Which—to judge by the way the rubber palm trees and little straw huts were tilting all the way over and bouncing back up—was exactly what the ground in the film set was: a painted muslin sheet. Tracey was too sleepy to be amused by bad effects, but as she lapsed into her doze again, she heard several girls laughing.

"This stinks," she heard Liz whisper.

"Oh, in 1923 it was probably the latest thing," Tracey mumbled.

She woke up again to hear the warbly music playing. "Is it over?" she asked.

"No," Liz whispered. "The dopey girl is climbing up a well."

"How'd she get into a well?" Tracey asked. She opened her eyes long enough to watch one of the film's main characters make a painstaking climb up out of a well. The scene would have been a lot more suspenseful, she decided, if she'd watched the picture from the beginning instead of in parts. But that was a fate she wouldn't wish on a dog. Even the girls who were awake and paying attention didn't look interested.

"What in the world got into their heads that made those stupid nuns get this film?" Liz demanded under her breath. "Are they punishing us? Maybe they're mad that we lost the division championships."

"When's it going to be over?" Tracey asked as she closed her eyes again.

"Never. That's part of our punishment."

But Tracey didn't have long to doze before she felt Liz poking her in the ribs.

"What? What?" Tracey exclaimed, jumping up.

"Look! Look!" Liz exclaimed, pointing at the screen. "Look! That's why they got the film. That's why!"

Everyone was in the same temper as Liz, though nobody else was as loud. Tracey could hear an under-current of angry murmurs.

She paid attention to the screen. "I don't get it," she said. "Why's the girl standing at the altar like that?"

"Don't be a dope, Jacamuzzi," Liz said. "She's becoming a nun. She's becoming a nun! That's why they got this stupid film. Gyp!" she yelled.

"Gyp!" several other girls exclaimed.

"She should've just stayed in the well," Tracey said.

The lights in the auditorium came up. One of the girls was running the film, so there were no nuns close enough to complain to. They'd all been in the back, watching. Now they were gone. The bell rang to end the school day.

"Gyp!" Liz yelled.

"Cool it, Liz," Tracey said as they stood up to leave. "No one's here to listen."

All the girls were annoyed and muttering about getting gypped out of their money. But Tina McCorkle slid out of her row and said, "I don't know. I really liked it."

"Oh, shut up!" Liz yelled at her.

Tracey brandished the sword. "Off with her head!" It made Tina run away, and Liz, caught by surprise, laughed.

"Come upstairs and just cool it," Tracey told her. "If you go yelling at the nuns, it's only going to get you in trouble."

"They took our money and spent it on a propaganda film about becoming a nun," Liz complained.

"Yeah, and you got Mary to put her hand into a mousetrap," Tracey said. "So I still think you're one up on her. Let her have her day. Come on."

"She's gonna have her day, all right," Liz muttered. She followed Tracey out of the auditorium and up to the room.

Tempers and attitudes in the hall that night were as bad as Tracey had ever seen. She felt some of her schoolmates' annoyance, but it was not as sharp for her. She probably would have fallen asleep during any film, just as she had the year before.

She admitted to herself that all of them constantly played jokes at the nuns' expense. It didn't seem possible that Sister Mary could have had the imagination to pick a bomb of a movie just to get revenge. Mary would more likely have canceled the movie altogether. But she had gotten revenge on them, whether she had meant to or not, and Tracey's sense of fair play told her they should take the loss gracefully.

Nobody shared her sense of justice, not even Liz, who said the idea was stupid.

"This was everybody's money," she pointed out. "Every brownie, every narc, every good kid, every bad kid, every ballplayer, every pusher. We all paid the same amount to vote on our movie. Mary cheated everybody."

Scooter, Peggy, and the rest of the team agreed with Liz, so Tracey kept her mouth shut. Privately, she saw the funny side of it—Sister Mary had burned them worse than they had yet been burned, and she didn't even realize it. She probably thought some of them were thinking of signing up for the convent, when really most of the girls were wishing they could burn it down.

There was no homework on Color Day, and study time was not enforced, so they all stayed in little clusters that night, complaining about how unfair everything was. Some of the girls were pretty extreme. There was talk that the tougher town students were going to have their boyfriends call in bomb threats the next day. That had been done before, though, and Sister Mary was wise to it. She would just conduct another locker search, notify the police, and conduct business as usual. Other girls were talking about finding green paint and stenciling dolphins all over the walls of the school in honor of *Green Dolphin Street*. Tracey thought a stunt like that had a lot more class than the old bomb-threat routine.

Liz cooled down by the end of the evening and suggested that they circulate a petition demanding their money back, and an apology for showing them a film that they all hated. This suggestion carried some weight, and the clique that had assembled in Tracey and Liz's room agreed to start a petition the next morning at breakfast. Tracey's classmate Amy, who was a good writer, offered to type one up. She was given the commission and immediately left to take care of her duty.

"Good," Tracey said as they got ready for bed. "Nobody gets out of hand, and Mary gets a petition. That's handling things like they always tell us to handle them—reasonably. If Mary doesn't listen to us, we can go to St. Bernard."

"What an eye for politics you have," Liz told her.

Tracey grinned at her but didn't answer. For her, the night was peaceful. She lay awake and looked at the sword and shield, which, in the dimness of the room, reflected the faint light with glints of gold. Next year, when the games started again, she would follow Liz and Scooter out and would be the first under the banner, carrying the sword and shield of the team.

No gift had ever humiliated her so much, for she knew she didn't deserve it. Yet the gift had revived her too. She wasn't much of a light, but she was the only one at MoJoe. And some of the girls, apparently, had listened and were watching.

Maybe she didn't have to be perfect, just honest about being such a sinner. For an instant, she thought she could almost grasp where she had been wrong all along, why she had failed so much. But then the moment of understanding was gone. She was only herself, with a tin sword and a shield painted to look like bronze, and an impossible commission from her peers to stand for moral strength and love of truth.

Tracey fell asleep, and the night passed quietly. Or almost quietly. At about two o'clock, she woke up suddenly, but not from a nightmare or night terror, she thought. Something outside of herself had awakened her. She looked around the room without sitting up.

"Are you all right?" Liz whispered.

"Sure, fine," Tracey whispered back. "I wasn't having a bad dream."

"No? You sounded like you were."

Tracey was used to waking up from a nightmare with a sense of panic and disorientation. She wasn't feeling either of these, nor was she unable to talk. Really bad dreams left her with a momentary aphasia when they jolted her awake.

"What did I do?" she asked Liz.

"You called out in your sleep and said for something to get off you."

"Well," Tracey said after a moment's puzzlement, "I'm OK." She went back to sleep.

Everybody seemed in better spirits the next morning. When Tracey got back from the showers, she saw that her sword and shield had been moved from where she had set them up the night before.

"Are these tripping you guys up?" she asked her roommates.

Nikki glanced at her. "They've been there all morning. None of us have tripped."

"I had the sword lying straight out last night, not propped up," Tracey said.

"I moved it when I first got up," Liz said.

Nikki glanced at Liz. "You did? I was first one up, and I thought it was upright when I passed it on the way out."

"Oh, well, it's no big deal," Tracey said. "As long as they're not in anybody's way. I'd better get them locked up with the banner and spears today."

"That's a good idea," Liz said.

"Hey," Nikki said, looking out the window as she tied back her hair. "There's something burning on the lawn."

Tracey and Liz glanced out the window. Toni came over to look.

"Looks like compost or leaves or something," Toni said.

Just then Peggy knocked and came in. "Breakfast," she yelled.

"Here we come," Liz yelled back. "Let's go, kids! Everybody got what they need?"

Conversation out in the halls was loud and brisk. Everybody was rested from a night with no homework. As the crowd of girls hurried down the center stairs and past the main doors, they saw a sign posted on the inside of the doors. The print was large and bold. It said:

SECOND VIEWING: *GREEN DOLPHIN STREET.* USE CENTER DOORS ONLY.

"Who'd want to see that junk again?" Amy asked. She had the petition under her arm.

Scooter and Peggy threw open the center doors. "All I see are the grounds," Scooter said.

"Yeah, and Mr. Szymansky's trash pile," Peggy added. "About as exciting as that movie."

"He's burning that on good green grass," Debbie Dibbley said. "Sister Mary's going to be mad. She keeps telling him to burn his stuff behind the kitchen."

"Come on," Tracey told them. "Breakfast is waiting."

Breakfast was good that morning: pancakes. While everybody was eating, the first carload of town students burst into the dining room.

"What are they doing here?" Liz asked. Town students usually went straight to the classrooms.

"Oh!" Tina McCorkle shrieked, coming up one of the aisles between the tables and getting everybody's attention. "The film is on fire! The film is on fire! Get one of the extinguishers!"

"That was the movie?" Liz exclaimed, jumping up. "Mary's going to kill us all."

Tracey jumped up too, aghast at the boldness of whoever had done such a thing.

Amy instantly ripped up the petition and dunked it into her glass of milk.

"What are you doing that for?" Tracey asked her.

"I don't know anything about any of this!" Amy exclaimed. "Nothing! Nothing! I really liked *Green Dolphin Street*."

"Oh, I don't know, Amy," Dibbles began in her singsong voice. "You had an awful lot to say last night—"

"Dibbles, shut up," Liz told her, but even she couldn't resist a smile. Amy's quick sense of guilt was unnecessary. The idea that anybody would ever connect meek and timid Amy with such a bold stunt was ridiculous to everyone but Amy.

"Well, OK," Dibbles said. "But what will we say if Mary asks—"

"Shut up!" Liz said again. This time Dibbles obeyed her, shooting her a mischievous smile that Liz acknowledged. Amy dumped the sodden petition onto her tray and mixed it with her paper napkin.

"Amy—" Tracey began.

"Shut up, shut up, shut up!" Amy said.

Liz shot Tracey a grin, and Tracey returned it. Their biggest chore was going to be just keeping Amy calm. None of them made a move to go outside to see the burning film. Nobody wanted to be near it when Mary arrived. They all sat back down.

"I guess homeroom will be extended today," Liz said. "I expect a rather *looong* announcement on the PA system."

"It was wrong to burn that film," Tracey said after a moment. "I mean, it didn't even belong to the nuns. It belonged to someone else."

"Oh, they'll take it out of our hides one way or another and make payment," Liz said. "That's what worries me. At least a bomb threat wouldn't have cost us all anything. But now we all get in trouble for one person's brainy idea of getting even." She drained her milk.

"What I want to know is, who could get the film?" Tracey asked. "It was locked in the school office. Nobody has a key."

"Be thankful for that," Liz told her. "Because if anybody did, that person would be Mary's number one suspect. And any person who had a key wouldn't be stupid enough to have done this." She shook her head. "Somebody figured out something. I wish I knew how they did it."

Liz's prediction that homeroom would be extended had not been exaggerated. Guarded looks of suppressed glee went back and forth as Sister Mary reprimanded all of them over the PA system. She expressed her shock and horror—first, at their behavior during the film, laughing at the earthquake scene and groaning through the well scene. There was no reference to their booing at the initiation into the convent, but everybody knew she was maddest about that, second only to her outrage at whoever had burned the film.

"I will know," she concluded her speech. "I will know who conspired to burn that film and how it was done."

The girls looked at each other, wondering what punishments she would contrive.

"All outings to the town library are canceled! All softball games are canceled! The sock hop scheduled for the week before commencement is canceled! All sports practices are canceled!"

"Dessert on Sundays is canceled!" Dibbles quipped under her breath from two seats behind Tracey.

"All candy concessions after school are canceled! All field trips are canceled!" Mary continued.

"Summer is now canceled!" Peggy whispered to Dibbles and Tracey from across the aisle. Tracey put her face in her hands to hide a smile.

"Use of the bathrooms is now canceled!" Dibbles added. A tremor of suppressed giggles ran up the aisle.

"Use of the bicycles is canceled." Mary's disembodied voice was sounding a little breathless from reading the list so fast. "Use of the gymnasium is canceled for uses other than gym class. Use of the grounds for walking or jogging is canceled."

She waited several seconds, perhaps catching her breath, perhaps waiting for the horror of all these restrictions to sink in.

"The drinking water has been cut off," Dibbles's low voice continued up the aisle in mimicry of Sister Mary. "Beginning at one o'clock, all students will be buried alive, starting with those freshmen whose last names begin with A."

"Girls!" Mary exclaimed. "I want to know who did this awful thing. If you have any idea at all about who conspired to destroy that film that was not ours, I want you to report to me immediately. Everybody will suffer until I find out the persons guilty of this crime against the film company and against this school."

"Poison has already been introduced into the food supplies," Dibbles's voice continued. "Whoever has any information about the conspiracy will be given a shot of antidote—"

"Well, Kean, you going?" somebody asked out loud to Sandra Kean.

"Cool it!" Tracey exclaimed, just as St. Bernard ordered, "Silence!"

Everybody looked at Sandra and then at Tracey before resuming the downcast look expected of them while they were being rebuked.

Sandra also looked at Tracey for a moment before looking down at her desk. Tracey realized with a sensation of guilt that she had been out of touch with Sandra ever since basketball had started. She had suspected, from the other girl's lower profile, that she was working on breaking her tie with Sister Mary and had not been quite as cooperative this year as last. No doubt she was in the uncomfortable position of still bearing the girls' mistrust, while also facing Sister Mary's pressure to cooperate.

At least no one was after Sandra this year. Her compliance with the students' unwritten code would have earned her that much. But Tracey's guilt was not eased. She had ascended that year, and she could have helped Sandra more. She should have helped Sandra more.

Mary's tirade over the PA brought the question of Mary's narcs to the forefront of everyone's mind. Most of the girls from whom Mary could get information were freshmen, who didn't understand what was going on when Mary called them in and talked nicely to them. But Tracey doubted that any freshman would know who had burned the film. Such an audacious and well-planned act would have been hidden even from roommates and friends. Whoever had masterminded it—and Tracey figured it had taken at least two people—had carried it out smoothly enough to show skill in secrecy. *Like a real pro*, she thought. Someone who knew all the ins and outs of MoJoe. Someone who knew all the ins and outs of boarding schools in general. A bold and brilliant strategist, someone with a very close friend who could keep her mouth shut. *Someone just like Liz and me.* The realization startled her.

As though in confirmation of her thoughts, the PA suddenly came on again. "I want to see Liz Lukas and Tracey Jacamuzzi in my office at once! The rest of the basketball team will follow in ten minutes."

Everybody stared at Tracey as she stood up. All eyes followed her as she went to the front of the room. She looked at St. Bernard. "I'm excused, Sister?"

Even St. Bernard looked shocked, as though the awfulness of such an idea had struck her.

"I didn't do it," Tracey said to her. She looked at everybody else, a little surprised to see them all wondering such a thing.

"Of course not," St. Bernard agreed heartily. Too heartily. Tracey turned and left.

"You two are rebels!" Sister Mary greeted Tracey as she entered Mary's school office, a much smaller room than her large private office near the main entrance of the residence hall. Liz was already there, standing up. She looked at Tracey with a grim smile.

"Look at me, Tracey Jacamuzzi, and tell me what you know about that film," Mary ordered.

"Sister Mary, I slept through most of the showing yesterday, and this morning I saw it burning on the lawn," Tracey said, unafraid.

"Am I to believe that?" Mary demanded.

"You can believe what you want. She doesn't know anything about it!" Liz exclaimed hotly.

"Silence!" Mary exclaimed.

"I don't know anything about it," Tracey told her. "I don't believe in destroying other people's property, Sister. Stuff like that is a sin."

Mary was silent for a moment. She rocked back on her heels as though trying to decide whether or not to believe Tracey. Tracey knew Mary well enough to see that she already did believe her. But the opportunity to interrogate her would give Mary a certain satisfaction.

"Did you sleep through the whole night?" Mary asked her.

"Yes," Tracey said, and then, "No, I didn't."

"Well, what is it, yes or no?" Mary demanded.

"I didn't get up during the night, but I had a bad dream and woke myself up. I do that sometimes."

"All the time," Liz added.

"How did you wake yourself up?" Mary asked.

"I don't know. I woke up Liz too," Tracey said.

"She yelled out for someone to get off her, and I woke up and asked her if she was OK," Liz said. "She said she was, and we both went back to sleep."

"So you're both corroborating each other's claims that neither of you left your room last night," Mary said.

Tracey shrugged. "Nikki or Toni might have woke up when I yelled. Call them in and ask them. But that's all I know about last night."

"Sometimes CPR hears Tracey yell in her sleep," Liz added. "Ask her."

"That only happened once that we know about," Tracey corrected her. "She came down to check on me," she added for Mary's benefit.

Mary hesitated, but Tracey could see that she realized both of them were innocent. But Mary still had a score to settle for the mousetrap. This was as good a time as any.

"I am displeased with both of you—" she began. It sounded like a long harangue was on the way, so Tracey bent her knees slightly and put her hands behind her back to take it as comfortably as possible.

Mary's lecture did go on for a long time, and neither Tracey nor Liz answered back or argued. Tracey just wanted to leave and get to class. Perhaps more incensed by their silence, Mary prolonged her speech almost to the end of first hour, making the rest of the basketball team wait in the outer office with Mrs. Sladern. Then she called them in and yelled at the whole team together. It was almost nine-thirty when they finally got away.

Not only had all recreational activities been canceled, but nobody was even allowed out on the grounds for any reason. Tracey couldn't go down to the retirees' wing to visit Sister Lucy. She went to Sister St. Gerard to ask her to intercede with Mary, for Sister Lucy's sake at least.

"I'll try, dear," St. Bernard said, apparently moved by Tracey's request. "I know that sometimes it upsets you to go and see Sister Lucy. Maybe a short break would be good for you."

"It's only once a week, Sister," Tracey said. "I ought to go. She doesn't have anybody else."

"I will ask Sister Mary, but I don't know if anything can move her this time, even if the request were made on behalf of poor Sister Lucy." St. Bernard saw the regret in Tracey's eyes. "I tell you what," she said. "I'll visit Sister Lucy until the restriction is over. I'm sure I can make the time."

"Thank you, Sister," Tracey said, honestly grateful.

That had been Tracey's biggest worry about the restrictions. She did need books from the library for some of her oral reports, but she could get town girls to pick them up for her. Her status as a basketball player meant that there were people who liked doing favors for her.

April passed very quietly. There was no softball season, no field trips, almost no privileges at all. The end of the school year was so close, most of the boarders preferred that their silence continue. They did not want the culprits to turn themselves in. It would be a tremendous victory.

Tracey wondered, though, about the guilty people. If she had done it, she would have turned herself in rather than have everybody who lived in the hall punished so severely, even if they were willing to endure it. Whoever was responsible, she suspected, must be feeling the guilt right now, wondering whether to come forward.

She felt a little worried that she couldn't practice basketball. She had never had more than two weeks off from practice, and that had been because of her sprain. The weeks of inactivity were now piling up on her: first one, then two, then three, then a whole month. She was becoming used to not practicing.

She and Liz went to Father Bing, and he seemed distressed.

"But," he told them, "my hands are tied. Vandalism is a crime, girls. It must be treated as a very serious offense. I have given Sister Mary her way in this, no matter what it takes."

"Father," Liz said, "whoever did it won't come forward now. It's back to us against the nuns."

He sighed and looked troubled. "I'll speak with her, girls. But I doubt that I can help much."

May came, the Blessed Virgin's month. Tracey no longer felt able even to walk in the May procession. It was a heathen ceremony from beginning to end. But rather than make her disapproval public as she had done the year before, she simply kept quiet. On the day of the May procession, she would go to the chapel and wait for it to be over. If she got in trouble, she got in trouble. If St. Bernard—who would be the one to notice her absence—made an issue out of it, well, she would have to face it.

But nobody was paying the May procession much attention. After six weeks of restrictions, with commencement only a few weeks away, everybody was on edge. Grades were better for the entire school, mostly because there was nothing to do but study.

The second week of May, Liz burst into the room with big news. "They caught one of them!" she exclaimed.

"Who?" everybody asked.

Liz shrugged. "I saw Father Bing hurrying off to Mary's office, and he told me."

"Let's go see who's not here," Tracey suggested.

The four roommates went up and down the halls to see. All of the people who seemed likely to be on a suspect list were accounted for. Amy was gone, and Sandra Kean was gone, and a couple of other really good or timid kids were gone, but no one people could seriously suspect.

Dinner came and went, and everyone but Sandra Kean was accounted for.

"No way," Liz exclaimed in the room after dinner.

"That's a town student they've got in the office down there, and Sandra Kean's somewhere else. You'll never get me to believe that she did anything like this."

Suspense was high. At long last, Sandra Kean came up the middle steps.

"Hey, come here," Liz called to her in a whisper. It was study time.

Sandra shook her head, looked down, and went to her room. Liz sneaked after her but was back in a minute, shaking her head.

"She told me to leave her alone," she said. "I asked her if she'd done it, and she said she didn't know what I was talking about and just to leave her alone."

They were all in an agony of suspense until study time was over, and then half the hall flocked to Sandra's room. Sandra wouldn't answer their questions.

"Just go away!" she exclaimed when she opened the door and saw almost everybody there. Her roommates looked angry and disgusted.

"Did you do it?" Peggy asked.

"I don't know what you're talking about," Sandra said. "Just leave me alone. Leave me alone!"

Tracey couldn't even see into the room, but Liz suddenly backed away. "Come on, she's crying. Let's go," Liz said.

The whole story came out the next morning. Sandra Kean had turned herself in for burning the film. But under the cross-examination of Sister Mary, her own confession had failed her. She had not known how to get a key to the office; she had not known where in the office the film had been stored.

"What motivates some people?" Liz asked. "Why turn yourself in for something you didn't do?"

"Maybe it was a way to redeem herself to everybody else," Tracey guessed. "You know, take the rap to set everybody else free."

"Yeah, or earn some respect for a brilliant strategy against Sister Mary," Liz agreed. "So now what has she got?"

"Now everybody thinks twice as bad of her," Tracey said. She sensed that Liz was upset for Sandra's sake. As rough and tough as Liz could be, she had a keen understanding of other people's weaknesses. She had never taken part in ridiculing any of Mary's narcs.

"Maybe I should go tell Mary that Sandra and I both did it, and I used her for a lookout and didn't tell her where I got the key from," Liz said at last.

"Oh, sure," Tracey said. "And you might make a better story out of it than Sandra did, but Mary's going to see through you in the end."

"You think so?" Liz asked.

Tracey sighed and gave her friend a long look. "All Mary needs is something to hang over your head, Liz. There's nothing she'd like more than that. Because you're the only person in this school who's not scared of her. What she really wants is to get a handle on you." At Liz's silence, she added, "Besides, it's wrong to tell a lie, even to help out somebody. If you want to help Sandra, just be nice to her."

"She's scared of me," Liz said. "But you're right. I'll try."

The extent of Sandra Kean's suffering soon became clear. Everyone's restrictions were lifted by the end of May, except for Sandra Kean's. Because she had confessed to a crime she had not committed, and thereby sheltered the guilty persons, her restrictions lasted all the way to commencement.

Both Liz and Tracey tried be friendly to her, but Sandra—as usual, not knowing friend from enemy—shunned them both and put on an attitude of not needing anybody's help or pity.

But there were things other than Sandra to think of. Summer was bearing down on them fast. Liz's family was going to Vermont again, and Liz promised to write to Tracey.

"Dibbles is staying for summer school, I think," Liz told her. "Maybe you can help her a little with the b-ball."

"I'll do my best," Tracey promised.

It had been quite a year; in some ways better than she once would have dared hope. She was on the team, respected—even admired—by some of the girls, and not just for her basketball skills. She had a good friend in Liz, and at last she had made peace with Maddie Murdoch and shed some of her fears of Sister Mary. But in other ways, it had been the worst year of her life, and it was marred with nightmares that had not completely gone away. Sister James Anne was dead, and Tracey's faith was still more shaken than she had ever thought a Christian's faith could be.

But good or bad, time was inexorable. Her life was a stream running out of control, taking her with it in its current. All she could do was hang on and ride through it.

The previous summer had been a small island of happiness at MoJoe, a summer that Tracey had enjoyed to its fullest degree. But this summer, without Sister James, was lonely.

As the days after commencement lengthened and memory after memory of her old friend came back to her, she began to realize how much she had grown and changed over that last summer. She had become old enough and familiar enough with Sister James to simply enjoy her company, not always needing comfort, guidance, or even attention. They had talked often, and it had been Tracey's first taste of real friendship, the kind of friendship that adults had—they could simply enjoy things together and enjoy each other's enjoyment. Books, old movies, ideas, past events—everything really, had made up their conversations. Until Sister James Anne had become to Tracey a real person, not just somebody to depend upon.

Now, Tracey could finally leave the school grounds to visit Sister James's grave in the cemetery. The visit was anticlimactic, even though she had long awaited the day and had brought flowers for the grave. All that was there was a little rectangle of grass, a flat bronze plaque on the ground, and a cup to stand flowers in. This wasn't Sister James or even a memory of her. The memories were all back on campus.

Tracey had expected to throw herself hard into her work that summer, maybe even offer to help St. Bernard in the garden. But she found that physical labor would be only a small part of her duties. Whoever assigned summer jobs had dictated that this year's chore for Tracey was not to clean the gym, but to inventory the school library.

Tracey's heart sank at the very idea. She didn't like paperwork and nearly rebelled at the thought of spending three months cooped up inside, writing out titles and making book labels.

As it turned out, the job had more variety than mere office work. On the second day, Sister Redemption took her up to the fourth floor of the hall and handed her two keys.

"This one unlocks all the doors this way," Redemption told her, "and this one unlocks all the doors down this way."

"But what's this got to do with the library?" Tracey asked.

Sister Redemption swung open one of the doors. Tracey glanced inside. On the farthest wall, metal bed frames were stacked upright. But everywhere else, on top of the built-in dressers and in the closets, were boxes and boxes of books. And there were books in separate stacks and books on the dusty windowsill.

"Why aren't these in the library?" Tracey asked.

"We've been waiting for you, dear," Sister Redemption told her with a wry smile.

Tracey grinned in spite of herself and said, "But these must have been up here for years."

"Some for two years, some longer. They need to be inventoried. We'll throw away those that are too worn for good use or whose subject matter is inappropriate for a high school—"

"Don't you know what books are here?" Tracey asked.

Redemption shook her head. "Some have been given to us from estates or from people doing housecleaning, and some we purchased with our library budget from other libraries that were cleaning house." She glanced at Tracey. "If we can't rebind a book, we simply throw it away. I'll leave those decisions up to you. Remember, we are on a limited budget. We rebind few books. If you inventory any books whose subject matter you doubt, make a separate list and I'll review it." She gave Tracey a long stare. "I expect you to exercise judgment, Miss Jacamuzzi."

Tracey cocked an eyebrow. "Sister, I don't like dirty books any more than you do. I wouldn't put them in a library."

The answer satisfied Redemption, and she left Tracey to her chore.

At first, Tracey had been a little startled at having the entire project dumped in her lap. They were leaving a lot up to her judgment. But then, the number of books was incredible, and she realized from an inventory of the space available in the school library that Redemption was using her only as a first screening. There wasn't room downstairs for more than a fourth of the books up here, if that many.

The books, then, were more of a problem than anything else. It was probably only the sisterhood's strict frugality that had prompted the storage and now the inventorying of the whole mess. Most schools would have scanned over the books as they had been donated and would have thrown away the unwanted books immediately.

Well, she thought, it sure made for an interesting summer job, if you didn't mind spiders and bookworms.

As she began sorting through the books, Tracey saw that the work would be sometimes boring, and at other times frustrating. Frustrating, because she found a great many books that caught her attention and impelled her to flip through the pages, glancing at woodcut illustrations or reading snatches here and there. She knew that she wasn't supposed to be doing that, and several times she caught herself and resumed her work, worrying about what Redemption would say about her slow progress.

Happily for Tracey, Redemption wasn't immune to lapses like that herself, and at the end of Tracey's first day, she seemed pleased with the two stacks of books, one inventoried and the other destined for the trash bins out back.

"Well," she said pleasantly as Tracey stood and dusted herself off, "we ought to get through this lot by the end of the summer. Anyway, you should. I'll be leaving in two weeks, but I think you're off to a good start."

Tracey had decided from the start that any picture books she found in the storage rooms would be good gifts for Sister Lucy. The school library had no room for picture books, and the old woman's mind found little these days to enjoy or even comprehend. Their one-sided conversations were all on Tracey's side these days. Sometimes it seemed as though Sister Lucy didn't even know she was there. Tracey didn't have the gentle art that so many of the attendants had of recalling Sister Lucy's mind with a joke or a squeeze of her hand or a couple of kisses on her cheek.

Even when they recalled her, Sister Lucy's mind didn't stay long. But she might like having color pictures to look at, and they would certainly spare Tracey from what amounted to talking to herself for an hour or two each week in Sister Lucy's presence.

Sadly, few of the books in the first storage room were anything like picture books. If any of them had been published after 1930, Tracey never saw it. The stacks consisted mainly of old books on religion or science and medicine. Most were in very bad repair, ripping out of their own bindings by their sheer weight.

Aside from the bad repair, they didn't have much appeal for an all-girls' high school. Tracey had some doubts about throwing away half the contents of this room, but then, she might be doing Redemption a favor. Besides, Redemption, who was adept at sarcasm, might ask her exactly what purpose she thought the old trade book, *Impossible Objective: Man on the Moon* might serve at MoJoe.

The religion books caught Tracey's attention more, and she went through these very slowly. She had argued with herself about throwing away all of the Catholic ones, but that didn't seem honest. The question was pointless, however, because most of the books were in too bad of shape to keep, or they were not Catholic at all. Nor were they orthodox Protestant, either. Some were about the Salvation Army and some were about metaphysics—she threw these away—and some had titles she didn't understand, with words like *gnosticism* and *mysticism*. She stored these for Redemption, assuming that they would get thrown away anyway.

One thick book had no cover at all, and she heaved it onto the throwaway pile. The book after it had its covers, so she opened it to find the title page. She saw that it was a book on Protestantism, illustrated with woodcuts.

THE HISTORY
of
PROTESTANTISM
by the
Rev. J. A. Wylie, LL.D.
Volume II

She smiled at the stilted figures in the illustration, and for a moment her curiosity was piqued by what she took to be a Roman Catholic account of the rise of Protestantism. She flipped the volume open and read a few lines, then quickly shut the book.

It was not a Catholic version of Protestantism. It was Protestant, and it was all about the Reformation.

Tracey could almost feel her eyes burning in her head. She had heard snatches of information about the Reformation from the preacher at the Baptist church. She had read bits about it in the old book on false doctrines. It had intrigued her to realize that Roman Catholicism and Protestantism—a biblical Protestantism —had once fought a pitched battle. Her pastor had said that the ramifications were still being felt throughout the world, that America itself had been born from Protestant thought so well expressed by Reformers.

Somewhere back in history, people had asked the exact same questions she had asked. They had made the same decisions. *But they were always sure,* she thought. Now she could find out why and how they had stayed so sure and had not made the mistakes she had made.

Back in sixth grade at St. Anne's, Tracey had learned that a Reformation had taken place. Her sixth-grade history book had included a huge picture of a small Martin Luther in a very big church. There had been a few paragraphs about a former monk who had gotten angry at church abuses and had left the church to found a church that he thought was what God wanted. Sister Steven Elaine had pointed out that Luther had said that faith alone was all it took. Everybody in the class could see that he was wrong, couldn't they?

The impression Tracey had gotten that day in sixth

grade was that Martin Luther had made his big change in about one afternoon, and by the next Sunday everybody had a choice of which church to go to. Some had become Lutherans, and little Lutheran churches had started springing up all over the place, just like McDonald's franchises. But, of course, all of the Lutherans were wrong.

After her conversion, Tracey's pastor, the Murphys, and her own reading had made her realize that the Reformation was a much bigger thing than she had first thought. But she still didn't know how long it had lasted —at least a few years, she would have guessed.

The little bit she had learned about John Foxe while doing library work in town had made her realize how big a thing the Reformation must have been—and how impossible it would be to study it out, unhampered by her teachers or even her classmates. There hadn't been time enough; there hadn't been an organized way to do it.

Now, here was a whole book on it. No, at least two books. The coverless book that she had discarded was the first volume, and there was a third volume next in the stack. Not two, but three volumes on the Reformation.

She was amazed that anybody would have had the foresight to sit down and write out an organized account of the whole thing; she knew that some of the Reformers were from different countries. Exactly when they had all gotten together to hammer out their theses and letters and bulls and books was still unknown to her. But she knew that they had produced a lot of writings, and she knew that the pope or popes of those years had harassed them. Some had died at the stake for their beliefs.

Tracey decided that she would read Wylie. If any parts of his books were dull, she would just skip them. That was one of the advantages of summer reading.

## SEVENTY-TWO

One thing the Wylie books gave Tracey, other than interesting information, was escape. You could dive into books this big, she thought. You started by wading through a page or two of fine print, and soon you became oblivious to the print itself, even the illustrations, as the story took hold of you and brought you under its spell.

For a girl who had already read the *Iliad* in English class and had done reports on *Plutarch's Lives* for World History, Wylie was very readable. Tracey began at the beginning of the first volume and started by getting to know the church fathers and the history of the Waldensians.

Wylie became almost like a friend to her, and her mind painted pictures of a gentle, bearded old professor who told her all of these stories. She liked him a lot. He didn't mind who she was or what she had done. All she had to do was open the book, and she was drawn into the friendly world of Reverend Wylie, who, aside from his understanding of history, also seemed to have a pretty good understanding of how hard it would be to spend four years in a Catholic school when you believed the simple and straightforward Gospel.

And Reverend Wylie, unlike the pastor she had known at home, did not seem like a thundering kind of preacher. His text ran with a kind of gentleness, a sorrow for the sins of others, and a compassion for sinners and saints alike. Tracey had never met such a wise and kind man; while she was reading and thinking, it never occurred to her that she had never really met him at all.

The first two weeks of vacation passed. Redemption left; Sister Mary was already gone for her usual circuit of seminars and retreats and vacation. Tracey worked unsupervised, and she chose her own hours: six to twelve. After lunch, which she ate with the summer school students and sisters, she retired to her room to read through the hottest part of the afternoon.

She practiced basketball from suppertime until dark, and then it was back for more reading. She knew she ought to take advantage of summer freedom and ride a bike into town for her favorites of coffee and Tastykakes, or even just to ride around. But it was easier just to read.

Sister Lucy had been unavailable sometimes when Tracey went to visit her on Saturdays, but Tracey tried each week to see her. One Saturday afternoon, she wandered down to the retirees' wing. It was a pleasant June day, and the early afternoon still had a touch of the freshness of morning. Whistling "Pieces of April" by Bread, she strolled down the hill. Maybe it would be one of Sister Lucy's better days.

An ambulance that was not a local rescue-squad

ambulance was pulled up to the retirees' wing, its back door open.

Such an event usually indicated a fresh sorrow in the wing. Somebody had either died or was having some kind of attack, Tracey supposed. She went in through one of the side doors to stay out of the way of the medical attendants.

But when she got inside, she was greeted by one of the attendants, who, apparently, had been waiting for her.

"Tracey," she said, detaining her with a hand on the arm.

It didn't take any more words than that.

A wave of trembling that surprised even Tracey washed over her.

"What?" she gasped.

"Sister Lucy—"

"Don't say she's dead!" Tracey exclaimed.

"Be quiet," the attendant rebuked her. Tracey first felt relieved because she saw that Sister Lucy wasn't dead, and then ashamed for saying such a thing so loud in a nursing home.

"What, then?" she asked.

"Sister Lucy is leaving us, dear." Tracey took the woman's hand off her arm and looked at her with all of the sternness that the woman had just shown her.

"What do you mean, leaving? Where is she going?" Tracey demanded.

"To a place where the care for her will be much better," the attendant told her. "We really aren't equipped to care for her as she requires—"

Just then an old woman's scream rang through the hall, carrying grief, terror, stark loneliness. It quickly subsided into a wail of sorrow. Sister Lucy, whatever her mental abilities were, still knew what going away meant, from both sides of the question.

Tracey heard a quick rush of feet, and the kind voices of the nurses and attendants who genuinely loved the poor old woman. But it was too much for her.

"It will be too hard for her if you see her now—" the attendant began.

"I'm getting out of here!" Tracey exclaimed, and before the woman could answer or stop her, Tracey was gone. She ran with long strides like a deer, burst through the double doors, and shortened her stride to a sprint up the hill.

*Why? why? why?* she demanded of God. *Why her? Why this now, at the very end of her life? God, why do You persecute people so much?*

She stopped at the top of the hill, a little shocked at herself for her frankness with God, but not ashamed.

*If You ever loved me, if You have any hope of loving me, if there's anything really good in God, then do something now—God, help me—*

The cry from her heart stopped with the sound of a car engine, and she realized that she had been staring at Maddie Murdoch's car even as she'd come running up the hill. It was now trundling toward the front gate, away from Tracey.

Tracey stood still, half tempted to run after it and half resolved not to. She didn't want to create the answer to her own prayer, and she didn't want to beg comfort from Mrs. Murdoch. If there was no hope that God would ever be her comfort, or if He wasn't real, she might as well know it.

But the car stopped halfway to the gate. The red tail-lights brightened, and the vehicle backed up—slowly at first, then more quickly, back to the small cleared place in front of the bike barn where Mrs. Murdoch had been parked. She got out of the car and came around the front of it, looking at Tracey in puzzlement.

Then Tracey's shock at what was happening in the retirees' wing hit her again. She looked back at the ambulance that was going to take Sister Lucy away forever, and she looked at Maddie, who was walking toward her slowly. Next thing Tracey knew, she was running toward Maddie, arms out, and she was crying.

Maddie Murdoch caught her without a question.

"Maddie," Tracey cried, "oh, for God's sake, stop them!"

"Who, dear? What's going on?" Maddie asked.

Tracey couldn't say it. The sheer force of her crying wouldn't let her form the words.

"Stop them!" she exclaimed again.

Maddie didn't ask again. She pulled Tracey's head against herself, firmly, not allowing her to flail her arms or cry out. "Tell me what's happened," Maddie said, her voice quiet and sober. "I'll help you if I can."

Being forced to be still brought Tracey back to herself. Her sense of shock and outrage gave way to genuine sorrow for the confused old woman who was being taken away. There was no doubt that Sister Lucy would receive good care; Catholic nursing homes were always good. But she would be with people as bad off as she was, far away from the only place she'd known as home. And Tracey couldn't even visit her. Tracey's frenzy of anger and frustration subsided into tears of grief as sincere as those she had shed over the death of Sister

James Anne. There was nothing Maddie could do. Tracey calmed down, and Maddie let her go.

"Look," Tracey said, and pointed at the ambulance.

"Poor dear," Maddie whispered. "Is Sister Lucy going away, then?"

Tracey nodded. "Why does God do this?" she asked with a sob. "Why does He do this to people?"

Maddie didn't respond. Tracey supposed Maddie's answer was that Sister Lucy had never trusted in God alone for help. That she was outside the cover of His protection. She wondered how a God who was supposed to be a God of love could so conveniently turn off the cries of people who didn't know Him.

But then Maddie said softly, "I don't know the mind of God in this, but maybe, dear, it is His last bid to gain Sister Lucy's attention."

The answer was so surprising that Tracey looked up at her.

"When we're all alone, Tracey, not when we're with our friends," Maddie said, "when we're sick and afraid, that's when we cast ourselves upon God. When every hope is blighted; for some of us, when our own minds are dissolving under us, and we know it—then we trust God and God alone." Her eyes were sober. "When we truly walk alone, then we truly walk with God."

These thoughts were new to Tracey. There was something in Maddie's words that spoke to her not only of Sister Lucy, but also of herself.

"I wouldn't wish it on anybody to plumb depths like that," Maddie said. "But God is good, and God is sovereign. It's as true now as it was when Sister Lucy had friends and her intellect." She looked directly at Tracey, but there was not a trace of judgment in her eyes. "People believe that God comes at chosen times to call them to Himself. But I believe that at every moment of our lives, at every instant, He is calling us to Himself. Every word we say, and every thought we think, reveals our reply to Him."

"Oh, Maddie," Tracey whimpered. That was all she said. The fire of revolt had gone out of her, but she felt very sad for Sister Lucy. She had worked and worked and tried to do the right thing for Sister Lucy, but nothing had done any good.

"Walk with me to my car," Maddie invited, and with her arm firmly around Tracey, she led her away from the sight of the retirees' wing, with its dismal ambulance.

## SEVENTY-THREE

Tracey had learned that there was no room in life for someone who got floored by grief. Her initial panicked flight shamed her, and she felt some embarrassment at crying so stormily in front of Maddie Murdoch. It seemed like Maddie always popped up when shock and grief—or anger—had disarmed Tracey entirely. She had only seen Tracey at her worst.

So even though Sister Lucy's horrible banishment was even then taking place, Tracey steeled herself against her revulsion and sorrow. She clamped down on her emotions and made herself deathly calm. Maddie had kept a tight hold on her arm as they walked back to the car, but as Tracey disciplined herself into silence, she felt Maddie's hand loosen and drop away.

"I came up to see you," Maddie said.

"You did?" Tracey asked.

"I have some time later this afternoon, and I thought I might take a carload of girls into town. I wanted to ask you first."

That would be because Tracey was stuck at MoJoe

all summer, Tracey supposed. Another kindness from the Irish woman. But Tracey was in no shape for an outing. "That's really nice of you," she said. "I . . . I guess I better stay here. Dibbles has to study during the week, so we usually play basketball on Saturdays."

"Dibbles?" Mrs. Murdoch looked amused by the nickname.

"Debbie Dibbley," Tracey said with a slight smile. "I'm helping her try to make the team next year. She's short, but she's pretty good, and Liz says she'll be real good for the team."

"There speaks the Valkyrie," Maddie said, smiling back at Tracey.

What Tracey really wanted to do was to get alone and think over what Maddie had just said about being thrown onto God alone. The memory of the words rang true in her heart—like a knife inside her, but not a bad knife. A true knife.

If Maddie were right, then Tracey had unmasked her reply to God all in that one moment. She had been telling herself for months that she was not a very good Christian. What if, under everything, what she really believed was that God was unkind? Perhaps this idea should have dismayed her more, but it did not. If He was forcing her to see this truth about herself, the only possible reason was that He wanted her to see that she was wrong. He was kind. It was a stern kindness, obviously. But if He were cruel, He would merely let her be destroyed in her ignorance, or perhaps He might fool her to ensure her destruction, but a cruel God would not let her see what she was really thinking about Him. A cruel God would not allow such honesty.

"Are you all right now, dear?" Mrs. Murdoch asked.

"I guess," Tracey said, her mind returning to what Sister Lucy was experiencing. Like an unexpected attack, the big wedge of grief almost cut into her again: stomach first, then heart. She put her arms up around her head without thinking, then caught herself and changed the gesture to push her hair back. But it took her a second to catch her breath and force away the shock and pain again. She dropped her hands. "I never did her much good," she said, her voice sounding weary even to her. "But it wouldn't have made much difference in the end."

"Nobody can say that until the end comes," Maddie said. "And only the Lord knows when to say it's the end."

"I guess you're right," Tracey said.

"Do you ever let people kiss you, Tracey?" Maddie asked all of a sudden.

Tracey looked at her blankly. Maddie leaned toward her, one hand touching Tracey's chin, and quickly kissed her cheek, a soft, cool kiss that reminded Tracey of George Macdonald fairy tales. His heroines were always tall and good like Maddie. She felt the honor of this kindness from someone like Maddie, though what prompted it puzzled her.

At Tracey's lack of response, Maddie smiled and said, "Well, I'd best be going, then, and take care of my errands. I hope to see you soon, dear."

"Thank you, Maddie," Tracey replied, remembering how Maddie had been there, almost like an answer to prayer. If Maddie had not come, Tracey would still be out in the hockey field somewhere, crying her heart out, mad at God, and absolutely comfortless.

She stood by as Maddie got into her car and drove away. By that time, the ambulance and Sister Lucy were both gone. Tracey's last act of grief over Sister James and Sister Lucy was to swear by her sword and shield that she'd never go into the retirees' wing again. It would have been easier for both herself and Sister Lucy if they'd never met.

She meant to go up to her room and think about what Maddie had said. It had made a big impression on her in her anguish, and it had sounded true enough to sit and think about for a long time. But when she got up to her room and saw the volume of Wylie lying open on the floor, silent and alone, she threw herself onto her bed and dismissed everything from her mind. She couldn't bear to think of Sister Lucy, to carry the knowledge of the old woman's sorrow and confusion. She pushed all of it away. A minute later, she was asleep.

In her sleep she saw the figure of the Valkyrie painted on the gym door. It moved, with a stilted sort of step, and came off the door. It had been painted by a heavy-handed person, and the result was an awkward, muffled figure whose skin was far too thick—as thick and baggy as rubber—and whose joints were far too stiff to allow it much flexibility. With a stick-figure gait, it tried to stride up the hill away from the gym.

"Come with me," a voice said to her, and suddenly, instead of the clumsy Valkyrie, Tracey found herself looking at Maddie Murdoch.

"No, I can't," she tried to say, but her mouth was covered over, swathed in some muffling material. She realized with a jolt of horror that she was no longer Tracey Jacamuzzi, but the Valkyrie from the door. Maddie reached over and pulled the thick skin away from her eye, revealing it to the world.

"No!" Tracey yelled. She covered her revealed eye with her hands. She staggered and tried to run away from Maddie, the shreds of the painted-on skin hanging from her face like strands of latex. The fastest stride she could manage was a hobbyhorse, rollicking kind of run, hampered by uneven legs and uneven knees. Maddie was coming after her.

The woman tackled her at the knees, brought her down on the grass, and tried to get astride her.

"No!" Tracey yelled, and for a moment she remembered the ring of faces over her. She tried to keep Maddie from pinning her, but Maddie jammed a knee against her chest and forced her back down onto the grass. Maddie reached down, took hold of the Valkyrie ear, and pulled from that side, peeling away all of the rubbery, latexlike paint that was her face.

She yelled and arched her back, rolled out from under Maddie, and tried to scramble away. Maddie would have dived onto her again, but she brought her feet up just in time and kicked as Maddie lunged forward. Her feet caught Maddie square in the chest and threw her back several feet.

Tracey, or whatever she was in the dream, struggled to her feet, the wind blowing cold in her revealed face, and staggered away.

A moment later Maddie brought her down again. This time, Maddie grabbed for whatever she could get hold of. She dug fingers as hard as steel pins into Tracey's shoulders, and she pulled on Tracey's skin as Tracey wrenched away from her and struggled to her feet. Enormous layers of the Valkyrie skin came down off of her arms, pulling shreds of her basketball uniform with it, as though she were wearing the uniform under the layers of paint. It hurt. She screamed, "Stop it! You'll kill me! Liz, help me!"

"This won't kill you," Maddie said. She tackled Tracey, and this time, freed from much of the encumbering skin that had housed yet hampered her, Tracey could fight much better. She levered her forearm against Maddie's chin, forcing her head back, preventing her from seeing what to tear away next.

But Maddie contrived some way to throw her, and Tracey somersaulted over Maddie and landed flat on her back on the grass, stunned for a moment. Maddie did not tackle her again but took quick advantage of the moment and pulled away the skin from her waist. "Stop!" Tracey screamed as she heard it tearing off her legs. Then she realized that she was not being stripped down to her bones. Nor was she even being stripped naked. Under the thick, heavy skin, under the layer of basketball uniform, there was another set of garments that was not being ripped away. She stopped fighting for a moment and looked down at the two intact legs peeping out from a tangle of Valkyrie skin and uniform. She looked at Maddie in puzzlement.

"Will you stand now?" Maddie asked, and Tracey stood up. Maddie pulled away the shreds and rags of skin and uniform from her shoulders, revealing bright skin underneath, and a brilliant white tunic with red piping.

"Whose clothes are these?" Tracey asked. But Maddie, busily pulling away remnants from Tracey's legs and back, was working too hard to answer. Tracey turned in a circle to survey the hill around them, littered with the debris that Maddie had pulled off of her. She had expected, for some reason, that the marks and

489

swelling on her eye would still be there under the layers of skin that had been pulled away. But when she reached up to touch it, the eye was normal and whole. She gasped in surprise and woke up.

Sunlight poured in through the room's solitary window. For a moment, before Tracey's eyes adjusted, the glare was almost too bright to be endured, and in her confusion she thought it was the dawn of a new day. She put her arm across her face until the dazzling sensation lessened. Then she blinked and sat up. The room was too warm. It had heated up from the direct rays of the sun.

After a moment, she stood and went to the window to breathe the fresh air and cool off. Her foot nicked the edge of the open volume of Wylie, and she scooped it up. These books were too old to be left on the floor. One accidental kick might break some of the pages loose from their brittle bindings. Holding the book carefully, she carried it to the window and looked outside.

The grounds were silent. Sister Lucy was gone. As gone as Sister James: never to return. And it had not been a peaceful exit. Tracey glanced down at the open pages.

Wylie had written about people who had suffered, and they had suffered well. There had been no complicating side issues for them—no fathers who hated them for obscure and inexplicable reasons, no mysterious strangers who met their mothers in dark motels. No people who might be truly saved and then again might not. Only bright conversions, crystal-clear doctrines, dark dungeons, and transforming fires at the end. In her own case, she seemed to suffer just as much for not having faith as for having it.

Maddie had said that at every moment of people's lives, God was calling them to Himself. Every word they said, and every thought they conceived, revealed their replies to Him: from hearts that believed and from hearts that did not believe.

*I don't think I believe in You enough*, she prayed. *But I want to. Won't You help me? Can't You answer my questions, even if I never become a very good Christian like Reverend Wylie?*

Then she remembered that Maddie had appeared at the very moment she had prayed for help. She suddenly felt better, less separated from God. She had been given the books by Wylie, and she had been given Maddie's answers. For now, maybe that was enough, because both of them had helped her to make better sense of things. For all she knew, there would be other answers coming. She closed the book and, after a moment, set it on the desk.

Her mood changed as she realized the time. Only two hours left before supper. The day was flying by.

*No matter how bad things get—or how sad—there really is only today*, she thought. *Only this present moment. And it's time to practice basketball.*

She dismissed everything from her mind and looked around for her basketball shoes.

SINCE 1894, Moody Publishers has been dedicated to equip and motivate people to advance the cause of Christ by publishing evangelical Christian literature and other media for all ages, around the world. As a ministry of the Moody Bible Institute of Chicago, proceeds from the sale of this book help to train the next generation of Christian leaders.

If we may serve you in any way in your spiritual journey toward understanding Christ and the Christian life, please contact us at www.moodypublishers.com.

*"All Scripture is God-breathed and is useful for teaching, rebuking, correcting and training in righteousness, so that the man of God may be thoroughly equipped for every good work."*
—*2 TIMOTHY 3:16, 17*

## MOODY
### PUBLISHERS

**THE NAME YOU CAN TRUST**